THE ESSENTIAL

Herodotus

Translation, Introduction, and Annotations
by
William A. Johnson

New York Oxford
OXFORD UNIVERSITY PRESS

Oxford University Press is a department of the University of Oxford. It furthers the University's objective of excellence in research, scholarship, and education by publishing worldwide. Oxford is a registered trade mark of Oxford University Press in the UK and certain other countries.

Published in the United States of America by Oxford University Press
198 Madison Avenue, New York, NY 10016, United States of America.

For titles covered by Section 112 of the US Higher Education Opportunity Act, please visit www.oup.com/us/he for the latest information about pricing and alternate formats.

Library of Congress Cataloging-in-Publication Data

Names: Herodotus, author. | Johnson, William A. (William Allen), 1956- translator.
Title: The essential Herodotus : translation, introduction, and annotations / by William A. Johnson.
Description: New York ; Oxford : Oxford University Press, [2016] | Includes bibliographical references, glossary, and index.
Identifiers: LCCN 2016003365 | ISBN 9780199897957 (pbk.)
Classification: LCC PA4003 .E5 2016 | DDC 938/.03—dc23
LC record available at http://lccn.loc.gov/2016003365

Printing number: 9 8 7 6 5 4 3 2 1

Printed by R.R. Donnelley, United States of America

Brief Contents

Contents

Preface

My first exposure to Herodotus was as a boy, when I picked up a volume called *The Portable Greek Historians,* put together many years ago by Moses Finley. It was not until some years later, when I first came to study Herodotus in Greek, that I became aware of how deeply misleading was Finley's handy volume, which effectively made Herodotus's work a rather straightforward history of the Persian War, albeit with a bit of storytelling at the front, and some fun facts about Egypt in the middle.

But Finley's book *was* handy, and, like Finley, I hope by offering a volume with selections (instead of the daunting 700-page whole) to serve a broad audience of those who are curious about the first history written in the west, or curious about ancient Greece, or just plain curious. The selections attempt to give a rich and balanced sense of what the whole of the history is like, and the brief comments and many maps and illustrations are designed to help guide the reader who may feel a bit at sea in such novel materials. I have, in short, tried to take my lifetime of study of our first historian and produce a guided tour to what is surely one of the most fascinating works to survive from antiquity.

WILLIAM A. JOHNSON
Duke University

About the Translator

WILLIAM A. JOHNSON, Professor of Classical Studies at Duke University, works broadly in the cultural history of Greece and Rome. He has lectured and published on Herodotus, Hesiod, Plato, Cicero, Pliny (both Elder and Younger), Gellius, and Lucian, and on a variety of topics relating to books and readers, both ancient and modern. His books include *Readers and Reading Culture in the High Empire: A Study of Elite Reading Communities* (Oxford, 2010); *Ancient Literacies* (Oxford, 2009), and *Bookrolls and Scribes in Oxyrhynchus* (Toronto, 2004).

Introduction

> In history everything is directed toward getting at the truth, while in poetry most things are directed to giving pleasure; however (it must be said) there are countless fabulous tales in Herodotus, the Father of History. . . .
>
> —CICERO, *DE LEGIBUS* 1.5

How can someone write history before the idea of writing history has been invented? This question animates, directly or indirectly, a deep wellspring of modern scholarship, as we try to understand better the aims and methods of the great work by Herodotus, the "father of history"—that is, the man who first, to our knowledge, wrote a "history" recognizable as such. This question is also behind much of what makes first-time readers of Herodotus as perplexed as they are charmed. Why in a *history* do we have stories of the mythic heroines Helen and Medea, of Arion miraculously saved by a dolphin, of the fairytale thieves who trick the Egyptian Pharaoh? Why in a *history* do we have scientific analysis of the origins of the Nile's flooding, lengthy catalogues of bizarre barbarian customs, descriptions of animals that include not simply the peculiarities of crocodile and hippopotamus, but gold-digging ants and winged serpents whose bones Herodotus claims to have seen himself?

Herodotus does not claim to *write history*: that had not yet been invented. What he claims is to "present to the public" a *historiê*, the Greek word that means "inquiry" or "investigation" or "researches" and from which our word *history* derives. In trying to understand what Herodotus is up to, the centrality of the concept of *historiê* is important to bear in mind. What we are getting is the staging, as it were, of an active inquiry or investigation into certain matters. What those matters are will become clearer as you work into the text; and while they include elements that are like history as we tend to think of it (by which I mean, especially, traditional political and military history), you will also find a much broader set of interests that motivate this active inquiry, a set of interests that finds relevance and meaning in affairs far beyond politics and military campaigns. Moreover, you will come to know (and to enjoy immensely) the active inquirer, that genial and rather sly persona that Herodotus adopts as he "presents"—stages—his own struggles to wrestle this enormous mass of knowledge into shape, and thereby to extract significance and, at times, deep meaning.

But how can it be that *history* is something that someone invents? Isn't the *historical* what it is? The answer to that is yes and no. True, the people are real (for the most part) and the situations (for the most part) are real too: Xerxes is a historical Persian king, and the conflict between Greeks and Persians known as the Persian War did happen. We may quibble on any number of details, or even quarrel over major events or outcomes, and we may further take the stand that the "truth" of these details and events is unrecoverable, but all will still agree that there exist real details, events, and outcomes to argue over and try to recover. But the moment the historian sits down to *write history,* that is a different matter. A historian creates a *narrative* that selectively presents evidence, and from analysis of that evidence inferences and conclusions are drawn. To create a massive catalogue of every detail we know about each person and event, no matter how trivial (darning of socks, eating of meals, stray conversation), for all those Americans whose testimony survives for the period 1861–1865 may be the stuff from which a history could be made, but it is not the writing of history. A military history asserts that there was a great war then, either the Civil War or the War between the States (two tellingly different options), which was fought for one or several reasons, including economic clashes, political intransigence, outrage at slavery, and so forth. A social history asserts a point of focus, let's say slavery, and arranges in some comprehensible fashion some of the ways by which slaves and the social institution, slavery, responded to the changing circumstances of the war and its many pressures and developments. An economic history might use data that show how meals and other contingencies changed over the course of the war, but that history will not simply list the meals, transactions, and other bits of evidence: it will construct from those many bits an argument, a *narrative.* None of this means that a good history is uncomplicated or unnuanced. But a history simply has to select what evidence is useful, what evidence is telling, and needs then to signal what the evidence suggests, to draw conclusions, however ambiguous or fragile, in a narrative that is coherent. That is a different matter from marshaling a raw array of "facts," even while we also now understand better, in our hyper-politicized world, how "facts" too can be variously constructed and construed.

We must be clear, then, that Herodotus is not claimed to have invented *history,* but rather is claimed (rightly or wrongly) to have invented the western tradition of *writing history.* Those who study this are studying *historiography,* literally the writing (*-graphy*) of history. What distinguishes Herodotus's writing are certain features that will quickly establish themselves as essential historical conventions, such as the focus on real-world events, the setting of events on a well-defined timeline, the collecting and reasoned analysis of evidence so as to establish the "facts," the attention to the causes and outcomes of events, the presentation of the whole as a coherent prose narrative in (roughly) chronological order. There are antecedents for many of the parts, as we shall see—the handling of the narrative, in particular, owes a great deal to the *Iliad*—but the whole seems to be something new and is the basis for

Thucydides' decisive intervention, after which the conventions of western historical narrative are firmly set.

Herodotus's overall purpose is defined at the front of the work: *so that time not erase what man has brought into being, and so that the great and marvelous deeds, manifested both by Greeks and by barbarians, not be without glory—and in particular to answer the question, for what reason these peoples came to war against one another.* The fighting he mentions is the Persian War, a war of great importance to the Greeks, since it demonstrated their ability to fight back an enormously powerful invader and led directly to Greek control over large parts of the eastern Mediterranean—which in turn led to the great economic and cultural expansion that we call the rise of Athens or, less admiringly, the Athenian Empire. For the Greeks, the defeat of the Persians and the economic and cultural advancement in its wake is of a piece with what come to be central ideas of Greekness: high ability in warfare, high attainment in matters cultural, willingness to fight for freedom.

Of the man, Herodotus, aside from what we can infer from his writings, we know little: merely that he was born in the city of Halicarnassus in Caria, on the southwestern coast of present-day Turkey, and that he seems to have emigrated to a Greek colony in what is now south Italy, in a town called Thurii, where perhaps he died. His life, then, spanned the Mediterranean, beginning at the far east of the area influenced by the Greeks and ending far to the west. From his work, we can infer that he traveled widely (although how widely is debated). He writes as though he did not fight in the Persian War (480–479 BC), but he was able to interview people who had; the latest secure reference in his work is 430 BC. Scholarly consensus makes him a boy or youth at the time of the war, and we guess that his life span was roughly from about the 480s to the 420s BC. Many (including myself) think it important that he wrote his work during the run-up to and start (431 BC) of the Peloponnesian War, that grim, protracted struggle between the two great Greek city-states, Athens and Sparta. It is also important to bear in mind that Herodotus is neither Athenian nor Spartan and that, while there is no Greek "nation" in antiquity, he assumes a loose commonality of identity among "the Greeks," who include not only Greek speakers of the mainland and Aegean islands (current-day Greece), but also Greek speakers along what is now the Turkish coast (Ionia). Greek speakers in this world view are opposed to those whose speech sounds like *bar-bar-bar,* that is, the barbarians. In this time, the dominant state among the barbarians was, of course, that of the Persians, whose empire was the largest yet created. What it was that brought the Persians and Greeks into contact and then into conflict was the question that motivated Herodotus's lifetime of inquiries, a set of investigations ranging widely over time and space that resulted in the extraordinary work he left behind.

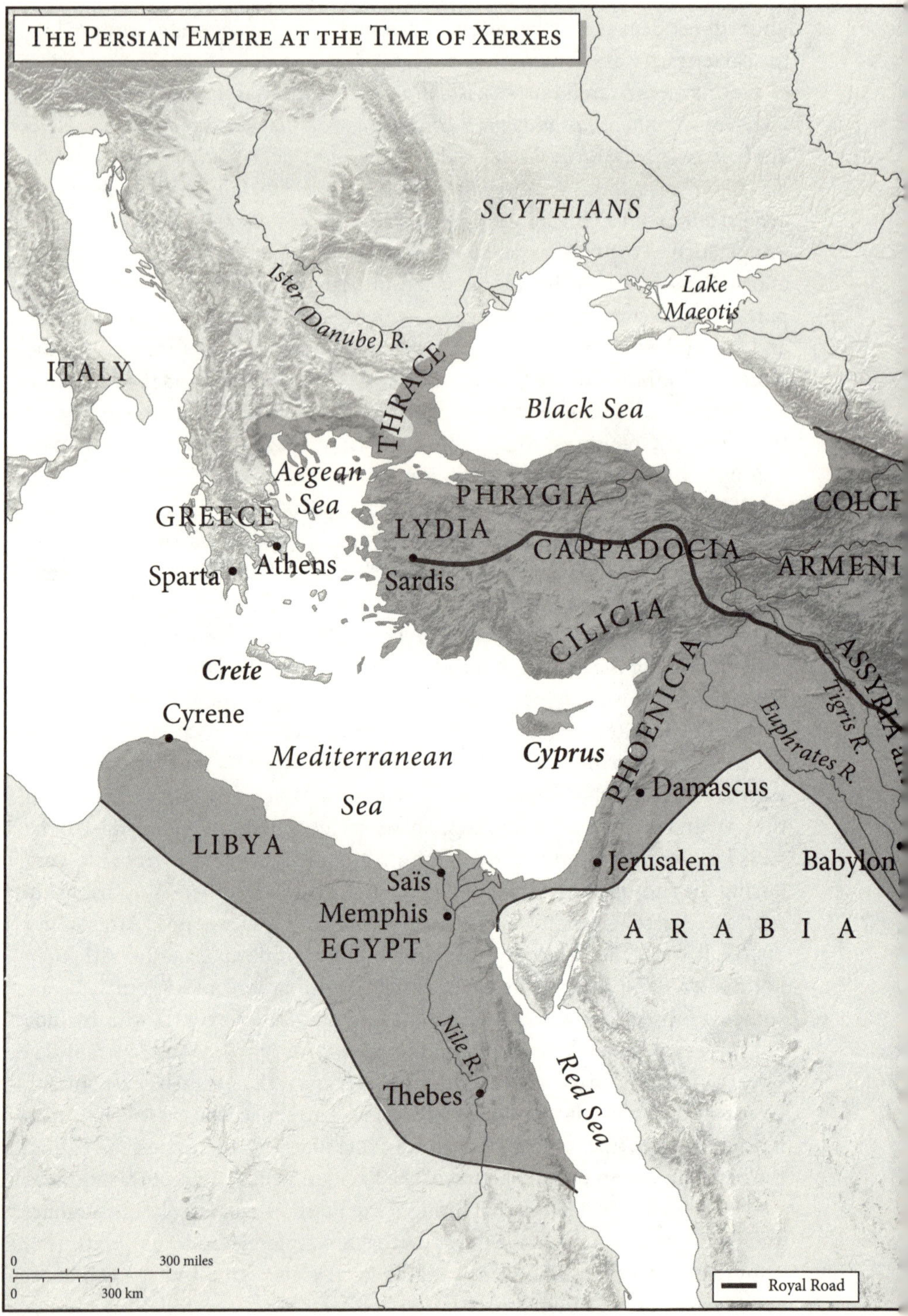
THE PERSIAN EMPIRE AT THE TIME OF XERXES
SCYTHIANS
Ister (Danube) R.
Lake Maeotis
ITALY
THRACE
Black Sea
Aegean Sea
PHRYGIA
COLCH
GREECE
LYDIA
CAPPADOCIA
ARMENI
Athens
Sparta
Sardis
CILICIA
ASSYRIA
Crete
PHOENICIA
Tigris R.
Euphrates R.
Cyrene
Mediterranean Sea
Cyprus
Damascus
LIBYA
Jerusalem
Babylon
Saïs
Memphis
EGYPT
ARABIA
Nile R.
Red Sea
Thebes
0 300 miles
0 300 km
Royal Road

MAP 1

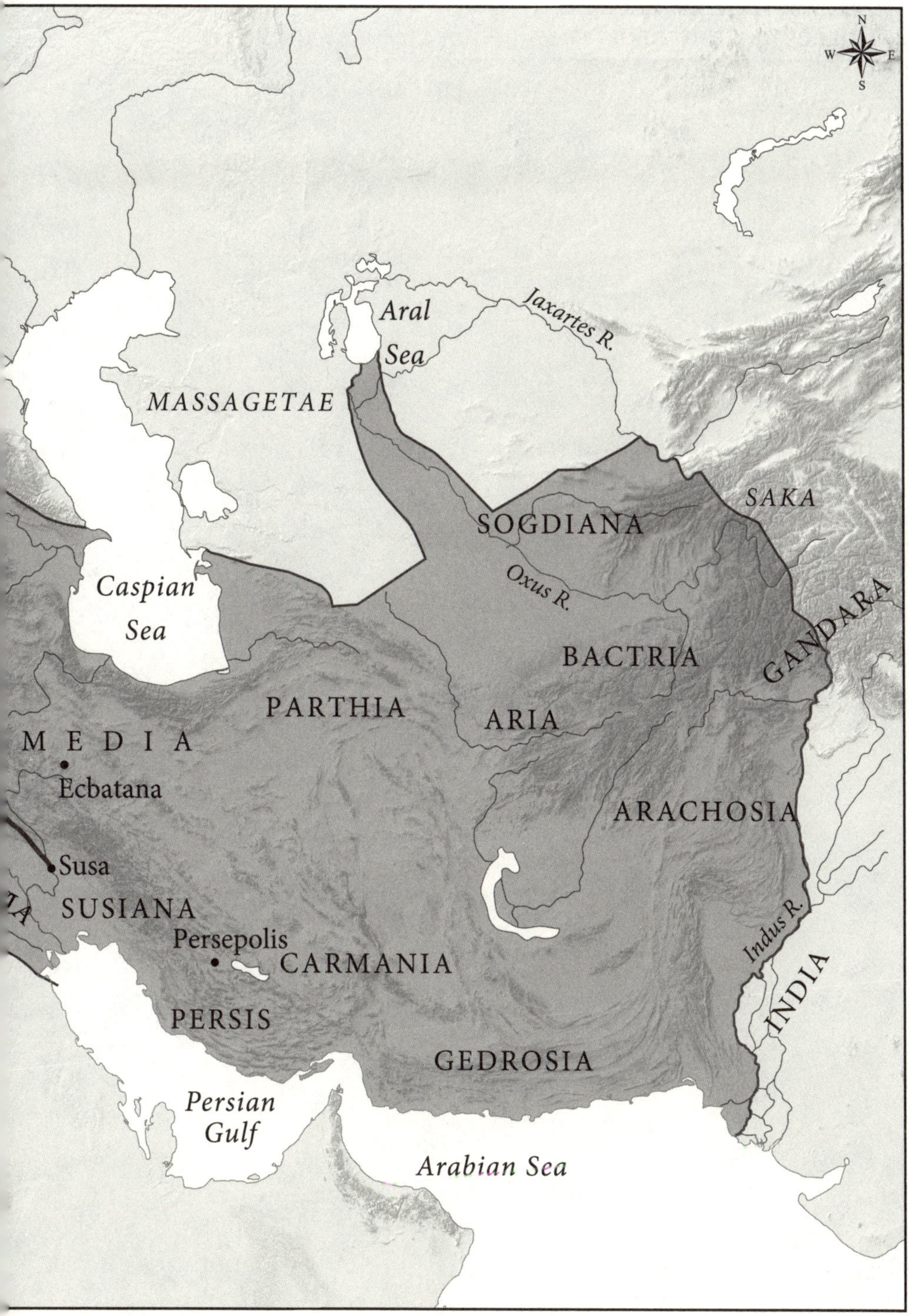
N
W
E
S
Aral Sea
Jaxartes R.
MASSAGETAE
SAKA
SOGDIANA
Caspian Sea
Oxus R.
GANDARA
BACTRIA
PARTHIA
ARIA
MEDIA
Ecbatana
ARACHOSIA
Susa
SUSIANA
Indus R.
Persepolis
CARMANIA
INDIA
PERSIS
GEDROSIA
Persian Gulf
Arabian Sea

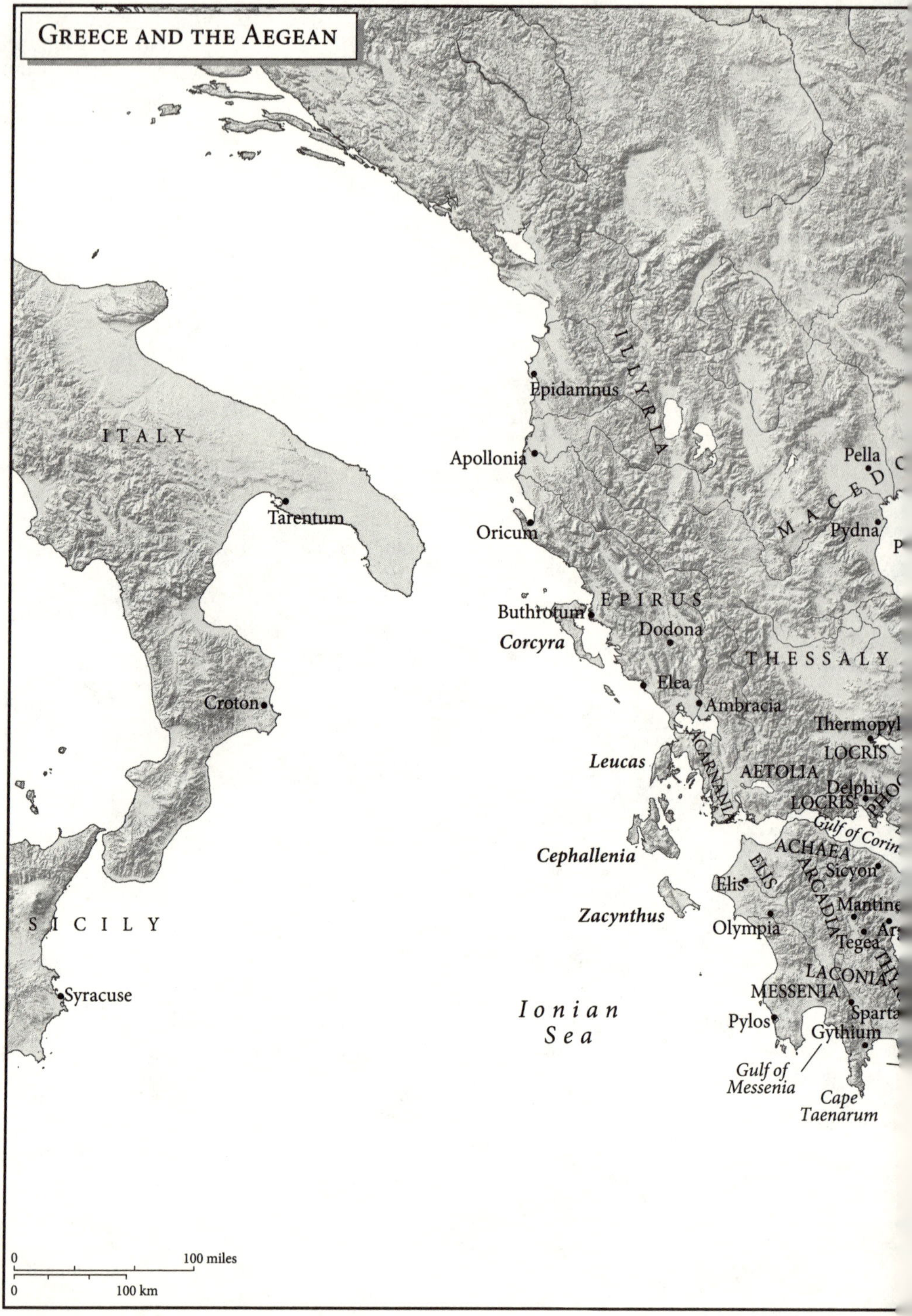
Greece and the Aegean
ITALY
Tarentum
Croton
SICILY
Syracuse
Epidamnus
ILLYRIA
Apollonia
Oricum
Pella
MACED
Pydna
EPIRUS
Buthrotum
Corcyra
Dodona
THESSALY
Elea
Ambracia
Leucas
ACARNANIA
AETOLIA
LOCRIS
Delphi
LOCRIS
Gulf of Corin
Cephallenia
ACHAEA
Sicyon
ELIS
ARCADIA
Elis
Zacynthus
Olympia
Tegea
LACONIA
MESSENIA
Sparta
Pylos
Gythium
Ionian Sea
Gulf of Messenia
Cape Taenarum
0
100 miles
0
100 km

MAP 2

N
W
E
S
Black Sea
Byzantium
Chalcedon
Perinthus
Amphipolis
Abdera
Thasos
Samothrace
CHALCIDICE
Aegospotami
Lampsacus
Sestus
Cyzicus
Abydus
Mt. Athos
Imbros
Troy
Lemnos
TROAD
PHRYGIA
Tenedos
Methymna
MYSIA
Aegean
Sea
Mytilene
Lesbos
Scyrus
EUBOEA
GREATER PHRYGIA
LYDIA
Hermus R.
Chalcis
Eretria
Smyrna
Sardis
Chios
Chios
Erythrae
Clazomenae
ATTICA
Colophon
Athens
IONIA
Andros
Samos
Ephesus
Maeander R.
Ceos
Tenos
Samos
Priene
CARIA
Miletus
Delos
Didyma
Paros
Halicarnassus
Caunus
Lake
Naxos
Siphnos
Cos
Caunus
LYCIA
Cnidus
Melos
Rhodes
Thera
Rhodes
Crete

Central Persons in Herodotus

The chapter number at the end of each entry refers to the passage where the person is introduced, or where his or her most notable action occurs.

Arion (*a-reye'-on*). A celebrated citharode who was forced to jump overboard by thieving sailors, but who was saved when a dolphin, sent it seems by Apollo, appeared and carried him to land. (1.23)

Aristagoras (*a-ri-sta'-goh-ras*). The tyrant of Miletus who started the Ionian Revolt. (5.97)

Artabanus (*ar-ta-bay'-nus*). Uncle and wise advisor to Xerxes. (7.10)

Artemisia (*ar-te-mee'-si-a*). Queen of Halicarnassus who captained a ship in Xerxes's fleet and through a combination of scheming and wisdom became one of his trusted advisors. (8.68)

Astyages (*a-steye'-a-jeez*). The brutal despot who ended the line of Median kings; he was overthrown by Cyrus the Great. (1.107)

Atys (*a'-tis*). The son of Croesus whose life was accidentally taken by the stranger Adrastus, who had sworn to protect him. (1.34)

Cambyses (*cam-beye'-seez*). King of Persia after Cyrus. He attacked and conquered Egypt, but in the course of the campaign went mad. He died on his way back to Susa to suppress a revolt by the False Smerdis. (3.1)

Croesus (*croy'-sus or cree'-sus*). King of Lydia, legendary for his wealth. He built a mighty empire but then made the mistake of attacking the Persians. His empire was conquered and absorbed by Cyrus the Great, after which he became a wise advisor to the Persian court. (1.26)

Cyrus (*seye'-rus*). Cyrus the Great was the first of the Persian kings. He overthrew the dynasty of the Medes by deposing Astyages. (1.108)

Darius (*da-reye'-us*). Darius the Great followed Cambyses as king of Persia. He was one of the Seven who detected the schemes of the Magi when they seized power; the Seven seized power back, and through various maneuverings Darius became the new king. In the Constitutional Debate, Darius argued that kingship is the best form of government for Persia. (3.70)

Deioces (*day'-oh-seez or dee'-oh-seez*). First king of the Medes, who ironically came into a tyrant's power through his reputation for justice. (1.96)

Demaratus (*de-mar-ay'-tus*). Exiled king of Sparta, who attended Xerxes at court and on the march, and was one of a succession of wise advisors to the king. (7.3)

Ephialtes (*e-fee'-al-teez*). The Greek from Malis who led Xerxes's soldiers around the mountain at Thermopylae, thus making it possible to surround and defeat Leonidas and his Three Hundred. (7.213)

Eurybiades (*yoo-ri-bee'-a-deez*). Spartan commander of the combined Greek naval forces at Artemisium and Salamis. (8.49)

Gyges (*geye'-jeez*). A spearman in the Lydian court who through a strange sequence of events brought the kingship to the Mermnads, the clan of Croesus. (1.8)

Harpagus (*har-pa'-gus*). Aristocrat and steward under King Astyages, who was commanded by the king to kill the baby Cyrus. (1.108)

Helen of Troy (*he'-len*). Legendary queen of Sparta and wife of Menelaus; her seduction by Alexander (also known as Paris) led to the Trojan War. (1.3)

Hippias (*hip'-pee-as*). Son of the Athenian tyrant Peisistratus who assisted the Persian forces at Marathon. (6.107)

Histiaeus (*hi-sti-eye'-us*). The scheming tyrant of Miletus who both kept the bridge intact for Darius's retreat from Scythia and worked to start the Ionian Revolt. (4.137, 6.1)

Leonidas (*le-oh'-nee-das*). Spartan king who led the Three Hundred at the battle of Thermopylae. (7.204)

Mardonius (*mar-doh'-ni-us*). A son of one of the Seven (Gobryas), he acted as an infantry general both under Darius, before Marathon, and under Xerxes, where he goaded Xerxes to invade and, later, assumed the command when Xerxes returned to Asia. (6.43, 7.5)

Miltiades (*mil-tee'-a-deez*). Athenian leader and victorious general at the battle of Marathon. (4.137, 6.109)

Otanes (*oh-ta'-neez*). The first of the Seven to divine the scheme of the Magi, by which they had put power into the hands of an imposter. In the Constitutional Debate (3.80), Otanes argued against monarchy and advocated that the Seven set up a democratic government in Persia. (3.68)

Peisistratus (*pay-si'-stra-tus*). Early and mostly beneficent tyrant of Athens, who through various schemes seized the tyranny three times. His descendants, known as the **Peisistratids**, continued to advocate for tyranny, and thus showed up repeatedly at the Persian court. (1.59)

Psammetichus (*psam-me'-ti-kus*). 7th-century BC Egyptian king who created an experiment to find out which people were the oldest. (2.2)

Smerdis (*smer'-dis*). The real Smerdis was Cambyses's brother, whom he had murdered. The "False Smerdis" was one of the Magi, who briefly seized control of the Persian empire by pretending to be Cambyses's brother at a time when Cambyses had gone mad. The False Smerdis was overthrown by the Seven. (3.30)

Solon (*soh'-lon*). An Athenian statesman famous for his wisdom, who journeyed to Sardis and offered advice to King Croesus. (1.29)

Themistocles (*the-mis'-toh-kleez*). A powerful and controversial leader of Athens, who commanded the Athenian part of the Greek fleet and through rhetoric and scheming drove the Greek strategy at Salamis. (8.57)

Tomyris (*toh-meye'-ris*). Queen of the Massagetae, who defeated and killed Cyrus when he invaded their territory. (1.205)

Xerxes (*zer-xeez*). King of Persia after Darius, who carried on and implemented Darius's plan to invade Greece. (7.2)

The Great Kings of Persia (The Achaemenids)

Name	Lifetime	Reign	Patrimony
Cyrus the Great (Cyrus II)	600–530 BC	559–530 BC	Son of Cambyses I
Cambyses (Cambyses II)	?–522 BC	530–522 BC	Son of Cyrus the Great
Darius the Great (Darius I)	550–486 BC	522–486 BC	Son of Hystaspes
Xerxes (Xerxes I)	519–465 BC	486–465 BC	Son of Darius the Great
Artaxerxes (Artaxerxes I)	?–424 BC	465–424 BC	Son of Xerxes

Timeline

	GREECE	PERSIA, NEAR EAST, EGYPT
ARCHAIC PERIOD 750–490 BC		
c. 750	Overseas colonization of western Mediterranean begins	
	Iliad and *Odyssey* composed (c. 750–675)	
700		Deioces becomes king of the Medes
687		Beginning of the Lydian empire (687–546) under Gyges
664		Psammetichus I (r. 664–610) becomes pharaoh, and establishes Naucratis on the Nile as a permanent Greek trading station
630	Sappho born in Lesbos	
612		Beginning of the Median empire (612–550) under Cyaxares after capture of Nineveh
c. 600	Beginnings of science and philosophy (the "Presocratics")	Lydians are the first to mint coins
594	Solon's reforms in Athens give rise to limited democracy in Athens	
569		Amasis (r. 569–526) becomes pharaoh and establishes close relations with Greeks as Persian power threatens
561	The beginning of tyranny in Athens under Peisistratus; he and his sons will rule Athens until 514	
560		Croesus becomes king of Lydia (r. 560–546)
559		Cyrus I (the Great) becomes king of the Persians (r. 557–530)

	GREECE	PERSIA, NEAR EAST, EGYPT
550		Cyrus I defeats the Median king Astyages; he now rules the Medes as well as the Persians
		Beginning of the Achaemenid Persian Empire (550–330)
	Sparta becomes the dominant power in the Peloponnese	
546		Cyrus defeats Croesus at Sardis and adds Lydia to his empire
539		Cyrus defeats Babylonian army at Opis and adds Babylonia to his empire
530		Cyrus dies in battle and his son Cambyses II becomes king of Persia (r. 530–522)
526		Cambyses launches his attack on Egypt; Pharaoh Amasis dies and his son Psammenitus ascends to the throne
525		Cambyses conquers Egypt, capturing the new pharaoh Psammenitus, and adds Egypt to his empire
522		Cambyses dies without an heir
521		Darius I (the Great) emerges as the Persian king (r. 521–486)
518		Darius begins the building of Persepolis, a new capital for the empire
513		Darius attacks Scythia
510	Cleisthenes expels the tyrants from Athens and in 507 institutes reforms; democracy takes root	
499	Outbreak of the Ionian Revolt	
498	Ionians with the help of Athens burn Sardis	

494	Ionian Revolt winds down (ending in 493)	Persians capture and destroy Miletus, thus restoring rule over Greeks in Ionia
490	First Persian Invasion: Athenians defeat Datis and his Persian army at Marathon	Darius sends Datis to attack Greece
486		Darius' son Xerxes becomes king of Persia (r. 486–465)
485		Xerxes crushes rebellions in Egypt and Babylon
480	Second Persian Invasion: Battles of Thermopylae and Artemisium, capture and burning of Athens, Battle of Salamis	Xerxes attacks Greece
479	Battles of Plataea and Mycale, end of Persian Wars	Xerxes leaves Greece and marches to Babylonia to crush a rebellion
CLASSICAL PERIOD 478–323 BC		
478	Formation of the first Delian League, led by Athens	
472	Aeschylus (525–456) produces the *Persians*, a tragedy about the Persian invasion	
469	Birth of Socrates (469–399)	
468	Sophocles (496–406) stages his first tragedy	
465		Xerxes assassinated and Artaxerxes I (r. 465–424) assumes the throne
461	Outbreak of hostilities between Athens and Corinth	
460	Pericles leads Athens through its "golden era" (c. 460–430)	
449	Acropolis building program, including construction of the Parthenon (447–432)	
445	Hostilities end with a 30–years' truce; Athens is at the height of her power	

	GREECE	PERSIA, NEAR EAST, EGYPT
440s and 430s	Herodotus at work on his history of the Persian War	
431	Outbreak of the Peloponnesian War between Athens and Sparta	
	Thucydides begins work on his history of the Peloponnesian War	
423		Darius II (r. 424–404) becomes king of Persia
404	War ends with Athens defeated, leaving Sparta now as the first power in Greece	

THE RESEARCHES *of*
Herodotus of Halicarnassus

BOOK I
Prologue

The first sentence ("Herodotus of Halicarnassus here presents to the public his researches . . .") reads much like an epigraph and acts as the title to the work. It also gives critical signals to the reader as to the contents and program (research, creating a written record, great deeds, glory, causes, war). The exact formulation of the sentence is interesting, since it implicitly announces strong ties to three different genres: (1) the first words, identifying the author in the third person, follow in the tradition of early proto-historians who accumulated lists of peoples and places and their stories; (2) the definition of the core activity as "researches" (*historiê*, the word that will gradually come to mean a "history") signals common cause with proto-scientists who were trying, through collection and analysis, to sort out how the material world works; and (3) the emphasis on preserving "glory" (*kleos*) is the signal goal of the Homeric epics, and thus offers this work as an alternative to poetic memorialization. The narrator is implicitly declaring that he will be doing something quite new that takes over elements from a variety of literary predecessors.

In the section to follow, the narrator characteristically picks up the final phrase of the first sentence ("for what reason these peoples came to war against one another") and turns to examine the question there introduced, the cause of the Persian War. This section—"The Snatchings of Women"—puzzles modern readers and probably puzzled some ancient ones as well. Several moves are simultaneously in play. The first is to take mythological persons and historicize them as real people involved in an escalating series of kidnappings and retribution. Secondly, though, the narrative does not carry the authority of the narrator ("Herodotus") but is explicitly a report of specific and irreconcilable viewpoints—what the Persians, the Phoenicians, the Greeks say. The third move is a surprise ending: at the conclusion of the narrative, the whole is set aside (in a figure that Classicists call a "priamel") in favor of what the narrator himself can reasonably know. Here at the front, then, there is an implicit discussion of the difficulties inherent in formulating a valid narrative for the distant causes of complex historical events—what we would now think of as a question of historical method.

Proem: The Opening Sentence

PR. Herodotus of Halicarnassus here presents to the public his researches (*historiê*), so that time not erase what man has brought into being, and so that the great and marvelous deeds, manifested both by Greeks and by barbarians,[1] not be without glory (*kleos*)—and in particular to answer the question, for what reason[2] these peoples came to war against one another.

The Snatchings of Women

Some motifs to watch for: the four rounds of attack or reprisal (Io, Europa, Medea, Helen), culminating in a landmark war; the continuing cycle of revenge; the mutability of human fortune. In Greek mythology, Io and Europa are lovers of Zeus subjected to the jealousy of Hera; Medea is a foreign princess seduced by the hero Jason; Helen is the queen of Sparta (wife of Menelaus) seduced by Paris, an act that led to the Trojan War.

1.1 Among the Persians those who tell the stories of things past[3] say that the
Phoenicians were the cause of the quarrel. By their account, the Phoenicians
arrived at our Sea[4] from what is called the Red Sea[5] and, settling what is now
their homeland, they immediately set about long sea voyages. They transported wares from Egypt and Assyria and traveled to many a land, among
them Argos, which at this time was the preeminent power in the territories we
now call Greece. To Argos, then, the Phoenicians came and there they set out
their wares. On the fifth or sixth day after their arrival, when nearly everything was sold out, quite a few women came down to the seashore, and among
them was the king's daughter. Her name—and on this point the Greeks
agree—was Io, daughter of Inachus. The women were standing near the stern
of the ship, bargaining for the wares their hearts most desired, when the Phoenicians gave the signal and rushed upon them. Most of the women escaped,
but Io, along with others, was captured. The Phoenicians (say the Persians)
1.2 loaded them onto the ship and made sail for Egypt. Thus it was that Io came to
Egypt. Or so say the Persians, telling a story quite different from the Greeks.[6]
This, they say, was the first act of injustice.

Next, they say, certain of the Greeks (whose names they cannot recall) traveled to Phoenicia, to Tyre, and carried off the daughter of the king, Europa.

1 Barbarian, Greek *barbaros*, means people who are not Greek speakers. Non-Greeks tend (from the Greek point of view) to be less civilized, but the essential contrast here is Greek versus non-Greek rather than civilized versus uncivilized.

2 The Greek word here, *aitiê*, means the reason or cause, but also the blame and responsibility for an action.

3 These authorities (*logioi* in the Greek) appear to be people specially designated to recall traditional materials, originally and probably also here referring to an oral tradition of cultural memory.

4 The Mediterranean.

5 Herodotus uses *Red Sea* for both our Red Sea and the Persian Gulf; here the latter is meant.

6 In Greek mythology, Io was bedded by Zeus, and then, fleeing a horsefly sent by Hera to torment her, wandered to Egypt in the form of a white cow. There she resumed human form and gave birth to Epaphos, whom the Greeks identified with the Egyptian bull-god Apis.

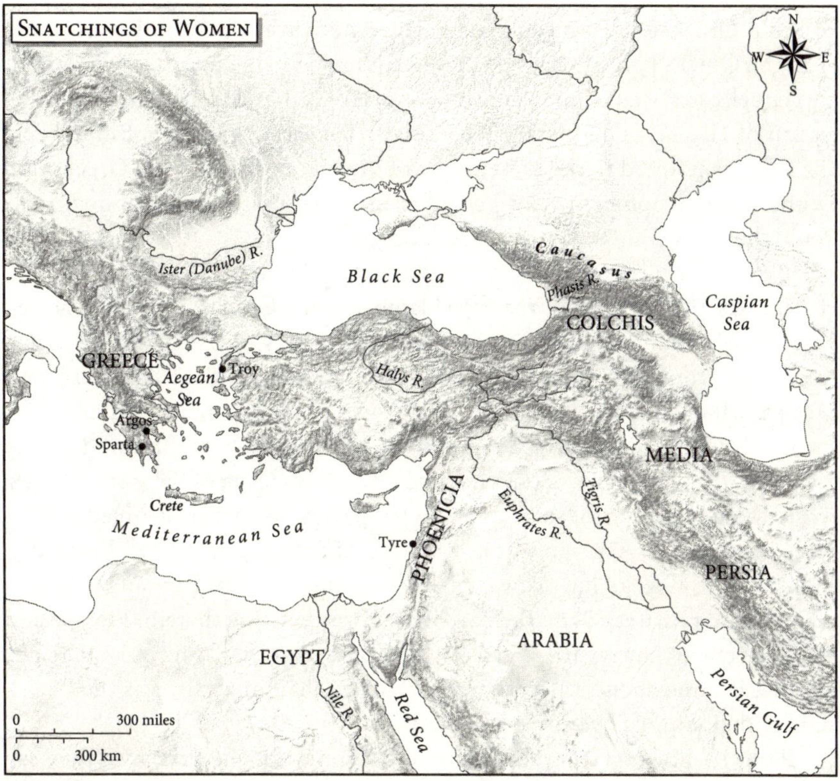

MAP 1.1

These men, then, would have to be the Cretans.[7] And so, up to this point, the score was even.

But after that, say the Persians, the Greeks were to blame for the second act of injustice—for they sailed down in a long ship to Aea, a city in Colchis on the river Phasis, and once they had done what they had come to do, they kidnapped the daughter of the king, Medea.[8] The Colchian king sent a herald to Greece, and demanded both monetary recompense for the kidnapping and the return of his daughter. But in reply the Greeks said that the barbarians had not given reparations for the kidnapping of Io from Argos, and therefore they would give none to the Colchians.

The Persians go on to say that in the second generation after this, Alexander 1.3
the son of Priam[9] was inspired by this story, and so wanted to seize a wife

7 In Greek mythology, Zeus came to Europa in Tyre in the form of a beautiful white bull; she climbed on his back, whereupon the bull swam to Crete and there they slept together.

8 "What they had come to do" was to capture the golden fleece: this is the mythological tale of Jason and the Argonauts, in which Jason and the witch-princess Medea fall in love and Jason brings her back to Greece to horrific consequence (murder of her brother, his uncle, their children). In the myth, Medea is the granddaughter of the Sun.

9 An alternate name for Paris, whose seduction and snatching of Helen led to the Trojan War. In mythology, Helen is the daughter of Zeus, king of the gods.

from the Greeks—convinced that he would not have to pay for this any more than the Greeks had. Thus it was that he kidnapped Helen. After deliberation the Greeks first sent a messenger to the Trojans, and demanded both the return of Helen and monetary recompense for the kidnapping. But in reply the Trojans pointed to the kidnapping of Medea, saying that the Greeks had neither given recompense nor given her up when that was demanded. How could they now want reparations from others?

1.4 So far, there were only kidnappings involved, but from this point forward, the Greeks, they say, were greatly to blame. For the Greeks invaded Asia well before the Persians invaded Europe. "In our view," say the Persians, "to kidnap women is wrong, but, once the deed is done, to make it the basis for serious reprisal is foolish—sensible men treat the snatchings of women as affairs of no great moment, since clearly the ladies would not have been captured if they were not willing. We men from Asia make no great matter of these snatchings, while the Greeks for the sake of a single Spartan woman assembled a great force, traveled to Asia, and destroyed the kingdom of Priam.[10] From this moment, the Greeks have always been our enemy." The Persians, you see, claim as their own Asia and the barbarian races dwelling therein; Europe and
1.5 the Greek race they regard as entirely separate. That then is how the Persians say that it came about: the capture of Troy, by their analysis, was the beginning of their enmity against the Greeks.

About Io, however, the Phoenicians disagree with the Persians. They say that they did not kidnap her to take her to Egypt. Rather, in Argos she had slept with the captain of the ship, and when she learned that she was pregnant, ashamed and afraid of her parents, she sailed with the Phoenicians of her own accord, so that she not be found out. Such, then, are the stories of the Persians and Phoenicians.

For my part, I am not going to address these stories, nor opine whether it happened this way or some different way; rather, the man I myself know to have first initiated unjust deeds against the Greeks—this is the man I will focus upon as I work my way into the story. And along the way I will tell of both the small and the great cities of men, since many of those that were great of old are now small, and those that were great in my day were small in the past. Knowing well that human fortune is ever changing, I will record the story of both great and small alike.

not sure if they are true

great ↔ small
↳ cyclical history
↳ history like humans baby → adult

10 Priam was the king of Troy at the time of the Trojan War. The Spartan woman is Helen.

Croesus and Tales of Lydia

Croesus is legendarily wealthy ("as rich as Croesus") and was in historical fact king of Lydia in the 6th century BC. We do not know what sources Herodotus had available to him as he tried to put together a depiction of Croesus and his reign. It is possible that Herodotus consulted with chroniclers in the Lydian capital; but Lydia was immediately adjacent to Greek Ionia, and the names and stories and details may well all come from Ionian sources. Certainly an important source was someone close to the oracle of Apollo at Delphi, as we will see.

The way Herodotus strings together his narrative repays study. At first, the initial series of stories—Gyges, Arion, Solon, Atys, and Adrastus—may seem rather random, and like set pieces, designed to entertain more than to inform us about the "history" of the times. Entertain they do, but each story also sets up ("prefigures" is the term scholars use) motifs or themes that will recur, in both the Lydian tales and throughout the *Histories*. The recurrence of these key motifs and themes is critical to providing the reader a sort of road map to how Herodotus's universe works. Power leads, *naturally*, to an urge to expand one's power. Arrogance of power leads, *inevitably*, to a downfall. Divine advice can be beyond human comprehension. Violation of norms leads, *by justice*, to correction. It is hard to tease out how much of this is psychological insight, how much an assertion of historical predictability ("history repeats itself"), and how much an affirmation of divine control over human affairs (meaning both "fate" and "divine justice"). This mix of history, psychology, ethics, and metaphysics makes Herodotus's *Histories* less comfortable as a "historical" text, but also potentially rich—in the manner of literature—in the questions it raises and the provisional answers it provides.

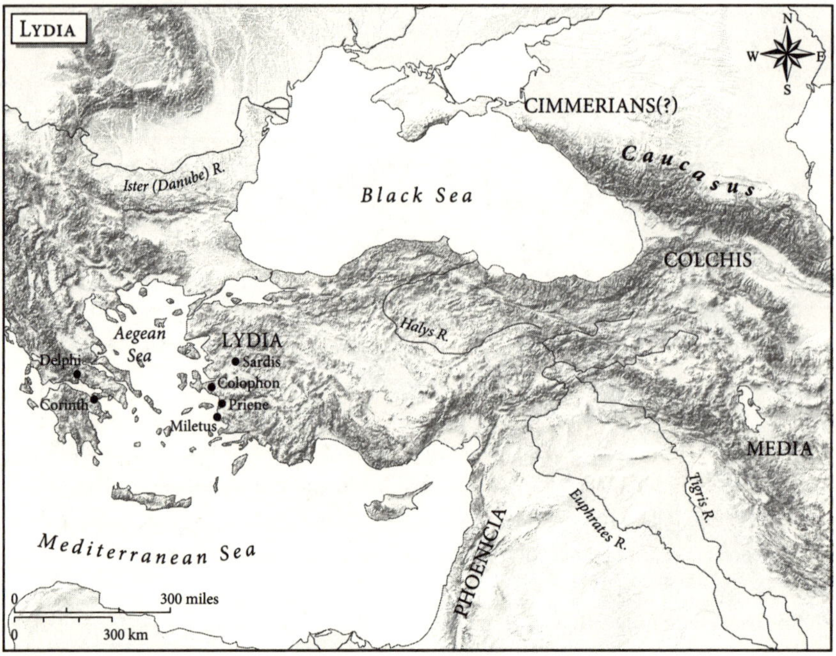

MAP 1.2

Croesus

Croesus was king of Lydia in c. 560–546 BC. The man "first within my own knowledge" (1.5) thus predates Herodotus by 2–3 generations, which is typical of what modern scholars define as the limits to accuracy for orally transmitted information. Characteristic of the narrative style is the introduction of the focal subject, Croesus, followed immediately by a long detour into the background, which here includes the previous four generations.

1.6 Croesus was by birth a Lydian, son of Alyattes, and ruler of the peoples this side of the Halys, a river that flows from the south between Syria and Paphlagonia, and drains northward into the sea called the Euxine.[11] This man Croesus was, to my knowledge, the first foreigner to subject Greeks to the paying of tribute, and to make others of the Greeks his allies—his subjects being the Ionians, Aeolians, and Asiatic Dorians, and the Spartans his allies. Before the reign of Croesus, all Greeks were free: for the invasion of the Cimmerians into Ionia, though before Croesus's time, was not really a conquest of the cities, but rather a raid that led to the cities' plunder.

Gyges and the Wife of Candaules

Some key motifs: the hubristic claim of the ruler ("fairest woman of them all"); the ruler's rejection of sound guidance from an advisor; the strength of action of the

11 The Black Sea.

queen; the transgression of a cultural boundary ("a deep disgrace to be seen naked"); retribution; reliance on the oracle; and the curse that will come to pass in the fifth generation.

The royal power, which had belonged to the clan of the Heraclids,[12] passed 1.7
into the family of Croesus—the clan called the Mermnads—in the following way. Once there was a ruler of Sardis named Candaules (whom the Greeks call Myrsilus), and he was descended from Alcaeus the son of Heracles. In fact the first of the Heraclids to be king of Sardis was Agron son of Ninus son of Belus son of Alcaeus, and Candaules son of Myrsus was the last. Before Agron, those ruling over this land were the descendants of Lydus son of Atys, from whom the entire *Lydian* people are given their name (they were previously known as the Maeonians). From the line of Lydus, the command of an oracle gave control of the kingship to the Heraclids, the descendants of Heracles and a slave-woman belonging to Iardanus. The Heraclids ruled for two and twenty generations of men, five hundred and five years, each son taking up the kingship from his father—up to the time of Candaules son of Myrsus.

Now this king Candaules fell passionately in love with his own wife, and so 1.8
much so that he considered his wife much the fairest woman of them all. Among his spearmen there was a particular favorite, Gyges son of Dascylus. Candaules discussed the most important matters with Gyges, and, because he thought so much of his wife, he especially liked to talk about his wife's beauty. Things were destined to work out badly for Candaules, and so after but a little while he said to Gyges, "Gyges, I don't think you believe me when I say how lovely my wife is. Since 'ears are less easily convinced than eyes,'[13] let's arrange it so you can see her naked." Gyges cried out and said, "Master, what a terrible thing to say—that I look upon my own mistress naked! 'A woman without clothes is also without shame.' Long ago rules of propriety were discovered by men, rules that must be taken to heart. Among these rules is this: that a man look to his own. I believe you—she is the most beautiful of all women!—and I beg you: don't ask me to do something so against the customs of our land."

So saying, he tried to resist, afraid of what terrible things might happen to 1.9
him. But Candaules answered, "Gyges, you needn't be afraid of me—I am not saying this in order to test you; nor of my wife—no harm will come to you from her. I will work the whole business so that she will never know you have seen her. I will station you behind the open door of the room where we sleep. After I go in my wife too will come to bed. A chair sits near the entrance: on that she will lay her clothes as she takes them off, one by one, and you will have plenty of time to look her over. When she steps from the chair to the bed and her back is turned to you, be careful then that she not see you as you go out the door."

12 The suffix *-id* or *-ad* means "descendants of," thus this clan claimed the Greek hero and demigod Heracles (Roman Hercules) as their ancestor.

13 "Eyes are more accurate witnesses than ears" is a proverbial saying attributed to the Greek wise man Heraclitus (as quoted by Polybius, 12.27), who was active in the generation before Herodotus. The proverb Gyges quotes in return is from an unknown source.

1.10 Not able to get away, Gyges gave his consent. So Candaules, when he decided it was time for bed, brought Gyges to the room. Soon afterward the wife arrived too. Gyges watched as she came in and took off her clothes. When the wife went to bed and her back was turned, he stirred and slipped outside—but the wife saw him as he was going out. She understood then what her husband had done; and yet she neither cried out in her shame nor gave any indication that she knew. For she had resolved to take vengeance on Candaules. Among the Lydians, and indeed among almost all foreign peoples, it is a deep disgrace for even a man to be seen naked.[14]

1.11 For the time being, then, she revealed nothing and held her peace. But as soon as it was day, she got ready the servants particularly loyal to herself, and summoned Gyges. Thinking she knew nothing of what had happened he came when summoned—there was nothing unusual in the queen's calling for him. But when Gyges arrived, the wife said, "Gyges, I am giving you a choice. There are now two paths open to you and you can take whichever you wish. Either kill Candaules and take me as your wife and Lydia as your kingdom, or, to stop you from obeying Candaules in everything and seeing what you shouldn't, you will die at once. One of you must die: either he who contrived this, or you, who looked on me naked and acted against the customs of our land." For a while Gyges was dumbstruck at her words, but then he begged her not to force him to make such a decision. He did not persuade her, though, and he saw that dire necessity truly lay upon him: either his master must die or he himself must die at the hands of others. He decided to live. He then spoke up and asked, "Since you force me to kill my master against my will, come, let me hear in what way we shall make our attack." And she answered, "The assault will be from the very spot where he exposed me naked; and you will attack him as he sleeps."

1.12 The plot was ready, then, and when night fell Gyges followed the wife to the bedchamber—for Gyges was trapped, and there was no way out: either he or Candaules had to die. She gave him a dagger and hid him behind the selfsame door. Later, as Candaules was taking his rest, Gyges slipped out and killed him, and thus came to possess both the wife and the kingship.

1.13 So Gyges gained hold of the kingship,[15] and his rule was made firm by sanction of the oracle at Delphi. That came about like this. The Lydians thought the violent death of Candaules a monstrous business and were up in arms, but the supporters of Gyges and the rest of the Lydians came to an agreement: if the oracle chose him as king of Lydia, he would be king; and if it did not, he would give back the rule to the Heraclids. The oracle in fact chose him, and thus Gyges was made king. The Pythian priestess at Delphi added, however, that the Heraclids would have vengeance on a descendant of Gyges in the fifth generation. But to this prophecy both Lydians and their kings paid no attention—until it came to pass.

1.14 Thus the Mermnads came to possess the rule, taking it from the Heraclids, and as soon as Gyges became king he sent a large number of offerings to Delphi.

14 This fact was baffling to Greek men, much of whose sport and exercise was done in the nude.

15 687 BC. For differences in chronology between Herodotus's account and what modern historians reconstruct, see the table below.

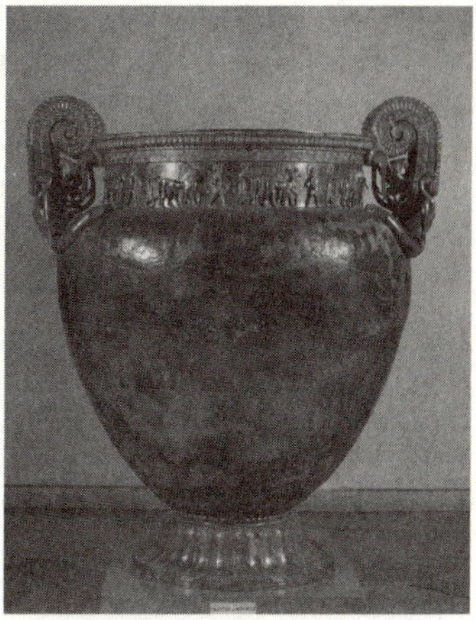

FIGURE 1.1 Wine crater

Indeed of all the silver offerings in Delphi, the greater part are his; and apart from the silver he dedicated a great deal of gold too, among which particularly worth notice are the golden craters, six in number, that he set up there. These stand in the treasury of the Corinthians (though, to tell the truth, the treasury was not the gift of the Corinthian people but of Cypselus son of Eëtion), and have a weight of 30 talents.[16] This man Gyges was, to my knowledge, the first foreigner to set up offerings at Delphi—that is, the first after Midas son of Gordias, the king of Phrygia. Midas set up as an offering the royal throne where he sat to make judgment, a piece well worth seeing; and this throne lies in the same spot as the craters of Gyges. The gold and also the silver which Gyges dedicated is called "Gygian" by the Delphians, after its dedicator.

When he became king Gyges, like others before him, invaded the territory of Miletus and Smyrna, and occupied the lower town of Colophon. But no
other great deed was worked by him in his reign of thirty-eight years. With 1.15
this then as his story we will let him go and turn to make note of the deeds of Ardys, son of Gyges, who took over the kingship after his father. This man seized Priene, and invaded the territory of Miletus; and it was during the time of his rule over Sardis that the Cimmerians, driven from their homeland by the nomadic Scythians, came to Asia and seized Sardis, all but the acropolis.

Early Kings of Lydia: Ardys, Sadyattes, Alyattes and the War against Miletus

Ardys ruled for forty-nine years, and was succeeded by Sadyattes his son. 1.16
Sadyattes was king for twelve years, and after him came Alyattes. Alyattes

TABLE 1.1: THE KINGS OF LYDIA

Name	Reign according to Herodotus	Reign according to modern historians
Gyges	716–678 BC, 38 years	687–652 BC
Ardys	678–629 BC, 49 years	652– ? BC
Sadyattes	629–617 BC, 12 years	? (c. 630–610 BC)
Alyattes	617–560 BC, 57 years	? (c. 610–560 BC)
Croesus	560–546 BC, 14 years	560–546 BC

16 About 775 kg, 1700 pounds. A *treasury* was a small building in which were collected votive offerings from kings and cities. (See Figure 1.3.) Cypselus was the first tyrant of Corinth (7th century BC).

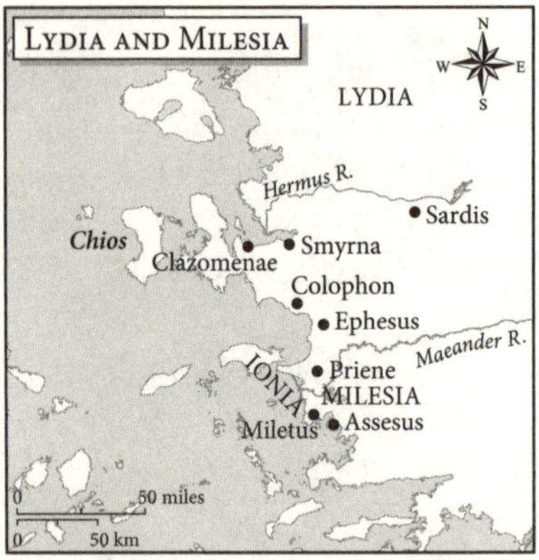

MAP 1.3

made war on the Medes and Cyaxares (a descendant of Deioces), drove the Cimmerians out of Asia, seized Smyrna (which was founded by the people of Colophon), and attacked Clazomenae. With these he did not fare as he hoped, but rather suffered a great defeat. As for the other deeds he performed during his rule here are the ones particularly worth narrating.

1.17 He fought with the Milesians—a war he inherited from his father. He marched on Miletus and besieged the city in a way worth describing. Just when the crops became full-grown he would invade with his army, marching in with pan flutes and wind harps and reed pipes soprano and alto in tone. And once they reached Milesian territory, they did not knock down the farm buildings, nor did they burn them or tear off the doors, but rather throughout the countryside left the buildings standing. But they did destroy the orchards and the crops in the field, and after that they went back home. The Milesians had control over the sea, you see, and so it was pointless to try to blockade them with his army. This then was the reason the Lydian king did not destroy the farm buildings: so that the Milesians would have farmsteads from which to set out to do the sowing and the work in the fields, and thus he would have something to attack and lay waste when the farm-work was done.[17]

1.18 In this manner Alyattes made war for eleven years, and during that time twice heavy blows were inflicted on the Milesians, one at the battle of Limeneium in their own territory and one in the valley of the Maeander. Six of these eleven years Sadyattes son of Ardys was the one ruling Lydia and attacking the Milesian territory with his army—and Sadyattes was also the one who started the war. For the last five years following these six it was then Alyattes, Sadyattes' son, who waged the war. So, Alyattes inherited the war from his father, as I have explained, but he pursued it with passion.

None of the Ionians, excepting only the men of Chios, came to the Milesians' relief in this war; and the Chians' help was by way of even return, since the Milesians had supported the Chians in their war against the Erythraeans.

1.19 Now in the twelfth year, as the crop was being burned by the army, an important thing happened. Just as the crop began to burn, the flames, blown by a strong gust of wind, set afire the temple of Athena of Assesus, and the temple burned to the ground. At the time, no one thought much about it, but afterward, when the army had arrived back in Sardis, Alyattes fell ill. The sickness

17 Greek readers will have been struck by the similarity of this strategy to the annual Spartan invasions of Attica (the area around Athens) in the Peloponnesian War. (Herodotus wrote his work during the run-up and start of that war: see Introduction.)

lasted longer than it should and so he sent a delegation to consult the oracle at Delphi—though it's unclear whether someone advised this or he himself thought to send to the god and ask about his sickness. When the emissaries arrived at Delphi the Pythian priestess declared that she would give no reply until they rebuilt the temple of Athena they had burned at Assesus in Miletus.

That's what I know from listening to the Delphians. The Milesians add to it this 1.20
detail. Periander the son of Cypselus was bound very closely by guest-friendship[18] to the man who was king of Miletus at that time, Thrasybulus. So, as soon as he learned the oracle's reply to Alyattes, he sent a messenger to tell Thrasybulus, allowing him to make plans in full knowledge of the situation that lay at hand.

That's what the Milesians say happened. In any case, Alyattes, when he 1.21
heard what the oracle had to say, immediately sent a herald to Miletus because he wanted to make a truce with Thrasybulus and the Milesians for whatever time it would take to rebuild the temple. So the herald went off to Miletus. Thrasybulus, however, knew all about the matter, and understood full well what Alyattes wanted to do; so he made a clever plan. He ordered brought to the public square all the grain in the city, public and private, and bade that at his signal everyone should drink and carouse with one another.

Thrasybulus arranged all this intending that the herald from Sardis see a 1.22
great mound of grain lying there and the people enjoying themselves, and report this back to Alyattes. And that is what happened. The herald saw exactly that, conveyed the king's appointed message to Thrasybulus, and returned to Sardis; and for this very reason, as my inquiries have confirmed, the desire for peace came about. Alyattes had expected that there would be a fierce grain shortage in Miletus, and that the people would be at their wit's end from distress and misery; yet the herald when he came home from Miletus reported the very opposite of what Alyattes had anticipated. Afterward, then, peace came about for these peoples, to the point that they became mutual guest-friends and allies. Alyattes built not one but two temples to Athena in Assesus; and he recovered from his illness. That then is the story of Alyattes' war with the Milesians and Thrasybulus.

Periander at Corinth: Arion and the Dolphin

A characteristic narrative move is the introduction of "digressions" such as the story here, which flows from the incidental mention of Periander and interrupts the narrative of the war against Miletus. The songs Arion performs are religious in nature and his performance in costume marks him as a pious figure singing in honor of the god. Some key motifs: the mutability of human fortune; divine rescue of the pious and retribution for the impious; corrupting allure of riches. Periander is a historical figure, ruler of the powerful Greek city of Corinth.

18 Guest-friendship (*xenia*) was a formalized connection between powerful people, involving hospitality and help, and carrying forward over generations.

1.23 

MAP 1.4

Now Periander son of Cypselus—the one who told Thrasybulus about the oracle—was the ruler of Corinth. The Corinthians say, and the Lesbians agree, that it was during his lifetime that a very great marvel occurred—when Arion of Methymna was carried to Cape Taenarum on the back of a dolphin. Arion was a citharode[19] second to none of that age, and he was, to my knowledge, the first man to compose and name the dithyrambic song,[20] and the first to train a choir to perform one, at Corinth.

1.24 The story goes that this man Arion, having spent most of his time at the court of Periander, had an urge to sail to Italy and Sicily. Once there he made a lot of money and then wanted to come home to Corinth. He trusted no one so much as the Corinthians, so he hired a ship of Corinthian men and set sail from Tarentum. But when they got on the open sea, the Corinthians hatched a plot to throw Arion overboard and take his money. Arion found out and beseeched them, offering them the money and begging for his life. The sailors would have none of it, though, ordering him either to kill himself, if he wanted to be buried on land, or to jump into the sea right then and there. Under threat and at a loss, Arion then begged them to let him stand on the quarterdeck in his robes and to sing; and he promised after singing to make an end of himself. The prospect of hearing the best singer in the world was a pleasant one to the sailors, and so they withdrew from the stern to the middle of the ship. Arion

FIGURE 1.2 Citharode

19 A citharode (see Figure 1.2) sang while accompanying himself with a large lyre (the *cithara*) meant for performance to large audiences. Successful singers were the rock stars of the era, able to fill entire theaters and thereby make great sums of money.
20 The innovation claimed here was that he trained choruses to sing and dance to songs that included a mythic story in addition to the music and dance; this particular type of formal song was known as the *dithyramb* and is credited by Aristotle as being the first step toward what will become Greek tragedy.

put on all his robes, took up the cithara, and standing on the deck he sang the Orthian Song[21] all the way through; then, when the song was over, he threw himself into the sea, just as he was, with all his robes. The crew sailed away to Corinth, but—the story goes—a dolphin took Arion on his back and carried him to Cape Taenarum. Once he reached land, Arion went to Corinth, still in his singing robes. On his arrival he described everything that had happened, and Periander, not believing him, held Arion under guard at the palace, while keeping an eye out for the sailors. And when the sailors arrived, he summoned them, asking what news they had of Arion. The sailors said that he was safe and sound in Italy and that they had left him doing well in Tarentum. But no sooner had they spoken than Arion presented himself, dressed just as he was when he jumped off the ship. Stunned and confused, the sailors confessed, no longer able to deny what was manifestly proved against them. That's the story the Corinthians and Lesbians tell, and there is in fact a statue of Arion, a small bronze one, at Cape Taenarum—the figure of a man riding upon a dolphin.

Alyattes—the Lydian who had waged war against the Milesians—then 1.25
died, after a reign of fifty-seven years. In thanks for his delivery from disease he became the second of this dynasty to set up an offering at Delphi: a huge crater of silver and a crater-stand welded of iron. This crater-stand is truly worth seeing, even among all the offerings at Delphi, since it is the work of Glaucus of Chios, the only man ever to discover how to weld iron together.

Croesus and Solon

Solon stands in as representative of archaic Greek wisdom. Solon was a famous man, one of the "founding fathers" for what would become democratic Athens; he is said to have died in c. 559 BC, and if that is right then the meeting here described is entirely legendary. Note the strongly schematic oppositions in play: between Eastern arrogance (hubris) and Greek wisdom; excess and moderation; selfish materialism and selfless piety (to family and the state as well as the gods). Some other key motifs: the figure of the wise advisor (twice: once heeded, once ignored); the hubristic claim of the ruler ("the most prosperous"); the uncontrolled urge to imperial expansion; the mutability of human fortune.

On the death of Alyattes, his son Croesus succeeded to the kingship, at the age 1.26
of thirty-five years. The first of the Greeks he attacked were the Ephesians. The Ephesians, surrounded and under siege, tied a rope from the old city wall to the temple of Artemis, thereby putting the city under the goddess's protection—a distance of seven stades.[22] The Ephesians were the first he attacked; but he attacked in turn each of the Ionians and Aeolians, on one pretext or another, laying on a grave accusation where he could find it, and petty excuses for the rest.

21 A traditional high-pitched hymn sung in honor of the god Apollo.

22 A long distance, about 3/4 of a mile, 1200 meters. The strategy is to make the entire city sacrosanct by using a physical link from the sacred temple to the city wall; by implication, Croesus does not respect the sanctity thereby conferred and conquers the city anyway.

1.27 Once he had subjected the Greeks on mainland Asia to the paying of tribute,[23] Croesus then formed a plan to build ships and attack the Greek islands. When he had everything ready for the construction of the ships, Bias of Priene came to Sardis, as some tell the tale, or as others tell it, Pittacus of Mytilene,[24] and in reply to Croesus's inquiry about what news there was from Greece, said (and so stopped the ship building), "King, the islanders are buying up thousands of horses, intending to march on you and Sardis." Croesus, taking the remark seriously, said, "Ah, ye gods, I pray you make this come to pass, that the islanders meet the sons of the Lydians on horseback!"[25] The Greek then replied, "King, you eagerly pray to catch the islanders on horseback and on land, and no doubt with justice. But what do you think the islanders pray for? As soon as they heard that you were going to build ships to attack them, don't you think they prayed to catch the Lydians on the sea? There, they can expect to take vengeance on you for the Greeks of the mainland, whom you made your slaves and now hold as such." Croesus was delighted at the moral of the story—he thought the Greek spoke shrewdly—and so he decided to leave off the building of the ships. That then is how he came to make an alliance of guest-friendship with the Ionians who lived on the islands.

1.28 Over time, almost all of the peoples in Asia who live on this side of the river Halys were under his sway. The Cilicians and the Lycians proved exceptions, but Croesus made everyone else his subjects: the Lydians, Phrygians, Mysians, Mariandynians, Chalybians, Paphlagonians, Thracians both Thynian and Bithynian, Carians, Ionians, Dorians, Aeolians, Pamphylians.

1.29 So, then, did Croesus subdue all these peoples and make them part of the Lydian empire. To Sardis, now at its height of prosperity, came all the Greek wise men of the time, one by one. And among these was Solon, an Athenian man. Solon had been asked by the Athenians to set up written laws and then had gone abroad for ten years—claiming to be off on a world tour, but in fact so as not to be forced to repeal any of the laws he had made. (The Athenians couldn't make changes themselves, you understand, since they were constrained by mighty oaths to use for ten years whatever laws Solon set in place.)

1.30 For this reason, then—but to see the world too—Solon had gone abroad, paying a visit to the court of Amasis in Egypt and also, now, to the court of Croesus in Sardis. On his arrival, Croesus received him hospitably and entertained him as a guest in the palace. Later, on the third or fourth day, Croesus had his servants take Solon around the treasure rooms and show him the magnitude of his prosperity. Solon gazed upon it all and examined it carefully.

Not worth

23 Paying money as annual tribute to the king marks these Greeks as no longer free, in Greek terms effectively the "slaves" of the Lydian king. Herodotus's readers might also think here of the contemporary Athenian Empire, by which democratic Athens subjected many Greek states to the paying of tribute.

24 Bias of Priene and Pittacus of Mytilene are usually included in lists of the canonical Seven Sages of Greece.

25 The Lydians were famous for their exceptionally well-trained and effective cavalry, whereas the inhabitants of the small Greek islands would have had little opportunity to develop this skill. Conversely, the islanders were famed for their skills in fighting at sea.

When the moment seemed right, Croesus asked, "Athenian friend, many a report has come to our court about you, your wisdom and your travels, how for love of knowledge and to see the world you have traversed many a land. So now, I cannot resist asking whether there is one who is the most prosperous of all you have seen?"[26]

Croesus put the question fully convinced that he himself was the one, but Solon, uninterested in flattery, spoke out the truth: "King, yes I have—Tellus the Athenian." Croesus was taken aback. "And why," he asked sharply, "do you judge *Tellus* the most prosperous?" Solon said, "Tellus had sons in a time when the city was doing well, beautiful, refined sons, and he lived to see from each of them grandchildren, and the grandchildren survived and flourished; moreover, he had wealth, at least by our standards, and in this prosperity he ended his life in most glorious fashion—for at a time of war for Athens he came to the aid of his fellow citizens in Eleusis, put the enemy to flight, and died with great bravery, for which the Athenians gave him a public burial on the very spot where he fell, and honored him greatly."

Solon's account of the great prosperity surrounding Tellus goaded Croesus, 1.31
and so he asked who was the next most prosperous man he had seen, thinking to carry off second prize at least. But Solon said: "Cleobis and Biton. These two, Argive in race, had livelihood enough, and in addition had remarkable bodily strength. They were both prize athletes, and the story is told that once, when the Argives were celebrating a festival for the goddess Hera, it was critical that their mother be brought to the temple by cart—but the oxen were not back from the field at the appointed hour. Want of time prevented them from doing anything else, and so the young men put on the yoke and dragged the cart themselves. The mother rode in the cart, traveling a distance of forty-five stades,[27] and thus arrived at the temple. This they accomplished, in full view of the entire crowd, and then enjoyed the best possible end of life—and the god made clear thereby that it was better for a man to die than to live. You see, the Argive men standing round were congratulating the young men on their strength, and the Argive women were congratulating the mother for the fine sons she had. The mother, greatly overjoyed with what her sons had done and what the crowd had said, stood opposite the cult statue and prayed for the goddess to give to Cleobis and Biton, who had honored her greatly, the best thing that mortal man can receive. Following this prayer, they sacrificed and feasted, and the youths lay down to sleep on the temple floor. And they never stood again—caught by life's end. The Argives made statues of the youths, since they had proved to be outstanding men, and set these up as offerings at Delphi."

26 The Greek word here, *olbios*, sometimes translated as *happy*, means blessed with good fortune, but can also mean rich in material goods. The entire passage is suffused with a fundamental ambiguity as to whether human happiness or material wealth is the subject; both devolve from divine favor.

27 About 5 miles, 8 km. This is a remarkable feat: ox carts were crude and heavy, and roads were primitive.

1.32 So Solon gave out the second prize for good fortune[28] to these two, and Croesus, seething, said, "Athenian friend, do you so disdain my good fortune that you rank me below mere private citizens?"

"Croesus," said Solon, "you ask me about human affairs, but I know only that the divine is always begrudging and baffling. Over a length of time there are many sights that no one wants to see, and many ills to suffer. I reckon the limit of a man's life at seventy years. These seventy years add up to twenty-five thousand and two hundred days, not counting the intercalary months;[29] and, if every second year you add a month to align seasons and calendar, there will be thirty-five intercalary months over the seventy years, and those months add up to one thousand and fifty days. The sum total of days over the course of seventy years is, then, twenty-six thousand two hundred and fifty, and of these not one day among them ever brings the same experience as another day. So you see, Croesus: for mankind all of life is but chance—what each day happens to bring.

"You appear to me to be very rich, and a king over many men; but that which you ask me, I cannot yet say, not until I hear that you have come nobly to the end of your lifetime. For the rich man is in no way more prosperous than the man who has only enough for a day, unless the good fortune follow that he who has many fine things also ends his life well. Many very rich people are without true prosperity, and many of those with modest livelihood have great fortune. The man who is very rich but not really prosperous has advantage over the fortunate man in only two ways, but the fortunate man has advantage in many. The rich man is more able to fulfill his desire and also to bear a great and ruinous fall, and in these things he holds the advantage; whereas the fortunate man has not the same capability for a ruinous fall nor for fulfilling desire, but his good fortune keeps these at bay, and he is sound of limb, without illness, without experience of evil, with good children and good looks. If in addition to all that he ends his life well, here then is the man you seek, here is the one worthy of the name "prosperous." But before he dies, you must hold back: do not yet name him "prosperous" or "blessed" but only a man of good fortune.

"No mortal man is able to have everything, just as no country is able to provide everything for itself, but has one thing and lacks another; and that country which has the most, is the best. Similarly the body of a man is not at all self-sufficient, but has one thing and lacks another; and he who continues to hold onto the most, and then ends his life in blessed fashion, this man, King, is in my view the one who justly carries the title. One has to look to the

28 The terms change here, from *olbios* ("happy, rich") to *eudaimoniē*, which is the usual Greek word for "happiness" but also refers to being blessed, literally "favored by the gods."

29 The calculation is simplified, as if there were 360 days in a year. In fact the calendar year was based on 12 months of 29–30 days, totaling 354 days a year. To bring the solar and calendar years into (approximate) alignment, the Greeks had to adjust by adding an extra month (the intercalary month) every other year. In this calculation, Solon displays his firm control over matters of science and mathematics, one aspect of his wise man persona.

Handwritten margin annotations: move to life + happiness than wealth; Self-sufficiency → happiness; Not your own doing; YOU never KNOW; Never know what the future brings; wait till end to really know → at best only today, not secure → Nothing bad, or by chance after death

end of everything, how it turns out: the god who gives many a glimpse of the heights of prosperity is also the god who overturns them by the roots."

So spoke Solon. Croesus was not at all pleased, nor was he impressed; and 1.33
so he sent him away, thinking the man surely a simpleton, who dismisses all the good that lies to hand and urges to look to the end of everything.

Atys and Adrastus

This tale, another legend attached to the figure of Croesus, explores further the mutability of human fortune, this time with an emphasis on the sort of irony we associate with Greek tragedy: the one who thinks to see the dream's meaning is blind to the god's intention; the protector unwittingly becomes the killer; the effort to thwart what is fated leads to fate's fulfillment. Motifs include then the limits of mortal understanding; the inescapability of fate; the ambiguity of divine messages. How the arrogance of Croesus exposed in the Solon episode relates to the tragic events here would have been clear to a Greek: to think oneself the best is to display hubris, since it shows a lack of awareness of mortal limitations; and the divine reaction to hubris is nemesis, the retribution that brings an arrogant man to ruin.

After Solon was gone, a mighty retribution (*nemesis*) from the god came to 1.34
lay hold of Croesus—in all probability because he considered himself the most prosperous of all men. That very night a dream stood over Croesus in his sleep, and declared unerringly the evils that were to come to pass for his son. Croesus had two children, one of whom was crippled—he was deaf and mute—and the other far the first of those his age in every way. That one's name was Atys. The dream was about this Atys, and it revealed to Croesus that he was going to die from the blow of an iron spear. When Croesus awoke he thought it over, and he was frightened by the dream. So he brought in a bride for his son; he stopped sending him on military expeditions altogether, even though Atys had often been in command; and, gathering up from the men's quarters the spears and javelins and all such instruments of war, he heaped them up in the storerooms, to be sure that a spear hanging on the wall didn't chance to fall on his son.

Croesus was busy with his son's wedding when there came to Sardis a man 1.35
gripped by misfortune, with blood on his hands, a Phrygian by birth and of royal ancestry. This man came to the palace of Croesus asking for ritual purification, as was the custom of that place, and Croesus purified him—the purification ritual for the Lydians is similar to that of the Greeks. Once he had performed the customary rites, Croesus asked where the man came from and who he was, saying, "Who are you and what part of Phrygia do you come from, to sit here by the fireside?[30] And what man or woman did you slay?" The man replied, "King, I am the son of Gordias son of Midas, and my name is

30 This echoes a recurrent line in Homer's *Odyssey*, "Who are you? Who are your parents? Where do you come from?" and thus gives the scene an epic atmosphere. The warning dream is likewise a motif taken from Homer.

Adrastus.[31] Against my will I killed my own brother, and I am here now being driven from the land by my father, stripped of all material possessions." "You are the offspring of men who are my guest-friends," answered Croesus, "and so you have come to friends. You will stay here in my palace, and you will lack nothing in material goods. As for this misfortune of yours, bear it as lightly as you can: that will do you the most good."

1.36 And so Adrastus came to live at the court of Croesus. In this same time there appeared on Mount Olympus in Mysia a great and monstrous boar. Hurtling down from the mountain the boar would ravage the crops of the Mysians. Time and again the Mysians would go out to fight the boar but do him no harm while being hurt themselves. At last, then, messengers from the Mysians came to the court of Croesus and said, "King, a great and monstrous boar has appeared in our land, and he is devastating our crops. We have done our best to kill him, but without success. We therefore make this request: send us your son and your pick of young men and dogs, so that we can drive the boar from our land." That then was their request. But Croesus, mindful of the dream, said, "Say nothing further about my son—I cannot send him along, as he is newly married and that is at the moment his main concern; but I will send my pick of the young men and the whole of my pack of hunting dogs, and I will command these to try their best to drive this wild beast from your land."

1.37 So Croesus replied, and the Mysians were satisfied. But just then Croesus's son came in, having heard of the Mysians' request. And when Croesus refused to send the son along with them, the young man said, "Father, before now, gaining distinction by going to wars and to hunts was all that was fine and noble. These days you keep me barred from both, though surely you haven't seen in me either cowardice or faintness of heart. What face am I to put on as I go to and from the central square? What sort of man will people take me for? And what of my newly wedded wife—what kind of man will she think she's living with? Either let me go to this hunt, or tell me some compelling reason why doing it this way is better."

1.38 Croesus then replied, "Son, I am doing it this way not because I have noticed cowardice or anything else ignoble in you; rather, a dream vision stood over me in my sleep and told me that you would be short-lived, that you would die from an iron spear. It was in reaction to this dream that I hurried along your marriage and do not send you along on the present expedition; I was being protective, looking for how I might steal you from fate, for my lifetime at least. For you are really my only child—that other one, the cripple who cannot hear, I don't consider my own."

1.39 The young man replied, "It's understandable that, after you saw such a vision, you were protective of me. But it's only right for me to point out what

31 In Greek Adrastus means "unable to escape/be escaped," and that will dovetail with the ironic conclusion to the story. (*Adrasteia* is also a name for *Nemesis*, inescapable divine Retribution.) Atys is a real Lydian name, but to a Greek sounds like the word for "Ruin" (*atê*).

you don't understand about the dream, what it has made you forget: you say that the dream said that I will die from an iron spear. But what sort of boar has hands, and thus what sort of iron spear are you afraid of? If it said that I would die by a tusk, or anything else appropriate to a boar, then you certainly ought to be doing exactly what you're doing. But as it is the dream said 'from an iron spear.' Therefore, seeing that the fight here is not against men, let me go."

Croesus replied, "Son, your view of the dream does in a way outdo mine, 1.40
and so you win. I change my mind: you are allowed to go to the hunt."

So spoke Croesus. He then sent for the Phrygian Adrastus, and when he 1.41
arrived said to him, "Adrastus, I performed the rites of purification for you when you were struck by a nasty misfortune—for which I do not reproach you—and I have welcomed you into my house, covering your every expense. Now—since you owe me a kindness in return for the kindness I rendered you—I need you to be my son's bodyguard as he sets forth to the hunt, to keep away the danger of thieves and criminals along the road. In addition to all that, it is but right that you too go where you can prove your valor and excellence: this is in your ancestry, and, besides, you are strong and able."

"King," replied Adrastus, "I would not otherwise go to this contest: some- 1.42
one with fortune as bad as mine ought not to be with those of his age who are prospering, nor even to want to be, and for that and other reasons I would hold myself back. But as it is, since you urge it and I want to please you—for I do owe you a kindness in return—yes, I consent to do this, and you may expect that your son, whom you ask me to guard, will return home free from harm, as least so far as that lies in the power of the one guarding him."

So Adrastus replied. He then went along, equipped with his pick of young 1.43
men and dogs, and when they got to Mount Olympus they looked for the beast and found it. The men were standing about in a circle hurling their spears at the monstrous boar. Then the stranger and guest-friend, this man who had been cleansed of murder, the one called Adrastus, hurled his spear at the boar, and he missed; but he hit—the son of Croesus. And so the son died, struck by the blow of an iron spear, and the dream's prophecy was fulfilled. Someone then rushed to tell Croesus what had happened; arriving at Sardis, he described to Croesus the fight with the boar and the fate of his child.

Croesus was distraught at the death of his child, and all the more bitter 1.44
since the killer was the very one he himself had made pure. In grief and anger at this turn of fortune, with terrible cries he called upon Zeus the Purifier as witness of what he had suffered at the hands of his guest; and named also Zeus, Protector of the Hearth and Zeus Guardian of Friendship, the former because he had welcomed into his home and fed the stranger, unaware that he was to be the murderer of his son, and the latter because the one sent as a defender had turned out to be the worst of enemies.

Later, the Lydian men came along, carrying the corpse, with the killer fol- 1.45
lowing along behind. Setting himself before the corpse, he offered himself to Croesus, stretching forth his hands, telling him to slay him upon the corpse.

He spoke of his earlier misfortune; and since he had also destroyed the very one who purified him, his life was not worth living. As Croesus listened, even in his own great personal misery he took pity on Adrastus, and he said to him, "Stranger and guest-friend, I have all the justice I need of you, since you condemn yourself to death. You are not to blame for this disaster, or only in the sense that you did something unwittingly; no, it is some god, I suppose, and he signaled to me long ago what was going to happen." And so Croesus buried his son in fitting manner, and once the area near the gravestone was clear of people, Adrastus son of Gordias son of Midas, the killer of his own brother and killer of the one who cleansed him, recognizing that he was the most ill-fortuned of all he had known, stabbed himself and fell upon the tomb.

Croesus Tests the Oracles

Oracles in Greece had deep influence on human affairs. The oracle of Apollo at Delphi, in particular, acted as an instrument to resolve serious political and diplomatic problems, even wars, as we will see. At Delphi, the oracle was delivered by the Pythian priestess, who in response to a request would become possessed by the god and (in literary accounts, at any rate) would speak out the god's reply in perfect hexameter verses. Some key motifs: mortal arrogance toward the divine ("testing" the oracles); the ambiguity in divine messages. The lengthy catalogue of Croesus's sacrifices and gifts exemplifies the theme of eastern luxury and material excess.

1.46 For two years Croesus sat about mourning deeply for the loss of his child. But then it came to pass that the dynasty of Astyages son of Cyaxares was overthrown by Cyrus son of Cambyses and the power of the Persians was growing; whereupon Croesus left off his grief, and began instead to ponder how he could hold back the Persians before they became truly great. With that as his aim, he quickly fashioned a test for the oracles of the Greeks and the one in Libya too: among the Greek oracles, he sent messengers to make consultation at Delphi, at Abae in Phocis, and at Dodona; at the shrines of Amphiaraus and of Trophonius; at Branchidae in Miletus; and as for Libya, he sent yet others to consult the oracle at Ammon. And this is why he sent these messengers to test the oracles: he had in mind that if he found an oracle that had true knowledge, he would then consult it a second time, and ask whether he should make war upon the Persians.

MAP 1.5

1.47 To test the oracles, he sent off messengers with this set of instructions: reckoning from the day they set out from Sardis, on the hundredth day forward they were to consult the oracles, asking what exactly Croesus son of Alyattes and king of the Lydians was doing; and they were to write down whatever divine utterance each oracle delivered and bring that back to him. No one now is able to say what the rest of the oracles responded; but at Delphi, as soon as the Lydians came to the temple to consult the god and asked what they had been instructed to ask, the Pythian priestess said in hexameter verse: *I know the number of the grains of sand and the measure of the sea; / I understand the mute and hear the one who does not speak. / A smell comes to my senses, of a tortoise hard of shell, / boiled in bronze with the flesh of lamb: / bronze laid underneath, and bronze set on top.*

Such were the prophetic verses of the Pythian priestess, and so the Lydian 1.48
messengers wrote them down and went on their way, back to Sardis. Now as the other messengers brought back the oracular responses and appeared before him, Croesus unrolled each scroll and looked upon what was written, and not one of them pleased him; but when he heard what had come from Delphi, at once he offered prayers and praises. The oracle at Delphi he considered the one true oracle, since it alone had revealed what he had done. For, after he had sent the sacred messengers off to the oracles, Croesus watched for the day appointed and devised something that would be impossible to puzzle out or imagine: with his own hands he cut up a tortoise and a lamb and boiled them in a bronze cauldron with a bronze lid set upon it.

That then was the Delphic oracle's response to Croesus. As to the reply of 1.49
the oracle of Amphiaraus at Oropus, no report survives and so I am not able to say what the oracle replied once the Lydians had performed the customary rites at the temple; but I can say that he considered this oracle also to possess unerring truth.

After all this, he worked to gain the Delphic god's favor[32] with great sacri- 1.50
fices: he slaughtered every kind of domestic beast as sacrificial victims, three thousand in count; he heaped up couches overlaid with gold and silver, and golden chalices, and purple robes and gowns, and burned them in a great sacrificial fire. And he gave commands to the Lydians, that everyone sacrifice everything they could to the god. After he was done with the sacrifices, he melted down heaps of gold, beyond measure, and had it beaten into ingots, making each six palms in length, three palms in width, and one palm high.[33] There were one hundred and seventeen of them: four of refined gold, weighing two and a half talents each, and the rest ingots of gold alloyed with silver, two talents each in weight.[34] He also had a statue of a lion made, of refined gold, weighing ten talents. This lion, when the temple at Delphi burned down, fell off the ingots (whereupon it stood), and now is set up in the Corinthian Treasury; it now weighs six and a half talents, for three and a half talents melted away in the fire.

32 Apollo.

33 Each palm is about 3 inches (7.5 cm).

34 Each talent is about 57 pounds (26 kg).

1.51 Once the ingots and the statue were finished, Croesus dispatched them to Delphi and other things too: two wine craters (Figure 1.1), large ones of gold and of silver; the golden crater was set up on the right of the temple's entryway, and the silver crater to the left. These too had to be moved when the temple burned down: now the golden one is set up in the Treasury of the Clazomenians, weighing eight and a half talents plus twelve minas,[35] and the silver one stands in a niche in the front hall of the temple, with a capacity of six hundred amphoras[36]—the Delphians use it to this day as the mixing bowl for wine when they celebrate the feast day called Theophania. The Delphians claim that the craters are the work of Theodorus of Samos, and I think so too: the workmanship is not that of just anyone, or so it looks to me.

FIGURE 1.3 Delphic treasury building (pictured here is the Athenian treasury)

Croesus dispatched also four large silver casks, which have been set up in the Corinthian Treasury; and he also made an offering of two lustral basins, one gold, one silver. The gold one has an engraving that claims it as an offering of the Spartans, but that is not correct: this vessel also is from Croesus. A Delphian man who wanted to curry favor with the Spartans made that engraving; his name I know but I will not record it. There is, however, a statue of a boy with water running through his fingers, and that is a gift of the Spartans—but not the water vessels themselves.

Croesus dispatched many other things too that did not have his name inscribed, including perfectly circular cast silver bowls, and a golden statue, over four feet high, of a woman (which the Delphians say is an image of Croesus's baker). And, finally, Croesus dedicated his wife's necklaces and the sashes from her waist.

FIGURE 1.4 Lustral basin (perirrhanterion) used to purify those entering a temple

1.52 Such were his dispatches to Delphi. To the oracle at Amphiaraus, once he had learned of the hero's valor and ill fate,[37] he

35 A mina is 1/60 of a talent, thus about 1 pound or 1/2 kg.

36 An amphora is a large jug that contains about 10 gallons (40 liters). The capacity of this crater—6000 gallons, 24,000 liters—seems to many commentators fantastically large.

37 In Greek myth, the hero Amphiaraus fought as one of the "Seven against Thebes" and was swallowed up by a sudden chasm in the earth. His tomb was the site of the oracle associated with him.

dedicated a shield of solid gold and a spear also all of gold, the shaft as golden as the spearhead. In my time these were both still lying in Thebes, in the Theban temple of Ismenian Apollo.

When the Lydians were ready to take the gifts to the two oracles, Croesus 1.53
gave instructions to ask the oracles if he, Croesus, should make war upon the Persians, and if he should make an alliance with some other power. When they arrived at their destinations, the Lydians made their offering, and then made inquiry of the oracles with these words: "Croesus, king of the Lydians and other peoples, inasmuch as he considers you alone the true oracles among mortal men, has made offerings befitting your powers of divination. So now it is you he asks, if he should make war upon the Persians, and if he should add some other power as an ally to fight alongside him." Such was their inquiry; and both oracles came to the same judgment, making this prophecy for Croesus, that *if he should make war upon the Persians, he would destroy a great kingdom*; and they also advised him to investigate which among the Greek states were the most powerful and to make those his allies.

When Croesus heard the report of the divine prophesies, he was very 1.54
pleased with the oracles, having now every expectation that he would destroy the kingdom of Cyrus. So he sent again to the Pythian priestess and—having found out how many Delphians there were—he gave two gold coins to each man in Delphi. In return, the Delphians gave Croesus and the Lydians the right to consult the oracle first, exemption from all fees, and the honor of front-row seats at the games; and furthermore set up that for all time any Lydian who wanted to could become a citizen of Delphi.

Once he had bestowed the coins on the Delphians, Croesus consulted the 1.55
oracle a third time—having found revelation of truth in the oracle before, he was hungry for more. And so he inquired of the oracle as to whether his monarchy would last a long time. The Pythian priestess responded with these verses: *At which time a mule becomes king of the Medes, / then, tender-footed Lydian, beside the river Hermus of many pebbles / you must flee: do not stand your ground, and be not ashamed of cowardice.*

Of all the prophecies he had heard from the oracle, Croesus found this by 1.56
far the most pleasing. He now had every expectation that he and his descendants would rule without end—surely, he thought, the Medes could never have as their king a mule instead of a man.

Croesus Seeks an Ally

Just at the moment when the narrator seems ready to depict the Lydian attack on the Persians—the ultimate focal point for the story of Croesus—there is a long pause while the narrator sketches out the early history of Athens and Sparta. This retardation of the narrative's forward movement (a technique Herodotus takes from Homer) is important, since it substantially alters the reader's perspective. The focus on Delphi and now Athens and Sparta re-centers the narrative on Greece, highlights the two Greek city-states that will come to predominate, and rewrites eastern events as events that include the west, even though in fact the alliance with Sparta will have no actual impact on the Lydian–Persian conflict.

Croesus next turned his thoughts to investigating which among the Greek states was the most powerful, so that he could make those his allies. And on inquiry, he found that the Spartans and Athenians were preeminent. . . .

BACKGROUND: ATHENS

We feel a slight shift in what follows to a voice that relies less on folkloristic storytelling and more on presentation and evaluation of "historical" sources, probably a reflection of the move from eastern kingship stories to the oral traditions of Greek family clans. That does not, however, preclude the insertion of what we now see as typical motifs, such as the wise advisor (here ignored), the opposition of Greek cleverness and of eastern credulity (here interestingly complicated), the duplicity of tyrants, the influence of oracles. Also introduced is the important question of what makes for a well-ordered state and the relation of that to the fundamental opposition between tyranny and freedom.

1.59 Of the two Greek powers, Croesus learned that in Athens the entire surrounding territory of Attica had been torn apart and held down by Peisistratus, son of Hippocrates, who by that time had become tyrant of the city. His father Hippocrates was but a private citizen when, as a spectator at the Olympian games, he met with a great omen. He had just finished making his sacrifice, when the cauldrons, standing there full of meat and water but not yet on the fire, started to simmer and boiled over. A Spartan, Chilon,[38] saw the omen—he happened to be standing right there—and gave Hippocrates this advice: "Best would be never to bring a childbearing wife into your house; but, if you have one already, send her away at least; and if you already have a child, disown it." Such was Chilon's advice, but Hippocrates was not inclined to listen. And so it came to pass that there was born to him a son, Peisistratus.

In course of time fighting had broken out between two of the Athenian factions[39]—the Shore Party under Megacles son of Alcmaeon and the Plain Party under Lycurgus son of Aristoleides—and Peisistratus already then harbored thoughts of tyranny. So, he put together a third faction, pretending to be the leader of those from the hill-country, and then carried out his plan.

First Peisistratus stabbed himself and his mules—to wound not to kill—and then he drove his mule-team to the central market of Athens, pretending that he was running away from foes who (he claimed) had tried to kill him as

38 Often included in the list of the "Seven Sages" of antiquity (along with Solon, Bias, Pittacus, Thales, and others).

39 The factions were defined territorially, since the terrain led to different ways of life with different political interests: 1. Shore Party = traders and fishermen, 2. Plain party = landowners of large farms, 3. Hill Party = herdsmen and farmers who worked smaller plots in the hill-country. Political reality was, of course, more complicated, but Herodotus here uses the terminology current in his day.

he was driving out of town. He asked the people to grant him a bodyguard—he who had already distinguished himself as their general in the campaign against the Megarians, capturing Nisaea and working other great deeds as well.

The people of Athens were completely taken in, and so they granted him a chosen force of three hundred citizens—who did not, however, serve as Peisistratus's spearmen,[40] but as his clubmen, for they accompanied him wielding wooden clubs. These men then joined cause with Peisistratus, rose up, and took possession of the acropolis. In such a way did Peisistratus take over as ruler of Athens,[41] but he neither meddled with existing magistracies nor did he change the laws. Rather, he governed the city in accordance with the law as constituted, arranging state affairs properly and well. After not much time 1.60
had passed, however, the factions of Megacles and Lycurgus made a truce and combined forces to depose him and send him into exile. That, then, is how Peisistratus first came to rule Athens, and yet lost the rule before his tyranny was firmly rooted.

As soon as the two factions had driven Peisistratus from power, they began once again to fight with one another. Megacles was getting the worse of these factional struggles, and so he sent a messenger to Peisistratus, to inquire if he would be willing to take Megacles' daughter as wife in return for the tyranny. Peisistratus accepted the offer on the terms prescribed. The two then devised a plan for his return that I find the silliest imaginable—especially inasmuch as from of old the Greeks supposedly were distinguished from barbarian peoples in being more savvy and many removes from credulity and naïveté, and yet at that time these men perpetrated a scheme as silly as this on Athenians, who are said to be foremost among Greeks for their intelligence.

Here was the plan. In the Attic village of Paeania, there was a woman named Phya, who was

FIGURE 1.5 Athena in panoply

40 This alludes to tyrants in general and in particular the Persian king, who, as we will see, goes about with a large bodyguard of spearmen.

41 561/560 BC.

MAP 1.6

almost six feet tall and very good looking as well. They fitted out this woman with a panoply of armor, put her onto a chariot, and showed her how to carry herself so as to present a striking figure; and then they drove the chariot to Athens, sending in advance heralds who, as soon as they reached the city, made proclamation as they had been instructed, saying, "Men of Athens, receive Peisistratus with kindly heart, he whom Athena, honoring him above all men, escorts to her own acropolis herself."[42] So proclaiming, the heralds roamed the city far and wide. Immediately the rumor spread throughout Attica that Athena was acting as escort to Peisistratus, and those in the city, believing the woman to be a goddess, prayed to this mere mortal, and received Peisistratus back.

1.61 In this way Peisistratus took back the tyranny[43] and, as they had agreed, he wedded Megacles' daughter. But Peisistratus already had young children, and

42 The Athenian Acropolis, whose Parthenon was Athena's temple. (Athens is named for its guardian goddess, Athena.)
43 c. 557 BC.

Megacles' clan, the Alcmaeonids, was said to be under a curse; he therefore did not want to have children with his new wife. So he had sex with her, but not in the way that custom dictates. At first, the wife kept the matter secret, but after a while—I don't know whether in answer to a question—she told her mother, and her mother told her father. Megacles thought this a horrific disgrace Peisistratus had brought upon him, and so, in his anger, he now let go his disagreements with the opposition.

When Peisistratus learned of the plot forming against him, he left Attica altogether, going to Eretria, where he gathered his sons to take counsel. The advice of his son Hippias won the day: to retake the tyranny. So they tried to collect money from all the cities that had any sort of obligation to them. Many gave a great deal of money, and the Thebans the most of all. I will not make a long story of it: time passed and eventually all the preparations were made for Peisistratus's return. Argive mercenaries had come from the Peloponnese, and an enthusiastic volunteer named Lygdamis had arrived from Naxos,
bringing both money and fighters. Finally, in the eleventh year, they set forth 1.62
from Eretria and returned to Athens.

Once in Attica, they occupied Marathon first. There, as they were encamped, their partisans from the city came to join them; and others poured in from the villages—those for whom tyranny was more welcome than freedom. And so their numbers swelled. The Athenians in the city had paid Peisistratus little attention while he was collecting money and even after he occupied Marathon. But when they learned that he was marching from Marathon against the city, they lent their support in the fight against him, coming out in full force to oppose the returning exiles. Peisistratus's men meanwhile marched from Marathon to attack the city. The forces met as they came to the temple of Athena in Pallene; there, they took up positions opposite one another. At that moment, by guidance of the goddess, the seer Amphilytus of Acarnania came to stand alongside Peisistratus, and spoke these verses: *the cast has been made, the net is spread out, / and the tuna will come, darting along the shoals through the moonstruck night.*

Possessed by the goddess, Amphilytus spoke forth this oracle, but it was 1.63
Peisistratus who grasped its meaning. Saying that he was following the prophecy, he led his army to the attack. Now at that time the Athenians who had come down from the city had turned to lunch; after lunch quite a few were playing dice, while others were taking a nap. Peisistratus's army swooped upon the Athenians and routed them.

With the Athenians in flight, Peisistratus next devised an exceptionally smart strategy, so that the Athenians would not regroup but would remain scattered. He mounted his sons on horseback and sent them forth; as they overtook the fleeing Athenians, the sons told them what Peisistratus had ordered, that they need not worry for retribution if each went back to his own
house. The Athenians did as they were told. 1.64

So, Peisistratus came to rule Athens a third time[44] and this time he made the tyranny take root, albeit with mercenaries and a great influx of money—some from Athens and the rest from Thrace. Some of the Athenians had not yielded and refused to flee, and from these he took their children as hostages and sent them to live in Naxos (which he had defeated in a war and handed over to Lygdamis). In addition, following the advice of an oracle, he purified Delos, working it like this: as far as one could see from the sacred precinct on Delos, he had the graves dug and the corpses relocated to another part of the island.

Thus did Peisistratus set up his tyranny at Athens, with some Athenians killed in battle, and others—including those of the Alcmaeonid clan—exiled from their homeland.

BACKGROUND: SPARTA

By Herodotus's time, the Spartan state consisted of the Spartans proper, called the Spartiates, and inferiors who sustained them. The Spartiates lived in extraordinary circumstances (soldierly brotherhoods, in effect) that demanded fierce concentration on physical virtue and led to their famous excellence in warfare. The well-ordered government apparatus that supported this military state was much admired in antiquity. Tegea was the last region to fall in Sparta's gradual assertion of control over much of the Peloponnese (the entire south of Greece). Some key motifs: ambiguity of the divine message (one riddle they get right, the other wrong); the important influence of the Delphic oracle in warfare and diplomacy; the researcher's duty to consider carefully conflicting sources.

1.65 Such were the conditions in Athens at this time, as Croesus learned, but of the Spartans, he learned that they had just put behind them great troubles and had recently achieved victory in their struggle with Tegea. In the time of the kingship of Leon and Hegesicles,[45] the Spartans had come to be consistently victorious over their enemies, faltering only against the Tegeans. Now in earlier times, the government of the Spartans had been bad, worse than almost any of the Greeks, as they were poorly organized as well as isolated from others. But they changed into a model state in the time of Lycurgus. He, a Spartiate and a man of some note, traveled to Delphi to consult the oracle. When he entered the great hall of the temple, the Pythian priestess spoke without hesitation these verses: *You, O Lycurgus, have come to my rich temple, / a man dear to Zeus and all those who have their homes on Olympus. / Yet I hesitate: is it to a man, really, or to a god that I give this prophecy? / Nay, 'tis to a god, or so I believe, O Lycurgus.* There are those who say that the priestess also dictated to him the elements of the government as now constituted for the Spartans. But the Spartans themselves tell this story, that Lycurgus imported

44 547/546 BC.

45 The Spartans had two kings at any given time; Leon and Hegesicles ruled in about 575–560 BC.

the constitution from Crete when his nephew, Leobotas, became king of the
Spartans and Lycurgus was appointed his guardian. As soon as he was made
guardian, Lycurgus changed the entire law code and took steps to make sure
that the new laws were not violated. Afterward, he implemented the institu-
tions that have to do with war—the soldierly brotherhood, the bands of thirty,
and the common meals—and, in addition, the offices of Ephor and Elder. In 1.66
this way the Spartans evolved into a model state, and when Lycurgus died,
they set up a temple and worshipped him as a great hero.

With a well-ordered government, good land, and plenty of men, Sparta grew quickly and flourished. No longer did it seem sufficient to pursue peaceful ways. In particular they came to look down on their neighbors, the Arcadians—surely the Spartans were their superiors, they thought—and so they came to consult the oracle at Delphi about that entire land. The Pythian priestess prophesied them this: *You ask me for Arcadia, do you? What you ask is great, and I will not grant it. / Many men there are in Arcadia, rugged acorn-eaters, / and these will stop you. Yet I will not begrudge all: / I will grant you to beat the Tegean land with stomping feet, / and to plot out its fair plain with a measuring line.*

The Spartans held back from the rest of Arcadia once they had heard the oracle's decree, but they attacked the Tegeans, bringing leg irons with them. Relying on the cryptic oracle, they thought they would enslave the Tegeans. But they were worsted in the fight, and those who were captured alive were made to wear the very fetters they had brought with them; and they worked the soil, plotting out the Tegean fields with a measuring line. The leg irons that had bound the Spartans were still extant in my day, hanging as dedications about the temple of Athena Alea in Tegea.

In this earlier war, the Spartans had always fared badly against the Tegeans. 1.67
But by the time of Croesus, when Anaxandrides and Ariston were kings at Sparta,[46] the Spartans had now gotten the upper hand. Here then is the story of how they did it. Since they were always being beaten by the people of Tegea, they sent sacred messengers to Delphi to inquire of the oracle, "To which of the gods should we pray, so as to gain superiority over the Tegeans?" The Pythian priestess prophesied them this: to bring back to Sparta the bones of Orestes, son of Agamemnon. But they were not able to discover where the tomb of Orestes was, so they sent to the god a second time, asking in what land Orestes lay. In reply to the sacred messengers, the Pythian priestess spoke these verses: *In the level plain of Arcadia there lies a place, Tegea, / where two winds blow by brawny force / and there is stroke upon stroke, and pain is laid upon pain. / There the earth that gives forth grain holds the son of Agamemnon. / Bring him back, and you will be lords over Tegea.*

On hearing the oracle, the Spartans were just as far as ever from finding the bones of Orestes, though they looked everywhere, until Lichas, one of the

46 c. 560–550 BC.

Agathoergi (as they are called), figured it out. Now these Agathoergi are the five eldest citizens who retire from the Spartiate cavalry each year. By law, they spend the first year of retirement in service as emissaries for the state,
1.68 busily doing whatever the Spartans send them to do. One of those, Lichas, made his discovery, partly by chance and partly by wits, while he was traveling in Tegea under a truce in effect at this time.

Lichas came upon a smithy working with iron and as he watched him beat and shape the iron he marveled at the workmanship. When the smithy noticed his amazement, he paused from his labor and said, "Spartan stranger, I suppose you would be really amazed, if you had seen what I saw—you who make my ironwork into such a marvel. I wanted to build a well in this courtyard here, but when I tried to dig the hole I came upon a coffin over ten feet long.[47] I couldn't believe that there used to be men that much bigger than men today, and so I opened it: and I saw a skeleton just as big as the coffin. Once I had measured it all, I covered the coffin back up." The Tegean man simply stated what he had seen; Lichas, however, pondered what had been said, and came to the conclusion that this was Orestes, just as the prophecy had spoken. This was how he interpreted it: the smithy's two bellows were the winds; the hammer and anvil the "stroke upon stroke"; and the beaten iron the "pain laid upon pain," guessing that this meant the ills brought upon men by iron's discovery.[48]

Such was his interpretation, and so he traveled back to Sparta and told the whole story to the Spartans. The Spartans then made a show of bringing a charge against him and sending him into exile. Lichas came to Tegea, told the smithy about his troubles, and tried to rent the courtyard—but the smithy was not renting it out. In time, though, he persuaded the smithy and took up residence there; whereupon he dug up the grave, collected the bones, and carried them back to Sparta. From that time,[49] whenever the Spartans and Tegeans came to fight, the Spartans had far the upper hand, they who, by then, controlled much of the Peloponnese.

1.69 All this Croesus learned through his inquiries. He then sent to Sparta messengers, laden with gifts, to ask for an alliance. On arrival they said, "Croesus King of the Lydians and other peoples, has sent us to say this to you: 'Spartans, the god at Delphi proclaimed an oracle, telling me to make Greece my friend and ally. I have made inquiry and find that you are the preeminent state in Greece, and I therefore, in accordance with the oracle, call on you to fulfill my wish to be your friend in peace, and your ally in war. I say this without trickery or deceit." Such was the message that Croesus announced through his heralds.

47 Over 3 m. "Seven cubits" says the Greek.

48 According to Hesiod's *Works and Days* the "Iron Age" is the current era, when food no longer grows on its own and the gods keep separate from men (and thus there are no longer demigods, the offspring of gods and mortals); rather, in the Iron Age life must be hard-won through the toil of farming with iron plows and fighting wars with iron weaponry.

49 c. 550 BC.

The Spartans in turn had already heard of the oracle that had come to Croesus, and were pleased at the Lydian embassy. So they swore oaths to guest-friendship and military alliance. In fact, certain kindnesses from Croesus had created a bond even before this. The Spartans had sent to Sardis to buy gold, wanting to use it for a statue of Apollo (the one that now is set up at Thornax in Laconia), but Croesus had bestowed it upon the buyers as a gift. For this reason too, then, the Spartans welcomed the alliance—as well 1.70
as because he had made them first choice among all the Greeks—and they declared themselves ready whenever he should send for them. Wanting to give something in return to Croesus, they also made him a bronze crater, engraved with fine figurines round its rim, and having a capacity of three hundred amphorae.[50] But this cauldron never reached Sardis, and there are two stories told as to why. The Spartans say that when the crater was on its way to Sardis, it went by Samos, and the Samians found out about the shipment, sailed out with their long ships, and seized it. The Samians, however, say that on its way to Sardis the Spartan embassy was delayed, and then learned that Sardis and Croesus had both been captured—so they put it up for sale in Samos. There some private citizens bought it and set it up in the temple of Hera. And when the ones who sold it got back to Sparta, perhaps they would then say that the Samians had seized it.

Croesus Attacks Cyrus

By this point in the narrative, the reader has been well trained to notice and reflect upon recurrent motifs like the wise advisor, the ambiguity of oracles, and so forth; and we will cease to note these. Two new motifs arise that prefigure important future events. First is the contrast of hard, rugged, poor peoples with those who are more "soft" and used to wealth and luxury. Second is the idea of critical natural boundaries (here the river Halys) that delineate "natural" divisions among people; the one who crosses such boundaries is taken to be a transgressor (a type of hubris), and thus a military attack can set in motion the machinery of divine retribution. Importantly, in Herodotus there is seldom a single chain of causation: the narrative characteristically puts forward a mix of impersonal (including divine), political, and personal (often family-related) motivations.

Now as to Croesus, he had mistaken the oracle's meaning and thus began 1.71
to make plans to attack Cappadocia, fully expecting to overcome Cyrus and crush the power of the Persians. While Croesus was making his preparations for the Persian campaign, a man came to offer him advice—a man the Lydians considered wise even before but whose words now brought him to very high repute. His name was Sandanis, and this is what he said: "King, you prepare to march on men who wear trousers of leather, and whose other clothing is

50 Half the size of the crater described at 1.51, but still huge: roughly 3000 gallons, 12,000 liters.

leather as well;[51] who eat not as much as they want but as much as they have; who possess a rugged, rocky land. These men do not drink wine—they have only water—and do not eat figs, or any other delicacy. If you defeat them in battle, what will you get from them, they who have nothing? But if you are defeated, think what fine things you will lose. Once they have a taste of our luxuries, they will hold them tight, and never let go. For my part, I give thanks to the gods that they have never made the Persians think to march on Lydia." The Persians, you see, had no delicacy or luxury before the Lydians made their attack. But Croesus did not listen to what Sandanis had to say.

1.72 The Cappadocians are called "Syrians" by the Greeks. The Syrians, before the Persians came to power, were subject to the Medes, who at this time were ruled by Cyrus. The border between the kingdom of the Medes and that of the Lydians was the river Halys, which flows from the Armenian mountains through Cilicia, with the Matieni on the right and the Phrygians on the left, but then turns and flows northward, there skirting Cappadocia on the right and Paphlagonia on the left. The Halys thus carves off almost the entire western part of Asia, the lowland from the sea off Cyprus all the way up to the Black Sea. Here the peninsula of Anatolia is at its most thin, a five-day journey by land.[52]

1.73 Many were the reasons that Croesus marched on Cappadocia: for lust of land, wanting to add territory to his empire; because a trusted oracle had told him to; but also because he wanted to take revenge on Cyrus on behalf of Astyages. Now this man Astyages the son of Cyaxares was Croesus's brother-in-law as well as king of the Medes (that is, until Cyrus son of Cambyses came to overthrow him). And this is how Astyages came to be Croesus's in-law. In a time of civil strife, a band of Scythian nomads came as refugees to the land of the Medes, and at that time Cyaxares son of Phraortes son of Deioces held the kingship. In the beginning he treated them well—they were suppliants after all—and he held them in great esteem, asking them to teach some Median youths their language and also their skill in archery.

The weeks passed; time after time the Scythians went on the hunt, and time after time they brought something back. But one day it so happened that they failed to catch anything. They arrived at the court empty-handed and Cyaxares (who it seems had a nasty temper) mistreated them badly, far beyond the bounds of decency. To have suffered such an outrage was intolerable as well as undeserved, and so the Scythians formed a plan of action: taking one of the boys who had been given over for them to teach, they killed him and cut him up. They then prepared the meat just as they would game, took it to Cyaxares as though a gift from the hunt, and got out of the country as fast as they

51 Greeks and Lydians wore tunics and robes made of fabric, so this will seem obviously uncomfortable and distinctly less civilized.

52 "Five days" is a conventional expression, meaning "a few days." The actual distance is far greater, at least 285 miles (460 km).

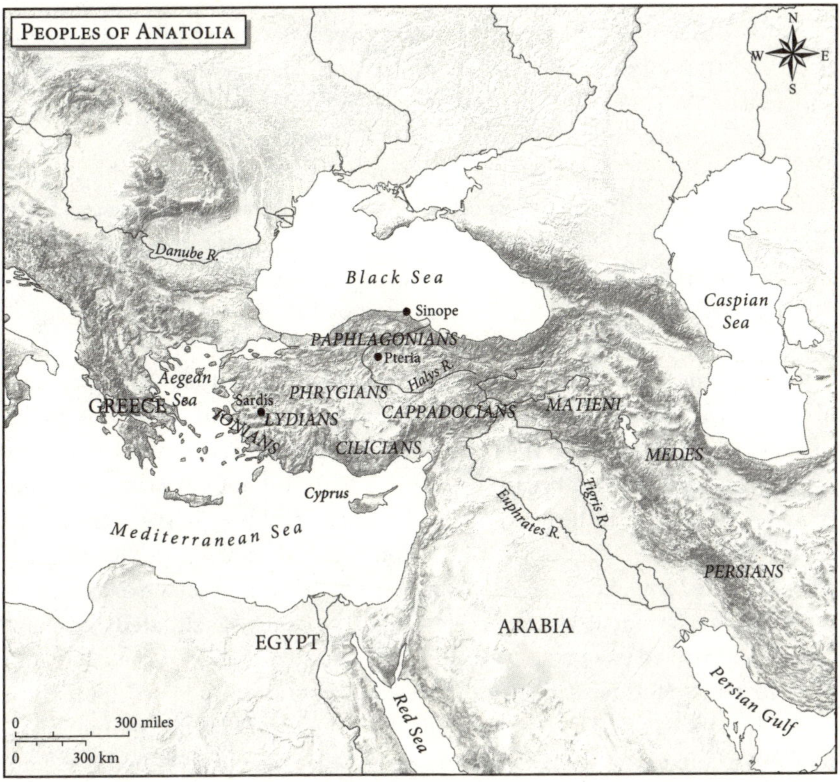

MAP 1.7

could—to Sardis, to the Lydian king Alyattes son of Sadyattes. So, Cyaxares and his fellow diners partook of this meat, even as the Scythians presented themselves as suppliants to Alyattes.

Cyaxares demanded the Scythians be handed over, but Alyattes refused; 1.74
and so war broke out and for five years the Lydians and Medes fought. Often the Medes won, but just as often the Lydians were the victors. One battle was even fought at night. Also, in the sixth year of this evenly fought war, the two sides were joined, and it so happened, just as the battle was raging, that the day suddenly turned to night. This transformation of daylight to darkness had been foretold to the Ionians by Thales of Miletus, who fixed as the year this very one in which the eclipse occurred.[53]

The Lydians and Medes, when they saw night replacing day, stopped from their fighting, and both sides were anxious to broker peace. Appointed to negotiate the truce were Syennesis of Cilicia and Labynetus of Babylon. These two quickly agreed to swear oaths to peace, but also made a marriage connection part of the deal: they decided that Alyattes would give his daughter

53 Probably the eclipse of 28 May 585 BC. Thales was considered the earliest of the Seven Sages.

Aryenis to Astyages, the son of Cyaxares, reasoning that without a strong bond the treaty too would not remain strong. These peoples make sworn oaths using the same rituals as the Greeks; but, as an added seal to the oath, they also slit the skin on their arms, and lick up each other's blood.

1.75 This was the Astyages whom Cyrus overthrew, even though he was his mother's father, and Cyrus presently held him as prisoner—for reasons I will discuss later on. It was in objection to this very coup that Croesus sent to the Delphic oracle in the first place, to ask whether he should march upon the Persians. When he got the prophecy, a cryptic one as we have seen,[54] Croesus—convinced that the oracle favored himself—marched into Persian territory.

When Croesus reached the river Halys, my opinion is that he crossed over along existing bridges. But Greeks generally tell a different story, that Thales of Miletus got him across. The story goes that Croesus was at a loss as to how to cross the river (since the bridges of our time did not yet exist), and that Thales, who was with the army, worked it out so that part of the river flowed left of the army and part to the right. And this is how he did it. Starting upstream of the camp, he had them dig a deep channel in the shape of a crescent moon, so that it went along the back of where the camp was situated; the channel ran out from the ancient river bed and, once it had passed the camp, ran back in again. In this way, with the river split between the two channels, it proved possible to ford the river on both sides. Others tell yet a different story, that the whole of the river was diverted, and that the old river bed dried up. This, however, I cannot accept: for how then could they have crossed the river on their way back?

1.76 Now when Croesus had crossed the river with his army, he came to the part of Cappadocia called Pteria—the most powerful polity in the land, situated in the area near the city of Sinope on the Black Sea. There they set up camp. Then, they pillaged the Syrian farmsteads; captured the main city, enslaving its inhabitants; and overran all the towns round about. And so the Syrians—who had no responsibility for any of this—were driven from their homes.

Cyrus meanwhile collected his own army, enlisting all he could from the lands along his route, and came to face Croesus. Before his army had set out to march, Cyrus had sent heralds to the Ionians, urging them to revolt from Croesus—but they did not do as he asked. So, Cyrus arrived and set up camp opposite Croesus. There, in the territory of Pteria, the armies pitted strength against strength. The battle was fierce; many men fell on both sides; at last night came on and they separated, but neither side had won—so hard did the two armies fight.

1.77 Croesus blamed the size of his army—his fighting force was far fewer in number than that of Cyrus—and when Cyrus did not come out to fight on the next day, he marched back to Sardis. What he had in mind was to summon

54 See 1.53.

the Egyptians in accordance with their treaty (he had made an alliance with the Egyptian king Amasis, before he made the one with the Spartans), to send for the Babylonians (whose king was Labynetus at that time, and whom he had also made his ally), and to tell the Spartans to be there at the time appointed. Once the allies had all gathered and his own army assembled, his thinking went, they would march upon the Persians—at the start of springtime, right after winter had passed. Such were his thoughts, and so on arriving at Sardis he sent messengers to these allies, telling them to gather at Sardis four months hence. As for the current army, the one that had fought with the Persians, he sent away all the mercenaries and they scattered to their homes. As he saw it, there was no chance that Cyrus, whose army had been fought to a standoff, would march against Sardis.

As Croesus was thinking this through, the outer parts of the city started to swarm with snakes. And as the snakes appeared, the horses left off grazing in the pastures and came to gobble them down. Croesus recognized the sight as an omen, as indeed it was—and so he quickly sent sacred messengers to Telmessus, where there were seers who could interpret such things. Though the messengers got there, and the seers told them what the omen meant to convey, they could never tell it to Croesus—for before they had sailed back to Sardis, Croesus was captured. What the Telmessians revealed was that a foreign army was to come against the land of Croesus, and once it came it would conquer those native to the land. "The snake," they said, "is a child of the earth, and the horse a warrior and one who comes from afar." Such was the reply that the Telmessians fashioned for Croesus, at a time when he was already captured, but when they knew nothing yet of what had happened to Sardis and to Croesus himself. 1.78

Cyrus Counterattacks: The Siege of Sardis

Even as Croesus was marching home after the battle of Pteria, Cyrus found out 1.79
that Croesus was intending to disband his army for the season. Taking stock of the situation, he concluded that his best course was to march upon Sardis at once, before the Lydians could assemble their forces a second time. No sooner was this resolved than done; marching his army into Lydia Cyrus arrived as herald of his own coming, outpacing all news of the attack. Croesus was stunned—matters had worked out so entirely opposite to what he had expected—but he nonetheless led the Lydians out to give battle. And at that time, there were none in Asia more manly and valiant than the Lydians. They fought from horseback, carrying long spears, impressive in their equestrian skill.

The two armies joined battle on the great unwooded plain that lies before 1.80
the city of Sardis. There several rivers, among them the Hyllus, join and dash their streams together into the largest of Lydian rivers, the Hermus; and the Hermus itself flows down from the mountains sacred to Cybele and disgorges into the sea near the town of Phocaea. Here, as he saw the Lydians taking up

their battle positions, Cyrus grew fearful of the cavalry, and so set in motion a plan that Harpagus, one of the Medes, had suggested. In the army's baggage train were camels carrying the food and equipment; these he had gathered and stripped of their cargo. He then had men mount them, using horse harnesses and saddles, and moved them into position—in front of the rest of his own army and opposite the horse of Croesus. He ordered the line of infantry to follow the camels, and behind the infantry he positioned the whole of his regular cavalry. When all was arranged, he instructed his men to kill without mercy every Lydian they encountered; but not to kill the Lydian king Croesus, not even if he resisted as they were trying to capture him.

Now the reason Cyrus had placed the camels opposite the Lydian cavalry was this: horses are frightened of camels and they can tolerate neither the sight nor the smell of them. Cyrus's stratagem had this aim, then: to render Croesus's horse useless—for the Lydian cavalry was the centerpiece of their prospects for victory. And in fact when they did join battle, the horses turned back as soon as they caught sight and smell of the camels, and Croesus found his hopes dashed. Yet even then the Lydians were not at all cowardly; rather, as they absorbed what was happening they leapt down from their horses and joined the infantry in the fight against the Persians. Time passed; many men fell on both sides; but the Lydians were forced to flee. Crowding into the city walls they now found themselves under siege.

1.81 So the Persian siege of Sardis began. Croesus, on the assumption that the siege would last a long time, sent messengers out to his allies. The first messengers had gone to tell the allies to assemble at Sardis in four months, but these he now dispatched to request immediate assistance—for he, Croesus, was under siege.

1.82 Among the allies to whom he sent were, of course, the Spartans, and at this very time the Spartans were involved in a dispute with the Argives over a region called Thyrea. The Spartans had occupied Thyrea, effectively annexing it from the Argolid. (At this time all the land to the west, extending as far as Males, belonged to the Argives, and not just the mainland but also Cythera and the other islands.)

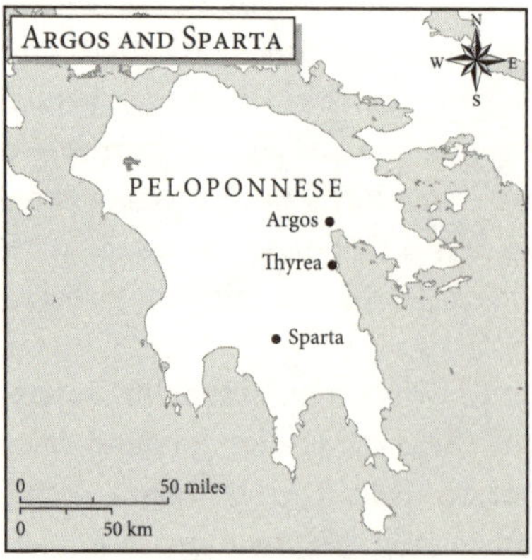

MAP 1.8

The Argives arrived in force to liberate the occupied territory, and thereupon the two sides negotiated an agreement. Three hundred from each side were to do battle to the death; the land would belong, then, to whichever side prevailed. Moreover, the bulk of the armies were to leave, each to their own land, not staying to witness the fighting—the thought being that if the armies were present, the side being worsted would intervene and try to defend their men. With this agreed upon, the armies withdrew, and the ones chosen, three hundred on each side, stayed behind. These now began to do battle. The fight was an even match and in the end, as night fell, only three—out of six hundred—were left: the Argives Alcenor and Chromius, and the Spartan Othryades.

The two Argives, joyous at their victory, rushed home to Argos. The Spartan Othryades, however, stripped the armor off the Argive corpses and dragged it to his camp, where he took up his position. The next day both sides came to learn the result of the contest. For quite a while they both claimed victory, the Argives saying that more of their men had survived, the Spartans that these men had run away, as anyone could see, and that their man had stayed and stripped the enemy corpses of their armor. In the end the quarrel grew violent and they fell to fighting. Many were killed on both sides; but the Spartans were victorious.

Ever since then, the Argives have worn their hair short, they who had before required men to wear their hair long; they made it a law, with a curse added thereto, that no Argive man should grow out his hair, nor any Argive woman wear golden jewelry, before they reclaimed Thyrea. The Spartans did exactly the opposite: they who had never worn their hair long before, from this moment forward always had long hair. As for the one Spartan left from three hundred, Othryades, they report that he was ashamed to return to Sparta, since the rest of the band of brothers had died. So he cut himself down on the spot, there in Thyrea.

These were the matters occupying the Spartans when the messenger came 1.83
from Sardis, asking help for Croesus, whose city was under siege. The Spartans, despite their own difficulties, set out to lend assistance as soon as they heard the message. But just as they completed their preparations and were ready to launch the ships, a second message came, that the Lydian city was taken, and that Croesus had been captured alive. And so the Spartans left off, despite their distress at his great misfortune.

Here is how Sardis was captured. On the fourteenth day of the siege, Cyrus 1.84
sent horsemen along the ranks, announcing a reward for the first man to scale the city wall. The army then made an assault in force, but without success. But when all the others had given up, a Mardian man, named Hyroeades, made an attack by climbing a part of the acropolis where no guard was posted. The Lydians, you see, had no fear of the wall being breached here, since the acropolis was sheer and impregnable on that side.

In that spot alone had Meles, an earlier king of Sardis, not led the lion that his concubine had borne to him. (Understand that the Telmessian seers had predicted that Sardis would be impossible to capture if the lion were brought about its walls.) Meles had led the lion around the rest of the city wall, to each spot where the acropolis was vulnerable; but he did not bother with this sheer and impregnable spot, where the acropolis faces Mount Tmolus.

The day before, this Mardian man, Hyroeades, had seen one of the Lydians climb down from the acropolis to pick up a helmet that had rolled down; noticing this, he set it in his heart. And so the next day he climbed up along that very route, and other Persians after him. More and more went up and over the wall and so Sardis was taken; and the Persians fell to plundering the entire city.

1.85 As for Croesus, this is how things turned out. He had a son who, as I mentioned earlier, was unable to speak, though a fine young man otherwise. Back in his time of prosperity, Croesus had done everything for him he could think of, including sending an inquiry to Delphi about his son. The Pythian priestess had spoken these verses in reply: *Croesus, born of Lydia, king of many, great fool: / Do not wish to hear in your palace the cry you pray so much for, / of your son speaking. Much better for you that it never be. / For he will speak his first words on a day of ill fortune.*

When the city wall was breached, one of the Persians, not recognizing Croesus, came up intending to kill him. Croesus saw his attacker but in his misfortune was beyond caring—it did not matter to him if he was struck and killed. But the son—the one who could not speak—when he saw the Persian attacking, was seized with terror at the calamity before him and broke out with a sound, saying *"Do not kill Croesus!"* These were the first words he uttered; and after that he spoke for the whole rest of his life.

1.86 The Persians occupied Sardis and took Croesus alive in the fourteenth year of his rule and on the fourteenth day of the siege. Just as the oracle had declared, a great kingdom had fallen—his own.

Croesus on the Pyre

The pyre is a large bonfire built to ceremonially incinerate corpses, and it is highly unusual to use it to burn people alive. In this famous and extraordinary scene, there are two allusions that cultured Greeks will have recognized. First is killing of enemies on the pyre. In Homer's Iliad, *Achilles honors his dead friend Patroclus with a funeral at which he slaughters and adds to the pyre twelve of the Trojan enemy* (Il. *23.175f); in the* Iliad, *this human sacrifice is a strong signal that Achilles' excessive grief is transforming him from great warrior to someone dehumanized, increasingly detached from any sympathy for the mortal condition. The sudden sympathy shown by Cyrus for his defeated enemy is, then, evocative of Achilles's mercy toward Priam in* Iliad *book 24. Second is the allusion to the "twice-seven" (and we will have noticed the emphasis on fourteen already in the story of Croesus). The phrase "twice-seven" is used of the seven boys and seven girls whom, in Greek mythology, the Athenians sent each year as human sacrifices to the Minotaur, a half-man and half-bull monster.*

The Persians seized Croesus and took him to Cyrus. Cyrus had had his men pile up wood for a great pyre, and now had them place Croesus upon it, bound in shackles, and alongside him twice seven Lydian youths. It is not clear what he had in mind. Perhaps he wanted to make a human sacrifice to

FIGURE 1.6 Croesus on the pyre. An Athenian painter named Myron decorated this vase not with the usual mythological episode, but with the scene of Croesus's death. Croesus is depicted sitting high up on a pyre, pouring a libation from a shallow bowl (to Apollo we assume), while a servant stokes the fire. Note the details not in our text: the intricately decorated throne, the royal scepter, the laurel wreath. Red-figure Attic amphora from the early 5th century BC

one of the gods. Or maybe he wished to fulfill some vow. But it may be that he put Croesus up on the pyre when he found out his piety to the Greek gods, wanting to see if some divinity would save him from being burned alive. In any case, this, they say, is what Cyrus did.

As Croesus was standing on the pyre, even in such great misery the words of Solon came into his mind, words spoken with the gods' inspiration, that "no one who is still alive can be called blessed." He pondered this in a deep silence; then sighed and groaned, and thrice called out the name "Solon!" Cyrus heard him and told the interpreters to ask who this was he called upon; so they approached him and asked.

For a time Croesus kept silent, not answering their questions; but then they used force. "He is the one whom I would have every king consult, regardless of the expense." What he said made no sense to them, so they asked him again what he meant. As they were persistent, and getting ready to use force again, he told the story—how Solon, an Athenian, had first come to Sardis, and though seeing for himself all of the Lydian's prosperity, he had made naught of it; how everything had turned out exactly as Solon had said; and how Solon's words were not so much for Croesus as for all mankind—though especially for those who think themselves prosperous or blessed.

Even as Croesus was telling his story, the fire was lit and the outer edges began to burn. But when Cyrus heard from the interpreters what Croesus had said, he had a change of heart, thinking, "I, a man, am burning alive another man, who as I am now once too was blessed." Besides, he was fearful of divine retribution, and was thinking how unstable were all human affairs. So he told his men to extinguish the blaze at once and to have Croesus and the Lydian youths step down. Try they did, but it was no longer possible to bring the fire under control.

1.87 The Lydians tell this tale of what happened next. Croesus, realizing that Cyrus had changed his mind, saw that the men were trying to extinguish the fire yet unable to get it under control. So he called out to Apollo in a loud clear voice: "If any of my gifts have pleased you, come to my side and save me from this evil!" With tearful cries he called upon the god; and suddenly in a clear and windless sky clouds gathered, a storm broke, a violent rainfall poured down—and the fire was extinguished.

Cyrus and Croesus

We get a view here of the complex intersection of human action, divine power, and preordained fate in the unstable fortunes of men. That the priestess herself explicates the god's riddling oracles is unusual, perhaps meaning to highlight the ironically close relation that Croesus has established with the god through his gifts and piety.

In this way Cyrus came to know that Croesus was a noble man, loved by the gods. Fetching him down from the pyre Cyrus said, "Croesus, what man persuaded you to march upon my land and make yourself my enemy rather than my friend?" "King," Croesus replied, "I did it myself, to your good fortune and to my bad. But the one to blame for all this is the Greek god, who encouraged me to attack. No man is so foolish so as to choose war over peace: for in peace, children bury their fathers, while in war fathers bury their children. No, I suppose it was dear to some god that things work out this way."

1.88 So spoke Croesus; Cyrus released him from his shackles and sat him at his side, holding him in great esteem. Indeed Cyrus and all those nearby gazed on him with wonder. Croesus, lost in thought, kept silence. After a while he looked up and turned his attention to the Persians who were plundering the Lydian capital. "King," he said, "should I say what I am thinking, or is it better to keep quiet for the present?" Cyrus told him to speak out as he pleased. So Croesus put this question to him: "What is it that these men of yours are actually accomplishing with their rushing about?" Cyrus said, "Why, they are despoiling your city and plundering your possessions." "But," Croesus replied, "it is not my city nor my possessions that they despoil; these things no longer have anything to do with me; no, they are grabbing and taking away *your* things."

Cyrus grew worried at Croesus's remark, so he sent the others away and asked Croesus his view of the present goings-on. Croesus said, "Since the gods have handed me to you as your slave, I think it right to let you know what I foresee. The Persians are by nature violent men and not used to riches. If you let them plunder and store up a great mass of wealth, this, I think, will be the outcome: expect the one who has stored up the most to challenge you. If this account seems right to you, do as follows: position your spearmen as guards at each of the city gates, and have them take the loot from each soldier as he carries it out, telling him that the property must be tithed—a tenth of it must be offered up to Zeus. In this way you will not be hated, as you would be if you took the loot by force; instead, the soldiers, thinking that you are doing what is right, will willingly hand it over." 1.89

Cyrus was delighted at these words, as he thought it excellent advice. Thanking Croesus, he bid his spearmen do exactly as Croesus had suggested. Then he spoke to Croesus, saying "Croesus, I see that you, once a king yourself, are willing to serve me well in both word and deed. Therefore ask for a gift, whatever you want to have, and it shall be yours immediately." "Master," he said, "you will do me a great favor if you let me ask a question of the god of the Greeks, the one I have particularly honored. I wish to send him these shackles, asking if it is his custom to deceive those who have done him well." Cyrus asked what offense prompted such a request. In return Croesus told him the whole story, his original plan and the oracle's reply, laying special emphasis on the rich offerings he had made, and how it was at the urging of the oracle that he came to attack the Persians. 1.90

He ended by asking once again that he be allowed to reproach the god in this way. Cyrus said, laughing, "This you will have from me, Croesus, and whatever you request in the future as well." So Croesus sent to Delphi men of Lydia, instructing them to set down the shackles at the entry of the temple, then to ask if the god was not ashamed that his oracles had urged Croesus to attack the Persians and thereby check the power of Cyrus, when from that he had gotten these first fruits—shackles. Asking this, they were then to inquire if it was the custom for Greek gods to be so thankless.

The Lydian men arrived at Delphi and did as they had been told. In reply the Pythian priestess said, "It is impossible even for a god to escape fate 1.91

preordained. Croesus has now paid for the crime of his ancestor of the fifth generation past, a spearman of the Heraclids, who, caught in a woman's scheme, killed his master, and held kingly power and office not rightly his. Apollo Loxias wanted that Sardis fall not in Croesus's time but in the time of his children—but the Fates proved impossible to turn aside. What favor the Fates allowed, however, Apollo brought to pass: for he held off the capture of Sardis for three years. Have Croesus understand this, then, that the capture of Sardis was three years later than was preordained; and also this, that Apollo was the one who helped him when he was being burned alive. As for the oracle, Croesus finds fault unjustly. The words of Apollo Loxias were: *if he makes war upon the Persians, he will destroy a great kingdom.* But Croesus needed to come and ask one more question—did the oracle mean his own kingdom or that of Cyrus?—if he was going to plan properly. Neither understanding what was said nor asking additional questions, Croesus himself clearly was the one to blame. Moreover, when he asked his last question, and the god spoke about the mule, not even this did Croesus understand. The mule was in fact Cyrus, he who was born from people unlike in race and breeding: his mother an aristocrat, a Mede and the daughter of Astyages king of the Medes; and his father, low-born, a Persian and the Medes' subject, an inferior who took as wife one to whom he should have been the slave." So did the Pythian priestess reply, and the messengers brought the reply back to Sardis, where they relayed it to Croesus. Croesus listened and came to realize that the fault was not the god's but his own.

1.92 Such then is the tale of Croesus's rule and the first subjugation of Ionia.

The Marvels and Customs of Lydia

As a sort of quiet coda to Croesus and the Tales of Lydia, the narrator appends a catalogue of extraordinary things about Lydia: the marvels, natural and man-made, and the customs. This is the first instance of what will be a habitual part of the rhythm to Herodotus's tales, and the reader will come to recognize these catalogues, and this deep interest in what is extraordinary in other cultures, as typical features.

I must add that Croesus sent many offerings to Greece beyond those already mentioned. In Boeotian Thebes he dedicated a golden tripod to Ismenian Apollo; in Ephesus golden statues of oxen and many of the marble pillars; in the temple of Athena Pronaea at Delphi, a huge golden shield. These were the ones still in existence in my day; but others of his offerings had already perished. For example, in Milesian Branchidae, as my inquiries have uncovered, Croesus set up dedications equal in weight and quality to those at Delphi. The offerings to Delphi and Amphiaraus came from money that was his own, part of what he inherited from his father; but the rest came from the property of a man who was his enemy, a man who before Croesus's kingship conspired to promote Pantaleon as the next king of the Lydians.

This Pantaleon was the son of Alyattes, Croesus's brother though not of the same mother—Croesus was born to Alyattes by a Carian woman, Pantaleon by an Ionian. But Alyattes named Croesus, not Pantaleon, as the next king. So, when Croesus took over, he had this conspirator torn to shreds in the torture chamber. The estate, already pledged to the gods, Croesus then sent as offerings to the shrines, as I have described. So much then for Croesus's dedicatory offerings.

Lydia does not have much by way of marvels to record, at least not like other lands. An exception is the gold dust that washes down from Mount Tmolus. As for man-made monuments, Lydia does provide one that is much the biggest outside of Egypt and Babylonia. That is the tomb of Alyattes, the father of Croesus, which has a foundation made of huge stone blocks, with the remainder a mound of earth. The tomb was built by tradesmen, workmen, and prostitutes. In my day there were still five large pillars on the top of the mound, and they were engraved with inscriptions that said what parts each group had built; and when you add up the numbers, it proves that the prostitutes made the greatest contribution. (All daughters of common people in Lydia offer themselves as prostitutes, in order to collect money for a dowry; and they do this up to the point that they get married—the daughters thus give themselves away at the wedding.) The circumference of Allyattes' tomb is about four thousand feet and the width is thirteen hundred feet.[55] The tomb also has a large lake near it, Lake Gyges, which the Lydians say is fed by ever-flowing streams. So much then about the tomb. 1.93

Aside from prostituting the female children, the customs of the Lydians are similar to those of the Greeks. The Lydians were, to my knowledge, the first people to use coins struck from gold and silver,[56] and also were the first to set up retail shops. According to the Lydians themselves, the sports and games that they now have in common with the Greeks were their own invention; they invented this, they say, during the period when they colonized northern Italy. 1.94

The story goes like this. In the reign of Atys the son of Manes, a harsh famine gripped all of Lydia. For a while the Lydians held out, but as time went on and the famine did not stop, they sought relief. Various solutions were contrived, and so it was that at that time they invented the games played with dice and knucklebones and balls, and all games of this sort (excepting backgammon, however, which the Lydians do not claim to have discovered). The inventions helped fight the famine in this way: every other day, they played games all day long, to take their minds off food; on the other days, they stopped playing and ate. In this way they managed to survive for eighteen years. But the famine did not go away; rather, it pressed all the harder. So the king divided the Lydians into two groups, and made them draw lots, to decide

55 1200 by 400 m.

56 Probably right: our earliest surviving coins are in fact from 7th-century Lydia and are made of electrum, an alloy of gold and silver.

MAP 1.9

which group would stay and which would leave the land; the king continued to govern those allotted to stay, and his son those who were leaving. The son's name was Tyrrhenus.

Those selected to be Tyrrhenus's companions left the country, and came down to Smyrna. There, they built ships, put aboard all their household effects, and sailed away to seek land and livelihood. They passed by many a people as they made their way, but, finally, they came to Umbria in the north of Italy, where they founded cities and have lived ever since. Instead of being called Lydians they are named after the king's son, the one who led them there. Thus they are named, after him, the Tyrrhenians.[57]

But back to the Lydians themselves. As I have described, the Lydians had by now been subjugated by the Persians.

57 Also known as the Etruscans (and their territory as Etruria).

Tales of Cyrus and the Rise of the Persians

Just as with Croesus, Cyrus is introduced only for the tale then to backtrack and introduce his predecessors, the Median kings, as background. In formal terms the succession of Median kings prefigures the succession of Persian kings to come: first the founder (Deioces), then the failure (Phraortes, who disastrously loses his army), next the warrior and conqueror (Cyaxares, who conquers the Assyrians), and finally the brutal despot Astyages. Historians tend to accept these figures as early kings of Media, but for the two earliest kings there are significant differences between the accounts in Babylonian sources and in Herodotus. Moreover, though there is no question of the historicity of a Median nation of some sort, archaeologists have yet to uncover a Median cultural presence in the material record and the reality of an actual *empire* of the Medes has been doubted. At this remove—the reign of the first Median king is fully 250 years before Herodotus—there is, then, a mix of history and legend. As for sources to which Herodotus had access, we can guess that these were among the stories that circulated as part of the Persians' own stories about their origins as an empire.

The succession of Median kings also picks up on patterns already available to the reader. For example, the history of the Lydian kings from Gyges to Croesus established as normative the idea of a succession of eastern kings, increasingly imperialist, that led up to a final king guilty of a fundamental transgression—who then, by logic of the divine machinery, must pay the price, for himself and for his people. This, then, is the history that repeats itself, a sort of "history" that, again, interacts in a fascinating way with forces and motivations that are psychological and divine as well as political and military. The figure of Astyages, in particular, rewards comparison with the paradigm set by Croesus; the two share far more than the mere fact that both fall to the founding Persian king, Cyrus the Great.

Thematically, the central motif of *freedom* versus *slavery* comes to the fore, and this will now recur throughout the work. In Greek terms, to rule as king is to be the "master"; and to be ruled by a king is to be "enslaved." The concept of *political freedom* seems to us naturally core to democratic societies, but in Greece the centrality of freedom has a history as ideology quite apart from the rise of democracy in Athens. Even within an egalitarian democracy like the United States, the citizens are hardly "free" in all respects; and this suggests that in modern contexts, too, the word is used more metaphorically than we are accustomed to think.

Cyrus the Great

Note the way that the story here starts to take on a life of its own—it is the "story," not the narrator, that demands to go down this path of inquiry. The narrator, however, is the one who carefully evaluates which version of events to record.

1.95 At this point our story (*logos*) demands that we find out more about Cyrus, that man who destroyed Croesus's empire; and also how it was that the Persians came to rule Asia. I know three other ways that the story of Cyrus is told: but the one I will record is the story given by Persians whose aim is not so much to glorify Cyrus and his deeds, but to tell what actually happened.

The Assyrians had ruled eastern Asia for five hundred and twenty years when the Medes became the first of those to revolt. For freedom they fought, bravely and nobly, and it came to pass that, pushing off the yoke of slavery, they became free. Following the Medes' success, the other peoples of Asia re-
1.96 volted too. And so all the peoples on the mainland became their own masters, but they would once again return to a tyrant's rule. Here's how that happened.

Background: Deioces, and the Rise of the Medes

The tale of Deioces reads like a parable of the rise of tyranny, with the paradoxical (and thought-provoking) conclusion that it is the people's very longing for justice that leads them to loss of freedom. Despite his strict attention to justness, we sense something inappropriate in Deioces's "passion for a tyrant's power"; and note that this phrase uses the same Greek word that was used in the case of Candaules, that early king of the Lydians who, you recall, had a (curiously inappropriate) "passion" for his wife in the story of Gyges (1.8). Key motifs such as the tyrant's duplicity and the power of the public gaze (and the power of its denial) we have seen before.

Once there was a wise man among the Medes, named Deioces, the son of Phraortes. This man had great passion for a tyrant's power, and so he contrived the following. The Medes dwelt in small villages, and in his own village Deioces, a man of good reputation even before, now dedicated himself to act as a proper judge. At the time, there was a great deal of lawlessness throughout Media, and he understood full well that injustice finds its foe in the rule of law. The Medes in his village saw him as a man of character and thus chose him as their arbiter of disputes. Deioces in turn—since he was after power—made decisions that were rightful and just. From this he got many a good word from the villagers, so much so that people in other villages heard about Deioces and how he alone gave judgments that were truly just. So they too (who had met with unjust decisions before) now went often and gladly to Deioces to get him to act as judge. In the end, the people came to trust no one else.

1.97 Over time there were ever more people coming, as the word went about that his judgments turned out as the facts demanded. So Deioces—knowing that everything depended on him—now refused to go and sit in the place where he had sat as judge in the past,[58] and said that he would no longer issue any verdicts. "What good does it do for me," he said, "to neglect my own affairs while sitting as a judge for my neighbors every day?" Now, the villages had even more robbery and lawlessness than before. So, the Medes gathered in an assembly to discuss the current situation (with his friends being particularly outspoken, as it seems to me); and this is what they said. "If things keep going the way they are now, we will be unable so much as to live in this country. So, come, let us set up a king for ourselves. In that way the country will be well governed, and we can go back to our work and cease being uprooted by lawlessness."

By arguments such as these they convinced themselves to take on a king. Then 1.98
at once the question arose: whom should they make king? So much was Deioces on everyone's lips—his name proposed, his character praised—that in the end they agreed to appoint him. Deioces, for his part, demanded that they build him a palace worthy of a king and afford him the protection of a bodyguard. So, the Medes did this: they constructed a large, fortified palace at the spot he designated, and they let him pick his spearmen, chosen out of all the Medes.

Once power was his, Deioces forced the Medes to build for him a great citadel and to make the citadel strong, elevating this one city above all the other towns. Again the Medes obeyed, constructing large, strong walls about the city now called Ecbatana. They set the walls in concentric circles one inside another, devising it so that each wall stands higher than the one below by exactly the height of the towers. The fact that the land rises to a hilltop helps the design, I suppose, but the precise effect is still by contrivance. Altogether there are seven walls, and inside the innermost one stands the royal palace and treasury. As for the outermost wall, it is approximately the size of the city wall around Athens.[59] This outermost wall has white towers, the next black, the third crimson, the fourth cyan, the fifth orange. The towers of these five thus are painted, made of glazed bricks, but the two last walls have towers
coated with metal, one silver and one gold.[60] Such were the walls Deioces had 1.99
built to protect himself and his palace; as for the people, he bid them live round about, in the area just outside the walls.

Once the building was complete, Deioces became the first to establish certain remarkable protocols pertaining to the king: that no one be admitted to the king's presence; that all communication be made by messenger; that the king not even be seen by anyone. In addition, he made it an offense for any to laugh or spit in the king's presence.

58 There were no courts of law, and so, by convention, such "wise men" would sit at the town gate to offer themselves as arbiters.

59 Thucydides (2.13.7) tells us that the walls of Athens were 60 stades, about 6.5 miles (10.5 km). The comparison to Athens shows that part (not all) of the expected readership is assumed to live in or have traveled to Athens.

60 The description here suggests an elaborate type of ziggurat, but no citadel quite like this has been found. Ecbatana (near modern Hamadan in Iran) has not been excavated.

The reason Deioces worked to exalt himself was this: so that his familiars—those who had grown up with him, and were neither from lesser families nor lacking in manly virtue—not grow irritated and plot against him. He reasoned that, as long as they never saw him, they would come to
1.100 think of him as someone no longer at all like themselves. Once the protocols were in place and he had made himself strong in the kingly power, Deioces was careful to continue as a strict, stern judge. The people would write out their accusations and send them in to him; and he would write down his decision and send it back out. That's how he handled legal disputes, but he also arranged this: whenever he heard of someone abusing power, he had the man arrested and a verdict rendered in proportion to the wrongdoing. And everywhere throughout the kingdom there were spies and informers to bring him these reports.

1.101 Deioces, then, joined together a nation of the Medes under his rule—and unlike other kings, of the Medes alone. And these were the tribes that formed this nation: the Busae, Parataceni, Struchates, Arizanti, Budii, Magi.

1.102 Deioces ruled for fifty-three years, and at his death, the kingship passed to his son, Phraortes. Once king, the son was not content with ruling over only the Medes, so he first attacked the Persians and they first were made subject to the Medes. Afterward, since he had two peoples under his control and both of them rugged and fierce, he moved to conquer the rest of Asia, marching from one people to the next. In the end, he made an attack on the Assyrians—those who once held Nineveh and earlier had ruled over everyone, at that time bereft of allies (since they had all revolted) but still prosperous and strong. In the attack Phraortes himself was killed, and most of his army with him. He had ruled for twenty-two years.

1.103 At the death of Phraortes, the kingship passed to Cyaxares son of Phraortes son of Deioces.

A description of the reign of Cyaxares now follows. He was a greater warrior than his father and defeated the Assyrians. His reign lasted 40 years, during which there was an incursion by the Scythians into Asia; that ended when Cyaxares invited the Scythian leaders to dinner, got them drunk, and slaughtered them, thus winning back his kingdom.

TABLE 1.2: THE KINGS OF MEDIA

Name	Reign according to Herodotus	Reign according to modern historians
Deioces	700–647 BC, 53 years	727–675 BC
Phraortes	647–625 BC, 22 years	674–653 BC
(Scythians)	(included in reign of Cyaxares)	652–625 BC
Cyaxares	625–585 BC, 40 years	624–585 BC
Astyages	585–550 BC, 35 years	585–550 BC

The Birth and Upbringing of Cyrus

This fairy-tale birth narrative would have reminded the cultured Greek of the myth of Oedipus, since in both tales the exposure of the baby is central, as is the irony that mortals inevitably and foolishly bring fate to fruition through exactly the actions they take in trying to evade it. Infanticide was a fact of the real world in antiquity, but it was a drastic act, one that has the potential to destabilize, as the myths seem to contemplate. A particularly fascinating aspect of the tale is the notion that a person is inherently "free" or "slave"—in the Greek view, a man can be enslaved and yet "free" by nature, *since slavery is a characteristic of the family one is born into and not simply a social circumstance.*

After the death of Cyaxares, the kingship passed to his son, Astyages. Asty- 1.107
ages had a daughter whom he named Mandane. He had a dream in which this daughter peed and peed, so much so that the urine filled up his city, and then spilled out, overflowing all of Asia. He asked the Magi dream-interpreters what this vision meant, and each detail he learned from them filled him with fear. When Mandane was at the age to marry, he therefore did not give her to any of the Medes of her rank—in his fear of the dream vision—but rather to a Persian, whose name was Cambyses, and who, as he learned, was from a good family and of gentle disposition. And so he gave her to Cambyses, even though he considered Cambyses inferior to even the most middling of the Medes.

But in the first year of their marriage, Astyages had another vision. He 1.108
dreamed that from the genitals of this daughter sprouted a vine, and this vine spread out over all of Asia. Such was the vision, and so he consulted with the dream-interpreters again; he subsequently summoned his daughter from the Persians—then with child and nearing her delivery date—and when she arrived he put her under guard, having in mind to kill the child when it was born. This vision, you see, had been interpreted by the Magi to mean that the offspring of this daughter would come to supplant Astyages as king. So, Astyages kept her under guard, and when Cyrus was born, he summoned Harpagus, a kinsman and the steward of his properties, a man whom he trusted above all.

"Harpagus," he said, "there is a certain matter I want you to take care of. You must handle it flawlessly. Do not expose me to danger by going to others—or you will find yourself in a trap of your own making. Now, take the child born to Mandane, carry it to your house, and kill it. And afterward, bury it in whatever way you see fit." "King," Harpagus replied, "you have never yet had cause to find fault in the man before you, and I will continue to manage your affairs with care. If it is your will so to do, my duty is to serve you and to carry out your wish."

Such was Harpagus's reply. The infant was handed over to him, decked out 1.109
in fine burial garb. Harpagus returned to his house, in considerable distress, and when he got there he told his wife the whole story, everything that Astyages had said. "What do you intend to do?" she asked. He replied, "Not what Astyages has commanded—not even if his madness makes him worse

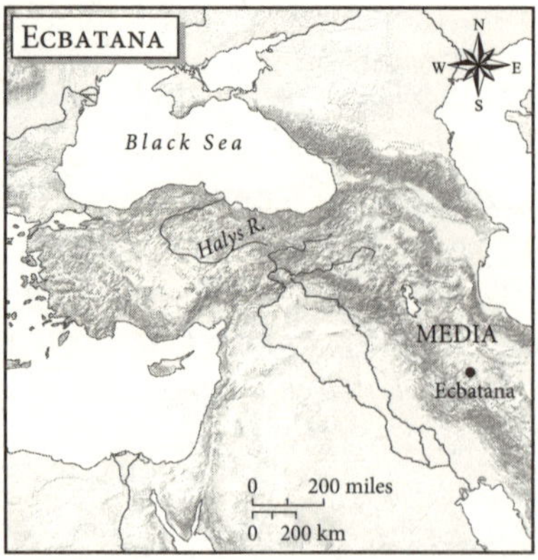

MAP 1.10

than he is already would I consent to take part in such a murder. Many are the reasons why. The boy is my kinsman. Astyages is old and without male issue: if the throne passes to this daughter when he dies—whose son he now wants to have me kill—what will I be left with, except the most extreme peril? No, for my own personal safety, the boy does have to die—but the killing has to be done by one of Astyages' servants and not one of my own."

1.110 So saying, he turned at once to send a messenger to one of Astyages' cowherds—one who tended a suitable pasture upon a remote, wild mountainside. His name was Mitradates. Living with the cowherd was a fellow slave, a woman whose name in Greek was Cyno, that is, "She-Dog," but in the Median language Spako (the Median word for dog being *spaka*). The cow pasture that Mitradates tended was on the lower slopes of mountains to the north of Ecbatana, toward the Black Sea. The rest of Media is completely flat, but there, on this side of the Saspires, the Median land is very mountainous, steep, and densely wooded.

The cowherd came with great haste to the summons, and Harpagus said, "Astyages bids you take this infant and expose it in a remote spot on the mountainside, so that he dies as quickly as possible. And he bids me add this: if you do not kill the child, but you keep it alive by some means, you will suffer a most grim death. I myself, by his command, will come to examine the corpse once it is exposed."

1.111 When the cowherd had heard all this, he picked up the infant and took the same road back home to the farmstead. Now his wife, who was ready to give birth any day, by some stroke of fate bore her baby while the cowherd was at the city. They were much in each other's thoughts—he, worried about his wife's delivery; she, about her husband's unusual summons from Harpagus. He arrived home before expected and, as soon as she saw him, the wife asked—before he could get in a word—why Harpagus had summoned him with such urgency.

"Dear wife," he said, "when I got to the city I saw and heard what no man ought ever to see, and what ought never to come to pass for our masters.[61] The whole house of Harpagus was filled with tearful cries and sorrow. Not knowing what to make of this, I went inside; and, as soon as I got in, I saw an infant fussing and crying, decked out in gold and wrapped in richly colored

61 "What one ought not to see" should remind the reader of the Gyges tale. As there, this is a signal that something has been done that transgresses a cultural boundary.

cloth. When Harpagus saw me, he told me to take the child, carry it home, and expose it on the most remote part of the mountainside, saying that this was the behest of Astyages, and making grave threats if I didn't do so. So I picked up the child and carried it off, thinking that it belonged to one of the servants—I could hardly have guessed where he actually came from! Anyway, I was confused when I noticed that he was decked out in gold and rich robes, and likewise by the tearful cries and sorrow that I had seen in the house of Harpagus. But straightway on the road I heard the whole story from the servant who was leading me out of the city, the one who had put the baby into my arms—that this was the child of Mandane daughter of Astyages and Cambyses son of Cyrus, and that Astyages had ordered that it be killed. And, look, here it is!"

With that, the cowherd uncovered the baby and showed it to her. Seeing 1.112
that the child was big and healthy and beautiful, she started to cry, grabbed her husband about his knees in supplication, and begged him not to expose it. But he explained that it was not possible to do otherwise. "Agents will come from Harpagus to examine the corpse, and if I have not done as ordered, the death they will mete out will be a gruesome one." Unable to convince her husband, the wife tried a second time: "I see that I cannot dissuade you from exposing the baby, so let's do as follows. Since necessity commands that they look upon a baby's corpse, take the one in here—the one I gave birth to while you were gone, a stillborn birth—and set that one on the mountainside; and let's raise the other, the son of Astyages' daughter, as if it were our own. In that way the masters won't catch you doing anything wrong, and it will work out for us not at all badly—our dead child will get a burial fitting a king, and this living child will not lose his life."

To the cowherd, this seemed good advice, given the situation, and so he 1.113
carried out her plan at once. He picked up the child he had been about to put to death and handed him over to his wife; his own dead child he took and laid in the crib that he had used for carrying the other. Decking out his own child with all the other's fine clothing and ornaments, he carried it to the most remote part of the mountainside and set it out. When his child had lain out for two days, the cowherd went into the city (leaving one of the other cowherds as a guard) and told Harpagus that he was ready to show him the child's corpse. Harpagus sent the most trusted of his spearmen, and through them he examined and verified the corpse; which they then buried, in actuality the cowherd's child. That one then was buried; the other child, the one later named Cyrus, was taken in and raised by the cowherd's wife (though presumably she named him something other than Cyrus).

When the boy was ten, something happened that revealed who he really 1.114
was. The story goes like this. In the village where the herdsmen lived, he was playing a game in the street with the other children. As part of the game the children chose him as king—this boy who was thought of as the cowherd's child. He ordered some to build him a palace, others to serve as his spearmen,

and no doubt one of them to act as the King's Eye,[62] and to someone he gave the privilege of conveying his messages—he assigned tasks to each. One of the children playing with them was, however, a child of Artembares, a man of repute among the Medes, and he refused to do what Cyrus ordered. So Cyrus bid the rest of the boys seize him, and when they obeyed, he whipped him, treating him very roughly.

This boy, as soon as they let him go, was extremely angry at what he had had to endure—so unfitting to his rank!—and so he went down to the city, to his father, complaining loudly of what Cyrus had done (though of course he did not say Cyrus, which was not yet his name, but spoke of the son of the cowherd). Artembares was incensed and went at once to Astyages, taking his son with him. He described the wrongs his son had suffered, concluding: "King, we have been assaulted, violently, by your slave—the son of a cowherd!"; and with that he showed the king his son's shoulders.

1.115 Astyages had heard and seen quite enough: he determined to punish the boy, as Artembares' honor required. So he summoned the cowherd and the cowherd's son. When both were before him, Astyages fixed his eye on Cyrus and said: "You, the son of a man like that, do you dare to strike in so outrageous a manner the son of a man like this, a preeminent man in my court?" "Master," he replied, "I did this to him with justice. The boys of the village—he is one of them—were playing a game and set me up as king, since I seemed best to fit the part. The rest of the boys did as they were commanded, but this boy did not: he refused to listen, and defied me—until I made him pay the price. If for this I deserve to be punished, then, look, here I am, at your disposal."

1.116 As the boy was speaking, a glimmer of recognition came to Astyages: the profile of the boy's face seemed similar to his own, the reply was more that of a free man than a slave, the timing of the exposure seemed to match the age of this boy. Struck by all this, he remained speechless for a while. He struggled to gather himself and then spoke—wanting to get rid of Artembares, so that he could get the cowherd alone and question him—"Artembares, I will act on this matter so that you and your son have no further cause for complaint." Artembares was then sent away, and at Astyages' bidding the servants led Cyrus inside.

Left entirely alone with the cowherd, Astyages asked him where he had gotten the boy and who had handed him over. The cowherd claimed the boy as his own and said that the woman who bore him was still at his side. "You are not thinking this through clearly—or do you like being tortured?"—and just as Astyages said this, he gave the signal for his spearmen to seize him. The spearmen tortured the cowherd and thus he came to reveal the facts of the

62 The famous "King's Eye" is a sort of chief inspector, who uses the "eyes and ears" of spies spread throughout the kingdom to ensure against plots and corruption detrimental to the king's interests (a practice pioneered by Deioces, the first king of the Medes: 1.100).

case. Starting at the beginning he told everything in detail, truthfully, ending with entreaties, begging for mercy.

The Punishment of Harpagus

Like several stories in Greek mythology, this story involves androphagy (the eating of a human). The archetypal myth is the story of Atreus, who in revenge killed the children of his brother Thyestes and served them for dinner; Thyestes's son Aegisthus in the next generation then takes his own revenge, killing Atreus's son, Agamemnon. In Herodotus's lifetime, Aeschylus's trio of tragedies, the Oresteia *(part of which is the play,* Agamemnon*) explored the difficulty of finding "justice" in this sort of perpetuated cycle of revenge and the role of city and civilization in formulating new modes of justice.*

Once he had gotten the truth out of him, Astyages thought no more about 1.117
the cowherd. Harpagus, however, he found much to blame, and so he bid the spearmen summon him. Harpagus appeared before him, and then he asked, "Harpagus, by what means did you make away with the child born from my daughter, the one I handed over to you?" Seeing the cowherd in the palace, Harpagus did not turn down the path of lies, for he did not want to be proven false and caught.

"King," he said, "when I took the baby, I debated with myself how to fulfill your intent and in no way fail you, but also not to be the actual murderer in your daughter's eyes—or in your own. So I did this. I summoned the cowherd and handed over the infant, saying that this was your behest, to kill it. And that was no lie—this was your very order. So, I handed it over, telling him to expose the child on a remote mountainside and to stay and watch until it died. And I made grave threats if he did not do exactly as commanded. When he had followed these orders and the child was dead, I sent my most trusted eunuchs[63] and—through them—I examined the corpse and buried it. That, my king, is how it came about, and the means by which the child met its death."

Thus Harpagus took the straight road, telling a truthful account—but 1.118
Astyages concealed the deep anger that dwelt within. First, he repeated for Harpagus what the cowherd had told him, and then, once he had gone through the whole story, he concluded with the remark that the boy was alive and that things had turned out for the best. "I have been greatly distressed at what was done to this child, and the falling out with my daughter has been no light matter. What a lucky turn of events this is! So, come, send your own son to join the newcomer, and sit beside me at dinner tonight—to the gods responsible for this I will give a thank-offering for his deliverance."

63 Persons of high rank in the east often used eunuchs as the servants most close to them, since these could be trusted to interact with the wife and other females without danger and could not normally aspire to high rank or rule.

1.119 On hearing this, Harpagus got on his knees and bowed before the king, thinking how great it was that his transgression had turned out to be just what was needed, and that by this stroke of luck he had even been invited to dine at the palace. So, he went home, and as soon as he arrived, he sent off his son—he had only the one, a youth of about thirteen years—telling him to go to Astyages' palace and to do whatever Astyages bid. Overjoyed, he told his wife all about his encounter with the king.

But as soon as the son arrived Astyages cut his throat, and he then chopped the body limb from limb, roasting some of the flesh and boiling the rest. When the meat was done, he set it aside in readiness. The appointed hour for dinner came along and the diners, including Harpagus, arrived. For the others, and for Astyages himself, the tables alongside were heaped with the flesh of sheep, but for Harpagus, it was the flesh of his own child—everything, that is, except the head and hands and feet, which lay apart in a covered basket.

Once Harpagus seemed to have had enough of the feast, Astyages asked him if he had enjoyed the meal. Harpagus said that he had enjoyed it very much. Those to whom it had been appointed now brought forth the head and hands and feet of the child, all covered up, and standing next to Harpagus they told him to uncover it and take whatsoever he desired. Harpagus did as he was told, uncovered it, and saw before him the remains of his son. As he gazed upon it, he did not lose control, but kept within himself.[64] Astyages asked him if he knew which beast's flesh he had feasted upon. Harpagus said that, yes, he knew, and that he approved all that the king did. With that reply, he picked up what was left of the flesh of his child and went home—intending, I suppose, to gather it all together and bury it.[65]

How Cyrus Became King

Here again the story contemplates the inscrutability of divine messages and the ways in which mortal foresight and preparation remain subject to fate. As often, there is an abiding irony in the tale—freedom for the (enslaved) Persians must mean slavery for the (free) Medes, and that prompts the involved reader to think further about the nature of just governance. Note also how quickly the narrative moves when it reaches the climactic engagement between the armies: the master stylist does not linger over battle details when that is not his focus.

1.120 Such, then, was the punishment that Astyages exacted on Harpagus. He next needed to figure out what to do about Cyrus, so he summoned the same Magi who first had interpreted the dream for him. Upon their arrival, he asked them again how they interpreted what he had seen in the dream. They

64 Just as the wife of Candaules controlled herself and did not cry out when she saw Gyges in her bedroom (1.10).

65 We have seen the motif of children served at a banquet before: recall that this was the crime of the uncivilized Scythians, who served to Cyaxares—interestingly, the father of Astyages—the flesh of boys from his household (1.73).

answered him as before, that the child would surely have been king had he survived and not died first. Then he told them: "The child exists, he is alive; and when he was living in the countryside, the other boys in the village set him up as king. And he did all that a true king would do, setting up spearmen and sentinels and message-bearers and everything else as though he was the ruler. So what now, in your view, does this seem to bode?"

The Magi replied: "If the child is alive and has been made king without anyone's intervention, then take heart and be of good cheer. For he will not be king a second time. Even prophesies sometimes extend to small matters, and as for dreams, their perfect fulfillment can be something entirely trivial." "Magi," he replied, "I too am very much of that opinion, that with the child named king the prophetic dream has been realized. This boy, in my opinion, is no longer anything to be afraid of. Yet, nonetheless, advise me and consider it closely: what is going to be the safest course for my house—and for you?"

"King," the Magi replied, "it is important to us too that your reign carry on and prosper. The rule will fall into the hands of outsiders, if it passes to this boy—for he is a Persian while we are Medes; we then would become the outsiders, made into slaves and ignored by the Persians. As long as you, a fellow Mede, remain king, we have our share of power and by your grace we enjoy great honors. Thus in every way it is in our interest to look out for you and your kingship. If now we foresaw anything frightening in the situation, we would tell you. But as it is, the dream has come to nothing; so we ourselves feel confident and no longer afraid, and we encourage you to take much the same attitude. As for the boy, send him away, out of your sight, back to the Persians and the ones who bore him."

Astyages was delighted to hear this. So he summoned Cyrus and told him, 1.121
"My child, driven by a vision I saw in a dream—one that did not come to pass—I tried to harm you; but your own destiny has kept you alive. Go now to the Persians, and good luck to you; I will send an escort to show you the way. When you get there you will discover your father and mother—and by that I do not mean Mitradates the cowherd and his wife."

With these words, Astyages sent Cyrus on his way. So Cyrus returned to 1.122
his homeland, to the palace of Cambyses, where his parents received him; and when they learned who he was they embraced him with great affection. They of course had thought he had died right after he was taken away, and they wanted to know at once how he had managed to live. So he told them, saying that, before, he had been very much in the dark, but on the way he had heard about what had happened—he had thought, he explained, that Astyages' cowherd was his father, but his escorts had told him the story from start to finish during the journey from the city. He also told them how the cowherd's wife had raised him, and he enumerated her virtues at length—the woman Cyno was everywhere as he told his story. The parents then took this name and—so that the child would seem to the Persians to have survived yet more

miraculously—spread the rumor that a she-dog had suckled Cyrus when he was exposed.[66] From that origin the legend has grown.

1.123 Now as Cyrus grew into a man he proved both the most valiant and the best-liked of his cohort—and so Harpagus tried to win him over, sending him presents, eager to take vengeance on Astyages. It was not possible, he thought, for a private citizen like himself to exact revenge, so as he watched Cyrus grow up he tried to enlist him as an ally—thinking that the wrongs Astyages had inflicted on Cyrus were not unlike his own. Indeed, even before this he had taken steps. Astyages' regime was brutal and repressive, so Harpagus had spoken with each of the Median leaders in turn, trying to convince them of the need to overthrow Astyages and make Cyrus king instead. He got them to agree; everything was now ready, and it was time to let Cyrus know of his plan. But Harpagus had no way to communicate—Cyrus was living among the Persians, and there were sentries posted on all the roads.

So he came up with this idea. Procuring a rabbit, he split open its belly—not removing the fur but leaving it intact—and inside the belly he placed a scroll. On the scroll he had written all that was necessary. He then sewed up the belly, and handed the rabbit to the most trusted of his servants, supplying him with nets too, so that he would look like a hunter. This servant he sent to the Persians, telling him to hand the rabbit to Cyrus and to tell him in person to cut open the rabbit with his own hands, and to have no else present when he did so.

1.124 All went just as planned. Cyrus got the rabbit, cut it open, and picked up the scroll he found lying inside. The message read: "Child of Cambyses, it must be that the gods watch over you—for how else could you have had such good fortune?—and so the time has now come for you to take vengeance on Astyages, your murderer. As you know, if he had had his way you would be dead; but as it is you survive, thanks to the gods—and thanks to me. Long ago, I suppose, you heard the whole story, what was done to you but also about me—what terrible things Astyages made me suffer. And why?—because instead of killing you, I handed you over to the cowherd. Now, if you will listen to me, you will become king over all the lands that Astyages rules. Persuade the Persians to rise up and march against the Medes. You will have all you could desire if Astyages appoints me as the general to face you, but it will be the same if some other of the Medes is appointed—the leaders, you see, are going to desert Astyages and take your side and work to pull him down. Everything here is ready: so do as I say, and do it quickly."

1.125 The message set Cyrus thinking. By what clever scheme could he get the Persians to revolt? On reflection, the best idea seemed to be to do as follows. Writing what he needed onto a scroll, he gathered the Persians together and

66 Similarly, the founding rulers of Rome, Romulus and Remus, were said to have been suckled by a she-wolf. This is a common folktale motif, one that shows the powerful destiny that attaches to kings; note here how the legend is included even as the narrator historicizes how it came to be.

then unrolled the scroll and read aloud, "Astyages hereby appoints Cyrus commander of the Persians." Then he spoke to them: "Now, Persians, I order each of you to be here tomorrow carrying a scythe." So he commanded. Now, among the Persians there are many tribes, and only certain of these did Cyrus assemble to revolt from the Medes. These (on whom the rest of the Persians rely) are the Pasargadae, Maraphii, and Maspii. The Pasargadae are the bravest of the three—and from that tribe come the Achaemenids, the royal family of Persia. The other Persian tribes are the Panthialaei, Derusiaei, Germanii (all of which are farming tribes) and the Dai, Mardi, Dropici, and Sagartii (all nomadic).

When all were there, carrying their scythes as ordered, Cyrus told them to 1.126
spend the day clearing brush from a very large field, roughly eighteen to twenty stades square,[67] full of thistle and weeds. And when they were done with the task appointed, he told them to wash up and come again on the morrow. In the meantime, Cyrus gathered together all the goats and sheep and cattle belonging to his father and had them slaughtered; and to that he added wine and bread in proportion, and so got ready to welcome the Persian army. Arriving the next day, the men were feasted as they lounged about on the newly mowed meadow. When they had finished eating, Cyrus asked them, "Which do you prefer, the work we did yesterday or what we have today?" They replied that there was a great gulf between the two: "Yesterday everything we had was bad; today, everything is good."

Picking up on their words, Cyrus then disclosed his whole plan: "Men of Persia," he said, "here is how it stands for you. If you are willing to do as I say, these and myriad other good things will be yours, and you will not have to work like a slave. But if you are not willing to act, countless pains will be yours, just like yesterday. So, do as I say, and take back your freedom. For my part, I think the gods had me born to take this very matter into my hands. And I think you are not inferior to the Medes in warfare or anything else. That then is how it stands. Come now, revolt against Astyages, and do it at once!"

The Persians embraced him as their leader and gladly asserted their 1.127
independence—they had long resented having the Medes as their masters. When Astyages heard what Cyrus was doing, he sent a messenger to summon him to the court. Cyrus, however, told him to give the king this message: "You, Astyages, will see me a good deal sooner than you might like." So, Astyages armed all his men, and—blinded by the gods—he appointed as their commander Harpagus, forgetting what he had done to him. The Medes marched out and met the Persians in battle. Some of them fought (those who were not in on the plot), and some deserted to the Persians; but most played the coward and ran away.

Such was the disgraceful collapse of the Median army. As soon as Astyages 1.128
heard the news, he railed at Cyrus, saying: "Not so easily will Cyrus take his

67 About 2 miles (3.5 km) along each side, almost 3000 acres.

pleasure." With those words, he first had the Magi dream-interpreters impaled, those who had persuaded him to let Cyrus live. Then, he armed the Medes left in the city, young men and old. He led them out to offer battle, but the Persians triumphed; and, with the loss of all his men, he himself was captured alive.

1.129 Harpagus stood next to the captive, Astyages, taunting and jeering, saying many cruel things—for he was thinking of that meal in which the king had had him feast on his own son's flesh—and among them was this question: "How does it feel to be Cyrus's captive slave rather than a king?" Astyages fixed his eye on him and asked in return, "Is this coup by Cyrus your doing?" Harpagus replied, "I wrote the secret message urging revolt, so, yes, by rights it is indeed my doing."

Astyages said, "Then you expose yourself, Harpagus, as both the stupidest and the most unjust man alive. Stupidest, since—if what has happened was really your doing—you could have been king, and yet you placed the power in the hands of another; most unjust, if, because of that dinner, you have enslaved the Medes. Now if you absolutely had to confer the kingship on someone else and not to keep it for yourself, the right thing to do was to entrust that honor to one of the Medes, not one of the Persians. As it is, the Medes—who are without blame in this affair—are now slaves, they who were masters before, and the Persians, once our slaves, now have become masters of the Medes."

1.130 That then is how Astyages' reign of thirty-five years came to its end. As a result of his cruelty, the Medes were made to bow to the Persian yoke, after

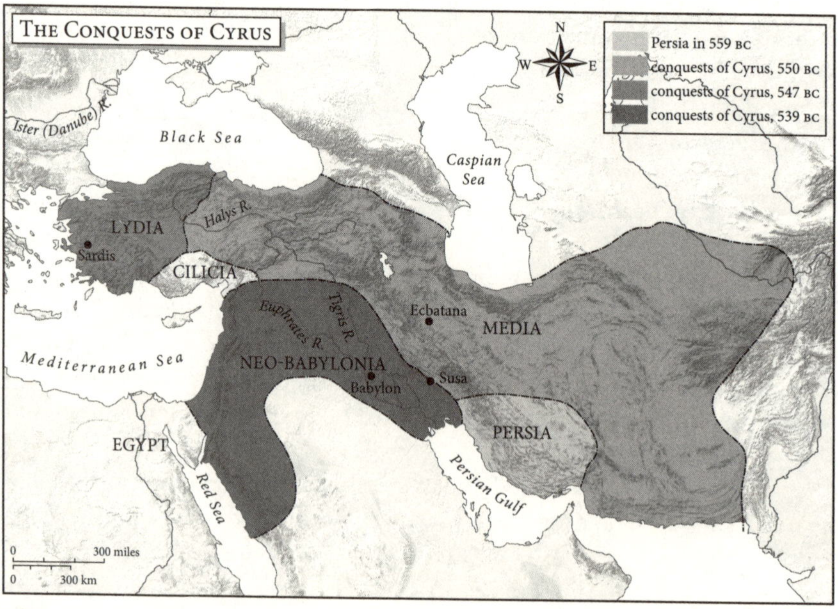

MAP 1.11

ruling for one hundred and twenty-eight years (excepting that time when the Scythians held sway) over upper Asia, the whole of the eastern, upland part of Asia beyond the river Halys.[68] In a later age they regretted their submission and rose up against Darius; but the insurgents were defeated in battle and again subdued.

In the time of Astyages, then, Cyrus and the Persians rose up against the Medes, and they ruled over Asia from that point forward. As for Astyages, until he died he was kept at Cyrus's court without further punishment.

Such is the story of Cyrus's birth and upbringing and how he became king. He later defeated Croesus—who, as I have already explained, was the aggressor, responsible for the first act of injustice.[69] With his victory over the Lydians, Cyrus thus came to rule over all of Asia.

We now skip a section in which the marvels, monuments, and remarkable customs of Persia are listed, much like the section at the end of the Tales of Lydia (1.92–94). That is followed by a lengthy account of Cyrus's reign, focusing on his conquests of Ionia and Asia Minor, and culminating in the story of his siege and capture of mighty Babylon. We pick up the tale as Cyrus now takes his army far to the north and the east, having decided to attack the Massagetae.

68 Falling roughly in the period 700–550 BC. See Table 1.2 on p. 48.

69 This is the same phrase used in the prologue, in the story of the Snatchings of Women (1.2, compare 1.5).

Cyrus's Last Campaign

This, the last of the tales of Cyrus, acts as a culminating episode in a variety of ways. As the geographical and ethnographical description in its opening chapters makes clear, the reader is now summoned to the edge of the known world, where the terrain is in part fantastic (gigantic islands in a river of uncertain identification), the neighboring tribes are semi-mythological, and the peoples are primitive, without culture, living off roots and the fruit from trees and having sex in open fields like cattle. Among these peoples are the Massagetae, whose queen's stately remarks help map them to the "noble savage" type, and whose bravery is foregrounded so as to prepare the reader for the bloodshed to come.

Several motifs should resonate with one or more patterns by now well established. The Araxes, a river which marks a critical cultural boundary (here, between civilized and uncivilized) is crossed, with all the ill omen that implies; Solon-like wisdom (here, from the savage queen!) is rejected; a divine omen is misinterpreted; a strong woman drives the events; wise advice is given (by Croesus), which seems sensible as military strategy yet leads only to further transgression—again, at a dinner! You will find others. The campaign against the Massagetae, in turn, sets up and prefigures the lengthy Scythian episode to come later on.

The episode is, then, full of the philosophical and ethical reflections we have come to expect. But there is also a deep vein both of historicity and reflection on the nature of historicity. Herodotus gives a mostly correct depiction of the geography of the Caspian Sea and its environs, hundreds of years before it was described with accuracy by anyone else in the western tradition. The precious details about the nomadic tribes are often taken as at least in part reliable, though we can hardly be sure. Yet the version here of Cyrus's last campaign is but one of several, as the narrator makes clear, and as often with history that predates written materials we have little more than Herodotus's own judgment for what is the "most plausible" account. (In this case, we know from antiquity three other accounts of Cyrus's last campaign, all Greek, and they vary in matters as basic as who Cyrus's enemy was.) We are, then, at the far edge of what oral traditions can preserve, even of major life events for a major figure like Cyrus the Great. Implicit in all this remains, then, an important methodological question: for such distant events, what sort of history can or *should* one construct, and with what sort of profit to the larger enterprise?

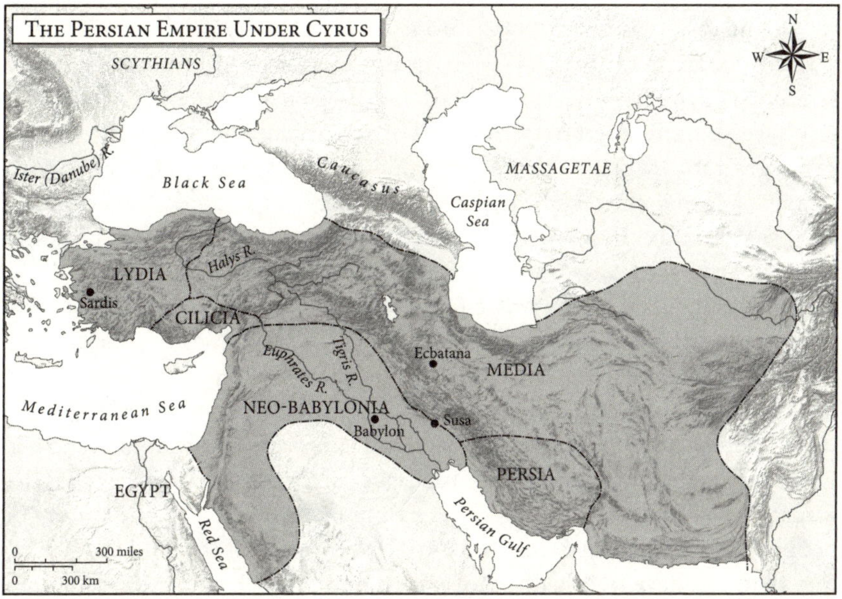

MAP 1.12

The Land of the Massagetae

Once Cyrus had conquered the Babylonians, his next desire was to put the 1.201
Massagetae under his sway. The Massagetae are said to be numerous and brave, a people that lives to the East where the sun rises, beyond the river Araxes and next to the Issedones.[70] Some also claim that the Massagetae are a Scythian people.

The Araxes is said by some to be bigger than the Ister, by others to be 1.202
smaller, and, they say, it is full of islands the size of Lesbos.[71] Several things are reported about the men who live on these islands. In the summertime they eat roots of all sorts dug from the ground, but store all the fruit they find ripe on the trees, so that they will have that to eat in the winter. These men have also discovered certain plants that bear a remarkable kind of harvest. Bands of men come together and sit in a circle around a fire, and throw the fruits of this plant onto the flames. As it smolders, the men sniff and become intoxicated on the fumes, just as Greeks do when they drink wine. As more is thrown on the fire, they get even more intoxicated, and eventually

70 The Issedones are a semi-mythical tribe often paired with the mythical Hyperboreans (literally, the Beyond-the-North-Wind people). As we shall see, adjacent to this tribe live the (fully mythical) tribe of one-eyed men.

71 A fantastic claim. Lesbos is a very large island in the Aegean Sea, over 630 square miles (1600 km^2) with 200 miles (320 km) of coastline. The Araxes itself is not firmly identified; scholars think that characteristics of perhaps as many as three rivers are conflated in the description he gives here and in book 4.

they stand up to dance and break into song.[72] Such, they say, is the islanders' way of life. In any case, this river, the Araxes, flows from the land of the Matieni, which is also the source of the Gyndes, the river that Cyrus divided into three hundred and sixty channels on his way to Babylon.[73] The Araxes disgorges into forty mouths, all but one of which, however, give way to swamps and marshes, and, they say, men there eat raw fish and regularly wear sealskins as clothing. The one clear and open mouth flows out to the Caspian Sea.

The Caspian is a sea unto itself, not connecting with any other sea. The Mediterranean—the one the Greeks navigate—and the sea beyond the pillars of Hercules called the Atlantic, and the Indian Ocean[74] are really one and
1.203 the same. The Caspian, however, is a second, distinct body of water. Its length takes fifteen days to traverse using oars, and the width, at the place where it is widest, is an eight-day voyage. Along the western side of the sea stretches the Caucasus, the longest and tallest of any mountain range. A wide variety of peoples inhabit the Caucasus, and most live entirely off the wild forest. It is said that they have trees with leaves of a special kind that, once crushed and mixed with water, are used to paint animal figures on their clothing. The animal figures do not wash out, but age with the rest of the fabric just as if they were woven in from the start. It is also said that these peoples have sex out in the open just like cattle.

1.204 The Caucasus hems in the part of the Caspian Sea to the west, but toward the east and the rising sun arises a great plain without bound as far as the eye can see. A very large part of this plain belongs to the Massagetae, that people that Cyrus was eager to march against. Many were the considerations that stirred up Cyrus and urged him on. Foremost among them was the manner of his coming to be, which seemed something more than that of a mere mortal; and, besides, there was the good luck that accompanied his military campaigns—it had proved impossible for any nation to escape, once Cyrus directed his army against it.

Cyrus Attacks the Massagetae

1.205 The Massagetae had a queen as their ruler, the wife of the dead king, a woman named Tomyris. Through a messenger Cyrus tried to woo her, pretending that he wanted her as his wife; but Tomyris saw that Cyrus was pursuing not

72 The plant is probably a kind of Indian hemp, from which hashish is made.

73 On his way to Babylon, Cyrus lost a favorite horse as they were fording the river Gyndes; in his fury, the king "punished" the river by splitting it into 360 small channels, aiming "to make it so weak that in the future even a woman can cross easily, without so much as getting her knees wet" (1.189, not included in the selections here).

74 Herodotus uses the name *Red Sea*, which can mean the modern Red Sea, Persian Gulf, or, as here, the sea to the south more generally. Herodotus was an exception in recognizing the Caspian as a landlocked sea; up to the Roman era, other Greek historians and geographers assumed it had a connection to the Indian Ocean. It is also remarkable that he knows that the Atlantic and Indian Oceans connect.

her but her kingdom, and so refused his proposal.[75] Cyrus then—since he was not getting anywhere by trickery—marched to the Araxes and openly prepared to make war on the Massagetae, working to bridge the river for the army's crossing and constructing upper works on the ships to be used as pontoons.

1.206 As Cyrus was working on this, Tomyris sent a messenger to say, "King of the Medes, why such haste, why so eager? You cannot know whether the end will turn out well for you. So, stop: rule over your own people, and be content to see us ruling over ours. Now of course you will not accept this advice—the last thing you wish is to be at peace. If, then, you are so very eager to try your chances with the Massagetae, come, leave off the hard work of bridging the river. We will withdraw from the river for a three days' march, and you can then cross over into our territory. Or, if you prefer, you withdraw to the same distance, and let us meet in your own."

When Cyrus heard the queen's message, he called together the leading Persians, and, once they were gathered, he set the issue before them, asking for advice as to which route to take. Their inclination was one and the same: they advised Cyrus to admit Tomyris and her army into their own territory.

1.207 But Croesus the Lydian was present and he criticized this advice, making quite a different argument. "King," he said, "I said long ago, when Zeus handed me over to you, that I would do whatever I can to turn aside any danger destined for your house. I have learned from my suffering, unpleasant though that be.[76] If you think that you are immortal and that you command an army that is also immortal, there would be no reason for me to make my opinions known. But if you know that you are human[77] and that you rule over others who are human too, learn this first and foremost: there is a cycle of human affairs, like a wheel, and as it revolves it does not allow the same people always to prosper. And so I have advice opposite to what these men have proposed. If we are willing to admit the enemy into our territory, this is the danger you face: if you lose the battle, you will lose your entire kingdom. Clearly the Massagetae, if victorious, will not run back but will march upon your dominions. If, on the other hand, you are victorious, you will not gain nearly so much as if you had crossed over into their territory, beaten them, and then were hunting them down as they fled. This follows the same logic as before: if you conquer the enemy you will march directly upon the dominions of Tomyris. Also, apart from this argument, it is a shameful, intolerable thing for Cyrus, the son of Cambyses, to give way

75 Just as Gyges by marrying the wife of Candaules was able to "inherit" the kingdom of Lydia, so Cyrus assumes that through marriage he could co-opt the territory as their new king.

76 This echoes Aeschylus's early encapsulation of the tragic paradox, that humans "learn through suffering" (*Agamemnon*, line 176).

77 Compare the famous inscription on the temple of Apollo at Delphi, "know thyself," for which the traditional understanding was not self-awareness in the modern sense but "know that you are a mortal with mortal limitations—and not a god."

to a woman and withdraw from his own territory. My advice, then, is to cross the river and march forward as far as they pull back and to try to prevail over them there. Now the Massagetae, I have discovered, know nothing of Persian luxury and have never experienced the finer things of life. So let's do this: slaughter many animals from the flocks and herds, in abundance, dress the meat, and set it out as a feast; and add to that large bowls of wine, abundant and strong, and other foods of every kind. Once that is done, leave the weakest part of the army behind and take the rest back to the river. Unless I am mistaken, the Massagetae, when they see the luxury before them, will indulge in it, and at that point what is left for us is to attack and reap the glory of great and mighty deeds."

1.208 Such were the conflicting opinions, and Cyrus abandoned his earlier decision, adopting the view of Croesus. He told Tomyris to withdraw while he made the crossing into her territory, and, as promised, she withdrew. Cyrus then handed over Croesus to his own son Cambyses, and proposed to hand the royal power to Cambyses as well, telling him again and again to honor Croesus and to treat him with kindness if the crossing into the land of the Massagetae did not go well. With this behest, Cyrus sent the two back to Persia. He then crossed over the river, his army with him.

1.209 After he had crossed the Araxes, when night fell and he was asleep, Cyrus had this vision in the land of the Massagetae: there appeared in his sleep the eldest of the sons of Hystaspes, with wings on his shoulders, and one wing cast its shadow over Asia and the other over Europe. Hystaspes was the son of Arsames, an Achaemenid, and his eldest son was Darius, a boy roughly twenty years old who had been left behind in Persia, not yet old enough to be part of the army. When Cyrus woke up, he reflected on the vision. He thought the vision was important, so he summoned Hystaspes and, taking him aside, said, "Hystaspes, your son has plotted against me and is trying to take over my kingdom. And I can explain how I know this so unerringly: the gods look after me and give me a sign of all impending troubles, and, in the night just passed, I saw in my sleep your eldest son with wings on his

FIGURE 1.7 From the palace of Cyrus at Pasargadae. Such winged figures were part of Persian royal iconography

shoulders, and one wing cast its shadow over Asia and the other over Europe. Given this dream, it has to be that he is plotting against me. So travel back to Persia as quickly as you can and see to it that—after I have conquered these peoples and return there—you bring your son before me for interrogation."

Cyrus said this because he thought Darius was plotting against him. But 1.210
in fact the god was revealing that Cyrus was destined to die here, in this land, and that his kingdom would be passed down to Darius. Hystaspes replied, "King, may no man born Persian plot against you, but if there is such a man, may he perish at once. You are the one who has made the Persians free men instead of slaves, and men who rule instead of men ruled by others. If a dream vision declares that my son is plotting a revolt, I surrender him for you to do with him what you will." Hystaspes replied in this way, crossed the Araxes, and went back to Persia to keep guard over his son Darius on behalf of Cyrus.

Cyrus advanced his army one day's march from the Araxes and did as 1.211
Croesus had suggested, after which he marched back to the river with the healthy part of the army, leaving behind those who could not fight. A third of the Massagetae force then fell upon them, slaughtering the soldiers Cyrus had left behind, overwhelming all resistance, a complete victory. But then the Massagetae noticed the food spread out before them. So, they lay down on the couches to feast, stuffing themselves with food and wine, and fell asleep—right as the main Persian force struck. The Persians slaughtered many and took many more alive, among them the son of Queen Tomyris, who had led the Massagetae as general. His name was Spargapises.

When Tomyris learned what had happened to her army and to her son, she 1.212
sent a messenger to Cyrus to say: "Insatiate of blood, Cyrus, do not exult in what has come to pass, that with the fruit of the vine—a fruit that makes you go mad as you engorge yourselves, spilling out ugly words once the wine fills up your belly—that with this drug, and not by fighting in test of strength, you tricked and overmastered my child. I offer you this advice. Take it. Give my son back to me and depart from this land, unpunished, even though you have committed this outrage[78] on a third of the army of the Massagetae. If you do not do this, I swear by the Sun, my god and master, I will glut you with blood, however insatiate of blood you be."

Such were the words the herald proclaimed, but Cyrus paid them no atten- 1.213
tion. Then Spargapises, the son of Queen Tomyris—once the wine had worn off and he grasped what a fix he was in—asked Cyrus to release him from his chains. And, as soon as he was released and his hands were freed, he killed himself.

That, then, was how her son died. Tomyris, however—since Cyrus had 1.214
not listened to her—gathered together her whole force and attacked. In my judgment, this was the fiercest of all the battles ever fought between

78 The Greek verb used here derives from *hubris*.

barbarian peoples. The battle, as I have found out, went like this: first, they stood apart and shot arrows at each other; next, when the arrows were used up, they fought hand to hand with spears and daggers. For a long time the fighters battled and neither side was willing to give way and run, but in the end the Massagetae prevailed. Most of the Persian army was destroyed where it stood, and among them was Cyrus himself. He had ruled for twenty-nine years.

Filling a wine sack with human blood, Tomyris looked among the Persian dead for the corpse of Cyrus, and when she found it, she pushed his head down into the sack. Befouling the corpse in this way, Tomyris said, "Though I am alive and have beaten you in battle, you have destroyed me by taking the life of my child, using a trick. You I glut with blood, just as I threatened." There are many stories told of the end of Cyrus's life, but this in my view is the most plausible.

The Marvels and Customs of the Massagetae

1.215 The Massagetae are very like the Scythians in the clothing they wear and in their way of life. The warriors, however, are both with and without horse (that is, there is infantry as well as cavalry), and they have spearmen as well as archers, along with some who regularly use battle-axes. They use gold and bronze for everything. Spear-points and arrowheads and the blades of battle-axes are made entirely out of bronze, while helmets and war-belts and chest-bands are decorated with gold. So likewise the breastplates of horses are made of bronze, but the metal parts of the bridle and the bit and the cheek-pieces are of gold. Iron and silver are not used for the simple reason that those metals aren't found there—while gold and bronze are plentiful.

1.216 They have the following special customs. Each man marries a woman, but they enjoy the women in common. (Some Greeks say the Scythians do this, but the ones who do this are not Scythians but the Massagetae.) When a man of the Massagetae feels desire for a woman, he hangs his quiver on the front of her covered wagon, and they have sex without fear of jealousy or retaliation. The Massagetae have no predetermined limit to their life span, but when a man is very old all the relatives come together and sacrifice that person, together with some sheep or cattle, and, boiling the meat, they have a feast. This is considered the happiest way to end one's life. Anyone who dies from sickness is not eaten but buried, and they think it a misfortune that he cannot be sacrificed. They do not sow crops, but live from domestic animals and from the fish that spawn in abundance in the Araxes River. They are milk drinkers. As for the gods, they worship only the Sun, and to him they sacrifice horses, with this as their reasoning: to the swiftest of the gods the swiftest of mortal creatures must be apportioned.

BOOK 2

Cambyses and Tales of Egypt

With what should by now be a comfortable rhythm, the narrative introduces Cambyses and his invasion of Egypt as the new focal subject, but then pauses to present background materials. In this case, those background materials will be a long and detailed excursus on Egypt, its geography, people, animals, monuments, and early rulers. This background will however continue not, as with Croesus (story of Gyges etc.) or Cyrus (story of Deioces etc.), for a few chapters, but for almost two hundred. Why Herodotus inserts such a long excursus at this point in his narrative remains a matter of active debate. In addition to Herodotus's announced interest in recording marvels and great works, scholars have seen here an analogy to the way that Greek epic poems are constructed: think of the *Iliad*, where the focal subject is introduced at the front (the quarrel between Agamemnon and Achilles), followed by several books of material that convey the magnitude of the contest and the personalities of principal heroes, with only sporadic return to the strict "plot" of the epic. Homeric scholars think of this as deliberate retardation of the narrative, designed to create a sense of the weight of events. That seems apt here.

In what follows, we will sense a distinct shift in register, one that would have reminded Greeks of contemporary proto-scientific inquiry. Even when Herodotus is not quite right, as for example with the source of the Nile, the logic, analysis, and evidence adduced are impressively different from the folktales of book 1; the experiment of Psammetichus at the front quickly detaches itself from pure storytelling mode—despite the fact that this is very ancient history he is trying to record. The sources, unlike book 1, are explicit and specific: Egyptian priests at Memphis, Thebes, and Heliopolis, who are charged with retaining knowledge of the past, and who do that through maintaining (among other things) archives of sacred writings. Recall in what follows that while Greeks will have known something of Egypt (about the pyramids, for example), few would have traveled there, and even fewer would have traveled beyond the trading sites near the coast.

Cambyses

2.1 At Cyrus's death, the kingship passed to Cambyses,[1] his son by Cassandane, daughter of Pharnaspes. Cassandane had died earlier, when Cyrus was still alive, and Cyrus mourned her so deeply that he issued a proclamation that everyone—all those he ruled—mourn as well. This woman, then, was the mother of Cambyses, and Cyrus his father, and Cambyses considered the Ionians and Aeolians[2] his patrimony, slaves inherited from his father; thus, when he gathered troops to make an attack on Egypt, he took with him the Greeks he had under his sway, along with others among his subjects.

Psammetichus and the Antiquity of Egypt

Motifs to watch for: experimentation as proto-science; specificity of sources; limitations of human knowledge about divine affairs. Here we also will see Herodotus engaging in rivalry with a near contemporary, Hecataeus, whom he alludes to without naming him. This passing allusion works as Herodotus's sly put-down—and claim of superiority over—Hecataeus's earlier work.

2.2 Now up to the time of Psammetichus,[3] the Egyptians thought that they themselves were the most ancient of all peoples. But when Psammetichus came to the throne, he set out to learn who in fact came first, and from that time onward the Egyptians have thought the Phrygians older than themselves, but themselves older than anyone else. This question—which people were the most ancient?—was, as Psammetichus found, impossible to settle by asking, and so he came up with an ingenious plan. He gave two newborn babies, taken at random, to a herdsman to raise among his flocks, bidding that no one speak so much as a word in their presence. They were to lie by themselves in a remote hut; at the times appointed the herdsman would bring she-goats to feed them milk, and in general take care of them. Psammetichus made all these arrangements because of this: he wanted to hear, once the children were past the age of meaningless baby-talk, what would be the first word they uttered. And so it came to pass. For two years the herdsman had done as he was told, but one day as he opened the door and went in both children fell at his feet, stretched out their hands, and cried out, "*bekos*." When he first heard this, the herdsman thought nothing of it. But as he frequented the hut and took care of things, he heard the word over and over; so he sent a message to his master and, when the king's order came, brought the children for the king to see. Psammetichus, after he had listened to them himself, tried to find

1 Cambyses' reign was 530–522 BC. The attack on Egypt was in 525 BC, against the Egyptian pharaoh Amasis.

2 The Ionians and Aeolians were the Greeks living along the mainland of current-day Turkey and the islands between that mainland and Greece.

3 Psamtik I, pharaoh from 664 to 610 BC.

out which people call something *bekos*, and discovered that this is what the Phrygians call their bread. With this as evidence, the Egyptians then had to concede that the Phrygians are the older people. That is the story I heard from the Egyptian priests of Hephaestus[4] in Memphis. The Greeks, however, tell many laughable stories, including this one: that Psammetichus cut out the tongues of some women, and these women then were made to keep the babies alive.[5] So much, then, for what the priests said about the rearing of the babies. 2.3

I heard much else in Memphis when I came to speak with the priests of Hephaestus. In fact, I also made visits to Thebes and Heliopolis for this very purpose: I wanted to know whether the priests there would tell the same stories as those told in Memphis. (Among the Egyptians, the Heliopolites are said to know the most about these stories.) Now, as for the tales I heard about the gods, those I am not eager to relate—aside from the bare names—since I think no man knows more than any other about divine affairs.[6] When I do speak of the gods, I therefore will record something only when the narrative absolutely compels it. But as to what the priests said regarding *human* af- 2.4
fairs, they agreed with each other on the following points. They said that the Egyptians were the first of all men to figure out the year by dividing the parts of the seasons into twelve. They figured this out, they said, from the stars. In my opinion, the Egyptians work out their calendar much more cleverly than the Greeks. The Greeks put in an intercalary month every other year because of the misalignment with the seasons,[7] while the Egyptians make the twelve months thirty days apiece, and then add five extra days every year; thus the annual cycle of seasons keeps pace with their calendar. The priests also said that the Egyptians first thought to give names to the twelve gods (which the Greeks took over from them), and that they first established altars and statues and temples for the gods; and that they also first carved figures in stone. For most of these things they pointed to a physical object as proof. They also said that the first human king of Egypt was Min. In his time, by their account, all Egypt except the Thebaïd was a swamp, and there was no land above water north of what is now Lake Moeris, which is a seven days' voyage upriver from the sea.

4 The Egyptian god Ptah. Greeks customarily substitute the one of their own gods whose powers most resemble the local divinity.

5 The phrase that begins this sentence echoes Hecataeus (whose work starts, "Hecataeus of Miletus tells these tales. I write the things that I think are the truth—for the stories that the Greeks tell are both many and laughable.") Probably the story of the cut-out tongues comes from Hecataeus, who wrote an ethnographical work that included Egypt.

6 Literally, the phrase runs, "men have equal understanding of divine affairs"—but in the Greek worldview this suggests an equal *lack* of understanding. Herodotus means that the understanding of divine affairs is not subject to human inquiry, and thus not a part of his investigation (*historiê*).

7 As we saw in the Solon episode (1.32) the Greeks used a calendar of 12 months of 29–30 days and in alternate years added an extra, "intercalary" month to keep the calendar aligned with the astronomical year.

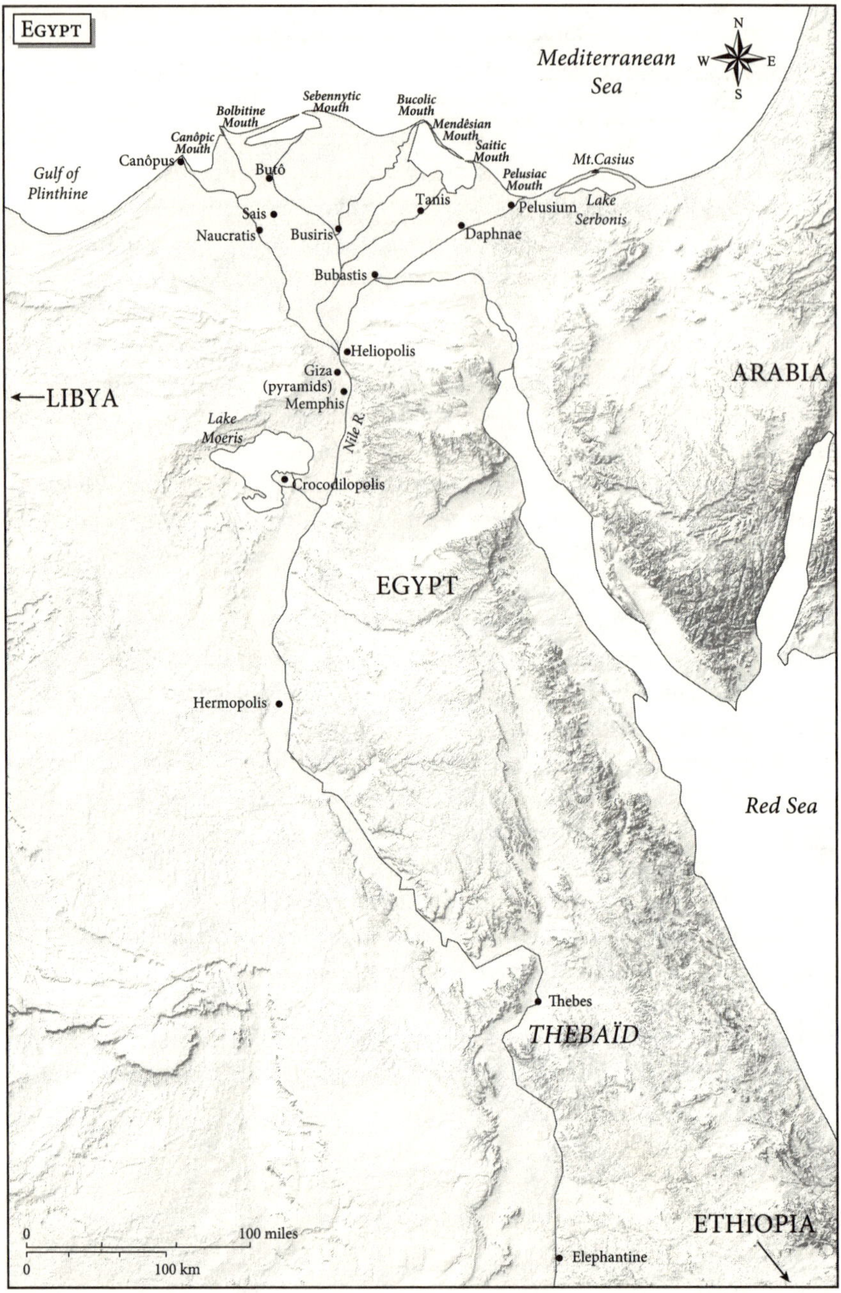
EGYPT
N
W
E
S
Mediterranean Sea
Sebennytic Mouth
Bolbitine Mouth
Bucolic Mouth
Mendêsian Mouth
Saitic Mouth
Canôpic Mouth
Canôpus
Gulf of Plinthine
Butô
Pelusiac Mouth
Mt.Casius
Tanis
Pelusium
Lake Serbonis
Sais
Naucratis
Busiris
Daphnae
Bubastis
Heliopolis
Giza (pyramids)
Memphis
ARABIA
←LIBYA
Lake Moeris
Nile R.
Crocodilopolis
EGYPT
Hermopolis
Red Sea
Thebes
THEBAÏD
0
100 miles
0
100 km
ETHIOPIA
Elephantine

MAP 2.1

Physical Geography of Egypt

The narrative voice continues in the mode of the proto-scientific. Geographical inquiry was an important part of the scientific thinking we associate with the Greek "Ionian Enlightenment" of the 6th and 5th centuries.

I think the priests' account of the land is right: it is clear to anyone who 2.5
looks, even if he has heard nothing about it—anyone who has intelligence, that is[8]—that the Egypt to which the Greeks now sail is alluvial land, the river's gift to the Egyptians, and that the land upriver for another three-day journey past the lake—though the priests said nothing about this—is also the same type.

The overall physical layout of the land of Egypt is as follows. First, when you sail in and are still a day's run from the land, if you let out a sounding line you will bring up river mud and find a depth of eleven fathoms.[9] This
makes it clear that the silt extends that far away along the coast. Moreover, 2.6
the length of Egypt's coastline (which I define as running from the Gulf of Plinthine to where Lake Serbonis sits below Mount Casius) is a distance of sixty *schoeni*. Men who have little land measure it by *fathoms*; those with more land, by *stades*; those with a lot of land, by *parasangs*; and those with a great abundance, by *schoeni*. The parasang is thirty stades, but each schoenus—an Egyptian measure—is sixty. The measurement of coastal Egypt in stades would be, then, three thousand six hundred.[10]

As for the part of Egypt that runs from the sea inland up to Heliopolis, that 2.7
is wide and entirely flat, full of water and marsh, and its length is about the same distance as the road that runs from the altar of the twelve gods at Athens to the temple of Olympian Zeus at Pisa. If you measured out these roads, you would find that, though the lengths are not exactly the same, there is only a small difference, no more than fifteen stades—for the road to Pisa from Athens is fifteen stades short of fifteen hundred, while the road to Heliopolis from the sea runs to the full count.[11]

But once you go farther inland from Heliopolis, Egypt becomes narrow. 2.8
On one side the Arabian mountains stretch alongside, running from the north to the south and the noonday sun, and extending inland all the way to what is known as the Red Sea (and in these mountains are the quarries that were cut for the pyramids in Memphis). Here, at the Red Sea, the mountains turn and end. Their greatest breadth from east to west is, as I learned, a two-month journey, and at the far limit of the mountains toward the east the land produces

8 This seems to be another dig at Hecataeus, Herodotus's predecessor, who also wrote on this question of alluvial deposits.

9 36 feet, 11 m. Ships would run along the coast when approaching the Nile, and thus the claim here is not that silt is found at 11 fathoms a full day's sail out from the Nile (which would be preposterous), but that silt is found at 11 fathoms that far away along the coast. This then naturally leads the inquiry to focus in turn on the size of Egypt's seacoast.

10 "Spectacularly wrong" (Lloyd): this translates to roughly 410 miles (675 km); the actual measurement is 295 miles, 476 km. Most of the other measurements in what follows are approximately correct.

11 About 165 miles, 265 km. Again, the point of reference targets a reader familiar with Athens and environs. (This will not always be the case.)

frankincense. Such then is the character of these mountains. On the side of Egypt toward Libya another rocky range stretches, containing pyramids and covered with sand, and running in parallel with the part of the Arabian mountains that bears southward. Starting from Heliopolis, then, there is no longer a great extent of land—that which is properly Egypt, that is—and the Egyptian territory stays narrow over the course of a four days' voyage. The land in between these mountains is a plain. At its narrowest point, there are by my estimate no more than about two hundred stades[12] between the Arabian mountains and those we call Libyan. Beyond that Egypt becomes wide again.

2.9 That then is the physical layout of the land itself. From Heliopolis to Thebes is a voyage upriver of nine days, a distance of four thousand eight hundred and sixty stades, or eighty-one schoeni. Here then is the sum total of Egypt's measurement in stades. The coastline, as I explained earlier, measures three thousand six hundred stades. The distance from the coast inland up to Thebes I will now tell you: it is six thousand one hundred and twenty. And between Thebes and the city called Elephantine there are one thousand eight hundred stades. . . .[13]

The Nile River

In examining the question of the source of the Nile flood Herodotus again pauses to refute rival narratives, with a sharp attack on contemporaries, to buttress his own general authority. He deploys arguments from analogy (2.20), and probability (22), and dismisses the traditions handed down from the poets (21, 23). His own explanation (24–26) will strike us as odd, but is internally consistent, given the state of scientific understanding, and not far off the mark. The actual reason for the annual flood does have to do with the seasonal movement of the sun (though it is the earth that moves, of course): winds move the wet air from the seasonal evaporation to the highlands of Ethiopia, from which come the floodwaters.

2.19 The Nile, when it floods, inundates not just the Delta, but also parts of Libya and Arabia, spreading out on either side over a two-day journey, more or less. Now as to why the Nile works the way it does, neither the priests nor anyone else was able to tell me anything.[14] I was particularly anxious to know why the Nile rises up and starts its flood at the summer solstice; and why the flood lasts for a hundred days—when it gets to just that count, the flood ebbs, returning the river to its bed, and then for the whole winter the river remains shallow, up to the time when the summer solstice comes around again. But I could not get anything about this from any of the Egyptians. I also asked them what there was about the Nile that made it naturally opposite to other

12 About 22 miles, 36 km.

13 Coast to Thebes: 680 miles (1100 km); the actual distance is about 550 miles (890 km). Thebes to Elephantine: 200 miles (320 km); actual distance 135 miles (220 km).

14 The priests would have offered mythological, not scientific, explanations.

rivers; and, similarly, I wanted to know why this alone of all rivers has no cool breeze blowing from it.

Now among the Greeks, men I will leave unnamed—since fame for cleverness is what they are after—have offered three different explanations for the behavior of this body of water. Of these, two I consider hardly worthy of remark, except to note what they are. One states that the Etesian winds[15] are the reason why the river floods, since the winds hold back the outflow of the Nile. But often the Etesian winds are not yet blowing, and the Nile does its flooding all the same. Moreover, if the Etesian winds were the cause, other rivers—all those that flow opposite to the winds—would have to flood just as the Nile does, and in fact they would flood more since these other rivers are weaker and have less of a current. Yet there are many rivers in Syria, and many in Libya, and none of them experience anything like the flooding of the Nile. 2.20

The other approach is even more ignorant than the one just described, as well as more fantastic in what it has to say. That one states that these things come about from the flowing of the Ocean, and that the Ocean flows round about the Earth.[16] 2.21

But it is the third approach to explaining the Nile's flood that by its very plausibility most misleads. This one—making no sense at all—claims that the Nile flows from melted snow.[17] But the Nile flows from Libya through the middle of Ethiopia, and ends up in Egypt. How in the world could it flow from snow, when it flows from the hottest lands into lands that are far cooler? Any man able to think rationally about this will find how unlikely this is—that the Nile flows from a snowy region. The first and greatest proof lies in the hot winds that blow from these regions. Secondly, the region is entirely without rain and without frost: yet wherever snow falls, by logical necessity there is precipitation throughout the region, to a distance of five days; so, if it were snowing at the source of the Nile, Egypt would have rain. Thirdly, the men there are black-skinned because of the extreme heat. And, finally, hawks and swallows stay throughout the year and do not migrate, whereas cranes flee the winter cold in Scythia in order to spend the winter in exactly these territories. If it did snow, even a little bit, in the regions through which the Nile flows or from which it springs, none of these things could possibly be—so logic dictates. 2.22

As for the story told about the Ocean, that admits no logical refutation, since it is a story told of something no one has seen. I at least do not know of any river "Ocean," and I suppose that Homer or one of the earlier poets must have found the name and introduced it into his poetry. 2.23

15 Winds of summer that start about the time of the solstice and blow toward Egypt from the north. We know from other sources that this is the theory of Thales of Miletus, an early "sage" whom we have seen before (1.74).

16 This is the theory of Herodotus's immediate predecessor, Hecataeus of Miletus. Again, the sharp put-down here is designed to increase Herodotus's own authority. That there is a great Ocean flowing around the flat disc of the earth is a mythical geography, mentioned by Homer and Hesiod (Herodotus will revisit the question of this "Ocean" at 4.8).

17 Again, we know from other sources that this is the theory of Anaxagoras of Clazomenae, a contemporary of Herodotus and thus a direct rival.

2.24 Now by rights anyone who criticizes the proposals of others should set forth his own view of this obscure matter—so, I will state my own theory as to why the Nile floods during the summer. *During the winter the sun is driven off its original course by the winter storms and comes to reside over upper Libya.* Those very few words say it all, given that wherever the sun-god is closest, one can reasonably infer that the land there is especially needy of water and that the local river channels run dry.

2.25 But here's the full explanation. As the sun crosses over the upper, inland part of Libya what happens is this. There, the air is constantly bright and clear, the land hot, the breezes never cool, and thus the sun has the same effect as it does elsewhere in summer as it passes through the middle part of the heavens: that is, as it passes it draws the Nile water up to itself, and pushes it further upland, and there the winds get hold of it and disperse the moisture. It thus stands to reason that the winds that blow from that land are the south and the southwest winds, those being much the winds most prone to rain. (The sun, as I see it, does not disperse all the water from the Nile every year, but some of it stays up near the sun.) Once the winter storms abate, the sun goes back to mid-heaven, and from that position it draws water up equally from all the rivers. During the winter, then, the other rivers grow big, swelling their stream with storm waters flowing down from the soaked and gullied earth; but over the summer, the rains abandon them and, drawn up by the sun, their waters recede. The Nile, by contrast, is without rain, and so during the winter, when the sun draws water only from it, the Nile flows far less than its natural flood during the summer. This is only logical: for in the summer its water is drawn up in equal proportion to other rivers, but during the winter it alone is depleted. I believe, then, that the sun is the cause of all this.

2.26 In my view the sun is also the reason why the air is always dry there, since the sun's heat dries out everything along its course—that's why it is always summer in the inland parts of Libya.[18] But imagine if the orientation of the seasons changed, and in the heavens north and south changed places, and the south wind stood where now the north wind stands—if that were the case, the sun, pushed from the mid-heaven by the winter storms and winds, would go to the upper part of Europe, just as now to upper Libya, and as it passed over Europe it would, I expect, make the Ister[19] behave just as the Nile does now.

2.27 As for the question of why no cool breeze blows from the Nile, my view is this: it is not logical that such a breeze would come from warm places—cool breezes are naturally wont to come from places that are cool. . . .

18 That is, during the winter the sun is diverted to reside over Libya; during the summer, all the Mediterranean countries are hot and dry, including Libya.

19 Danube River.

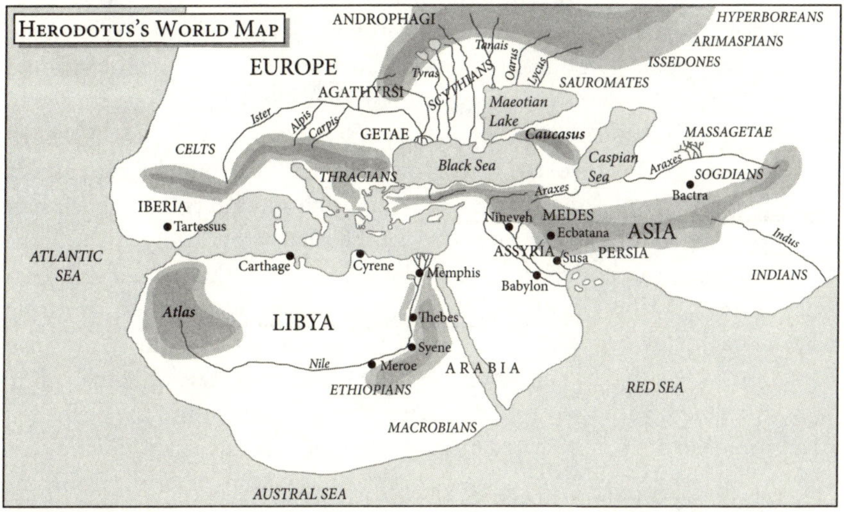

FIGURE 2.1

The Marvels and Customs of Egypt

The narrative now turns to marvels beyond the physical terrain. Behind much proto-scientific thinking in this period was the belief that geography and climate had a determining influence on peoples and their customs (scholars call this "environmental determinism"), and this idea could extend in surprising directions. In this case, the narrative, having established that the Nile behaves in a manner opposite to all other rivers, looks to a similar opposition in the customs of its people. What follows is a selection from a long section, of 64 chapters.

As for the Nile, enough has been said. Concerning Egypt as a whole, how- 2.35
ever, I will now speak at length, since nowhere else in the world are there so many marvels, and so many great works that defy description.[20] Surely that is reason enough to say more about this land.

EGYPTIAN CUSTOMS AND MANNERS

Not only do the Egyptians have their own peculiar weather and a river different from other rivers, but they also have made almost all of their habits and customs exactly opposite to the rest of mankind. Among the Egyptians, the women go to the marketplace and sell the wares, while the men stay at home and do the weaving. Other people push the loom's threads up, the Egyptians down. The men carry loads on their heads, the women on their shoulders. And the women pee standing up, the men sitting down. They ease their bowels inside, and eat outside in the roadways, saying that one ought to do shameful

20 The phrasing here—marvels (*thomasia*), great works (*erga*)—echoes the first sentence of the work, in which Herodotus presents one aim of his work as the celebration of the "great and marvelous deeds" of Greeks and non-Greeks. The word there translated "deeds" (*erga*) is here used more concretely and thus translated as (human) "works."

things out of sight, and things not shameful out in the open. No women are priests of the gods or goddesses, but men do this duty for all gods, male and female. Men are under no obligation to take care of their parents if they so choose, but all women must, whether they want to or not.

2.36 Elsewhere the priests of the gods grow their hair long, but in Egypt priests shave the head clean. For others the custom is for mourners to cut their hair while grieving, but Egyptian mourners let their hair grown long, on both the head and the chin, though it is otherwise kept short. Other men dwell apart from animals, but in Egypt the animals live in the house. Others live from wheat and barleycorn, but the Egyptians hold those who do so in great contempt—they make their flour from a kind of spelt, *zeia* as some call it. They mix dough with their feet, and clay with their hands; and they use their hands (instead of a scoop) when picking up dung. The Egyptians practice circumcision, while everyone else—except those who learned from the Egyptians—leaves the genitals as they were at birth. Men in Egypt wear two garments (tunic and mantle), women one. On sailing vessels, the reefing rings and ropes are fastened from the outer side of the sail, but the Egyptians fasten them from the inner side. Greeks write letters and move the abacus counters working from left to right, but the Egyptians from right to left. And even as they do this, they claim that they are doing it "rightly" and the Greeks "leftly"—by which they mean wrongly. They make use of not one but two alphabets, one called the hieratic (the "holy script"), and the other the demotic (the "common script"). . . .

THE SACRED ANIMALS OF EGYPT

The overarching theme continues to be the marvels of Egypt, with special focus on marvels that relate to Egypt's unusual terrain and climate. The voice remains in proto-scientific mode, with an impressive accumulation of detail, from the rareness of bears and wolves (extraordinary from a European perspective) to the exotic crocodile (accurately depicted) to the even more exotic hippopotamus (whom Herodotus seems not to well understand: the beast, despite the fact that the name means "river-horse" in Greek, has no mane, nor a horse's whinny). Cats, by the way, were unknown in classical Greece, so they too were exotic animals and their mummification and worship mystifying.

2.65 Despite sharing a border with Libya, Egypt does not contain a lot of animals. But what animals they have are all considered sacred, both domestic and not. Now, were I to tell you why the animals are held sacrosanct, I would have to range into divine affairs, something I particularly want to avoid—what I have touched upon already, I have included only where the narrative required. In any case, the Egyptians have a remarkable custom as regards animals and it works like this. Caretakers, men and women both, are appointed from the Egyptians as keepers, one for each type of animal, an honor that passes from father to child. In the towns each citizen performs his vows by praying to the god (whichever god is the right one for the particular animal), then shaving his children's hair, either the whole head of hair, or a half, or a third, and, finally, weighing the hair against a sum of silver: however much silver tips the scale is what he gives for maintenance of the animals. The keeper then cuts up as much fish as the silver will buy and feeds it to the animals. Such is the way the animals are maintained. Anyone who kills one of these animals on purpose, is punished by death; if by accident, the punishment is whatever the priests assign. But if anyone kills an ibis or a falcon[21]—whether on purpose or not—he needs must die.

FIGURE 2.2 Cat-headed goddess Bastet

Though there are a great many domestic animals in Egypt, there would be many more except for what happens to cats. 2.66
Once the females give birth, they no longer consort with the males, and males wanting to mount them are refused. In response the tomcats work this clever trick: they grab the kittens and secreting them away they kill them (but not for food). The females then, eager to replace the young they have lost, come back to the males—so strong is the desire for offspring among animals. What happens to the cats when something catches fire is a wonder. No one pays any attention to putting out the blaze. Instead, the Egyptians stand in a row, trying to shield the cats, while the cats, slipping through or leaping over, jump into the fire. If the cat succeeds, it is a cause of great mourning for the Egyptians. When a cat dies from natural causes, the people in the household shave the hair, but of their eyebrows only; and when a dog dies, the household shaves
the whole of body and head. Dead cats are taken to sacred huts in Bubastis, 2.67
where they are embalmed and buried. Dogs and jackals each man buries in his own town, in sacred tombs; and the Nile mongoose is buried in the same way. Field mice and falcons they cart to Buto, and ibises to Hermopolis. Bears and wolves are rare, not much more common than foxes, and so these they bury right where they find the corpse.

As for crocodiles, they have unusual characteristics that are worth remark. 2.68
Over the four winter months a crocodile eats nothing. It is a four-footed creature both of the land and of the water, in that it lays and hatches its eggs on dry land and spends most of each day there, but spends the whole night in the river, where the water gives more warmth than the night air and dew. Of all the creatures I know this is the one who grows to be the greatest from the least: a crocodile lays eggs no larger than a goose, and the size of the young is

21 The Egyptian god Thoth had the head of an ibis, while both Horus and the sun-god Ra had the head of a falcon.

in keeping with the egg, but as it grows up it reaches over twenty-five feet[22] or even more. It has the eyes of a pig, and great teeth and tusks of a size with its body. The crocodile alone of animals has no tongue, and does not move the lower jaw: rather, it and it alone moves the upper jaw to meet the lower. It has strong claws and a hide that is tough and covered with scales over the back. It is blind in the water, but very sharp-eyed out in the open air. Since a crocodile spends so much of its life in water, the inside of its mouth is teeming with leeches. Other birds and animals avoid the crocodile, but the Egyptian plover gives it help, and so they are on the best of terms. For when the crocodile crawls out onto land from the water and then gapes open his mouth (which it mostly likes to do while turned toward the west wind), the plover goes into its mouth and gobbles down the leeches: the crocodile is happy for the help and therefore does the plover no harm.

2.69 Some Egyptians hold the crocodile sacred; others do not, but treat crocodiles as enemies. Crocodiles are held especially sacrosanct in the area near Thebes and Lake Moeris. There, each cult keeps one crocodile, selected out of all, which they train and tame. On its ears are set earrings made of colored glass and gold,[23] and bangles on the front feet; specialty bread and sacrificial victims are provided as food. Every fineness is accorded these crocodiles so long as they live; and when they die, they are embalmed and buried in sacred tombs. By contrast, Egyptians who live near Elephantine do not consider crocodiles sacred, and even eat them. Egyptians call the animal not a "crocodile" but a *champsa*. Ionians named them *krokodeiloi*—Ionian for a lizard—because they thought they resembled the native lizards that live in their drystone walls.

2.70 Of the many and various ways of hunting crocodiles, I record here the one that seems to me most worth describing. The hunter puts a pig chine on a hook as bait, and casts it into the middle of the river; meanwhile, up on the riverbank, he has a live suckling pig, which he starts to slap. The crocodile hears the squealing, rushes toward the sound, and, coming upon the pig chine, gobbles it down. The men then pull on the rope and drag the crocodile to dry land. The first thing the hunter does is to smear its eyes with mud—once that is done, the beast is easily dispatched; otherwise, it can give a lot of trouble.

2.71 Hippopotamuses are sacred in the Papremis region of Egypt, but not elsewhere. Hippopotamuses have unique characteristics: they are four-footed, with cloven hoofs like cattle, snub-nosed, with the mane of a horse—though with showy projecting tusks—and the tail and whinny of a horse as well; in size like the largest ox; and a hide so thick that when it is dried spear shafts can be made of it.

22 8 m.

23 Crocodile mummies at Thebes have been found with holes drilled in the skulls, presumably for these earrings.

FIGURE 2.3 Crocodile mummies. In the Fayum area of Egypt crocodiles were connected with the crocodile-headed god Sobk and were therefore venerated. Hundreds of crocodile mummies survive, laid to rest in animal cemeteries specially set up by the temples for these sacred animal remains

2.72 Otters are also found in the river, and the Egyptians consider these sacred, along with the fish called the scale-fish and the eel; these, they say, are the hallowed creatures of the Nile river god, as is the Egyptian goose among the birds.

2.73 There is another bird that is sacred, named the phoenix. I never saw it, except in a painting, for he comes to them rarely—as the Heliopolites tell the story, only every five hundred years, when his father dies. If he truly looks like the painting, his wings have gold-tipped plumage that is mostly red, and in shape and size he is very like an eagle. And this is what they say the phoenix does (though I don't believe it): setting out from Arabia he carries his father encased in myrrh to the temple of Helios, where he buries him. To convey him, first the phoenix molds an egg-shaped lump of myrrh as big as he can carry, and tests whether he can carry it; if the test is successful, he hollows out the egg and puts his father inside; then, using more myrrh he plasters up the hole. (The egg with his father laying inside thus weighs the same as it did at the beginning.) So encased, the father is carried by the phoenix to the temple of Helios. That, then, is what they say this bird does.

2.74 In the vicinity of Thebes there are sacred snakes, not at all dangerous to men, which are small and have two horns growing from the top of the head: when these die, they bury them in the temple of Zeus, since, they say, these are the hallowed creatures of that god.

2.75 In Arabia, roughly opposite the city of Buto, is a place where I went to find out about the winged snakes. When I got there, I saw indescribable numbers of bones and backbones of snakes. There were heaps of spines—big heaps, and small, and smaller even still—and there were lots of them. Now the place where these spines lie strewn has a narrow mountain pass that descends to a great plain; and that plain joins to the plain of Egypt. The story goes that in the springtime winged snakes fly from Arabia into Egypt and the ibises meet them at the mountain pass here and do not let the snakes by but strike them down. The Arabians say that it is for this very deed that the ibis is greatly honored by the Egyptians; and the Egyptians agree that this is the reason why they honor these birds.

2.76 The appearance of the ibis is remarkable: jet black all over, but with the legs of a crane; a face with a sharply hooked beak; and as big as a corncrake. That's the appearance of the black ones—the ones that fight against the snakes—but the one more commonly found in inhabited areas (there are two kinds of ibis, you see) is bald over its head and the whole of its neck, and its feathers are white, except for the head and neck, the tips of the wings, and the tip of the rump (which are all jet black); its legs and beak are like the other

FIGURE 2.4 Ibis-headed god Thoth

one. As for the snake, the shape is like a water snake, and it has not wings with feathers, but ones pretty much like the wings of bats.

So much, then, about the sacred animals.

THE PEOPLE OF EGYPT

The people of Egypt who live in the arable parts of the country, by virtue of their 2.77
consistent practice of record-keeping, have far the most knowledge of things past of anyone I have encountered. Such is their collective memory, and here is their way of life. Every month, for three days in a row, they take an emetic, and through emetics and bowel purging they pursue bodily health, believing that all human diseases arise from the foodstuffs that nourish them. Even apart from this, the Egyptians are, after the Libyans, the healthiest of all men—because of the climate, or so it seems to me, that is, because in Egypt there is no change from one season to the next. For change is what causes human disease; and of all changes, seasonal shifts in the weather are the most likely to lead to illness.

The Egyptians are bread eaters, and make bread from barley (which they call *kyllestis*). They drink a sort of "wine" made from barleycorn,[24] since there are no grapevines in the land. Certain types of fish they eat uncooked but dried in the sun, and other types cured in brine. Among the birds they also eat quail and duck and other small species, uncooked but dried. But in general they roast or boil whatever birds and fish they get their hands on (except for the ones appointed sacred, of course).

At dinner parties of the wealthy, after the meal a man carries about in a 2.78
coffin the wooden likeness of a corpse, two or three feet tall, carved and painted to look like the real thing. Displaying the corpse to each of the guests in turn he says, "Look upon this as you drink, and be merry: for so you will be when you die." That, then, is what they do at drinking parties.

Egyptians follow the customs of their ancestors exclusively; none are im- 2.79
ported from abroad. Among many interesting customs is a ritual hymn, the *Linus Song*. This man, under various local names, is celebrated in song in Phoenicia and in Cyprus and elsewhere, including in Greece, where the song (which closely resembles the others) gives him the name *Linus*. Among the many things that surprised me in Egypt was, then, this one too: how did they come to have this very same song? They plainly have sung it from time immemorial. In Egyptian Linus is called *Maneros*, and the Egyptians tell the story that Maneros was the only begotten son of Egypt's first king; that he died an untimely death; that the Egyptians made this sorrowful song in his honor; and that this was the first and, for some time, their only hymn. . . .

The Egyptians made also these discoveries: which month and which day 2.82
belong to which god, and based on each man's day of birth what will happen to him and how he will die and what sort of person he will be. (There are versifiers among the Greeks who have made use of this too.) The Egyptians

24 Beer.

have determined the meaning of more portents than any other people. When a portent happens, they carefully record the outcome; and if a similar portent happens later, they expect the outcome to be the same.

2.83 As for prophecy, the art is vested in no one among men, nor in any one god, but in several: they have an oracle of Heracles as well as of Apollo, Athena, Artemis, Ares, and Zeus; and the oracle of Leto in Buto is held in particularly high regard.[25] There is no one way of consulting the god, however; each oracle is different.

2.84 In the practice of medicine, they divide it up so that each doctor is the doctor of a single disease and no more. There is a great plenitude of doctors, since there are doctors for the eyes, doctors for the head, doctors for the teeth, doctors for the gut, and doctors for diseases whose origin is obscure.

2.85 Grieving and burial among the Egyptians works like this: whenever a man of some note passes away, the womenfolk of the house all smear mud over their heads and even their faces; leaving the dead man in the house, they then wander the city beating their breasts (with their clothes girt round so as to expose them); and all their female relatives join with them. Opposite them, the men of the household also strike themselves, girded in the same way. Once this is done, they take the body for the mummification.

2.86 In Egypt, mummifying is a specialty trade and people make a living at it. When a corpse is brought in, the embalmers show the relatives wooden effigies of mummies, realistically painted. The most elaborate of these they claim as the type used for He-Who-Is-Not-to-Be-Named (it would be sacrilegious to record the name);[26] they then show a second that is not as good and cheaper; and finally a third that is the least expensive. Having made the presentation, they find out from the mourners which style they prefer for preparing the corpse. The relatives then agree on a price and go away, leaving the embalmers to their work.

The most elaborate type of mummifying is done as follows. The embalmers first use an iron hook to pull out the brains through the nostrils, at least the parts they can; the rest they remove using liquefying drugs. After that, they take up a sharp Ethiopian stone and slice along the flank, extracting the insides whole. They clean out the belly cavity, dousing it first with palm wine and then with an infusion of fragrant ground spices; then, they fill the belly with myrrh, pure and finely ground, and cinnamon, and other fragrances (but not frankincense); and sew it back up. Once all that is done, they exsiccate the corpse, covering it with soda ash for seventy days—this is the maximum time allowed for the drying process—and, when the seventieth day comes, they wash the corpse off. Now, taking bandages cut from fine linen, they smear these with gum arabic (which Egyptians often use instead of glue), and with a spiraling motion they wrap the body up from head to toe. The relatives then take the body and have a wooden coffin made in the shape of a man; in that

25 Heracles = Onuris, Apollo = Horus, Athena = Neith, Artemis = Bastet, Ares = Montju, Zeus = Amun, Leto = Wadjet.

26 This is the god Osiris, who in Egyptian mythology was the first to be mummified, by the jackal-headed god Anubis. Ritual imitation of that act was part of the journey to the kingdom of Osiris, where one could find eternal life in death.

they shut in the corpse, close the lid, and lay it in the tomb chamber, standing the coffin upright against the wall.

That's the way they handle corpses when money is no object, but those who 2.87
want to take the middle road and avoid so much expense manage it like this. They fill syringes with oil extracted from cedars, and inject that via the anus into the stomach cavity of the dead man, making no incision nor opening up the belly. Once they have made the injection, they stop the liquid from draining out the backside, and exsiccate the corpse for the stipulated number of days. On the last of those days, they retrieve the cedar oil from the stomach cavity by the route through which they injected it earlier. The cedar has so much potency that it liquefies and brings along with it the intestines and inner organs. The soda ash dissolves the flesh, and thus only the skin and bones are left. Once this is done, they hand over the corpse, taking no further trouble over it.

Finally, the way they handle mummifying for the most needy is to douse 2.88
the stomach cavity with purgatives, exsiccate the corpse for seventy days, and give it back to be borne away. . . .

The Kings of Egypt

After concluding his observations on the land and people of Egypt, Herodotus goes on to report what he learned from the priests about the Egyptian kings. (He tells us that the priests worked from a papyrus roll that listed 330 rulers.) The kings Herodotus catalogues are a mix of legendary and historical. Proteus is an Egyptian king mentioned in Homer and unlikely to translate to a particular pharaoh; Rhampsinitus is thought to be a legendary composite for the several Ramses pharaohs of the 19th and 20th dynasties (c. 1300–1100 BC); Cheops and Chephren are in fact the pharaohs who built the pyramids at Giza (4th Dynasty, c. 2600–2500 BC). Despite the uneven quality and coverage, Herodotus's account still forms much of the backbone for our understanding of Egyptian monarchical history. The account ranges from Min, the first human to succeed a god as pharaoh, to Amasis, pharaoh at the time of Cambyses's invasion. We pick up the catalogue while still in the legendary era of the very early pharaohs.

KING PROTEUS AND THE STORY OF HELEN OF TROY

This Egyptian version of the kidnapping of Helen seems to pick up where the proem (1.1–5) leaves off. Recall that the proem immediately raises the question of how to judge the historicity of traditional tales; that theme is revisited here, but to very different effect, in a tale with a profound mix of evocative storytelling and rationalistic inquiry. Three bits of background will help your own evaluation: (1) The emphasis on the guest–host relationship (xenia) is unmistakably Greek, despite the Egyptian setting, and Zeus Xenios ("Zeus protector of Guests/Strangers") was the god overseeing this sacred relation. (2) Greeks did not doubt that the Trojan War was an historical event and that Agamemnon, Menelaus, Priam, and so forth were historical kings and warriors. (3) As the Greeks tell the story, when the army was ready to

MAP 2.2

set sail for Troy, they were confronted with unrelenting contrary winds; the remedy for that turned out to be the requirement that Agamemnon, brother of Menelaus, make human sacrifice of his own daughter, Iphigenia—which he did. That sacrifice complicates the justice of the Greeks' revenge on Troy, to say the least; and the Egyptian version will complicate the notion of just reprisal further. As Charles Chiasson remarks, "The scrupulous observation of xenia by Egyptian characters (Thonis, Proteus) stands in provocative contrast to its violation by Greek characters (Paris, Menelaus)."

2.112 They say that the kingship next passed to a Memphite man, whose name in Greek is Proteus. Memphis today has beautiful and well-appointed grounds sacred to this king, situated to the south of the temple of Hephaestus, and in that precinct there is a shrine dedicated to Aphrodite Xenia. My own best guess is that this shrine in fact belongs to Helen of Troy, daughter of Tyndareus, judging both from what I heard about Helen's stay at the court of Proteus, and especially from Aphrodite's epithet, *Xenia*—which means "guest" or "stranger" in Greek. (There are many other shrines to Aphrodite, but nowhere else does she have the epithet *Xenia*.)

2.113 When I looked into the question, the priests told me that what had happened with Helen was this. Alexander,[27] they said, snatched Helen from Sparta and sailed off to his own land. But when he came to the Aegean Sea, violent winds blew him off course, to the sea off Egypt, and at that point, since the winds did not let up, he landed in Egypt, at Taricheae, along the mouth of the Nile known as the Canobic. On those shores there was, as even now, a temple of Heracles, and to this temple a slave, belonging to any man whosoever, could flee to safety; and if he succeeded in searing himself with the sacred brand, thereby marking his submission to the god, no one could then lay a hand on him. (This has been a continuous tradition from the founding of the temple down to my own time.) As it happened, some of Alexander's slaves found out about this tradition and ran away. Seating themselves at the temple as suppliants of the god, they denounced Alexander, eager to do him harm, telling the whole story about Helen and the injustice done to the house of Menelaus. Hearing their accusations were not only the temple priests, but also the officer set to guard that mouth of the Nile; his name was Thonis.

2.114 On hearing all this, Thonis at once sent a message to Memphis, to the court of Proteus, with these words: "A stranger has come, Trojan by race, but having

27 Paris, son of Priam, the king of Troy.

worked an ungodly deed in Greece: he seduced the wife of his host, and he comes to this land, driven by the force of the winds, bringing the wife and a great deal of plunder as well. Should we let him sail away unharmed, or seize what he has brought with him?" In reply, Proteus sent a messenger to say this: "Seize this man who has worked ungodly deeds against his own host—no matter who he is—and bring him to me, so that I may learn what he has to say."

So, Thonis seized Alexander and impounded his ships. After that, he 2.115
brought him up to Memphis, and Helen and the valuables along with him, and the suppliants too. When all were assembled, Proteus asked Alexander, "Who are you? From where do you sail?"[28] Alexander recounted his ancestry, declared the name of his country, and described the voyage on which he came. Proteus next asked him, "Where did you get Helen?" At that, Alexander strayed down the path of lies, no longer speaking the truth, and the suppliants challenged him, telling the whole story of his wrongdoings. When the questioning was over, Proteus made clear his views on the matter with these words: "If I did not place great store in never putting to death a stranger, no matter how many are driven off course by the winds and come to my land, I would make you pay the price for what you have done to this Greek man—you, vilest of men, who in return for a host's welcome worked a monstrous, ungodly deed, coming to the bedside of your host's own wife. But this was not enough for you: no, sweeping her off her feet you got her to run off with you. And even this was not enough: you now come bringing plunder from your host's house as well. As it is, inasmuch as I *do* place great store in not putting a stranger to death, I will do this. I will not allow you to take the woman here, nor the valuables. These I will keep safe for the Greek, until such time as he himself is ready to come and take them back. As for you and your sailors, I give you three days to raise anchor and sail somewhere else, out of my land; if not, you will be treated as an enemy."

Such is the story the priests told of how Helen came to live at the court of 2.116
Proteus. And I think that Homer knew this story too. Their version is not as suited to epic poetry as the other one, the one Homer used, so he deliberately set it aside; but in such a way that it's clear he knew this version of the tale. How is it clear? In composing the *Iliad* he mentions (without correcting himself elsewhere) the wanderings of Alexander, how in bringing back Helen he was blown about, coming to land at Sidon in Phoenicia. Homer mentions this in the part called the *Glory of Diomedes*, where he says:

> There lay the elaborately wrought robes, the work of Sidonian
> women, whom Alexander himself, the godlike, had brought home
> from the land of Sidon, crossing the wide sea, on that journey
> when he brought back also gloriously descended Helen.[29]

28 This echoes a characteristic phrase from Homer's *Odyssey* and is part of what gives the tale its Greek texture.

29 *Iliad* 6.289–292. Trans. R. Lattimore.

In these lines Homer shows that he knew about the wanderings of Alexander—Syria, you understand, borders on Egypt, and the Phoenicians, who inhabit Sidon, live in Syria.

2.117 This passage also shows beyond any doubt that the epic known as the *Cypria* is not the work of Homer, but of someone else. In the *Cypria*, it is said that when Alexander brought Helen from Sparta, he enjoyed fair winds and a calm sea, arriving at Troy on the third day; but in the *Iliad* Homer says that he was blown about while bringing her back.

So much, then, about Homer and the *Cypria*.

2.118 When I asked the priests whether or not what Greeks say about Troy is a laughable tale, they added more to the story, saying also this, that they had researched the question, and claimed Menelaus himself as the source for what they knew. After the kidnapping of Helen, they said, a great army did come to the land of Troy in support of Menelaus. Once the army had landed and set up camp, emissaries were sent to Troy, among them Menelaus himself. The emissaries approached the city walls and made their demands: the return of Helen, return of the plunder that Alexander had taken when he left, and monetary recompense too, as reparation for the injustice. To that, both then and later, with oaths and without, the Trojans gave always the same reply: they said they did not have Helen, nor did they have the plunder the Greeks were asking for; rather, they said, all this was in Egypt, and there could be no justice in demanding that they, the Trojans, pay reparations for what was in the hands of Proteus, the Egyptian king. But the Greeks took all this as mocking and trickery, and so they set to the siege; and, eventually, they captured the city. But when they took control of the citadel, Helen was nowhere to be seen, and their inquiries produced the same replies as before. So now the Greeks came to believe the story as first it was told, and dispatched Menelaus to the court of Proteus.

2.119 On reaching Egypt, Menelaus sailed up the Nile to Memphis. There, he told the king the whole affair, exactly as it had happened, whereupon the king welcomed him in grand style, and gave back Helen (who was safe and sound) along with all the stolen goods. Despite all this, Menelaus came to do wrong to the Egyptians. For when he was to set sail for home, contrary winds held him back, and this continued for a long time. So, as remedy, he came up with an ingenious but ungodly plan: he seized two of the native children and sacrificed them. But his deed became known, and so the Egyptians reviled him and tried to hunt him down; at which point Menelaus slipped away with his ships to Libya—where he went from there, the Egyptians are not able to say. This, then, is what the priests claim to know. Part, they told me, they learned from making inquiries, but the part of the tale that transpired in Egypt they knew for actual fact.

2.120 This, then, is what the Egyptian priests have to say. I personally am inclined to accept this tale of Helen, and here is my reasoning. If Helen really was in Troy, the Trojans would have given her back to the Greeks, regardless of what

Alexander wanted. Priam and the rest of the royal family were hardly so crazy that they would want to risk their own lives, and those of their children—and indeed the entire city—just so that Alexander could sleep with Helen. And even if they decided in the beginning to do as he wanted, once many Trojans had died fighting the Greeks, and (if I may use evidence from Homer himself) every time they went to fight two or three or more of Priam's own children were killed—with this sort of thing happening, I expect that, even if Priam himself were the one sleeping with her, the Trojans would have given Helen back to the Achaeans, anything to be rid of their woes. Moreover, the kingship was not to pass to Alexander, so things were hardly in his hands, even as Priam aged; rather, Hector, the elder son—and much more the man than Alexander—was destined to take the throne on Priam's death. And Hector was not the kind of man to indulge the wrongdoing of his brother, least of all when it had brought so many woes, both to Hector personally and to all the Trojans. No, they were not *able* to give Helen back, and though they spoke the truth, the Greeks did not believe them. Let me make my own view clear. It was a god who contrived this, so that the slaughter and utter destruction might show clearly to mankind the consequence: for great wrongdoing the gods' retribution, too, is great. That's what I have to say about my thoughts on the matter.

RHAMPSINITUS AND THE THIEF

The three schemes and counter-schemes mark this as a parable on the ways in which the Egyptians are the "wisest" of men; note also the prominence of folktale motifs (trickster succeeds in a series of trials to win riches and the hand of the princess). The failed scheming of kings is by now a well-explored motif.

Now the priests told me that from Proteus the kingship passed to 2.121
Rhampsinitus. As a memorial this king left behind the monumental gateway on the west side of the temple of Hephaestus. Across from it stand two statues, about thirty-eight feet tall. The one on the northern side they call Summer, and the one to the south they call Winter. The Egyptians kneel and bow and give reverence to the statue called Summer; but for the one called Winter they do the opposite.

This king had a great abundance of silver, so much so that none of the sub- 2.121(1)
sequent kings were able to accumulate more, or even to come close. Wanting to store the money safely in a treasure house, Rhampsinitus had a room built of stone blocks, as an extension off one of the outside walls of the palace. Now the stonemason who built this room came up with a clever scheme: he made one of the stone blocks removable, easily taken out of the wall by two men, or even by one. As soon as the project was complete, the king stored his money there. Time passed and the stonemason, nearing the end of his time of life, summoned his sons (he had two) and explained to them—looking out for them, so that they could have a limitless means of support!—how clever he had been in building the king's treasure house. He described in detail all about the removable stone, and gave its exact location. "As long as you keep this knowledge," he said, "you will be the keepers of the king's treasure." When the

stonemason died, the sons did not hold off for long; going to the palace by night they easily found the stone in the wall, wrested it free, and carried off lots of money.

2.121(2) When next the king chanced to open the treasure house, he was amazed to find jars with the silver missing—and there was no one he could blame, since the seal was intact and the room locked. A second time, and yet a third, when he opened the treasure house there always seemed to be less money (since the thieves could not control their looting), and so the king did this. He had animal traps made and had these placed around the jars that held the silver. Just as before, the thieves came and one of them went in, heading for one of the jars; but suddenly he was caught by the trap. As soon as he realized what a fix he was in, he called out to his brother and showed him how things stood. "Come quickly," he said, "and cut off my head before I am seen and recognized—in that way, you will not have to die too." This made sense to the brother, and so, persuaded, he did exactly that. Fitting the stone block back in place, he then went home, carrying his brother's head.

2.121(3) When the king entered the treasure house the next morning he was astonished to see the body of the thief, caught in the trap, but missing its head; and the room with no signs of a break-in, and with no other entrance or exit. Perplexed, he next did this: he had the corpse of the thief hung outside, from the city wall, and set guards to stand by it, ordering them to take hold of anyone they saw wailing or weeping, and to bring that person to him. So, the corpse was hung up. The son's mother, however, was terribly upset. She spoke to her surviving son, telling him to manage—by whatever means necessary—to take down his brother's body and bring it home. "If you do not," she threatened, "I will go to the king myself and tell him that you are the one with his money."

2.121(4) The mother was implacable, and, though the surviving son tried many times, he was unable to move her. So, he came up with another clever scheme. He saddled his donkeys, filled up some wineskins, and strapped them onto the animals. He drove the donkeys along the road, and when he was near where the corpse was hung and the men guarding it, he grabbed two or three of the wineskin spouts and loosened their fastenings. As the wine started to spill, he smacked himself on the head, shouting out that he didn't know which to turn to first. By now a lot of wine was spilling, and when the guards noticed, they took some jars and rushed to the road to fill them up—their lucky day! For his part, the thief cursed them all roundly, pretending to be very angry; the guards tried to cheer him, and gradually he calmed down—or so he pretended—and set his anger aside. Eventually, he drove the animals off the road and worked on repacking his gear. The guards and he continued to talk back and forth, and one of them made a joke and got him laughing. He handed them one of the wineskins then, and the guards sat down right where they were, thinking to have a party; they took hold of him and bid him stay and do some drinking too. Easily persuaded, he stayed. As he joined the party they gave him a rousing welcome, and so he gave them yet another of the wineskins. With so much to drink, the guards got very, very drunk, and, overcome by drowsiness, they fell asleep right there where they had been drinking. The thief waited until it was deep into the night and let down his brother's body. Then—to mark his contempt—he shaved off the right side of each guard's beard. He strapped the corpse onto the donkeys, and drove the animals home. Thus did he accomplish what his mother had commanded.

FIGURE 2.5 Young man pouring from a wineskin into a drinking cup

2.121(5) When the king learned that the thief's dead body had been stolen, he was terribly angry, and wanted more than anything to catch this trickster, whoever he was. Though I personally don't find it credible, this is the story they tell of what the king did next. They say that the king sat his own daughter in a chamber, and bid her to receive every man, regardless, but before having sex to make each tell her what he had done in life that was most clever, and what most ungodly. And if a man told her the thief's tale, she was to take him by the arm and not let him go. The daughter did as her father had commanded. Meanwhile the thief learned why the king was doing this, and wanting to outdo the king in his many wiles[30] he did the following. Getting a fresh corpse, he cut off an arm at the shoulder, and held it under his cloak as he went to the treasure house. When he entered, the king's daughter asked him just as she had asked all the rest. So, he told the story of his most ungodly deed, how when his brother had been caught in a trap in the king's treasure house he had cut off his head; and of his most clever deed, how he had gotten the guards drunk so that he could let down his brother's body after it had been strung up. Hearing this the daughter grabbed him. But the thief in the darkness had held out the arm of the corpse; that then was what she took and held fast, thinking that she had the thief's arm. The thief dropped it, went out the door, and got away.

When this was reported to the king, he was struck by the ingenuity and 2.121(6)
daring of the man, and in time he sent round to all the cities a proclamation granting amnesty and promising great things should the thief present himself to the king. The thief, persuaded, came to the court, and Rhampsinitus, greatly amazed, married him to his daughter, saying that he was far the wisest

30 The *Odyssey*, also the story of a trickster, begins: "Tell me, Muse, of the man of many wiles. . . ."

FIGURE 2.6 Pharaoh's golden headdress

of men; for, he said, the Egyptians are the wisest of men, and he, the thief, the wisest of the Egyptians.

2.122 The priests report that, later, this same king made a descent, while living, down to the spot the Greeks call Hades, and there played dice with the goddess of the underworld, Demeter. He won as often as he lost, and on his return to the upper world brought back a golden headdress she had given him. The Egyptians celebrate a ritual that, they say, reflects the Descent and Return of Rhampsinitus. (I know from my own observation that this ritual is still performed today; yet whether it actually is celebrated because of Rhampsinitus I cannot say.) This is the ritual. In a single day the priests weave a robe. They blindfold one of their own, and lead him, carrying the robe, to the road that goes to the temple of Demeter; they then come back, leaving him behind. The blindfolded priest, they say, is escorted by two wolves to Demeter's temple, twenty stades away; and then the wolves lead him back from the temple to the place where he began.[31]

2.123 As for what the Egyptians report, we should by all means make use of it wherever it seems credible. My principle, however, is to record, for each story, what is said as I heard it. Now the Egyptians say that Demeter and Dionysus are the rulers of the underworld.[32] And the Egyptians are the first to tell this story, that the human soul is immortal, and that when the body perishes the soul passes into another creature, always right at birth, and when it has passed through all the creatures of the land and the sea and the air, it passes once again, at birth, into the body of a man; and that the cycle of reincarnation lasts for three thousand years. Greeks tell this story too, some of old, some more recently, and claim it as their own; I know their names full well, but will not make them part of my record.

CHEOPS, CHEPHREN, AND THE BUILDING OF THE PYRAMIDS

Herodotus's account of how the pyramids were built has some difficulties in detail, but is broadly correct and is in most respects our best ancient account. A motif to watch for: the daughter's sacrifice for the father's ambitions, which here dovetails interestingly with the motif of the clever and effective female potentate.

2.124 The priests told me that as long as Rhampsinitus was king, Egypt was well governed and immensely prosperous, but, later, once Cheops[33] took the rule, he

31 2¼ miles, 3.5 km. The two "wolves" would be two priests ritually impersonating the jackal-headed divine heralds who accompany the king on his Descent and Return. The robe is probably a mark of kingship.

32 Demeter = Isis, Dionysus = Osiris.

33 Khufu, who ruled c. 2596–2573 BC.

FIGURE 2.7 The great pyramids at Giza (that of Cheops at right, Chephren center, and Cheops's daughter at left)

drove them to total misery. He closed all the temples first, and put an end to sacrificing; next, he forced all the Egyptians to labor on his behalf. Some he appointed to haul blocks of stone from the quarries in the Arabian mountains to the Nile; others he bid take the blocks (once they were shipped across the river) and haul them to the mountains we call Libyan. Gangs of one hundred thousand men toiled continuously, three months at a time. For ten years the folk labored to construct the causeway over which to haul the blocks of stone, and the causeway itself was a feat of engineering hardly less than the Great Pyramid itself. Or so it seems to me—five stades long,[34] sixty feet wide, forty-eight feet high at its tallest, and the whole made with polished stone and decorated with carvings of animals. Ten years, then, passed as they built the causeway, and during that same time they built underground chambers on the hill where the pyramids stand, the tomb chambers for Cheops himself, which he made into an island by running a canal in from the Nile. As for the pyramid itself, the building of that took twenty years. Each face of it is eight hundred feet wide and eight hundred feet tall, perfectly square at the base, made of polished stone blocks fitted with great precision; and none of the blocks are less than thirty feet in length.

The pyramid was constructed first in the manner of a flight of steps (called 2.125
variously *krossai* or *bomides*, that is, "tiers"), and once that was complete, the remaining stones were lifted into place by a levering device made of short pieces of wood. Using the lever, they lifted a block from the ground to the first row

34 About ½ mile or 1 km. The monumental causeway leading from the Nile valley to the desert hillock where the pyramids stand is here partly conflated with the building ramp.

of steps, and when the block was up there, the stone was placed on another lever located on the first row, and then heaved from there to the next row using that other lever. To move the stone either they had a separate lever for each row of steps; or they moved a single, easily transported lever from one row to the next—I record both possibilities since both are reported. The uppermost row was finished first, then the next one down, and last the bottommost row closest to the ground. They also carved on the pyramid in Egyptian script the amounts of radish and onion and garlic consumed by the workers; and, as I vividly recall, the interpreter who read me the inscription said that the cost for that was sixteen hundred talents of silver. If this is so, the amount one reasonably infers for the other expenses is huge—for the iron that the stonecutters used, and the bread and the clothing for the workers, given how much time (as already mentioned) they are said to have taken to build this monument, quite apart from the time, by no means small, that (I imagine) they spent cutting the stone blocks and raising them and digging the underground chambers.

2.126 So evil was Cheops that, needing money, he forced his own daughter to sit in a house to earn—by whoring—a certain sum of money (the priests did not say how much). The daughter went to work as her father commanded, but privately she had in mind to leave behind her own memorial; so, from each man who came to her she demanded a contribution of one stone block for her monument. From these stones (or so they say) was built the pyramid that stands among the three, in front of the Great Pyramid, itself one hundred and fifty feet along each side.

2.127 The priests told me that Cheops ruled Egypt for fifty years, and on his death the kingship passed to his brother, Chephren.[35] Chephren conducted himself in every way like his brother, and, like him, he built a pyramid, even though his is not as big as his brother's—I measured them both myself. Moreover, it does not have chambers that run underground, nor is there a canal from the Nile that flows to it like the other. Its first course of stone is Ethiopic red granite (instead of limestone), and it is forty feet smaller in size than the Great Pyramid, next to which it was built. Both pyramids stand on the same hill, roughly a hundred feet high. Chephren, they told me, ruled for fifty-six years.

2.128 For one hundred and six years, then, the Egyptians suffered total misery and for all that time the temples were barred from entry. The hatred of these two kings is such that the Egyptians do not much like to speak their names. In fact, they call the pyramids after the shepherd Philitis, a man who in that time and place tended the flocks.

Following, Herodotus gives a lengthy catalogue of Egyptian pharaohs down to the time of Cyrus, listing their names and the most notable events of the reign. The last in the list is Amasis, who as we know from the start of the Egyptian story (2.1) was king at the time that Cambyses the son of Cyrus ascended to the throne.

35 Khafre, in fact Cheops's son, erected not only the second great pyramid at Giza, but also the great Sphinx (which goes unmentioned by Herodotus, perhaps because it was largely buried by sand in this period).

BOOK 3

Cambyses Invades Egypt

Cambyses II succeeded to the throne at the death of Cyrus in 530 BC. The Persian invasion of Egypt is historical, as is Cambyses's death there in 522 and the crisis that arises from the fact that he dies without an heir. But, judging by evidence from Egypt and elsewhere, scholars believe that Herodotus's depiction of Cambyses is heavily influenced by Persian or Egyptian sources that are, in effect, anti-Cambyses propaganda. The story that Cambyses killed the sacred Apis bull, for example, is contradicted by evidence from Egyptian inscriptions. However that may be, the tale of Cambyses falls squarely within Herodotus's keen interest in stories that are tragic, several of which we have seen before, in which a figure at the peak of success loses control and thereby comes to ruin. In this case, though, the tyrant's loss of control is not the arrogance (*hubris*) of an imperialistic impulse that goes beyond natural boundaries (the Egyptian campaign itself is a great success, adding the vast territories of Egypt and Libya to the Persian empire). Rather, the tyrant's arrogance manifests itself in routine violation of the customs and laws (*nomoi*) of man and god. Throughout the tale, then, is a sort of meditation on control, on what constitutes a "law" or a "custom" that is *inviolate,* given that laws and customs are also so ethnically diverse and contradictory. Is it a sin for the Persian king to marry his sister, when he has just conquered Egypt, where, famously, pharaohs by custom do exactly that? We see, then, how philosophical questions now begin to frame the deep interest that Herodotus has shown throughout in the customs of different peoples.

Also deeply entangled in this series of stories is the question of *falsehood,* in the sense of deceptive appearance. We see in succession a false wife, a possibly false god, and the dramatic climax, which is the story of a false ruler of Persia! That culminating piece—the false ruler—immediately stirs, again, a more philosophical set of questions about what, specifically, does or should make someone the one who is accepted as the ruler; and that will lead directly to the story of the crisis that leads to the ascension of the next Persian king, Darius.

The Causes for the Invasion

Here we return to the account interrupted at the very start of book 2 (2.1). As so often, there is an immediate focus on the causes, and, also as often, there is more than one. (Scholars say that the cause is "overdetermined.") A section in book 1 we did not read tells us that Cyrus had already planned the invasion (1.153), and the Persian urge to imperial expansion is sufficient cause in itself. Here, though, Herodotus tells a story that gives the more personal motivation of retribution for a transgression involving a woman, which should remind us of the prologue to book 1 (1.1–5). This is followed by two variant accounts that the narrator rejects, thereby showing both the depth of his research (including both Persian and Egyptian accounts) and his steadiness of judgment. Motifs to watch for: deceit and falsity; the strength of action of the woman.

3.1 It was, then, against this king, Amasis, that Cambyses son of Cyrus made his invasion, taking with him the Ionian and Aeolian Greeks, along with others among his subjects.[1] And here's the reason why he invaded. Cambyses had sent a messenger to request the hand of Amasis's daughter, acting at the advice of an Egyptian in his court. But the Egyptian's advice was a plot—this Egyptian was resentful because he, of all the Egyptian doctors, was the one Amasis had handed over to the Persians, hauling him away from his wife and children, when Cyrus had sent a request for the best of the Egyptian eye doctors.[2] The Egyptian hatched his plot, then, out of resentment, persuading Cambyses to ask for Amasis's daughter so that either Amasis would hand over the girl and suffer, or not hand her over and become Cambyses' enemy. For his part Amasis, intimidated and alarmed by the Persian power, felt he could not refuse, but neither could he bring himself to hand her over. You see, he understood full well that Cambyses would keep her not as his wife, but as a concubine. So, on reflection, he did this. There was at that time a daughter of the late king Apries, tall and beautiful, and the only one remaining of her line; her name was Nitetis. Amasis had Nitetis decked out in fine robes and gold, and sent her to the Persians as though his own daughter. After a while, when Cambyses tried to greet her as "daughter of Amasis," the girl said to him: "King, do you not understand how Amasis has tricked you? He dressed me up and handed me over to you as though sending his own daughter, but in truth I am the daughter of Apries, the man who was his master, the man whom Amasis murdered after he led the other Egyptians in revolt." So she spoke, and this then was the reason why Cambyses son of Cyrus was driven, in great fury, to attack Egypt.

3.2 That at any rate is what the Persians say. The Egyptians, however, claim Cambyses as one of their own, saying that he is the offspring of this daughter of Apries. By their account, Cyrus was the one who sent to Amasis asking for his daughter's hand, not Cambyses. But they do not get the story right. How can it have escaped their notice (given that Egyptians know Persian

1 In 525 BC.

2 Egyptian doctors were renowned for their excellence and highly specialized (see 2.84).

ways as well as anyone), first, that it is not the Persian custom to make a bastard the king while a legitimate son is living, and, secondly, that Cambyses was the son of Cassandane the daughter of Pharnaspes, one of the Achaemenids, and not the son of an Egyptian woman? No, they give a distorted account just to pretend to be related to the house of Cyrus.

So much about that. 3.3

Yet another story is also told (though it is not reliable, in my view), that, once, one of the Persian ladies entered the king's harem, and when she saw that Cassandane had such tall and beautiful children she went into raptures, singing their praise. At that, Cassandane wife of Cyrus said, "And yet with children like this I, their mother, am held in contempt by Cyrus, while this migrant from Egypt holds the place of honor." So she spoke, in her resentment at Nitetis, and the eldest of her children, Cambyses, then said to her: "For that, Mother, when I am a grown man I will turn Egypt upside down, so that you can no longer tell which Egypt is Upper and which Lower."[3] It is said that Cambyses was about ten when he surprised the women by saying this. And, they say, when he became a man and was made king, he held on to this memory, and for this reason made war on Egypt.

Preparations for the Invasion

The description of the coastal geography is accurate, but there is and was no great river flowing through the Arabian peninsula. The many incidental details (some of which can strike the modern reader as a bit random) are a good example of how Herodotus deploys his selection of material so as to imply a much more vast array of knowledge at his disposal.

Here is another story that is told about the invasion. Among Amasis's allies 3.4
there was at that time a man from Halicarnassus, Phanes by name, a man with good sense in counsel and courage in battle. But Phanes grew angry with Amasis for some reason, and so he left Egypt by boat, intending to seek an audience with Cambyses. But Phanes, by no means an insignificant man among the allies, knew the Egyptian preparations in considerable detail, and so Amasis went after him in all earnest, sending a fast warship captained by the most reliable of his eunuchs. The eunuch caught Phanes in Lycia, but even so did not bring him back to Egypt. Instead, Phanes used his wits to escape, getting the guards drunk and slipping off to the Persians. Cambyses meanwhile was eager to attack Egypt, but was at a loss as to how to make the march—for the journey passed through a desert. When Phanes came, he described all of Amasis's preparations, and also explained how to make the march. "Send to the king of the Arabians," he advised, "and ask him to provide help and safe passage."

3 Ancient Egypt was divided into two lands, the northern area containing Memphis and the extensive Nile delta region, called "Lower Egypt," and the southern area upriver, including Thebes, called "Upper Egypt." After their unification in c. 3000 BC, pharaohs wore a double crown to signify their rule over the two lands.

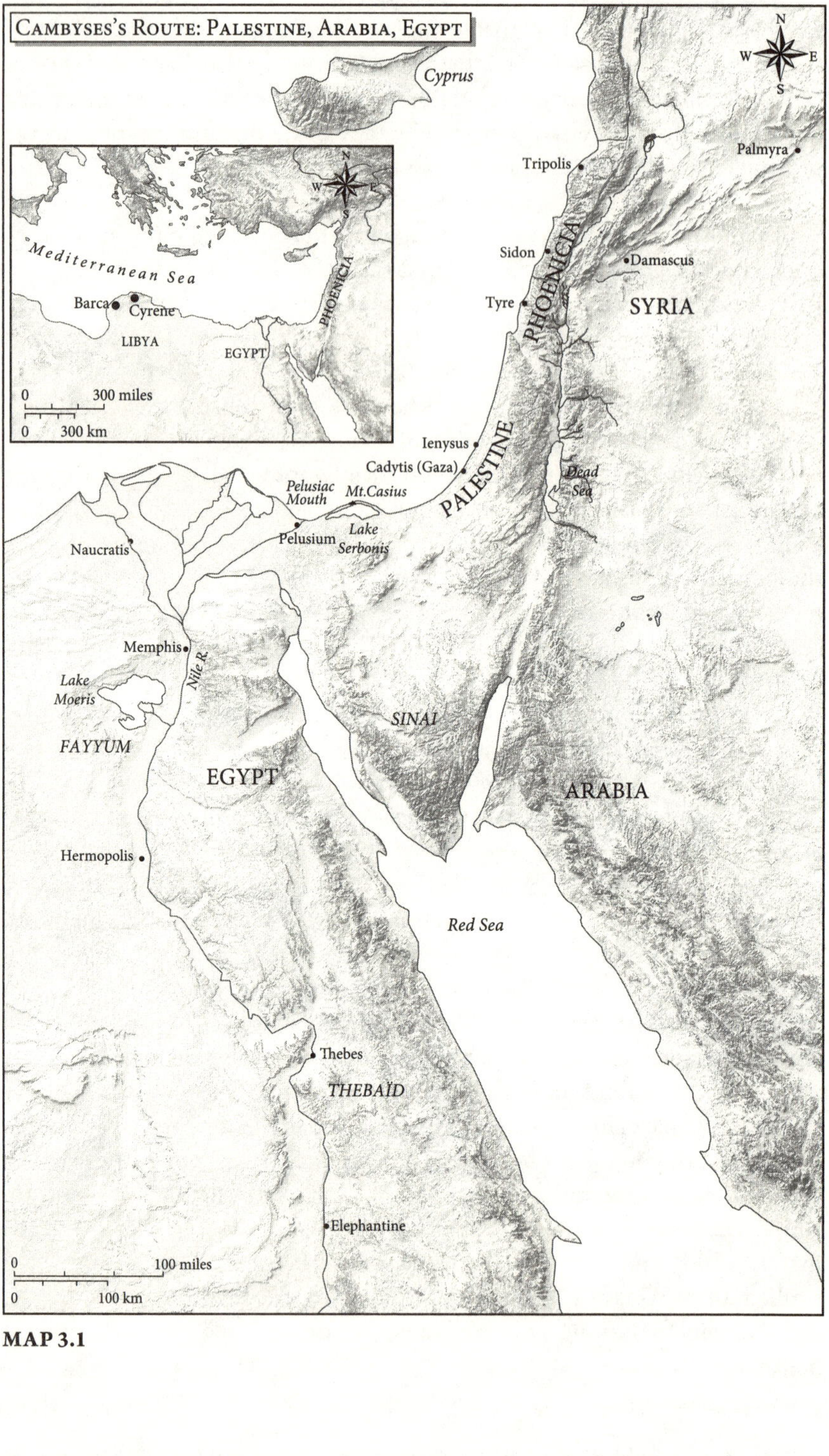
Cambyses's Route: Palestine, Arabia, Egypt
Cyprus
N
W
E
S
Palmyra
Tripolis
Sidon
Damascus
Tyre
SYRIA
PHOENICIA
Mediterranean Sea
Barca
Cyrene
LIBYA
EGYPT
0
300 miles
0
300 km
Ienysus
Cadytis (Gaza)
PALESTINE
Dead Sea
Pelusiac Mouth
Mt.Casius
Lake Serbonis
Pelusium
Naucratis
Memphis
Nile R.
Lake Moeris
FAYYUM
SINAI
EGYPT
ARABIA
Hermopolis
Red Sea
Thebes
THEBAÏD
Elephantine
0
100 miles
0
100 km

MAP 3.1

Now going through Arabia is the only obvious way to get to Egypt, given the geography: from Phoenicia up to the city limits of Cadytis[4] the land belongs to those Syrians called "Palestinian." From Cadytis, which is I think a city almost as big as Sardis, up to the city Ienysus, the trading posts along the coast belong to Arabia. The land from Ienysus up to Lake Serbonis—where Mt. Casius stretches to the sea—is held by the Syrians again. From Lake Serbonis (where, legend has it, the monster Typho is hidden), Egypt starts. The part from Ienysus to Mt. Casius and Lake Serbonis—not a small territory, but a three-day journey by foot—is a desert, without any water whatsoever. 3.5

I will now explain a relevant fact that few travelers to Egypt have come to understand. Twice a year, jars filled with wine are imported into Egypt from all over Greece and from Phoenicia besides—and yet there is hardly a single empty wine jar to be seen. One might well ask, where do they all go? Well, I will tell you. The chief magistrate of each town is required to collect each and every jar and bring it to Memphis, and men from Memphis then fill the jars with water and haul them to the Syrian desert. In such a way the imported jars, once emptied in Egypt, are transported to Syria to join the jars long since there. 3.6

And it was the Persians, soon after they conquered Egypt, who made the desert route into Egypt viable, equipping it with pots of water as I've just described. But at this time, when Cambyses heard the words of the stranger from Halicarnassus, there was no water supply yet available. So, he sent messengers to Arabia to ask for help and safe passage. That he got, both offering and receiving oaths as guarantee. . . . 3.7

And as soon as the Arabs had given their guarantee, they got to work. Filling up camel skins with water they loaded them upon all the live camels and drove them into the desert. There they awaited the army of Cambyses. That at any rate is the more reliable of the reports. But the less reliable version also needs to be recounted, since, like it or not, it's a story that's told. A great river flows through Arabia, named the Corys, and that river disgorges into the Red Sea. The story goes that the king of the Arabs had conduits made by stitching together ox hide and other animal skins, making them long enough to extend out into the desert, and that using these conduits he diverted the water from the Corys to a place in the desert where large reservoirs had been dug. There they collected and stored the water—a distance, from river to desert, of twelve days! And, they say, the king made three of these conduits, leading to three different reservoirs in the desert. 3.9

The Attack on Egypt

By now we are more comfortable with the curious way that Herodotus mixes history with proto-scientific explanations as well as vivid storytelling in the Greek tradition. Even so, the chapters here are a fairly extreme example, as the narrator

4 Gaza.

moves from a lurid account of Greeks(!) making human sacrifice and drinking blood, a tale that resonates with myth (though not impossible as history—scholars are divided) to a proto-scientific excursion on the reasons why Persian skulls are relatively fragile. Motifs to watch for: the telling portent; the foreign ruler appropriated as wise man (which cannot but summon Croesus to mind).

3.10 Meanwhile, at the mouth of the Nile called the Pelusiac, Psammenitus the son of Amasis lay in wait for Cambyses. Amasis, you see, was no longer alive when Cambyses made his march on Egypt—Amasis had died, having ruled for forty-four years,[5] during which time he experienced no great calamity. And when he died, he was embalmed and buried in the tomb he had built himself in the temple. But during the reign of his son Psammenitus, the Egyptians experienced their greatest portent ever: Egyptian Thebes had a rainfall, a city where, as the Thebans themselves say, it had never before rained, nor has it rained since, even up to now. Upper Egypt, you see, is entirely without rain. But that one time rain did fall on Thebes—though but a drizzle.

3.11 So, the Persians marched across the desert and set up camp near the Egyptians, intending to offer battle. Among the Egyptian mercenaries were Greeks and Carians, and they were angry that Phanes had led a foreign army against Egypt. This then is what they did. Phanes had left his children in Egypt. The Greeks and Carians had them brought to the camp and placed a large mixing bowl, in full sight of the father, in between the two armies. They led in the children one by one and cut their throats, streaming the blood into the bowl. Once they had finished with the children, they added wine and water, and the troops all had a drink of the bloody mix. With that, they joined in battle. The fighting was fierce and soldiers fell on both sides in great numbers; but finally the Egyptians turned and fled.

3.12 I personally witnessed something truly amazing at the site of this battle, something I found out from the natives. The bones of the men who fell in the battle lie scattered but separate (that is, those of the Persians lie to one side, and those of the Egyptians lie opposite, just as they were originally). Now, the skulls of the Persians are so fragile that you can, if you like, make a hole by tossing a pebble, whereas the skulls of the Egyptians are so strong that you can hardly break through even if you pound them with a rock. The natives explained the cause of this (and I was readily convinced): the Egyptians from the youngest age keep their head shaved, thereby thickening the bone by exposure to the sun. This is also the reason why they are not bald—you will see far fewer bald men in Egypt than anywhere else. Such then is the cause of their tough skulls, and as for the Persians, their skulls are fragile because they wear woolen caps from the earliest age, keeping their heads shaded. I saw very much the same at Pampremis, at the site where the Persians under Achaemenes son of Darius were destroyed by the Libyan Inarus.[6]

5 569–526 BC.

6 A much later battle that occurred in 462/461 BC when Herodotus was a young man.

So, the Egyptians turned and fled from the fighting, in total disarray. Once 3.13
they were trapped in Memphis, Cambyses sent upriver a ship from Mytilene[7] carrying a Persian herald, to negotiate terms. But when the Egyptians saw the ship heading for Memphis, they poured out from the city walls, sank the ship, and tore the men apart limb by limb, carrying the pieces back inside the city. After that the Egyptians were besieged and in time they surrendered. The neighboring Libyans, terrified by what had transpired in Egypt, surrendered without a fight, volunteering to pay tribute, and sending gifts to Cambyses. The people of Cyrene and Barca, equally terrified, did the same. Cambyses welcomed the gifts sent by the Libyans. But those from Cyrene he was not happy about, I think because they were too few—for Cyrene sent only five hundred silver coins. Taking the coins in his own hands, Cambyses tossed them to his troops.

So, Cambyses captured the citadel at Memphis,[8] and on the tenth day he 3.14
took Psammenitus, the Egyptian king, who had ruled for six months, and sat him before the gates of the city. Alongside him were other Egyptians, and Cambyses set out to make trial of his soul by doing this: fitting out the king's daughter in a slave's rags he sent her forth with a pitcher to fetch water, and along with her other young girls, gathered from the households of the Egyptian noblemen, also dressed as slaves. As the girls passed opposite their fathers with cries and tears, all the others howled and wept when they saw their daughters so reduced; but Psammenitus, when he saw them coming and realized what was happening, bent his head to the ground. Once the water-bearers had passed, Cambyses next dispatched the king's son together with two thousand other Egyptian youths of the same age. These were bound with a rope around their necks and horses' bits curbing their mouths, and were being led away as reprisal for the men of Mytilene who died at Memphis with their ship. (The royal justices had passed down this as their judgment, that for each dead Mytilenean ten noble Egyptians were to die.) Psammenitus saw his son coming and realized that he was being led to his death. The others, all those Egyptians sitting around him, wept and made a great stir; but Psammenitus acted exactly as he had in the case of his daughter.

When the youths too had passed, it happened that one of his former drinking companions passed by, an older man, someone who had lost everything he owned, with no more means than a vagabond, and now a beggar

FIGURE 3.1 Behistun Relief: Darius leads bound prisoners

7 An ally. The island of Lesbos was under Persian control, and its major city, Mytilene, was ruled by a pro-Persian tyrant.
8 525 BC.

following the army. As he passed in front of Psammenitus and the other Egyptians seated before the city gate, Psammenitus saw him; and the king wailed loudly and called out to his companion by name and struck his head in anguish. Now there were guards nearby who reported to Cambyses every one of Psammenitus's reactions as each procession passed. Cambyses thus knew what was going on, and was astonished. So, he sent a messenger to ask a question. "Psammenitus, our master Cambyses inquires why it is that, when you saw your daughter disgraced and your son lined up for execution, you neither cried out nor wept, but, when you see a beggar who is (as he has found out) in no way a kinsman, you honor him with your grief?" So he asked, and this is what Psammenitus replied: "Child of Cyrus, the affairs of my household are a woe beyond weeping, but the sorrow of a friend is worthy of tears, one who from great prosperity has fallen into beggary and so comes to the threshold of old age." What was said by the king seemed to be well said, and, as it is reported by the Egyptians, Croesus (who happened to be among the followers of Cambyses in his invasion of Egypt) wept, and others of the Persians alongside him wept too. And finally, pity overcame Cambyses himself. So, he instantly issued a command to release the king's son from execution, to raise Psammenitus from his seat at the city gates, and to bring the king to him.

3.15 Those sent to release the son found him no longer alive—for he was the first to be struck down; they did, however, raise Psammenitus from his seat and bring him to Cambyses' court. There Psammenitus lived for the rest of his life and was well treated. If he had known not to make trouble, he could have taken over Egypt to rule in Cambyses' name—for it is the Persian custom to honor the sons of kings, and even in times of revolt to punish the fathers and hand the rule to the sons. . . . But as it was, Psammenitus did stir up trouble; and he paid the price. Trying to rouse the Egyptians to revolt he was caught; and as soon as this became known to Cambyses, he drank bull's blood, thereby dying a swift death. And that was the end of Psammenitus.

After exhuming, mutilating, and finally burning the dead body of Amasis (a violation of both Egyptian and Persian custom) Cambyses marched on the Ethiopians, but he was forced to withdraw for lack of food and water. He next sent his army to attack Oasis in the Libyan desert, an important caravan town that hosted the oracle of Ammon; but the army fell prey to a massive sandstorm and perished to a man. (Most scholars believe this more likely a miracle story spread by the oracle than something that actually happened; the remains of Cambyses's army were announced to have been discovered in 2009, only to have the story exposed as a fraud.)

Cambyses and the Apis Bull

Nothing was more sacred to the Egyptians than the appearance of Apis, a god who appeared to mortals in the form of a bull. Motif to watch for: deception and falsehood.

FIGURE 3.2 Apis. The Apis bull was the most sacred of animals in Egypt, and to kill the Apis bull the greatest sacrilege imaginable. The bull was thought to be a god on earth, the incarnation of the great god Ptah. A new Apis was the cause for celebration throughout Egypt, and the animal spent the years of his life enthroned at his own court in Memphis. On his death, he would be mourned for 70 days, mummified, and placed in his own tomb at a special sanctuary at Saqqara

At the time when Cambyses made his way back to Memphis, it happened 3.27
that Apis appeared to the Egyptians, the god Greeks call *Epaphos*. At once the Egyptians put on their finest robes and started to celebrate the god made manifest. But Cambyses, when he saw what the Egyptians were doing, firmly believed that theirs was a feast of thanksgiving for his own ill fortune. So, he

summoned the magistrates of Memphis to his presence. The moment they walked in he asked, "Why do you Egyptians make a feast not when I arrived earlier, but now, when I have come here with most of my army destroyed?" They explained that a god was made manifest, a god whose habit was to appear only after long intervals, and that when he did appear all Egyptians celebrated with a feast. Hearing this Cambyses then said, "You lie, and because of this lie, you will pay the price—your death." So saying, he had them killed.

3.28 Next, he summoned to his presence the priests. They spoke along the same lines, and so Cambyses said, "I will see if in fact a god of kindly disposition has arrived among the Egyptians. Go and bring me this Apis." So, the priests went off to fetch him. Now this Apis, the god called Epaphos, is a calf from a cow no longer capable of conceiving. Egyptians say that a moonbeam comes down from the sky to penetrate the cow, and that the Apis is born of that union. The calf called Apis is black with distinctive markings: a white triangle on its forehead, the likeness of an eagle on its back, a tail with double the hair, and a mark like a scarab under its tongue.

3.29 This then was the Apis that the priests brought back, and Cambyses, half-mad as he was, drew his sword and, wanting to stab this Apis in the stomach, struck the thigh instead. Laughing out loud he cried out to the priests, "You stupid fools, are your gods like this, of blood and flesh and vulnerable to iron? Just the right god for Egyptians, to be sure! And as for you, you have made me the butt of your joke to your sorrow." So saying, he ordered those whose task it was to give the priests a good lashing, and as for the rest of the Egyptians, if they found any of them feasting, they were to kill them. So, the celebration broke up, the priests were punished, and the Apis languished from the blow to his thigh, lying in the temple. And when he died from his wound, the priests gave him burial, keeping it secret from Cambyses.

The Madness of Cambyses

This horrific litany of Cambyses's deranged abuses ends with a startling inversion of the civilized order, by which cannibalism can be seen to be just as normal as cremation. The moral, that each society's customs are "king," not subject to a universal (or hegemonic) idea of what is appropriate or "civilized," puts on display the open-minded, almost cosmopolitan worldview so characteristic of Herodotus. The passage is full of inversions, but watch in particular for the many ironic plays on the theme of madness/control and truth/falseness. Again, the narrative is quick to accommodate proto-science within the storytelling patterns: thus Cambyses's madness can be ascribed to the vengeance of the Apis god, or to a neurological disorder.

3.30 Now Cambyses in fact was none too stable before, but according to the Egyptians it was this wrongful act that put him entirely out of his mind. The first of the ills he worked was against his brother Smerdis—a full brother, of the same mother and father. Smerdis he sent from Egypt back to Persia, out of envy, since Smerdis alone of the Persians could draw back, if only a couple of inches, the bow that the Fish-eaters had brought back from Ethiopia.[9] And when Smerdis had gone off to Persia Cambyses saw a vision in his sleep. In the dream a messenger appeared, who had come from the Persians to proclaim that Smerdis was sitting on the throne of the king, his head touching the heavens. In response, Cambyses grew fearful: would his brother murder him and take the rule? So, he sent Prexaspes to Persia, the most loyal of his men, with orders to kill him. And, going up to Susa, that's what he did—either by taking Smerdis out hunting, or by luring him out to the Red Sea[10] and drowning him (both stories are told).

dreams wrongly inter?

This then was the first of the ills that Cambyses wrought, according to the Egyptians. The second had to do with the sister who accompanied him to Egypt. He made her his wife, though she too was a full sibling of the same parents. And he contrived to marry her in a way I will now describe. Before this, it was not at all the Persian custom for a man to marry his sisters. But Cambyses had fallen in love with one of his sisters, and wanted to marry her—and he had every intention of doing so, custom be damned! So, he summoned the royal judges and asked whether there was a law that allowed a man who so desired to marry his sister. The royal judges are select Persian men, appointed for life, unless they are discovered in misconduct. These were the men who tried cases for the Persians, and acted as interpreters of the ancestral laws, men to whom everything was entrusted. When Cambyses made his inquiry, they made a reply that was true to the law but also safe: "King, we have found no law that invites a brother to marry his sister; but we have found another law, dictating that the Great King can do whatever he wants." In that way, they avoided breaking the law even though fearful of Cambyses, and so as to avoid dying in defense of the law, they found a way around it—by coming up with another law that could be used to support his wish to marry his sisters. So, Cambyses married the sister that filled him with desire, and a little later he also made another sister his own. The younger of these was the one who had accompanied him to Egypt, and the one he now killed.

3.31

custom be damned ↓ breaking custom / trad.

Just as with Smerdis, two different stories are told of her death. The Greeks tell this tale. Cambyses set a lion cub to fight a young dog, and his wife was also there to watch. The puppy was getting the worst of it when his brother, also a puppy, broke his leash and came to help. The two young dogs working together then overmastered the lion cub. Cambyses was pleased by the show, but the wife sitting alongside began to weep. Noticing this, Cambyses asked, "Why are you crying?" and the woman said, "As I watch the young dog coming to help his brother in the fight, I weep, remembering Smerdis and knowing that there will be no one to avenge him." For saying this she was killed by

3.32

9 The Fish-Eaters (a primitive coastal tribe that lived along the Red Sea) were sent by Cambyses as envoys to the Ethiopians. The king sent back a bow with the instructions, "When Persians can draw so large a bow as easily as I, then let the Persians make war on the Ethiopians" (3.21).
10 Here the Persian Gulf is meant.

Cambyses, or so the Greek story goes. The Egyptians, however, say that once they were sitting at the dinner table and the wife took up a head of lettuce and stripped off the leaves. She then asked her husband whether the lettuce was better stripped bare or better whole. When he said, "Whole," she said, "And yet just as I have shorn this head of lettuce, so have you laid bare the house of Cyrus." In a rage, he stomped on her belly, which was then with child, and she miscarried and so died.

3.33 Such were the outrages that Cambyses wrought on his family, whether this had to do with Apis or something else—so many are the ills that can befall a man. Indeed, men say that Cambyses had an inherited disease, the one people call "sacred."[11] If so, it is hardly surprising that with the body wasting away from a terrible disease, the mind too would grow ill.

3.34 But there were also outrages that he wreaked on the rest of the Persians in his madness. For example, a conversation with Prexaspes is reported. Now Prexaspes he honored above all—this was the man who carried his important dispatches—and his son was the boy Cambyses appointed wine steward to the court, an office of great distinction. In this conversation, Cambyses is reported to have said, "Prexaspes, what sort of man do the Persians consider me to be, and what do they say about me?" He replied, "Master, the Persians praise you highly in almost every respect, but they do say that you are excessively fond of wine." Such was his reply, and Cambyses grew enraged, saying, "Now they say that I am too fond of drink, do they, that I have lost control, that I am not in my right mind? If so, what they said before was a lie!" Before, you see, Cambyses had asked a gathering of his counselors (among whom was Croesus), how in their view he compared with his father Cyrus. The counselors replied, "You surpass your father; for you have retained all the territory he had, and have added Egypt and control of the sea besides." Croesus, however, was sitting alongside and found himself dissatisfied with the Persians' reply. So, he said to Cambyses, "By my way of thinking, child of Cyrus, you have not equaled your father. For you do not yet have a son such as that man left behind in you." Cambyses, pleased by these words, praised the sound judgment of Croesus.

3.35 This was what Cambyses had in mind when now he spoke in rage to Prexaspes: "Let's find out whether the Persians who criticize me speak the truth or a lie, and who it is who has lost control. Do you see your son standing there by the doorway? If my arrow pierces him through the middle of the heart, then it proves the Persians wrong; if I miss, then it proves the Persians right, and shows that I am indeed out of my mind." So speaking, he drew his bow and shot the boy, and he ordered his men to split open the fallen body and investigate the wound. They found that the arrow was stuck right in the heart. Laughing and very pleased with himself, Cambyses turned to address the father: "Prexaspes, clearly I have not lost control and the Persians are the ones who are crazy. So, tell me: do you know of any other archer so deadly accurate?"

11 Epilepsy.

Prexaspes saw that he was not in his right mind, so, fearing for himself, he said, "Master, I think not even the archer god himself could shoot so well." That's what Cambyses did on that occasion; on another, he arrested twelve high-born Persians for a trivial offense and had them buried alive, head first.

With Cambyses behaving like this, Croesus felt duty-bound to offer some 3.36
guidance: "King, do not always indulge in the passionate impulses of youth, but hold yourself back, show some restraint. Prudence is a good thing, looking to the future is wise. You kill men who are your fellow countrymen, arresting them on a trivial offense; and you kill children. If you go on like this, watch out or the Persians will rise up against you. Your father Cyrus often urged me to offer you guidance, to give whatever good advice I have." Showing his good will, so did Croesus advise. But Cambyses said this in reply: "Do you dare to give me advice, you who took care of your own country so well, and who gave such good advice to my father, telling him to cross the river Araxes and attack the Massagetae—when they were perfectly willing to fight us on our own territory? No, you destroyed your own country through your incompetent leadership, and destroyed Cyrus by your bad advice, and it is time for you to pay! I have long since wanted an excuse to take care of *you*!" With those words, he grabbed his bow to shoot him down—but Croesus dashed away and ran out the door. Not able to shoot Croesus himself, Cambyses ordered his servants to seize and kill him. The servants, however, knowing the ways of their master, hid Croesus in an underground chamber, reasoning that if Cambyses came to regret his action and sought after Croesus, they could reveal him and get a reward for keeping Croesus alive; but if Cambyses had no regrets and did not want him back, they could dispatch him then. And indeed after a short time Cambyses did come to miss him, and when the guards heard this they announced that Croesus was still alive. To that Cambyses said, "I am pleased that Croesus is alive, but you who kept him alive are not to go unpunished: rather, you will die." And so he ordered.

These are but a few of the many outrages Cambyses wrought on Persians 3.37
and allies alike. Moreover, while he was at Memphis, he opened the ancient tombs and examined the mummies; and when he visited the temple of Hephaestus[12] he laughed out loud at the cult statue. For in the temple there is an idol very like the image of a Pataïcus (which is a statue of a pygmy, if you've not seen one) that Phoenicians use as a figurehead on the bowsprit of their triremes.[13] Cambyses also went into the temple of the Cabiri, where it is forbidden for any but the priest to enter. He ridiculed the idols there (which are similar to the ones at the temple of Hephaestus, and are said to be Hephaestus's sons), and in the end he even set them on fire.

And so it is in every way obvious that Cambyses was completely out of his 3.38
mind: otherwise, he would not have scorned the sacred and secular customs

12 The famous temple of Ptah at Memphis.

13 A trireme is a type of ancient warship with three banks of oars: see Figure 8.1.

as he did. If you ask people to select from all possible customs the ones that are best, they will examine the matter and choose their own—for everyone considers the religion and ways of his own people far the finest. Therefore it is improbable that anyone but a crazy person would scorn such things. That custom works this way for all peoples can be established by a great abundance of proofs, but among them is this one. Darius during his reign summoned some Greeks who were there and asked, "How much money would it take for you to eat your fathers when they die?"; and they said they would not do it for any price. Darius next summoned those among the Indians called the Callatiae, people who do in fact eat their parents when they die, and asked them (while the Greeks were there, and with interpreters making what was said intelligible), "How much money would it take for you to burn your dead fathers on a pyre?" They raised a great shout and asked that he not even say such a thing. So it is with customs, and I think the poet Pindar got it right when he said that *for all men, Custom is King*. . . .

King → People will not break customs for anything.
↳ Subjected to it.

Crisis and Constitutional Debate

Cambyses's despotic and erratic behavior leads to a year of crisis for the Persian empire, 522 BC, in which in quick succession a rival (the False Smerdis) declares himself the Great King, Cambyses dies on his way back to Susa, a group of seven intrigue to overthrow the imposter, and Darius then manages to gain the throne for himself. Readers had long doubted the colorful events Herodotus here depicts when in the 19th century a monumental inscription carved on a cliff face at Mt. Behistun (Bisitun) was gradually deciphered. That inscription—carved under and alongside large-scale figures in relief, measuring in total 15 by 9 feet (5 × 3 m), and 300 feet (100 m) up from the ground (Figures 3.1, 3.3)—turned out to be a document, in three languages (Old Persian, Babylonian, Elamite), that Darius the Great had had inscribed to give an account of his reign. The early part describes much the same situation—including the False Smerdis and the Seven—that Herodotus reports, a spectacular validation of Herodotus's accuracy. Today, scholars regard the inscription as official propaganda rather than straightforward documentation, and thus the account has again come to be viewed with some skepticism. But that Herodotus's rather romantic tale derives from official Persian "history" cannot be doubted; and the tale gains credence from examination of how commonly in antiquity rebels would muster support by false claims to authority (false Nebuchadnezzars showed up repeatedly in Babylon, and Darius had to defeat two of them as well as a second false Smerdis, according to the inscription). That the Persian empire was under considerable strain in the last year of Cambyses's reign is in any case not in question; and that seems to have been compounded by the fact that he died without legitimate heirs. The ascent of Darius may not have gone along the lines of the story presented here, but it certainly proved a vexed affair: the Behistun inscription lists nineteen revolts that Darius had to put down in his first year as king.

FIGURE 3.3 View of the Behistun Relief in situ

A False Smerdis Declares Himself King and Cambyses Dies

The theme of deception, truth/falseness, and the true/false ruler comes to a head and, almost predictably, familiar motifs like the riddling wisdom of oracles and dreams recur. That the Persian nobles take Cambyses's last words to be a manipulative lie (while in fact true) is telling, as is the use of physical evidence—not hearsay or judgment—to resolve whether this Smerdis is false or genuine.

THE MAGI REVOLT

3.61 But while Cambyses son of Cyrus, now utterly insane, lengthened his stay in Egypt, two of the Magi[14] back in Persia, brothers, decided to rebel. One of the brothers was the steward Cambyses had left in charge of the palace. He decided to revolt when he realized that the murder of Smerdis had been covered up and few of the Persians knew about it—most thought that Smerdis was still alive—and thus he formed a plan to seize the throne. He had a brother, you see—as I mentioned, this was his collaborator—who closely resembled Smerdis the son of Cyrus (that Smerdis who was Cambyses' brother and whom Cambyses had put to death); and not only was he very like to Smerdis, but, remarkably, he also had the same name, Smerdis. The Magian, Patizeithes, told his brother that he would take care of everything for him, and, once persuaded, he led him to the king's throne and sat him down. He then sent forth

14 The Magi—whom Herodotus also identifies as one of the Median tribes (1.101)—were members of a hereditary priestly caste, who oversaw sacrifices and libations and also acted as seers.

heralds throughout the empire, including to Egypt, proclaiming to the army that henceforth Smerdis son of Cyrus was the one to heed and not Cambyses.

The heralds all went to make this proclamation and that included the 3.62
herald dispatched to Egypt. He came upon Cambyses and his army in Syria, at Ecbatana, and standing in their midst made his pronouncement as ordered by the Magian. Now when Cambyses heard this, he assumed that the herald was telling the truth, and that he had been betrayed by Prexaspes (thinking that though sent to kill Smerdis he had not done so). Turning his eyes to Prexaspes he said, “Prexaspes, is this the way you carried out the task I set for you?” He replied, “Master, what the herald says is not true: your brother Smerdis has in no way revolted from you, nor will there be any trouble from that man great or small. I myself, doing as you told me, buried him, with my own hands. If the dead are arisen, then expect also Astyages the Mede to rise in revolt! But if things are as before, then there is no more mischief coming from that quarter. Here’s what I think: go after the herald, and let’s examine him closely as to who sent him to proclaim that the army heed a King Smerdis.”

What Prexaspes had to say made sense to Cambyses. So, instantly, they 3.63
sent after the herald, and when he arrived, Prexaspes asked, “My good man, you say that you come as a messenger from Smerdis son of Cyrus. Answer me this, and tell the truth, and you will go away without harm: did Smerdis present himself and issue this order in full sight, or was there an underling speaking on his behalf?” The herald replied, “I have not laid eyes on Smerdis son of Cyrus, at least not since the time when King Cambyses marched against Egypt. Rather, the Magian whom Cambyses appointed as steward of the palace, this was the one who gave the order, saying that Smerdis son of Cyrus had set these as the words to proclaim to you.” So spoke the herald, telling nothing but the truth. Cambyses then said, “Prexaspes, you did as ordered and are freed from all suspicion of blame. But who can this Persian be who is trying to seize power by commandeering the name Smerdis?” Prexaspes replied, “I think I understand what has come to pass, my King. The rebels are the two Magi: the one whom you left as the steward of your palace, Patizeithes, and his brother—whose name is Smerdis!”

When Cambyses heard the name, Smerdis, there came to him in a flash 3.64
the truth about the words the vision had spoken—the vision that appeared in his sleep, proclaiming that Smerdis was sitting on the throne of the king, his head touching the heavens. Understanding what a fool he had been to kill his brother, he cried out, “Smerdis!” And as he cried out, enraged at all these mishaps, he leaped onto his horse, thinking to march then and there to Susa and attack the Magian. But as he leaped, the cap to his scabbard fell off and the naked tip of the sword struck his thigh, and the wound was at exactly the spot where he had stabbed the Egyptian god Apis. Thinking the wound fatal, Cambyses then asked what was the name of the town they were in, and they answered: Ecbatana. Now, earlier the oracle at Buto had foretold that he would end his life at Ecbatana, and Cambyses of course had thought he

would die in his old age at the Ecbatana of the Medes, the city that served as the capital of his empire. But now everything was clear: the oracle had meant the Syrian town named Ecbatana. So, when to his question the answer was, "Ecbatana," the double blow of ill fortune, from the Magi and from his wound, brought him back to his senses. Fully grasping the prophecy, he said, "In this spot Cambyses son of Cyrus is fated to die." For the moment, that was all.

DEATH OF CAMBYSES

3.65 But some twenty days later he summoned the most respected of the Persians and to them he said, "Persians, it falls to me now to disclose to you what of all my affairs I have kept most secret. When I was in Egypt I saw a vision in my sleep—and would that I had never seen it! In the dream a messenger appeared, who had come from Susa to proclaim that Smerdis was sitting on the throne of the king, his head touching the heavens. I grew fearful that my brother would depose me and so I acted with more speed than good sense—as we know, it is not in human nature to avert what is fated to be. Fool that I am, I sent Prexaspes to Susa, to kill my brother. Once the murder was carried out, I was able to live without fear, it never occurring to me that, with Smerdis out of the way, another such might arise against me. Failing to grasp what was foretold, I needlessly murdered my own brother, and in consequence I have lost nothing less than my kingdom. For it was Smerdis the Magian, not my brother, whose rebellion the god revealed in my dream. That then is what I have wrought. Understand that Smerdis son of Cyrus is no longer with us: the Magi have seized the throne, Patizeithes, the one I left as steward of the palace, and his brother, Smerdis.

"The one who by rights should avenge this, my disgrace at the hands of the Magi, has suffered an ungodly fate, murdered by his own kin. With him gone, O Persians, it is critical that you carry out what is second best, and that is my wish as I end my life. Ye gods who watch over kings, I summon you to witness: you, all of you, but particularly you Achaemenids,[15] do not let the kingship pass back to the Medes! Since they have seized the kingship by deceit, use deceit to take it back, and since they have also used strength of arms, use your own strength—in force!—to regain it. If you do so, may the earth be fruitful and your women and flocks fertile, and may you be free for all time. But if you do not regain the kingship or do not at least try to take it back, I lay on this curse: may just the opposite happen to you, and, yet more, may each of the Persians die as miserably as I." So saying, Cambyses wept and wailed over all that he had done.

3.66 When the Persians saw the king weeping, they tore the clothes they had on and wailed loudly and long.[16] Soon after, gangrene set in about the bone

15 The Achaemenids, the ruling clan in this period, were a kinship group that claimed descent from Achaemenes, a (probably legendary) early king. In the Behistun inscription both Darius and the family line of Cyrus-Cambyses are said to descend from Achaemenes, probably a lineage fashioned by Darius to legitimize himself as ruler. The Persian Empire from Cyrus up to the invasion of Alexander the Great (550–330 BC) is often called the Achaemenid Empire.

16 Tearing clothes while weeping is typical of eastern habits of grieving.

and the thigh quickly began to rot. So it was that they carried out for burial Cambyses son of Cyrus, who had ruled for seven full years and five months, altogether childless, bereft of male or female issue. Much skepticism spread then among the Persians present about the plot of the Magi; rather, they thought that what Cambyses had said about the death of Smerdis was scandal-mongering, an attempt to engulf the whole of Persia in civil war.

THE FALSE SMERDIS IS FOUND OUT

The Persians, then, supposed that Smerdis son of Cyrus was the one on the 3.67
throne. For his part, Prexaspes fervently denied that he had killed Smerdis—with Cambyses dead, it would hardly be safe to admit that he had killed a son of Cyrus by his own hand. So, the Magian ruled without fear, now that Cambyses was dead, relying on having the same name as Smerdis son of Cyrus. He ruled for seven months, thereby filling out the remaining months of Cambyses' reign and making it a full eight years.[17] During that time, he delivered great benefits for all his subjects, proclaiming for all the nations under his rule a three-year release from military service and tribute, so that when he died all those in Asia (the Persians excepted) wished him back.

Such then was his decree at the start of his rule, but in the eighth month[18] 3.68
he was found out. Here's how that happened. There was a certain Otanes, son of Pharnaspes, by birth and wealth among the first of the Persians. This man Otanes was the first to suspect that the Magian was not Smerdis the son of Cyrus but who he really was. What raised his suspicions was that the Magian never ventured out from the citadel, and never summoned to his presence any Persians of rank. So, Otanes did as follows. A daughter of his, named Phaedyme, had been kept among the women in Cambyses' harem. At that time she belonged to the Magian, and he came to her bed as he did with the other wives and concubines of Cambyses. So, Otanes sent a message to her, wanting to know who was the man she was sleeping with: was it Smerdis son of Cyrus or someone else? She wrote back saying that she didn't know: she had never seen Smerdis son of Cyrus nor did she know who it was who was coming to her bed. Then Otanes sent a second message, to this effect: "If you yourself cannot recognize Smerdis son of Cyrus, ask Atossa who it is that you and she are living with—she will know her own brother, I should think!" But the daughter wrote back, "I have no opportunity to speak with Atossa, nor with any of the other women who live here. As soon as he assumed the throne, this man, whoever he is, ordered that the women disperse, each to a different part of the palace."

On hearing that, the situation seemed pretty clear to Otanes. So, he sent 3.69
her a third message: "Daughter, you were raised a noble woman, and it is your

17 In fact the first months overlapped with the end of Cambyses's reign. The Magian seems to have ruled independently for only about 3 months.

18 September 522 BC.

duty to take on whatever risk I as your father command. If this man is not Smerdis son of Cyrus but whom I suspect, he must not get away with coming to your bed and assuming the power of Persia—he must pay the price. Therefore do this: when he comes to your bed and you are sure that he is asleep, feel for his ears. If he has ears, know that you are sleeping with Smerdis son of Cyrus; but if he does not, with Smerdis the Magian." Phaedyme wrote back, pointing out how extremely dangerous doing this would be: "If he doesn't have ears, and I am caught touching them, no doubt he will kill me. But nonetheless I will do it." Such was her promise to her father. (Smerdis the Magian had had his ears cut off during the reign of Cyrus son of Cambyses for some not inconsiderable crime.)

This woman Phaedyme, the daughter of Otanes, then did all she had promised her father. When it was her turn for going to lie beside the Magian (the women come to the Persian king in rotation), she came in to sleep with him, and when he was fast asleep she felt for his ears. She determined that the man had no ears without difficulty, so, as soon as day broke, she sent a message to her father to let him know what had happened.

The Seven Overthrow the Magi

Note the strong characterization of the older man, Otanes, who instigates the plot but is cautious and deliberate; and the younger man, Darius, a headstrong man of action. Darius's sociological description of the motivations of truth-tellers and liars (3.72) seems meant to recall the story of Deioces (1.96–106), Cyrus's ancestor and the first king of the Medes—who also was made king at a time of crisis.

3.70 Otanes then took in Aspathines and Gobryas, Persians of rank and perfect for his purposes because of their personal loyalty, and explained the whole business to them. They too had suspected that this was how it was, and so readily accepted what he had to say. They then decided that each would add to the conspiracy one close friend—whomever each trusted most. So, Otanes brought in Intaphrenes, Gobryas Megabyzus, and Aspathines Hydarnes. Thus there were six. But then Darius son of Hystaspes arrived at Susa, coming from Persia, where his father was the satrap. The Six decided to add Darius to their ranks.

3.71 Now Seven, when they had come together, they pledged mutual loyalty and discussed what to do. And when it was time for Darius to express his view, he said, "I thought that I alone knew all this, that the Magian was the king and Smerdis son of Cyrus dead. That was the very reason I hurried here, to arrange death for the Magian. But since it has come to pass that you too know and not I alone, it is best to act at once, without delay. There can be no better plan." To him Otanes then said, "Son of Hystaspes, you are of a noble father, and you show yourself to be none his inferior. But rush not into this undertaking without a plan; let us proceed thoughtfully, and with due caution. We need more men before we try this." To that Darius said, "Listen, men: if you act along the lines Otanes suggests, you will die a painful death. Someone, surely, will betray us to the Magian, and get himself a lot of money in the bargain. You very much ought to have kept the plot to yourselves; but then you decided to bring in more, and you even added me. So, let us do the deed today. Otherwise, if you let this day slip by, mark my words: no one will get there first to accuse *me* of conspiracy: rather, I myself will go to the Magian to denounce *you*!"

Otanes could see Darius's anger and passion, and so he said, "Since you 3.72
push us to rush and will not admit delay, come, tell us, how are we going to get into the royal palace to kill him? You yourself, even if you haven't seen it, will have heard that guards are stationed there; how will we get past them?" Darius replied, "Otanes, in many situations words obscure but the deed can make all clear; and in many others, the words are clear, but no shining deed ever follows. You all know full well that it is not difficult to get past the guards stationed there. No one will refuse to let us by, we being who we are, whether out of respect or out of fear. But in any case I myself have the perfect pretext by which we can enter, since I can say that I have come from Persia and wish to convey a message from my father for the king. Yes, let us lie if we have to! In my view, those who lie and those who tell the truth are after the same thing. The liars lie when they profit by talking people into things; the truth-tellers speak the truth so that they can profit by getting people to trust them. Thus by different paths they come to the same end. And if there were no advantage to be gained, the truth-tellers would turn into liars and the liars into truth-tellers in equal numbers. Now as to the sentries, we will in due time reward those who let us pass; but whosoever tries to get in our way, mark that man as an enemy, and then let us force our way inside and do our business."

After that Gobryas spoke: "Friends, when will there be a better time to 3.73
regain the kingship—or, if we cannot take it back, to die? As it is we—Persians!—are ruled by a Mede, a Magian, a man with his ears cut off. Those of you who were at Cambyses' deathbed, you recall, do you not, that even as he was ending his life he put a curse on any Persians who did not try to regain the throne? We did not take that up then, because we thought that Cambyses spoke out of malice. So, here's my vote: let's do as Darius says and instead of breaking up our meeting let us go to attack the Magian right away." So spoke Gobryas, and all the others nodded assent.

But even as the Seven were plotting, the Magi were making their own plans, 3.74
as luck would have it. The Magi decided to make Prexaspes their ally, both because he had suffered shockingly at the hands of Cambyses (who, you recall, shot and killed his son); and because he alone knew that Smerdis son of Cyrus was dead (he being the one who killed him by his own hands); and, in addition to all else, Prexaspes remained the most respected among the Persian leaders. For all these reasons, they called him in and won him over as an ally. So, with pledges and oaths they made an agreement: he would keep to himself

and not broadcast to other men the trick they were playing on the Persians; and in return they promised him countless gifts of every sort. So, Prexaspes promised to do just as the Magi had advised. Then they approached him with a second proposal: that they would summon all the Persians before the palace wall, and he would climb up the tower to proclaim that the rule was in the hands of none other than Smerdis son of Cyrus. The reason they did this was that he feigned to be the most loyal to them among the Persians, and in the course of denying the murder had often asserted that Smerdis son of Cyrus remained alive.

3.75 Prexaspes declared his willingness. So, the Magi summoned the Persians, and told him to climb the tower and make his proclamation. Prexaspes, however, deliberately ignored what the Magi had asked him to say. Instead, he listed the ancestry of Cyrus, starting from Achaemenes; and once he worked through the genealogy up to Cyrus's time, he described the many good things Cyrus had done for the Persians. He then revealed the truth, explaining that earlier, when it was unsafe to say what had happened, he had kept all a secret, but that the present circumstances made it necessary for him to bring it all to light. "I was forced by Cambyses to kill Smerdis, and I did so with my own hands," he said. "It is the Magi who are now your rulers!" Finally, he put many a curse upon any Persian who did not take back the throne and punish the Magi—and then threw himself headfirst from the tower. Thus did Prexaspes, always a man of honor, honorably bring his life to a close.

3.76 Meanwhile the Seven, who had decided to attack the Magi without delay, had given prayers to the gods and were on their way, having no notion of what was up with Prexaspes. But when they were halfway there, they heard what Prexaspes had done. Stepping to the side of the road, they again began to argue. Otanes and his followers urged delay—"Let's wait until things calm down!"—while Darius and his followers pressed to do as they had decided—"Let's go now, and not wait!" And while they were arguing, seven pairs of hawks appeared, attacking two pairs of vultures with their beaks and talons. At the sight, all seven agreed to follow the plan of Darius. Taking courage from the bird-omen, they began to walk toward the palace.

3.77 When they reached the gates, things happened just as Darius had anticipated: as Persian men of rank, they were treated with respect by the guards, who had no suspicion of the sort of thing they were up to; and so the Persians were let pass without so much as a question, proceeding as though a god were helping them along the way. But then they came to the courtyard, and ran up against the eunuchs—the king's message-bearers—who asked them why they had come, scolded the sentries for letting them pass, and stopped them when they tried to go farther. Giving the signal, the Seven drew their swords, stabbed the eunuchs blocking their way, and made a rush for the main hall.

3.78 As it happened, both Magi were inside at that time, planning how best to react to what Prexaspes had done. When they noticed the eunuchs raising a great shout and clamor, both ran up, and as soon as they understood what was happening, they turned to defend themselves. One of them got to the bow first, so the other went for the spear.[19] Then they fought. Since the attackers were close by and hard on him, the one with the bow couldn't do much, but the other, the one with the spear, struck Aspathines in the thigh, and hit Intaphrenes in the eye—and Intaphrenes did in the event lose his eye, though not his life at least. In any case, these were the ones wounded by the Magian with the spear; as for the other, finding his bow useless, he fled into the bedchamber that opened onto the main hall, intending to bolt the doors—but two of the Seven, Darius and Gobryas, forced their way in with him. As Gobryas wrestled with the Magian, Darius stood over them in the dark room, uncertain what to do, worried that he would hit Gobryas if he struck. Gobryas saw him standing there doing nothing and asked, "Why don't you use your sword?" Darius said, "I'm worried, afraid I'll stab you by mistake." Gobryas replied, "Then push the sword up to the hilt, even if goes through us both!" Darius did as he was told: he thrust with his sword and as luck would have it hit the Magian.

So, they killed the Magi and cut off their heads. They left their two wounded 3.79
at the palace, both because of their lack of strength and to act as guards over the citadel. They themselves, now five, rushed down with shouts and cries, holding the heads of the Magi, and calling out for the rest of the Persians, describing how things stood and pointing to the heads, and killing any of the Magi who got in their way. For their part, the Persians, once they grasped the Magi's trick and what the Seven had done, they thought it right to do yet more; drawing their swords they killed as many of the Magi as they could find. And if night had not fallen, none of the Magi would have survived. This day, called the *Magophonia* ("Slaughter of the Magi"), is the most celebrated of the Persian holidays and is commemorated by a great feast. On that day no Magian is allowed to come out in the open; rather, the Magi keep to their homes all day long.

The Constitutional Debate

This extraordinary scene, in which the Persians debate which type of government would be best for them, has been deeply influential, much read and cited throughout classical antiquity and beyond. The conceptual classification of government into three types—government by the many, by the few, or by the one—is not a Herodotean innovation; we first find it in the previous generation in surviving Greek texts (Pindar, Pyth. 2.87–88), and it may well be older and it may well come from the East. But most doubt whether such a discussion could have happened in the Persian crisis of 522 BC. Be that as it may, Herodotus here imagines a very Greek sort of debate, put in Greek terms (down to the assumption of choosing magistrates by lot in a democracy). The theme of the true/false ruler returns, with a twist, at the very end.

19 In Persian iconography, the king is accompanied by one bow carrier and one spear carrier (see Figure 3.1); Herodotus seems to imagine here that these are the only weapons available to the Magi.

3.80 Five days later, when things had calmed down, the Seven, those who had overthrown the Magi, got together to consider the whole state of affairs. A debate ensued—one that some of the Greeks believe never happened, but one that happened nevertheless. Otanes spoke first. He urged them to put the government into the hands of the Persian people: "To my way of thinking, it is best that none of us be made king. Monarchy is neither agreeable nor beneficial. You have seen how far along the path of prideful arrogance (*hubris*) Cambyses came, and you have met with the arrogance of the Magi as well. How can a monarchy be a good system, when, without checks or balance, it allows the king to do whatever he wants? No, it would induce even the best of men, once king, to see things differently. Arrogance sprouts up from all the advantages kingship brings, and from the start envy begins to grow. Monarchy always has these two evils: filled to the brim with arrogance, but also with envy, the king comes to do a great many ungodly things. It should be that the tyrant is free from envy, since he can have all he desires. But human nature works in exactly the opposite way: when he looks at his fellow citizens, he resents the best men as long as they are alive and doing well, and he delights in the worst of the citizens, and, though a "best man" himself, happily believes their slanders. And here's something that really makes no sense: if you admire a king in measured terms, he is irritated that you do not serve him well enough; but if you praise him to the skies, he is mad at you for being such a flatterer. The worst thing about a king, however, is this: he upends the laws of the land, he violates women, and he kills men without trial. Now as for democracy, first, it rests on the most beautiful principle—equal justice under the law (*isonomia*)—and, second, it shares none of the habits of monarchy. Magistracies are appointed by lot,[20] and the magistrate is held accountable; and all decisions are referred to the people. I vote therefore that we get rid of the monarchy and hand power to the masses. For everything depends upon the people."

3.81 That then was Otanes' view. Megabyzus spoke next, and he bid them to hand power to an oligarchy. "I agree with Otanes' advice that we should end the monarchy. But when he tells us to hand power over to the masses, he gets it wrong: this is not very good advice. Nothing is more stupid and prone to arrogance than an uneducated crowd. It is unacceptable that we get rid of the arrogance of a tyrant only to fall under the arrogant power of an unrestrained mob. The tyrant at least understands what he is doing when he acts, but in the mob there is no understanding at all. How could there be, when there is no education, no refinement at home, and when the norm is to rush into things with all the thoughtfulness and caution of a rain-swollen river? Let those who intend bad things for the Persians advocate democracy; but as for us, let us select a group of the best of the Persians—among whom will also be

20 Greeks will have thought in the first instance of the democratic system at Athens, where magistrates were selected by lot (instead of executive appointment or democratic election), on the principle of equal share in the management of the government.

ourselves—and hand the power over to them. It is only reasonable that the best government will arise from the best men."

Such was the view of Megabyzus. Third to make known his view was Darius. "To me what Megabyzus says about the masses seems rightly spoken, but about the oligarchy he is wrong. In our debate three possibilities have been put forward as the best government—democracy, oligarchy, and monarchy—and I say that monarchy is far the champion. Now, clearly there could be nothing better than rule by one man, so long as he is the best. Using his good judgment, he can manage the masses without any problem, and he can keep secret all plans to counter our enemies. In an oligarchy, however, strong personal enmities tend to arise among the rival leaders. Each wants to be chief, each wants for his own agenda to prevail, and thus conflict comes. From that, factions arise, and from the factionalism, killing and mayhem. Eventually and inevitably the infighting results in the rule by one. This makes it plain that monarchy is far the best form of government. As for democracy, it is impossible that evils not attend such a rule. So abiding is the public malaise that bad and lowly men not only do not come into conflict but strengthen their ties: they work together in close collaboration to bring harm to the polity. This continues to the point that a leader of the people arises who puts a stop to these lowlifes; because of his actions, the man is admired and esteemed by the people; and, bathed in esteem, he becomes their ruler. This too, then, makes it clear that monarchy is the strongest form of government. In a word, then, and in conclusion, let us ask this question: where did our freedom come from, and who gave it to us? Was it from the people, or some oligarchs, or a king? We were freed by one man, the king, and in my view we should keep it that way; moreover, we would do well not to put aside our ancestral ways. That cannot be a better plan." 3.82

These then were the three views put forward, and of the three it was this last that the other four approved. And when Otanes saw his proposal defeated—he being the one who advocated equal justice under the law—he said to the rest, "My fellow conspirators, clearly one of us will be made king, whether by lot or by a vote of the Persian populace, or by some other means. I for my part will not contend for that prize: I want neither to rule, nor to be ruled. Therefore, I renounce any claim to rule, on the proviso that I myself and all my progeny never be your subjects." Such was his proposal, and the other six agreed; and so he did not participate in the contest, but took a seat to the side. Even now, his family alone among the Persians remains free and participates in public affairs only so much as it wishes—as long as none of the Persian laws are broken. 3.83

The rest of the Seven next tried to figure out the fairest way to set up the kingship. This is what they decided. Otanes and all his progeny would have as their perquisites that every year the king, whoever it was of the Seven, would give them robes from Media and gifts of all kinds, whatever was most valued by the Persians—reasoning that Otanes had first hatched the plot and 3.84

FIGURE 3.4 Darius I seated, with Xerxes standing behind him and Artabanus in front

summoned the conspirators, and that he thus deserved this special honor. They also decided that the Seven would all have the right to enter the royal presence unannounced, whensoever they wanted (unless the king was sleeping with a woman, that is); and that the king would not be allowed to marry into any family except that of his fellow conspirators. As for the kingship itself, the plan was this: they would go outside the city walls and just before dawn get on their horses; as soon as the day broke, the man whose horse first whinnied would be the one made king.

3.85 Now Darius had among his horsemen a clever man, named Oebares. Once the Seven broke up their meeting, Darius spoke to him: "Oebares, this is what we've decided to do about the kingship: we will get on our horses at daybreak, and the man whose horse first whinnies will be the one made king. So, if you have some clever scheme, get to it, so that I and no one else can be the one to take off this prize." Oebares replied, "Master, if the kingship hangs on this, take heart and be of good cheer: no one else will be made king but you—for I have the right solution." Darius said, "Well, if you have such a good trick, it's time to get to work—without delay—since the time appointed is tomorrow." At these words, Oebares went to work: during the night, he led outside the city walls one of the mares, the one that Darius's stallion had much passion for, and there he tied her up. He then brought along Darius's stallion, and over and over he led the stallion in circles around the mare, getting very close, right up to her—and finally he let the stallion mount her.

3.86 As the day began to dawn, the Six, just as they had agreed, got on their horses and rode along the city walls; and as soon as they got to the spot where the mare had been tied up during the previous night, Darius's stallion pranced up and neighed. And just as the horse did this a lightning bolt flashed and thunder rolled, though the sky was clear, as if the whole were foreordained; and so the choice of Darius was affirmed. The others leaped down from their horses and knelt and bowed in homage.

3.87 Such is one story of how Oebares got this to work. But others tell a different story (and both stories come from the Persians). They say that Oebares rubbed his hand on the private parts of the mare and stuck his hand in his pocket; at the break of day, when the horses were about to be released, Oebares took out his hand and held it under the stallion's nostrils. The stallion noticed, snorted, and gave out a neigh.

3.88 And so Darius son of Hystaspes was made king. . . .[21]

21 In the autumn of 522 BC.

BOOK 4
Darius Invades Scythia

Late in 522 BC, Darius I was made king of the Persians. The beginnings of Darius's reign were tumultuous—as mentioned, he had to put down 19 rebellions in his first year as king. Among these was the revolt of Babylon, whose recapture Herodotus describes, in a part we did not read, at the end of book 3. Having consolidated his power, Darius—with that imperialistic impulse *natural* to a Persian king—decided to launch an invasion of the territories at the far north of his empire. As with Cambyses's invasion of Egypt to the south, this attack both is a historical event and also has deep symbolism, as the Persians push to the limits of the known world in their urge to power and conquest. In this case, the Persians will come up against peoples who are almost mythical—the Black-Cloaks, the Man-Eaters, and the Sauromatae, descendants of the Amazons—and who are the last known peoples before utterly unknown, mythical territory is reached.

As with the Egyptian tales in book 2, the narrator will announce the attack but then pause to describe the peoples and customs and geography at considerable length. Much of what we know about these tribes at the far north (in modern-day Ukraine) comes from Herodotus. Where archaeology is able to weigh in, what Herodotus says is largely confirmed; but the light imprint of nomadic tribes makes it impossible to be certain how much is accurately depicted. Note in particular the many schematic oppositions: the Egyptians are (almost) the oldest people, the Scythians the youngest; the Egyptians were anciently settled with temples and huge monuments, the Scythian nomads lacked not only monuments but even walled towns; and so forth.

FIGURE 4.1 Scythians

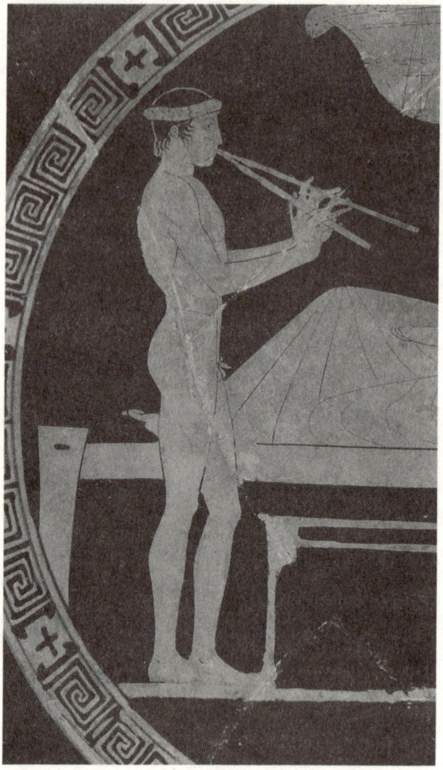

FIGURE 4.2 Boy playing *auloi*

Why Darius Attacked Scythia

As we have come to expect, there is both a rationalistic cause (expanding population) and a historical one, told in a storytelling mode. The phrase "who did the first wrong" should remind the reader of the proem (1.2, 1.5) and, by now, its many echoes. Reflection continues on what it means to be slave or free, both here and throughout the account of the Scythian campaign.

4.1 After the capture of Babylon, Darius marched with his army to attack the Scythians.[1] Asia was thriving—the population was growing, and a great amount of money had accumulated—and so Darius felt an urge to punish the Scythians. To his mind, the Scythians were the ones who did the first wrong, since, in an earlier era, they had attacked the Medes and beaten them in battle. As I mentioned earlier,[2] the Scythians had had command over upper Asia for twenty-eight years: while chasing after the Cimmerians, they had swarmed into Asia and put an end to the Medes' power—the Medes, recall, were the ones who had ruled Asia before the Scythians arrived. The Scythians, then, were away from home for twenty-eight years, but for all the trouble they had had with the Medes, yet more lay in wait for them on the return to their own territory: upon arriving, they found ranged against them a large and hostile army. For the Scythian women, when their men had stayed away for a long time, had come to live with the men who had once been their slaves.

4.2 Now as for the slaves, the Scythians blind all of them because of the milk they drink and the way they do the milking. They take blow-pipes made of bone, very much like the musical pipes called *auloi*, and position them in the genitals of female horses; they then blow air with their mouths, some of them blowing while others do the milking. They say they do it this way for the

1 Capture of Babylon 521 BC; expedition against Scythia c. 515 BC.

2 At 1.15–16 and 1.104–106.

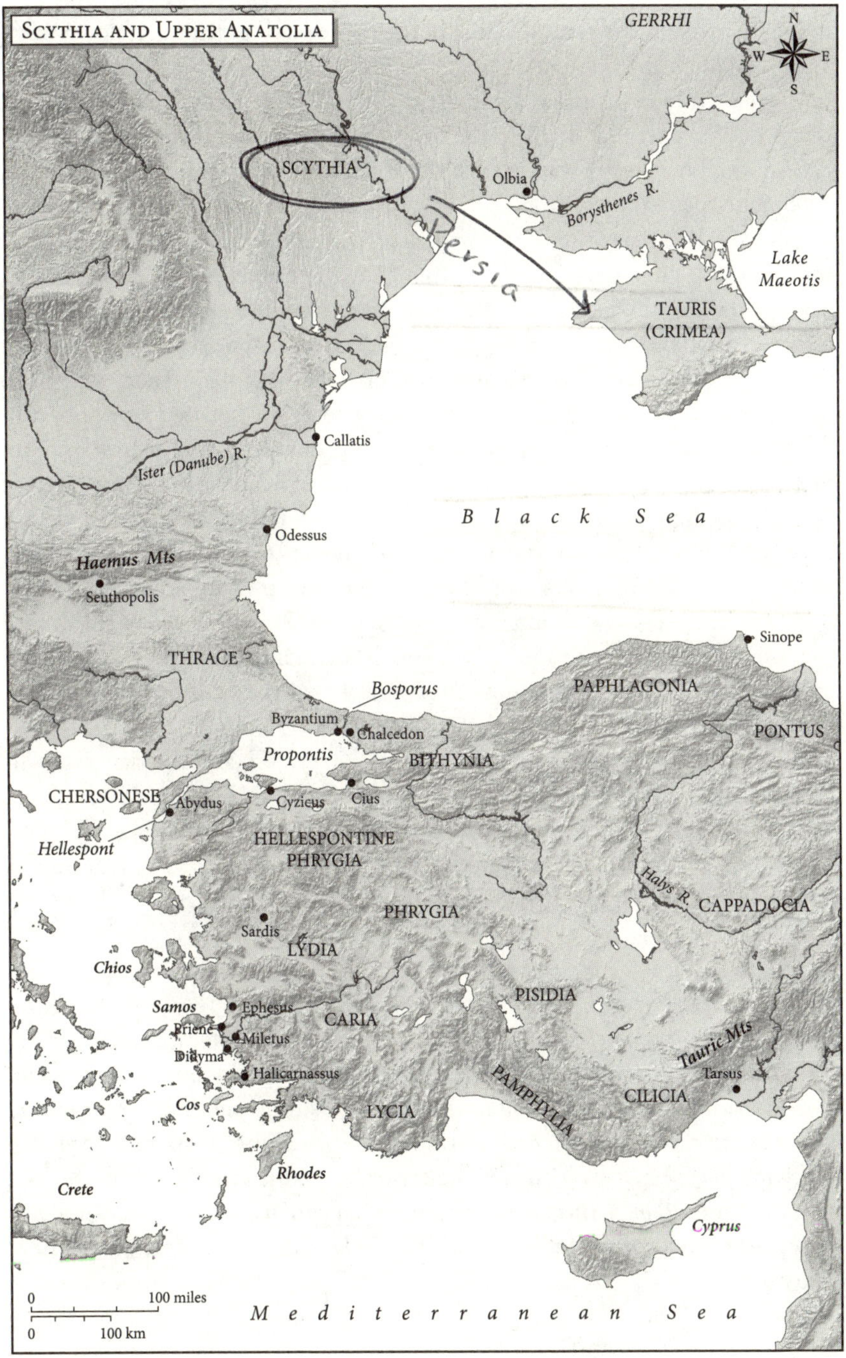
SCYTHIA AND UPPER ANATOLIA
GERRHI
N
W
E
S
SCYTHIA
Olbia
Borysthenes R.
Lake Maeotis
TAURIS (CRIMEA)
Callatis
Ister (Danube) R.
Black Sea
Odessus
Haemus Mts
Seuthopolis
THRACE
Sinope
PAPHLAGONIA
Bosporus
Byzantium
Chalcedon
PONTUS
Propontis
BITHYNIA
CHERSONESE
Abydus
Cyzicus
Cius
Hellespont
HELLESPONTINE PHRYGIA
Halys R.
CAPPADOCIA
PHRYGIA
Sardis
LYDIA
Chios
PISIDIA
Samos
Ephesus
Priene
Miletus
CARIA
Didyma
Halicarnassus
Tauric Mts
Tarsus
PAMPHYLIA
CILICIA
Cos
LYCIA
Rhodes
Crete
Cyprus
0
100 miles
0
100 km
Mediterranean Sea

MAP 4.1

following reason: the genital veins[3] of the horse swell as they are blown upon and the udders then descend. Once the milking is done, they pour the milk into deep wooden containers and set the blind slaves around these to churn the milk. The part that floats to the top they skim off: that part they consider choice, the lower layer less so. For these reasons, then, the Scythians blind every man they capture. They are, after all, not farmers but a nomadic people.[4]

4.3 So, from these slaves and the Scythian women a younger generation grew up, and they, when they found out about their heritage, resolved to stand up against the Scythians when they came back from Media. First, they constructed a defensive barrier, digging a wide trench that stretched from the Tauric Mountains to the broadest part of Lake Maeotis.[5] Then, when the Scythians tried to force their way in, they took up position opposite and fought. Many a battle later, with the Scythians unable to get the best of them in the fighting, one of the Scythians said, "Look at what we are doing, men of Scythia: by fighting with our slaves, we become fewer ourselves as we are killed and as we kill them have fewer to rule hereafter. Better, it seems to me, to leave behind our spears and bows, and each to pick up a horsewhip and approach them so. For as long as they see us bearing arms, they think that they are our equals or the sons of our equals; but when they see us with whips instead of arms, they will come to recognize that they are our slaves. Then they will no longer stay to fight."

4.4 The Scythians listened and did as he had suggested; and the slaves, bewildered by what was happening, forgot their resolve to fight, and ran away. Such, then, is the story of how the Scythians once had power over Asia, and how, driven out by the Medes, they returned to their own territory. Wanting to punish them for what they had done, Darius now massed his army for the attack.

R

Origins of the Scythians

Origins—how a people came to be where they are—are by nature inaccessible to the researcher, so Herodotus tells three tales, two traditional and one a speculative historical account that he finds attractive. The three golden objects that fall from the sky are probably meant to symbolize agriculture (plow/yoke), worship (drinking-bowl, i.e., a libation cup), and warfare (battle-ax). The plow/yoke is a surprise, since although there are some counterindications, Scythians in Herodotus are nomads, not farmers. In the second tale, the horses and bow are emblematic of who the Scythians are (nomadic archers).

3 The word here (*phleps*) can mean a vein, artery, or other vessel in the body, including the ureter, and it is not entirely clear what Herodotus has in mind. Sexual stimulation in milking is, however, paralleled in several modern pastoral societies, and that is probably what is behind this part of the account. Kumis, a fermented drink traditionally made from mare's milk, remains an important product for peoples of the central Asian steppes.

4 That is, since the Scythians did not need the slaves for complex agricultural duties, but simply to churn the milk, it is possible to blind them and thus keep them under control.

5 Sea of Azov.

The Scythians say that theirs is the youngest of all peoples, and the story of their origins goes like this. The first man to be born in this then-deserted land was named Targitaus. They say that the parents of Targitaus (a report I find unbelievable, but so they say) were Zeus and the daughter of the river Borysthenes. Such then was the ancestry of Targitaus, and from him were born three children: Lipoxais, Arpoxais, and the youngest, Colaxais. While these three held the rule there fell upon the Scythian land three golden objects, borne from heaven: a plow and yoke, a battle-ax, and a drinking-bowl. The eldest of the sons was the first to see them, and he came near, wanting to pick them up; but the gold blazed up and caught fire as he approached. He then went away and the second son approached, and he had the same result as his brother. These two, then, the blazing gold chased away, but when the third son came near, the fire was quenched, and so the youngest son brought the gold home. From this, they say, the elder brothers recognized that the entire kingdom was to be handed over to the youngest.... 4.5

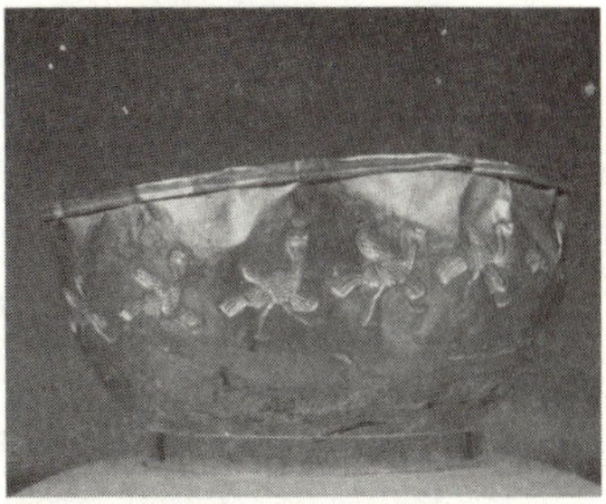

FIGURE 4.3 Scythian drinking-bowl, gold

That's what the Scythians say about themselves. But the Greeks who live around the Black Sea tell this tale. They say that Heracles when he was driving the cattle of Geryon came to the land where now the Scythians dwell, back when it was uninhabited. Geryon lived far beyond the Black Sea, dwelling on the island the Greeks call Erythea, near that Gadira[6] which is just outside the pillars of Heracles[7] and on the Ocean's shore. As for the Ocean, some Greeks say that it begins in the East, where the sun rises, and flows around the whole of the earth—that's the claim (*logos*), but they make no showing of proof. From Erythea, they say, Heracles came to what is now called Scythia. There, snow and ice overtook him, and as he was sleeping, using his lion-skin as a blanket, his grazing horses disappeared from under the yoke—the work of some divinity. 4.8

When Heracles awoke, he went in search of the horses, and traversing the whole of the land he came, finally, to the territory called Woodland. There he found in a cave a kind of viper-girl, double in form: a woman from the buttocks upward, and down below a snake. Seeing her, he was amazed, and he asked her if she had seen horses wandering about; and she said that she had them herself, and was not going to give them back until he lay with her. So Heracles bedded her: such was the price. She then put off the return of the horses, wanting for as long as possible to be with Heracles—he wanted to leave just as soon as he got them. But in the end she gave them back, saying: "It was I who rescued your horses when they came here, but you have given me my reward: for I have three sons who will be born from you. Speak now what I should do when they become 4.9

6 Modern Cadiz, on the Atlantic coast in the southwest corner of Spain.

7 The straits of Gibraltar.

adults, whether to settle them here (where I myself am the ruler of the land) or send them to you." So she asked, and, they say, he said this in reply: "When these boys become men, you will do right if you act as follows: he whom you see drawing this bow as I do now and putting on this war-belt as I do, have him dwell in this territory. But he who fails to do these things, send him out of the land. If so you do, you will be happy and you will have done as I command."

4.10 Heracles drew one of his bows (up to that time he had carried two) and showed how the war-belt fastened, and then handed over the bow and the war-belt, with a golden drinking-bowl hanging from the top of the buckle; making a gift of these, he went on his way. As soon as her sons had grown to manhood, she gave them names—Agathyrsos for the eldest, Gelonus for the second, and Scythes for the youngest—and told them of Heracles' message; and she then did as he had instructed. Two of the sons, Agathyrsos and Gelonus, were unable to do the task appointed and so they, exiled by the one who had given them birth, departed from the land. But the youngest, Scythes, performed the task and stayed. From Scythes son of Heracles the kings of the Scythians have always descended; and because of that drinking-bowl still to this day the Scythians carry drinking-bowls on their war-belts. Such then is the tale told by the Greeks who live around the Black Sea.

4.11 There is another story—which I am particularly attracted to—that goes like this. The Scythians were nomads living in Asia, but were hard pressed in a fight with the Massagetae; they thus fled across the river Araxes and moved into the Cimmerian land (and in fact it is said that the land the Scythians now inhabit belonged of old to the Cimmerians). As the Scythians were invading, the Cimmerians took counsel—for the invading army was a large one—and opinion was sharply divided. The common people urged that it made sense to leave, that there was no need to stay and risk their lives against so many, while the kings urged a more honorable course, that they should fight the invaders and defend their territory.

But the people were unwilling to listen to the kings, nor would the kings listen to the people. So, the commoners decided to leave without fighting, to abandon their land to the invaders; but the kings, reflecting on how many good things they had enjoyed, and how many evils would likely grip them if they fled the fatherland, thought it best to die and be buried in their own land. That's how they saw it, and so the kings took a stand opposite one another, in equal numbers, and fought. The commoners buried them—the whole lot had killed one another—beside the river Tyras (and their tomb is still in evidence). Once the burial was complete, the people made an exodus from the land. The Scythians moved in and took over the now deserted territory. . . .

The Marvels and Customs of Scythia

SACRIFICES

The use of human sacrifice and human blood as libation to the war god Ares marks these peoples as especially barbaric.

All the Scythians perform sacrifices in the same way, and they do it like 4.60
this. The sacrificial animal stands with its fore feet tied together, and the person doing the sacrificing, standing behind it and jerking on the cord, brings the animal down to the ground. As the animal falls, he calls upon the god he is sacrificing to, and then he throws a noose around the neck, and uses a stick to twist the cord and choke the animal, neither lighting a fire nor consecrating the victim nor making libations:[8] rather, he chokes the animal to death, skins it, and then turns to boiling the meat.

But since the Scythian territory is entirely without wood, they have in- 4.61
vented their own way of cooking meat. Once they skin the animals, they strip the meat from the bones, and, if they have them to hand, they toss the meat into locally made cauldrons, much like Lesbian craters, except that they are far larger. So, tossing the meat into these, they boil it—but by burning the animal bones underneath. If there is no cauldron to hand, they mix all the meat with water and toss it into the animals' bellies, and boil that over the burning bones. The bones burn very nicely,[9] and the bellies easily hold the flesh that is stripped off the bones. Thus an ox boils itself, and so also for each of the other sacrificial animals. When the meat is cooked, the one doing the sacrificing consecrates the meat and the entrails, and casts them in front of him. All sorts of domestic animals are sacrificed, but most commonly horses.

That at any rate is how they sacrifice to the rest of the gods, and such are the 4.62
beasts used, but the sacrifice to Ares is special. In each chieftain's district, they set up a holy precinct for Ares by piling up bundles of dry sticks over an area that is three stades[10] in length and breadth, but not so tall. At the top a flat, square space is fashioned from the sticks; the sides are straight up and down for all but one side, which is made so that you can climb up it. Each year the Scythians add to the heap one hundred and fifty wagonloads of dry sticks, since the stack always settles under the weight of the snows. On top of this sacred pile, an ancient iron sword is dedicated by each of the tribes, and this functions as the cult statue for Ares. To it—the Sword—they bring annual sacrifices of cattle and horses, and they sacrifice more of these than to any other of the gods.

When they capture enemies alive, they sacrifice one man out of every hundred, using not the same method as they do for cattle, but something different. First they pour wine over the victim's head, then they stab the man in the throat so that his blood runs into a bucket, and finally they carry the bucket up onto the heap of dry sticks and pour the blood down on the Sword of Ares. Even as they are doing that up above, down below, alongside the holy precinct,

8 Greeks consecrate the victim by sprinkling of purifying water and barley grains and cutting a lock of the victim's hair. To a Greek, Scythian practice would also be striking in that it does not involve the ritual shedding of blood.

9 In fact, bones do not burn well (dried dung is what is used in this area in absence of wood); the narrator here tries to explain rationalistically a ritual practice.

10 1800 feet (550 meters).

they cut away the whole right shoulder of the dead man, along with the hand, and toss it to the breeze. Once they do this for all of the victims they go away. Each arm lies wherever it falls, and the rest of the corpse lies separate.

4.63 Such then are the customs of sacrifice among the Scythians. Pigs they use not at all, indeed they are absolutely unwilling to raise pigs anywhere in their territory.

WARFARE

Part and parcel of the image of the noble savage that is being constructed is the emphasis on "savage." The use of gold for the skull-cup may seem surprising, but Scythia did in fact have many productive gold mines.

4.64 Their particular customs in warfare work like this. When a Scythian kills his first enemy, he drinks his blood. When he kills someone in battle, he takes the head to the king, since only by bringing the head can he exchange it for whatever loot they plunder—otherwise, he gets nothing. From the head, he strips off the skin, cutting in a circle around the ears; and he then grabs the head and shakes off the scalp; next, he uses an ox-rib to scrape away the flesh and kneads it until softened. The result, very like a cloth napkin, he keeps as his proud possession, fastening it to the bridle of his horse: for he who has the most of these human-skin cloths is judged the most brave. From these "cloths" they often make cloaks to wear, sewing them together just as one would a shepherd's coat from animal hides. Often, they also take the enemy dead and peel off the skin from their right hands, fingernails and all, and use this to make the covering for their quivers. Human skin is both thick and lustrous—in fact it turns out to be the most gleaming white of almost any skin. Oftentimes, they even skin a man whole, and then stretch it across a wooden frame and carry it about on horses.

4.65 Such then are their customs. As for the heads—not just from anyone, but from those who are their greatest enemies—each Scythian saws away the part below the eyebrows and cleans it up. A poor man then stretches raw ox-hide around the outside and uses it like that; but a rich man not only covers it with ox-hide, but also gilds it on the inside and uses it as his drinking cup. . . .

OATHS

4.68 When a Scythian king falls ill, he sends for the three soothsayers of best repute in the land, and these soothsayers take divination and mostly say that such-and-such (naming the person they mean) has sworn falsely on the king's hearth—for the Scythians by custom swear on the king's hearth when they wish to make a great oath. At once the man said to have sworn falsely is seized and led to the king; when he arrives, the soothsayers accuse him, saying that he plainly (according to their soothsayers' art) has made a false oath on the king's hearth and because of this the king has fallen ill. The man of course denies making a false oath, and protests loudly. At his denial, the king sends for twice-three other soothsayers, and if these too look into their soothsayers' art, and convict the man for falsely swearing, then they cut off his head at once; and the first three soothsayers divide up his property. But if the second group of soothsayers acquit the man, then other soothsayers are brought in, and yet again others. And if the majority of these acquit the man, it is decreed that the first soothsayers themselves must die.

And this is how they kill them: they fill a wagon full of dry sticks, and yoke 4.69
a team of oxen; then they put the soothsayers in chains, tie their hands behind the back, gag them, and shove them down into the pile of the sticks. Setting the sticks ablaze, they startle the oxen and drive them off. Often the oxen burn alive along with the soothsayers; often, though, the wagon poles burn in half and the oxen get away with only a scorching. Such is the way the soothsayers are burned alive, for this and for other reasons too—whenever they are condemned as false prophets. And not only does the king kill them, but he denies them progeny as well: the females are left unharmed, but every male child is put to death.

Now this is the way that the Scythians make sworn agreements. Pouring 4.70
wine into a large earthenware cup, they mix in the blood[11] of the two swearing the oath, lancing themselves with a sharp point, or slicing a bit of their flesh with a dagger. Then they dip into the cup their sword and arrows and battle-ax and spear and as they are doing that they lift up great prayers; and then they drink it down, both those swearing the oath and the most worthy of their followers.

BURIAL AND PURIFICATION

The burial of the retinue along with the king in preparation for the afterlife is known from cultures as far removed as Egypt and China. Nothing quite as extensive as here described has been found by archaeologists, but the same could have been said of China before the discovery of the terracotta warriors and horses outside Xi'an in 1974.

The tombs of the kings are in the land of the Gerrhi, at exactly the point 4.71
where the Borysthenes becomes navigable. There, when a king dies, they dig a great square-shaped pit, and once this is done they prepare the corpse. The body is waxed all over, the belly is gutted, cleaned, stuffed with cypress shavings, perfume, celery seed, and anise, and sewn back; they then carry it on a wagon to the next tribe. When the next tribe has gotten the corpse, they do just as the Royal Scythians:[12] they cut off part of an ear, shave their hair, make cuts in rings around their arms, tear at forehead and nose, and thrust arrows through their left palm.

From there they convey the king's corpse by wagon to the next tribe under Scythian rule, and all the tribes visited earlier follow them. When they have made the circuit, carrying the corpse to all the subject tribes, they find

11 There is a deliberate surprise in the sentence: the Greek custom was to pour in the wine and mix in *water*!

12 The Scythian king belongs to the "Royal Scythians," which considers itself the ruling tribe.

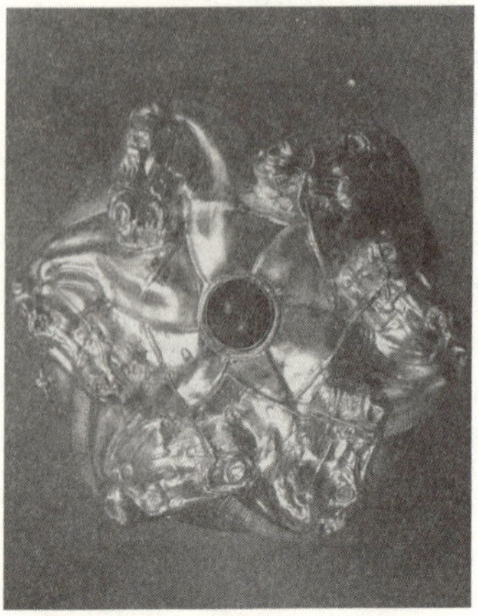

FIGURE 4.4 Scythian horse diadem, gold, from a 5th-century tomb

themselves at Gerrhi, the most remote of Scythian tribes, and at the burial place. First they set the corpse on a straw bed among the tombs, and then they fix their spears on either side of the body as posts, stretch over planks as beams, and roof it with plaited reeds. In the unused part of the tomb pit, they bury (having strangled them first) one of the concubines, the king's cup-bearer, cook, stable boy, steward, herald, and his horses, along with all sorts of other offerings, including golden jars (they don't make any use of silver or bronze). Once all this is done, everyone works to construct a great burial mound, each eagerly competing with the next to make it as big as possible.

4.72 After a year has passed, they do this. They take the most suitable of the servants (and these are Scythians by birth—the Scythians have no slaves bought with money, so the king chooses his servants from among his subjects), and they strangle fifty of these, as well as fifty of the finest horses. For all these they gut the body cavity, cleanse it, stuff it with dry husks of grain, and sew it up.

For the horses, they saw a wheel in half and to one half they affix two wooden posts and to the other half two others, and they construct many more in the same fashion, and plant each half wheel on the ground. They then drive a thick stake down the length of the horse up to the neck, and stand it up on the wheels, such that the front wheels support the shoulders of the horses and the back wheels support the belly, right beside the back legs. Both front and back legs hang loose. They put reins and a bit on each horse, and pull the reins to the front, and fasten them from pegs. On top of each horse they stand up one of the fifty strangled youths. They make them stand up by driving a straight stake alongside the backbone up to the throat; this stake is supported from below by being fastened into a sort of socket carved in the thick stake that runs through the horse. They set up these horses and riders in a circle about the tomb; and then they themselves ride away.

4.73 That then is how they bury their kings. As for the rest of the Scythians, when they die the closest kin lay the body in a wagon and cart it around from friend to friend. Each friend welcomes the procession and gives them a feast, laying out nearly as much food for the corpse as for everyone else. For forty days the dead are carted about in this way, and then they are buried.

Once they have made the burial, the Scythians purify themselves in a way worth describing. Each wipes his head with unguent and washes it, and then turns attention to cleansing his body. They stack three sticks leaning on each

other and tie about these a close-fitting covering of woolen felt. Then, they toss in rocks from a red-hot fire into a bowl that lies at the center of the felt tent.
Now there exists among the Scythians a kind of cannabis that grows in their 4.74
land, much like flax except broader and taller—the cannabis is much bigger there. The cannabis grows wild as well as under cultivation, and from it the Thracians make cloth much like linen. (No one, unless he has a great deal of experience, would be able to tell whether this cloth was of linen or of hemp; and if someone does not yet know about hemp clothing, he will think that this
cloth is made of linen.) This cannabis then is the plant whose dried buds[13] the 4.75
Scythians take and, slipping under the felt covering, throw upon the red-hot rocks. The buds that fall on the rocks smolder and produce a steam that is more powerful than any Greek vapor-bath. The Scythians rejoice in the vapor and howl with pleasure. This is what they use instead of a bath—they never wash their bodies with water. The Scythian women, however, pour out some water and make a poultice from cypress and cedar and frankincense wood by pounding these on a jagged rock, and when it becomes a thick mush from the pounding they plaster it all over their bodies and faces. From this the women possess a fragrant odor and, once the poultice is removed the next day, the skin is clean and sparkling.

"CUSTOM IS KING": THE STORIES OF ANACHARSIS AND SCYLES

To conclude this long section on the customs of Scythia, the narrator turns to two stories that exemplify how determinedly the Scythians keep themselves apart from other peoples. This complicates the schematic, since though the Scythians are the far-north people in contrast to the far-south Egyptians, they are also, like the Egyptians, most strikingly opposite to the Greeks. The Greeks, then, reside in the center, with these other peoples at the extremities of the world, with customs to match.

Like others, the Scythians are dead set against adopting the customs of 4.76
other peoples, and especially of the Greeks, as is shown by the stories of Anacharsis and, later, of Scyles. Now Anacharsis had toured many a land and had shown throughout his considerable wisdom. He was on his way back to his Scythian homeland when he sailed through the Hellespont and came to port at Cyzicus. There he found the people of Cyzicus celebrating a festival to the Mother of the Gods in opulent fashion, and Anacharsis vowed to the Great Mother that if he returned to his own home safe and in good health, he would celebrate her in the same way and at the same season as the people of Cyzicus, and would establish an all-night festival. So, when he arrived back in Scythia, he slipped down to a place called the Woodland (which is near an area called Achilles' Racecourse, and which happens to be full of trees of every kind), and secretly celebrated the goddess's festival in every particular,

13 Seed or seedpod reads the Greek.

with tambourine in hand and cult images hung from his neck. But one of the Scythians saw him doing this, and sent a message to King Saulius. The king came, and when he saw what Anacharsis was doing, he pulled out his bow and shot him dead.

Now, though, if anyone brings up Anacharsis, the Scythians say they know nothing of him—precisely because he traveled abroad to Greece and took up foreign ways. What I heard from Tymnes, the steward of King Ariapithes, was that Anacharsis was the paternal uncle of the Scythian king Idanthyrsus (and that he was the child of Gnurus, son of Lycus, son of Spargapithes). If Anacharsis was truly of this house, then one must conclude that he was killed by his own brother. For Idanthyrsus was the son of Saulius, and it was Saulius who killed Anacharsis.

4.77 And yet I have also heard a different story, told by the Peloponnesians, that Anacharsis was sent by the king of the Scythians to be a student in Greece. And when he returned back home, he reported to the one who sent him that the Greeks were preoccupied with getting every kind of wisdom, with the lone exception of the Spartans, but that the Spartans were the only Greeks who spoke and listened with wisdom and good sense. But this is nothing more than a story fabricated by the Greeks themselves—in fact, the man died as already described.

4.78 That then is what happened to Anacharsis on account of his foreign habits and close ties to the Greeks. And a great many years later, Scyles the son of Ariapithes had a similar experience. Scyles was one of the children of Ariapithes the king of the Scythians, and his mother, not a native but from Istria, taught him to speak and read Greek. Later, Ariapithes came to life's end when he was betrayed by Spargapithes, king of the Agathyrsi. At that, Scyles inherited the kingship and also his father's wife, whose name was Opoea. Opoea was a native Scythian, and she had had her own son from Ariapithes, named Oricus.

Though king of the Scythians Scyles was not at all content with the Scythian way of life—his mode of education had made him much more inclined to Greek ways. So he did this: whenever he was on campaign and took his army past the city of the Borysthenites (who themselves claim to be Ionian Greeks from Miletus), on arrival he would leave the army at the outskirts of the city. He himself would walk up to the city wall and as soon as the gates were closed behind him, he would put aside his Scythian robe and put on Greek garb. Dressed in this way, he went about the city, accompanied neither by his spear-bearers nor anyone else; and he had the gates guarded, so that no one among the Scythians might see his dress and behavior. Scyles, then, took on the Greek way of life, even making sacrifices to the gods in the manner of the Greeks. When he had stayed there a month or a bit more, he would put on his Scythian robe and go away. He did this often, over and over again, and had a house built in Borysthenes and married a local woman to be its mistress.

But it was fated that things turn out badly for him, and here is what brought 4.79
that about. Scyles conceived the desire to be initiated into the rites of Bacchic
Dionysus,[14] but when the rite was about to begin, a great portent came to pass.
His estate in Borysthenes was large and costly (this is the house I just mentioned), and all around were stationed sphinxes and griffins of white marble.
Upon that house the god[15] hurled his thunderbolt, and the whole of it burned
down—but Scyles went through with the initiation nonetheless. Now the
Scythians, for their part, are critical of the rites of Bacchus among the Greeks,
saying that it is not right to celebrate as a god this power that makes men go
mad. So, once Scyles was initiated into the mysteries of Bacchus, one of the
Borysthenites taunted the Scythians, saying, "You laugh at us, you Scythians,
because we follow the god Bacchus and the god possesses us; but now this
spirit possesses your king too, and he follows Bacchus and is made mad by the
god. If you don't believe me, follow, and I will show you." So, the leaders of the
Scythians followed, and the man from Borysthenes brought them back secretly and sat them in a tower to watch. And when Scyles came along with his
band of revelers and the Scythians saw him in his Bacchic frenzy, they took
it as a great disaster. They went back and told the whole army what they
had seen.

King has no Power—> All Custom

Later, when Scyles marched back to his own territory, the Scythians re- 4.80
belled against Scyles and put his brother Octamasades (son of Teres' daughter)
in charge. When Scyles learned about the revolt and the reason why, he
immediately fled to Thrace; whereupon Octamasades marched against the
Thracians. But when he came to the Ister,[16] the Thracians awaited him in
battle formation, and on the brink of engagement the king Sitalces sent this
message to Octamasades: "What need is there to try each other in battle? You
are my sister's child, and you have my brother. You give him back to me, and
I will hand over Scyles to you. Let neither you nor I risk our soldiers in battle."
Such was Sitalces' proposal—for his brother had fled in exile and was living
with Octamasades. Octamasades approved of the plan, handed over his uncle
to Sitalces, and got in turn his brother Scyles. Sitalces then took his brother
and left; and Octamasades cut off Scyles' head on the spot. Thus do the
Scythians privilege their own customs, and as for those who take on the customs of others, such is the price they pay. . . .

Darius Prepares to Invade

*The emphasis on the dimensions of the Black Sea here would have been useful to the
many readers who knew little or nothing of the region, but the deployment of numbers and explanation of research methods are also a means by which the narrator*

14 The Greek god of wine and its attendant revelry and "madness." Also known simply as "Bacchus."
15 Zeus.
16 This river (our Danube) forms the border between Scythia and Thrace.

shows how painstakingly he has inquired into every detail, thus underlining his authority as he moves into the main story of the invasion.

4.83 Darius made ready to attack Scythia, dispatching messengers with his orders: some were to muster foot soldiers, others were to supply ships, and yet others were to work on bridging the strait of Bosporus over to Thrace. But Artabanus, the son of Hystaspes and thus Darius's brother, was not at all happy about this campaign against the Scythians. "The Scythians are impossible to get at," he said, and he listed his reasons. The advice was sound, but it did not persuade Darius; and so the one brother ceased speaking of it, and the other, as soon as all was ready, started the march from Susa.

4.84 Then one of the Persians, Oeobazus, pointed out to Darius that all three of his sons were going to the war, and asked if one might stay behind with him. Darius replied, "Since you are a friend and make a reasonable request, all your sons will stay behind." Oeobazus was thrilled, thinking that his sons had been released from the expedition. Darius, however, gave the order to those appointed to kill the three sons of Oeobazus—and so they did stay behind, but with their throats cut.

4.85 So, Darius traveled from Susa to Chalcedon, arriving at the spot on the Bosporus where the bridge had been built. Setting forth in a boat, he sailed to the so-called Dark Rocks, which the Greeks claim were roaming islands in an earlier time. There he sat on the headland and gazed across at a sight to behold—the Black Sea which is of all inland seas the most extraordinary. It has a length of eleven thousand one hundred stades, and its width at the widest point is three thousand three hundred stades.[17] At the entryway into this sea there is a channel called the Bosporus (and that's where the bridge had been built) which extends for one hundred and twenty stades; and the Bosporus stretches all the way to the Propontis.[18] The Propontis itself is five hundred stades wide and fourteen hundred long, and it empties into the Hellespont, which is narrow, only seven stades wide, yet four hundred stades long. The Hellespont empties into the open sea, and that sea is called the Aegean.

4.86 Here is how one goes about making such measurements. On a long summer's day a ship travels roughly seven thousand fathoms, and about six thousand over the course of the night. From the sea's entryway to the river Phasis (which is where the Black Sea has its greatest extent) the journey takes nine days and eight nights, which makes one million one hundred and ten thousand fathoms; and that equals eleven thousand one hundred stades. The journey to Themiscyra (near the river Thermodon) from Sindica, where the Black Sea is at its widest, takes three days and two nights, which makes thirty-three thousand fathoms, or three thousand three hundred stades.

17 1260 miles (2000 km) × 375 miles (600 km); the actual measurement is more like 750 × 250 miles, 1200 × 400 km. His measurements for the Bosporus (length of 13.5 miles, 22 km), Propontis (57 × 159 miles, 80 × 250 km), and Hellespont (just under a mile wide, 45 miles long, 1.3 × 75 km) are not so far off.

18 Sea of Marmara.

MAP 4.2

This then is how I went about measuring the Black Sea and Bosporus and Hellespont. Issuing into the Black Sea is a lake that is not much smaller than itself, the Maeotis, which is thus said to be the "mother of the Black Sea."

Now when Darius had had his fill of gazing at the Black Sea, he sailed back 4.87
to the bridge, and from the bridge (which had been designed by Mandrocles of Samos) he took in the sight of the Bosporus too. Darius then erected two marble steles, one inscribed with Assyrian letters, the other with Greek, listing all the tribes and peoples he had brought with him—and his army was made up of every people in his empire. The assembled host totaled seven hundred thousand men, not counting the sailors but including the cavalry; and six hundred ships. It was these two steles that the Byzantines later brought to their city and used for the altar of Artemis Orthosia—except for one broken off stone, covered with Assyrian script, which was left near the temple of Dionysus in Byzantium. I imagine, then, that the part of Bosporus where

FIGURE 4.5 Cuneiform stele

Darius constructed the bridge was midway between Byzantium and the temple at its northern edge.

4.88 Darius was very pleased with the bridge, and so, next, he gave rewards aplenty to its designer, Mandrocles of Samos. Mandrocles took a part of his prize and commissioned a painting that depicted the whole of the bridge over the Bosporus, with Darius seated on a throne as his troops crossed over; this he set up in the temple of Hera, and to it he added an inscription that read:

> Mandrocles bridged the fish-filled waters of Bosporus,
> and as a memorial dedicates this picture to Hera;
> he bears a crown on his own head and glory to the Samians,
> all because he made perfect the vision of Darius the King.

4.89 So much then about the rewards and memorial for the man who bridged the Bosporus.

Darius now crossed over into Europe. Before crossing, he had directed the Ionians to sail up along the Black Sea to the Ister, and once there, to build a bridge over the river and wait for him. (The fleet was under the command of Greek Ionians and Aeolians, as well as the peoples of the Hellespont.) So, the fleet passed through the Dark Rocks and made straight for the Ister; and from there sailed upriver for two days. And when they reached the neck of the river, just above where the Ister starts to break apart into the channels of the delta, they built a bridge. Meanwhile Darius crossed the Bosporus and marched through Thrace. When he reached the springs that are the source for the river Tearus, he set up camp and stayed for three days.

4.90 Now the Tearus is said by the locals to be the best river for its curative powers, and especially effective for curing skin infections in both men and horses. The springs at its source number thirty-eight, all flowing from one
4.91 rock formation, and some of them are cold, others hot. . . . When Darius arrived at this river and set up the camp, he was very pleased with the river, and so he set up a stele here, too. It read like this: "The springheads of the Tearus provide the noblest and finest water of any river; to these has marched a man, on his way to attack the Scythians, who is likewise the noblest and finest of any man, and his name is Darius son of Hystaspes, King of the Persians and the whole of the continent of Asia." Such were the words inscribed.

4.92 Darius then decamped, and he came next to another river, named the Artescus, which flows through the land of the Odrysians. When he got there, he did this: pointing out a particular spot, he commanded every man to leave one stone as he passed by; and when the troops were done, Darius marched on, leaving behind great hillocks of stones. . . .

Darius Crosses the Ister

As usual, the narrative pauses at the critical moment when the king crosses the natural boundary. As with Cyrus's campaign against the Massagetae, the discussion concerns strategy; but that earlier tale also intimates that bad things are about to happen.

Once Darius and his army had reached the Ister, and all had crossed over, he ordered the Ionians to destroy the bridge and to follow him into the Scythian territory along with the soldiers from the ships. Just as they were on the brink of carrying out the order, Coes son of Erxander, the general of the Mytileneans, spoke to Darius (though he first asked whether the king would like to hear advice from anyone wanting to give it): "King, you are about to march against a territory where you will see neither farms nor settled towns. Let the bridge stand, and leave behind as guards these men, the ones who built it. If we catch up with the Scythians and do what we have in mind, this will be a way back for us; and if we have trouble locating them, our way out will be secure. Understand that I have never been afraid that the Scythians will beat us in battle; what I fear is that we'll get into trouble as we roam about this forsaken territory, unable to catch them. Now some might say that I am arguing this for my own sake, hoping to stay behind. But that is not so. Rather, I present you, King, with the best advice I have; and as for me I will follow you and would never be left behind." Darius was very pleased by this advice, and so gave him this reply: "Lesbian friend,[19] when I am back safe in my home by all means come present yourself to me, so that I can offer good works in return for such good counsel." 4.97

So he spoke; and then he tied knots, sixty of them, onto a leather strap. 4.98
Summoning the Ionian tyrants to council, he said this: "Men of Ionia, forget what I had earlier advised about the bridge. Now take this leather strap and do as I ask. As soon as you see me moving into Scythian territory, from that time forward untie one knot each day. If I do not appear within this time and the days you count by the knots run their course, then sail back to your own land. But up to that point, now that I've changed my mind, guard the bridge, and work with all your heart for its safety and protection. If so you do, you will have pleased me greatly." So Darius spoke; and then he pressed onward into Scythia.

Physical Geography of Scythia and Its Neighbors

Now on our side of Scythia there is Thrace, which projects out into the sea. 4.99
There is a bay on the northern coast there, and within that Scythia begins and the Ister has its river delta, flowing out to the east. I will now give you an idea of the size of the part of Scythia adjacent to the Black Sea, starting from the Ister. The ancient land of Scythia begins at the Ister and lies along the coast,

19 Mytilene was the principal city on the island of Lesbos.

with the Black Sea to the south and the noonday sun, as far as the city of Carcinitis. From there the land continues to run along the sea, but becomes mountainous terrain and lies out into the Black Sea; and that part is inhabited by the Tauri, as far as the so-called Rocky Peninsula, which itself extends as far as Lake Maeotis to the east. Let me make this clear: this part of Scythia has a sea on two of its four borders, one to the south and one to the east, very like the land of Attica, and it is here that the Tauri dwell—very much as if, in Attica, Cape Sunium, that is the part between Thoricus and Anaphlystus, projected a bit farther into the sea and were inhabited not by the Athenians but by some other people! Of course, in saying this I compare small things to large—Scythia is on a different scale—but in any case that's how the land of the Tauri is situated. Now for anyone who has not sailed past that part of Attica, I will give another example, this one from Italy: it would be as if in Iapygia some other people and not the Iapygians marked a boundary from Brundisium to Tarentum and settled on the promontory that stretches out into the sea there. These are but two examples of the many I could cite whose geography resembles that of the land of the Tauri.

4.100 North of the land of the Tauri, and next to Lake Maeotis on the east, Scythians inhabit the territory, as well as the part to the west of the Cimmerian Bosporus running up along Lake Maeotis as far as the river Tanais, which flows into the far corner of the lake.[20] Now in the area north of the Ister and inland, Scythia is bounded by these peoples: first the Agathyrsi, then the Neuri, then the Man-Eaters, and finally the Black-Cloaks.

4.101 The land of Scythia is more or less a square, with two sides bordered by water, since the side that extends up inland and the side running along the sea are very much equal. From the Ister to Borysthenes is a journey of ten days; and from Borysthenes to Lake Maeotis is also ten days. And from the Black Sea inland to the Black-Cloaks, who live at the north edge of Scythia, is a journey of twenty days. I estimate that an overland trip is about two hundred stades a day. So, the length of Scythia from east to west would be four thousand stades,[21] and the length inland from north to south would be the same. This then is the size of Scythia.

4.102 Now the Scythians conferred and decided that they could not fight the army of Darius alone. So, they sent envoys to the neighboring peoples. The kings of these peoples had already met, and were trying to plan how to deal with the great army marching against them. Assembled there were the kings of the Tauri, the Agathyrsi, the Neuri, the Man-Eaters, the Black-Cloaks, the Geloni, the Budini, and the Sauromatae. . . .

20 Herodotus's grip on the geography here seems to falter, since the part west of the Cimmerian Bosporus would be the eastern coast of Crimea; the shore north of that, along the west side of Lake Maeotis (Sea of Azov), is then counted twice. Some commentators take the description to include the southeastern shore of the Black Sea and the east side of the Sea of Azov. Probably Herodotus simply misunderstands the complicated situation of the Crimean peninsula and environs.

21 About 450 miles, 725 km.

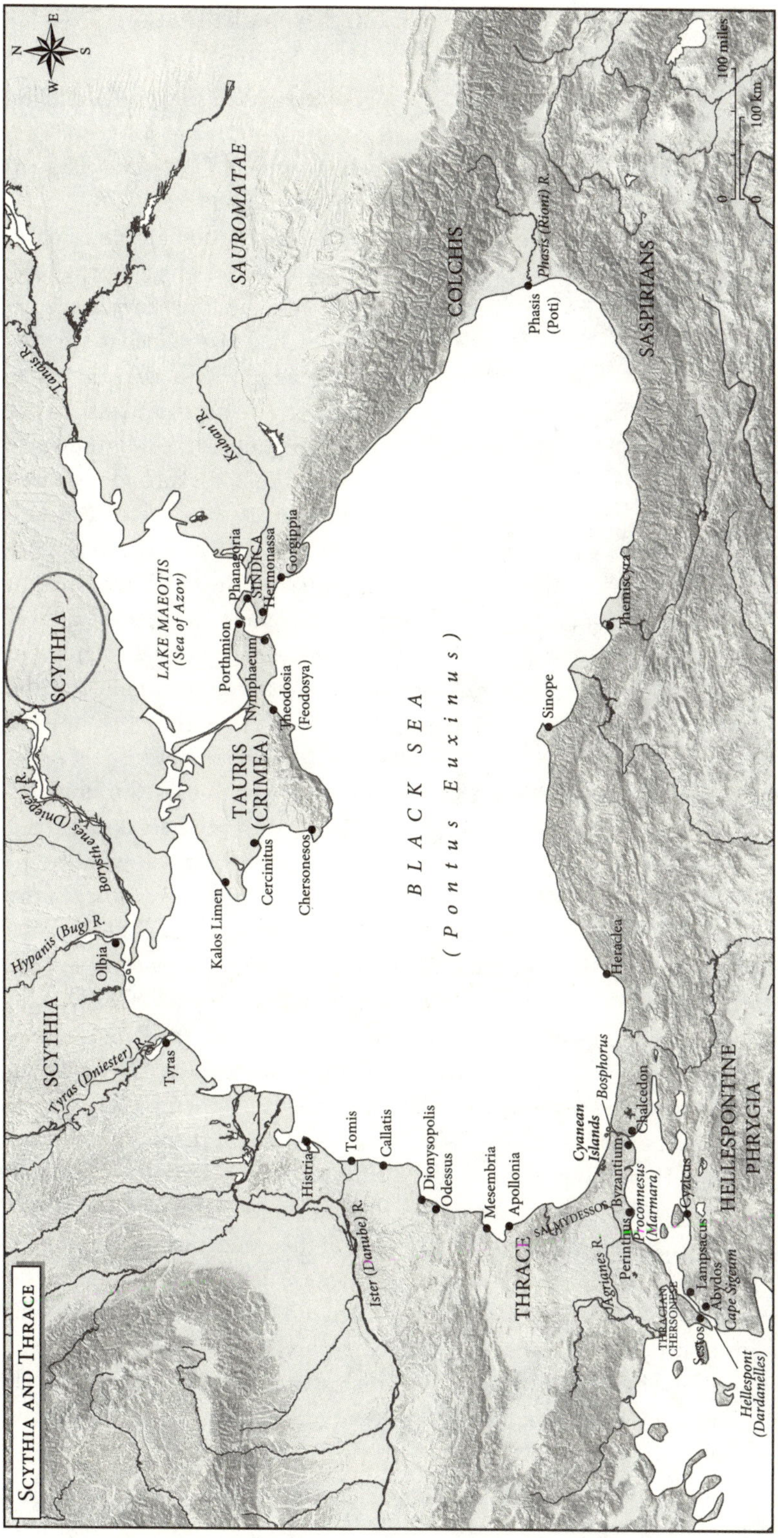

SCYTHIA AND THRACE
N
E
S
W
SCYTHIA
Tyras (Dniester) R.
Tyras
Hypanis (Bug) R.
Olbia
Borysthenes (Dnieper) R.
SCYTHIA
Tanais R.
SAUROMATAE
LAKE MAEOTIS
(Sea of Azov)
Kalos Limen
Cercinitus
Chersonesos
TAURIS
(CRIMEA)
Theodosia
(Feodosya)
Nymphaeum
Porthmion
Phanagoria
SINDICA
Hermonassa
Gorgippia
Kuban R.
COLCHIS
Phasis (Rioni) R.
Phasis
(Poti)
SASPIRIANS
B L A C K S E A
(P o n t u s E u x i n u s)
Sinope
Themiscyra
Heraclea
Bosphorus
Cyanean
Islands
Chalcedon
Byzantium
Proconnesus
(Marmara)
Cyzicus
HELLESPONTINE
PHRYGIA
Histria
Tomis
Callatis
Dionysopolis
Odessus
Mesembria
Apollonia
SALMYDESSOS
Ister (Danube) R.
THRACE
Agrianes R.
Perinthus
Lampsacus
Abydos
Cape Sigeum
THRACIAN
CHERSONESE
Sestos
Hellespont
(Dardanelles)
0
100 miles
0
100 Km

MAP 4.3

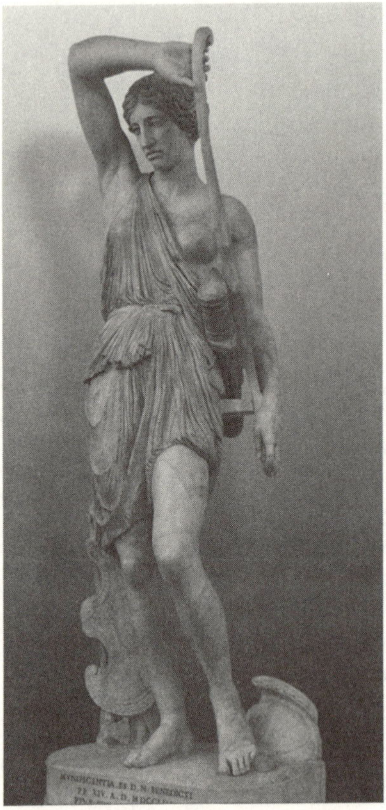

FIGURE 4.6 Amazon

Excursus: Sauromatae and the Amazons

This charming tale is a myth of how different peoples can come to live together in harmony, very much a central theme to the larger narrative.

4.110 About the Sauromatae a remarkable story is told. Long ago when the Greeks were fighting the Amazons (who are called *Oiorpata* in the Scythian language, which means "man-killers," *oior* being the Scythian for "man" and *pata* for "kill"), the story goes that the Greeks had defeated the Amazons near the river Thermodon, and sailed off in three ships with every Amazon they had been able to capture alive. On the open sea, however, the Amazons rushed them and slaughtered them to a man. But the Amazons knew nothing of how to steer with a rudder, how to reef a sail, or how to row with oars. So, after killing all the men, they were borne along by the currents and the wind, until they reached the Lake of Maeotis near Cremni, which is in the territory of the free Scythians.[22] There the Amazons got off the ships and made their way to inhabited country, where they took the first herd of horses they came across. Mounting the horses they then ravaged and plundered that part of Scythia.

4.111 The Scythians could not understand what was going on: the language, the clothes, the ethnicity of the Amazons were all unfamiliar to them, and they were at a loss as to where they had come from. Moreover, they thought the women were youths in the first blush of manhood. So, they fought them. But after the battle the Scythians carried off some of the dead, and so came to know that these were women. The Scythians took counsel: they no longer had any notion of killing the women; rather, they sent the youngest of their own men to them (estimating how many women there were), and told these to set up camp next to the women and take their cue from what the women did. "If the women chase you, do not offer battle, but run away; and when the women stop, go back and again set up camp close by." The Scythians, you see, had in mind to conceive children from these women. So, the young men were sent off and did as the elders said.

22 Also called the "Royal Scythians," this tribe at the far east of Scythia claimed itself superior to the others, designating the other Scythians their subjects. See also 4.71.

Gradually the Amazons saw that the youths meant them no harm, so they 4.112
relaxed; and every day the camps moved closer together. The young men, just like the Amazons, had nothing but their weapons and their horses, and they lived just as the women did, by hunting and raids.

Now each day at noon the Amazons were wont to go off by ones or twos, 4.113
and then to separate even further from one another, so as to have privacy for their daily needs. The Scythian men noticed this, and so they did exactly the same. And one of them sidled up to one of the women, all alone, and she did not push him off—instead, she let him have his way. She could not speak with him—they couldn't understand each other—but with her hand she gestured that he come again the next day to this very spot, and bring another man, indicating that there should be two men and that she would herself bring a second woman. The youth left, and told the others; and on the next day he came back to that spot, bringing another youth with him. And they found the Amazon and another with her waiting. When the rest of the young men heard what had happened, they too went out to tame an Amazon and make her their own.

After that, they combined the two camps and lived together, each man 4.114
keeping as his woman the one he had first had sex with. Now the Amazon language proved impossible for the men to learn, but the women did come to grasp the language of the men. So, since they now could understand each other, the men said to the Amazons, "We have parents, and property. No longer should we continue to carry on this way of life: let's leave this behind and live in the company of others. We will keep you, and no one else, as our wives." And the Amazons said in reply, "We could not live among your Scythian women—our ways are not at all the same. We shoot from a bow and hurl the javelin and ride on horses, and we know nothing of womanly affairs; your Scythian women do none of these things, but do women's work, staying with the wagon in a nomad's tent, going out not to the hunt nor anywhere else. How could we get along with women like that? No, if you want to keep us as your wives, and to do what's right, go to your parents and take a fair share of the common property. And then let us go and live by ourselves." The young men agreed, and did exactly that.

When they had gotten their share of the family possessions, the men re- 4.115
turned to the Amazons, and the women said, "A deep foreboding grips us as we think about how many times we have plundered the countryside here—and now we have robbed you of your fathers too. Why must we live in this spot? If we are truly the right wives for you, then come, let us get away from this land, we and you, and cross the river Tanais and find a home over there."

The young men agreed to this, too, and so they crossed the Tanais, traveling 4.116
to a spot three days east of the Tanais and three days north of Lake Maeotis. And when they reached the place they now inhabit, they stopped and settled. The women of the Sauromatae still embrace this ancient way of life—they routinely go to the hunt on horseback, both with their men and separately, they go to war, and their clothes and equipment are just like the men's.

4.117 As for the language, the Sauromatae speak Scythian, but make lots of mistakes because of their past—that is, since the Amazons never learned the language properly. Their marriage customs are remarkable too: no young woman marries before she has killed her first man in battle. And, because not everyone is able to do that, some women even grow old and die without ever having married.

The Neighboring States Take Counsel

4.118 So, the king of the Sauromatae as well as the kings of the other tribes were the ones in assembly when the Scythian envoys arrived, as I said earlier.[23] These envoys explained how the Persian, once he had come to control the whole of the other continent, had bridged the channel of the Bosporus and crossed over to this continent, had then subdued the Thracians, and was now bridging the river Ister, intending to bring every land under his sway. "You must not stand by and let us be destroyed; rather, join us in the fight against the invader. If you won't, we will have no choice but to abandon our territory or come to terms. Think what will happen to us if you are not willing to help! And think what will happen to you—there is no easy path here. The Persian has come not just to attack us but you too; once he has defeated us, he will never be content to let you be. And here is a mighty proof of our words: if the Persian marched against us alone, intending to avenge the time when we held them subject, by all rights he should have come straight to our country, holding back from all the rest; and then all could see that he was attacking the Scythians and no one else. But as it is, as soon as he crossed into Europe, he subdued all who were in his path—he now holds the Getae, our neighbors, under his sway, as well as the rest of Thrace."

4.119 When the envoys were done, the kings, all those who had come from the neighboring peoples, took counsel, and their opinion was divided. The kings of the Geloni and Budini and Sauromatae were of the same mind, and promised to help the Scythians. The kings of the Agathyrsi and Neuri and Man-Eaters and Black-Cloaks and Tauri, however, gave the Scythians a different response: "If we ignored the fact that you were the ones who first wronged the Persians and started this war, then what you ask would seem right to us, and we could comply and do as you ask. But as it is, you and not we attacked their country and ruled over Persia for as long as the god gave that to you; and the Persians, now that this same god has aroused them, are paying you back. We have done these men no wrong, nor will we now undertake to do so unprovoked. If the Persian[24] attacks our land as well as yours, and initiates the wrongdoing, then we too will not suffer this. But until we see that happening, we will keep to ourselves. It is our view that the Persian

23 4.102.

24 Meaning the Persian king.

comes not to attack us, but to attack those who were the cause of the quarrel and first acted with injustice." first wrong, reaction

The Scythians Lead and the Persians Follow

When Darius crossed the Ister with his 700,000 troops many chapters ago, it was hard to imagine how the Scythians could oppose such a mighty force. The several retardations of the main narrative (description of the geography, consultation with the adjacent tribes, excursus on the Amazons), however, not only create suspense, but contribute critical pieces of a solution to the puzzle: the Scythians will succeed by virtue of the size of the territory, the type of terrain, and the nomadic lifestyle of the Scythians and their neighbors.

When the Scythians heard back from the envoys, they decided not to chal- 4.120
lenge the Persians in open battle, since so many of the allies had refused to join them. Instead, they formulated this plan. They would split the army into two and retreat, and as they marched they would plug any well they passed by, choke the springs, and lay waste to the grasslands. One detachment, led by Scopasis, would be joined by the Sauromatae. They were to retreat straight toward the river Tanais near Lake Maeotis whenever the Persian turned that way; and when the Persian turned back to march on, they were to give chase and attack. The other detachment was to be made up of two combined divisions, the larger led by Idanthyrsus, and the smaller by Taxacis; these would be joined by the Geloni and the Budini. This part of the army was to keep one day ahead of the Persians, and continually withdraw and do all else in accordance with the plan: first, as they retreated, they were to head straight for the lands of the peoples who had rejected the alliance, intending to force those too to join the battle—they reasoned that if they did not willingly join the fight against the Persians, they could still get entangled in the fight whether they wanted it or not. Then, they were to turn back toward their own land and, whenever it seemed the right moment, to launch an attack.

This then was the Scythian plan for opposing the army of Darius, and they 4.121
dispatched the finest of their horsemen as scouts. As for the wagons and nomadic tents where all the children and women lived, these they sent away, and the flocks too (except what they needed for food), telling them to drive the wagons ever northward.

The wagons then moved out 4.122
in advance of the army. Soon the Scythian scouts located the Persians, at a three-days march from the Ister. Having found them, the scouts moved on,

FIGURE 4.7 Scythian horseman

keeping one day ahead; and each day they set up camp and destroyed all that one might harvest from the land. Now the Persians, as soon as they saw the signs of the Scythian cavalry, followed their trail—but the horsemen continually retreated. And then, going after one of the main Scythian forces, the Persians followed them to the east, where the Tanais flows. The Scythians crossed the river, and the Persians, in pursuit, crossed too. So, having traversed the entirety of the land of the Sauromatae, they came to the land of the Budini.

4.123 So long as the Persians were passing through Scythia and the land of the Sauromatae, they found nothing to damage, for this was a barren land. But when they invaded the land of the Budini, they found a walled city there, entirely empty (since the Budini had abandoned it), and that they set on fire. After that, they continued to follow the Scythian trail ever farther, until they had traversed the whole land and come to the desert. The desert itself is uninhabited, lying to the north of the Budini at the distance of a seven-days journey. Beyond the desert live the Thyssagetae, and from their country flow four mighty rivers, passing through the lands of the Maeotae and emptying into Lake Maeotis: these are the Lycus, the Oarus, the Tanais, and the Syrgis.

4.124 So, when Darius came to the desert, he halted his march and settled the army on the banks of the Oarus. There he constructed eight great forts, equidistant from one another, with roughly sixty stades[25] between each—the ruins of these were still standing in my time. And while he was busy with this, the Scythians he was pursuing circled to the north and headed back into Scythia. When the Scythians no longer appeared—they had disappeared without a trace—Darius left the forts half-built and turned back to the west, the whole time supposing that this was the whole of the Scythian army, and that they were now fleeing westward.

4.125 Marching his army at double pace he met up with the Scythians, now with the two detachments combined, just as he reached Scythia. He gave chase—but they kept ever one day ahead. Darius was unrelenting in his advance, so the Scythians withdrew exactly as planned, leading him into the lands of those who had rejected the alliance, first of all the land of the Black-Cloaks. The double invasion of Scythians and Persians threw the Black-Cloaks into utter turmoil, and the Scythians then led Darius down to the lands of the Man-Eaters. When these too were in disarray, they went next to Neuri territory, where more turmoil ensued; and then to the Agathyrsi. Now the Agathyrsi were watching their neighbors fleeing in panic and knew this was the work of the Scythians. So, as the Scythians were about to burst into their territory they sent a herald to warn the Scythians not to violate the border—"otherwise, you will have to fight us first." Such was their warning, and they then marched out to the borderland, determined to beat back the invaders.

25 7 miles, 11 km.

(The Black-Cloaks, the Man-Eaters, and the Neuri had done nothing to defend themselves when the Scythians and Persians invaded; rather, they forgot all about their threats and fled, panic-stricken, northward toward the desert.) So, the Scythians gave up going into the land of the Agathyrsi, turning back to their own territory and by that route leading the Persians out of Neuri territory.

Darius Challenges the Scythians to Fight

In reply to Darius's challenge, the free and noble savage will offer not battle but two riddles. One involves the ancestral tombs, whose detailed description at 4.71 seemed an ethnographical excursus but here becomes important background; essential to the tale is the irony that only in death do these nomads stand still and that the tombs are the only thing worth defending to the death. The second riddle receives two very different interpretations, one by Darius that in trying to see something positive for the Persians verges on incoherence, and the other by one of the Seven (Gobryas) with chilling implications. The psychological warfare here, as the Persians become increasingly bewildered, at first uneasy and gradually alarmed, is brilliantly depicted. That animals as common as donkeys and mules are exotics in this territory (4.129) shows how far outside of their natural sphere the Persians have wandered.

Long had the Persians chased the Scythians, and there seemed no end to it. 4.126
So Darius sent a horseman to Idanthyrsus, the Scythian king, to say this: "You strange man, why do you always run away? Instead, take your choice. If you think you can stand up against my army, stop all this roaming around and fight. But if you understand that you are not my equal, also stop your running, and bring to me, your master, gifts of earth and water, and let us come to terms."

To that, the Scythian king Idanthyrsus said, "Persian king, this is how it is for 4.127
me. I run away not in fear of any man, and neither before nor now am I running away from you; nor am I now doing anything different from what I normally do in peacetime.[26] I will also explain why I do not instantly offer to fight. We have no cities and no planted fields, and thus we have no need to fight for fear that our cities be captured, or our crops cut down before the harvest. But if you must fight us straightway, know that what we do have are the tombs of our forefathers. Come then, find those tombs and try to wreck them: then you will know whether we will fight or whether we will not. But before that—unless for good reason—we will not join battle. That's enough said about fighting. As for my masters, I have only these two: Zeus, who is my ancestor, and Hestia, the Scythian queen. Gifts I will send you, not earth and water, but what you deserve; and because you claim yourself as my master, I mean to see you weep."

The herald then left to report back to Darius. The Scythian leaders, how- 4.128
ever, were brimming with anger at the very mention of slavery. The part of

26 That is, as the chief of a nomadic people, he moves around with his people constantly as a matter of course.

their force that included the Sauromatae, led by Scopasis, they dispatched to negotiate with the Ionians (that is, the Ionians who were guarding the bridge over the Ister). As for the remainder of the force, they decided they were no longer to lead the Persians about; instead, they would attack the Persians every time they left camp looking for food. So, they watched for foragers from Darius's army, and did just that. These skirmishes went like this: the Scythian horse would rout the Persian horse, forcing them back to the infantry for support; and the Scythians, once they had chased back the horse, would turn back in fear of the infantry. The Scythians made forays of this sort at night as well.

4.129 Now I will tell you something quite amazing, something that helped the Persians and worked against the Scythians whenever they attacked Darius's camp—that is, the sound of the donkeys and the odd appearance of the mules. Scythia cannot sustain donkeys or mules; and in point of fact there is not one donkey or mule in all the Scythian territories, on account of the cold. So, the braying of the donkeys would unsettle the Scythian horse, and often when they attacked the Persians, as soon as the horses heard the noise from the donkeys, they would prick up their ears, and then rear and run away. Such was their wonderment—since they had never before heard such a sound or seen such a creature. From this, then, the Persians gained a small bit of advantage in the war.

4.130 But the Scythians could see that the Persians were alarmed by the constant skirmishes, and so they worked to get them to stay longer in Scythia, thinking that the longer they stayed the more they would suffer, lacking entirely of resources as they were. They worked it like this: from time to time they would leave some of their own flocks with the herdsmen and go off to another place. The Persians then would swoop down and seize the flock, and so would feel momentarily encouraged.

4.131 As all this happened over and over, Darius was gripped with uncertainty. The Scythian kings could see that, and so they sent to Darius a herald bearing four gifts: a bird, a mouse, a frog, and five arrows. The Persians asked the man who brought them, "What are these gifts supposed to mean?" but he said that he had been sent with no instructions other than to deliver them and return as quickly as he could. "I will let you Persians yourselves figure out what the gifts mean to say—if you are clever enough."

4.132 On hearing that, the Persians took counsel. It was Darius's view that the Scythians were surrendering and offering him land and water, giving this explanation: "The mouse lives in the ground and eats the same food as man, the frog lives in water, the bird is most like a horse, and by surrendering these arrows, they signal that they are giving up on their own valor." Such then was the view set forth by Darius. But Gobryas held a different view—he, you'll recall, was one of the Seven who had overthrown the Magian[27]—and he gave this as his interpretation of what the gifts meant to say: "Unless you become

27 That is, the false Smerdis (3.70–79).

2 inxrs

birds and fly to the heavens, or mice and burrow under the earth, or frogs and leap into the lakes, you will be struck down by arrows like these and never return home."

Such then were the explanations the Persians offered for the gifts. The Scythian detachment with the lone division—the one that had earlier been stationed as a guard near Lake Maeotis, and then was sent to negotiate with the Ionians—now reached the bridge crossing the Ister. "Men of Ionia," they said, "we come bringing freedom for you, if you are willing to listen. We know that Darius gave you orders to guard this bridge for sixty days, but for sixty days only, and that if he does not appear in that time, you are to go back to your own land. As long as you are doing just that, you are without reproach—from Darius or from us. Stay here for the days appointed but then depart from this land." The Ionians made a promise to do that, and so the Scythians pressed on, eager to return as soon as they could. 4.133

As for the Persians, after the gifts had been delivered to Darius the rest of the Scythian force, foot and horse, was drawn up in a line, ready to join battle. But then a rabbit ran out into the middle ground between the armies. And, as each Scythian noticed the rabbit, he gave chase. With there being much shouting and commotion among the Scythians, Darius asked what the noise was all about. And when he heard that the enemy drawn up opposite him was busy chasing a rabbit, he said to his retinue, "These men, my friends, have great contempt for us, and it now seems to me that Gobryas spoke rightly about the Scythian gifts. And since I too now think that this is how it is, we need a plan, a good one, so that we get back home safely." At that Gobryas spoke: "King, before I came, what I had heard gave me some insight into the difficulties these men would present, but now my education is complete; and I finally understand that they are toying with us. So I advise this: as soon as night falls, light all the fires and in every way do just as we usually do; but then let us tie up all the donkeys and trick the men unfit for the march into staying. Then let us get out of here, before the Scythians make their way to the Ister and destroy the bridge, or for that matter the Ionians decide to do something that can lead to our ruin." 4.134

Darius Retreats and the Scythians Give Chase

Darius's treatment of his troops will remind us of Cyrus and the Massagetae (1.207).

Such then was Gobryas's advice, and once night fell Darius made good use of it. He abandoned the sick and other men not likely to be missed if they were killed. He left behind the donkeys, too, tying them up there in the camp, so that they would provide sufficient noise. To the infirm men (the ones he was leaving because of their weakness) he gave the pretext that they were going to secure the camp while he took the healthier men out to ambush the Scythians. That then was what he told the men he left behind, and as soon as the fires were lit, he pressed on with all possible speed to the Ister. The donkeys, lonely with the bulk of men now gone, brayed even more loudly than usual; and 4.135

FIGURE 4.8 Bridge using ships as pontoons

the Scythians, hearing the donkeys, were fully persuaded that the Persians were encamped there.

4.136 At daybreak, the men who were abandoned, realizing that Darius had betrayed them, stretched out their arms in pleading, and told the Scythians all that had happened. As soon as they heard, the Scythians got the whole army together—the two divisions and the one that had now rejoined them, Scythians, Sauromatae, Budini, and Geloni—and they went after the Persians, marching straight to the Ister. But the Persian army had many foot soldiers, and did not know the roads, which were rough and hard to follow; while the Scythian army was entirely of cavalry and knew every shortcut. They therefore passed by one another, and the Scythians easily beat the Persians to the bridge. When they found out that the Persians were not yet there, they said this to the Ionians, who were in their ships: "Men of Ionia, the numbered days have passed, and you have not done right in remaining here. Before, you stayed out of fear; but now, cut the bridge and make a swift voyage home, rejoicing in your freedom and giving thanks to the gods—and to the Scythians. We will attend to that man who before was your master: no more will he march against any other people."

The Ionians at the Bridge and Darius's Arrival

There is considerable irony in the fact that the Ionian tyrants—Greeks!—are the ones debating whether to set Ionia free and let Darius's army be destroyed. That in turn prefigures the Ionian revolt against the Persians, which will be the subject of books 5 and 6.

4.137 At this, the Ionians took counsel. Miltiades, an Athenian who was general and tyrant over Hellespontine Chersonese, was of the opinion that they should listen to the Scythians and set Ionia free. But Histiaeus of Miletus was of the opposite view: "It is thanks to Darius that each of us is the ruler of our city. If the power of Darius is crushed, we will no longer be able to maintain control over our cities, neither I in Miletus, nor you in yours. As you well know, every city will want to become a democracy rather than a tyranny." And as soon as Histiaeus expressed this view, all changed their minds to support it—even though at first they had favored what Miltiades had said.

4.138 Those who cast their votes in support and were so esteemed by the Persian king were as follows.[28] The tyrants of the Hellespont were Daphnis of Abydos, Hippoclus of Lampsacus, Herophantus of Parium, Metrodorus

28 This chapter stems from a desire to record, for the rest of the Greeks, exactly who joined with the Great King at this critical moment.

of Proconnesus, Aristagoras of Cyzicus, Ariston of Byzantium. And the tyrants from Ionia were Strattis of Chios, Aeaces of Samos, Laodamas of Phocaea, and Histiaeus of Miletus—the very man whose advice was opposite to that proposed by Miltiades. From Aeolia was present only Aristagoras, from Cyme.

These then were the men who supported Histiaeus's view. They next decided on a plan that involved both action and words. First, they would cut the bridge along the Scythian side—but only so far as to be out of range for a Scythian archer—so as to seem to do something while in fact doing nothing, and also to prevent the Scythians from trying to force their way over the bridge and across the Ister. Second, even while they were cutting the bridge, they would make verbal assurances that they would do everything the Scythians desired. This, then, was the plan. So, Histiaeus spoke to the Scythians, replying for them all: "Men of Scythia, you come bearing good news, and have hurried here at just the right time. What comes from you to us is nobly brought; and what comes from us to you is our dutiful service in return. Look! As you see, we are even now destroying the way across, and we do so with great eagerness, in our longing to be free. And while we are busy cutting down the bridge, now is the time to hunt down Darius and his men—and once you find them, to take vengeance on them as they deserve, on behalf of us all." 4.139

And so the Scythians for a second time trusted the Ionians, thinking that they spoke the truth, and turned back to hunt down the Persians. But they missed the Persian route entirely. For this the Scythians themselves were to blame, since they had ravaged the grasslands and choked the sources of water. If they hadn't done that, it would have been easy for them to have found the Persians if they liked. But as it was, what had seemed the best of plans now proved to be their undoing. The Scythians went searching for their enemies in the parts of their land where there was pasture and water for the horses, supposing that the Persians too would make their escape along such a path. But the Persians kept close to the trail they had made when they first marched, and following that they found—not without difficulty—the bridge. By the time they got there night had fallen, and as they came up, the bridge, they saw, was cut away. And they were very afraid that the Ionians had abandoned them. 4.140

With Darius was an Egyptian man who had the loudest voice of anyone, and at Darius's bidding he stood on the bank of the Ister and called out for Histiaeus of Miletus. So, he shouted the name, and Histiaeus heard him at first shout, and put all his ships to work getting the army across the river and reconstructing the bridge. 4.141

That then is how the Persians escaped even as the Scythians were trying to hunt them down—missing them twice. The Scythians decided then that if you think of the Ionians as free men, they are the most cowardly and unmanly men ever; and if you speak of them as slaves, they are the ones most adoring of their master and least likely to run away. Such were the insults the Scythians hurled at the Ionians. . . . 4.142

BOOKS 5 AND 6
The Ionian Revolt

The narrative in book 5, as well as the opening chapters of the book to follow, centers on the tale of the Ionian revolt from Persian rule, which began with the rebellion of Miletus in 499 BC and effectively ended with Miletus's fall in 494. In typical Herodotean fashion, the causes are multiple and range from cosmic, or at least broadly human, forces (e.g., the natural Greek longing for freedom) to local and personal. Even the immediate cause of the revolt is overdetermined: Miletus rebels both because of a failed scheme by the tyrant, Aristagoras, whom Histiaeus (in Susa) had left as his deputy at Miletus, and as a result of the direct command of the equally scheming Histiaeus himself. Histiaeus we are expected to remember: though a leader of the revolt, he is the Ionian who deceived the Scythians and preserved the bridge for Darius's retreat over the Ister, explicitly preferring to preserve his own power (as Darius's approved tyrant of Miletus) over the liberation of the Ionian Greeks (4.137). And as the narrative develops, we gradually come to see that the revolt is not so much that of the Ionians, but of their tyrants. Actions and motivations are selfish and opportunistic, without the sort of concerted tactics needed to have a chance of winning; as Henry Wood put it, the whole reads much like a misguided slave rebellion.

Even the slim selections here will give some sense of the sprawling and convoluted character of this part of Herodotus's narrative, a confusing amalgam of small actions, skipping rapidly and somewhat disjointedly from place to place, from leader to leader, full of treachery and intrigue. The manner of narrative itself, that is, seems to suggest the messy and unruly nature of this rebellion by the many independent city-states of Ionia; as well as to raise essential questions about Greek unity and about the tangled correlation between Ionian Greeks and those of the mainland. The narrative thereby sets up brilliantly the depiction in books 7–9 of the coordinated Persian invasion, which will be laid out in grand, majestic, orderly fashion, and which is written from limited and distinct perspectives, in contrast to the scattered viewpoints in play here.

The vast geography and many peoples of the Mediterranean are now adequately in front of the reader. The narrative pauses one last time to emphasize the far reach of Persian power with a vivid portrayal of the 1500-mile route of the Royal Road that ran from Sardis to Susa. But from here on out the spotlight will remain on the Greeks and Persians.

Aristagoras Visits Sparta

The year is 499; Aristagoras is tyrant of Miletus as a stand-in for Histiaeus (Histiaeus is at Susa serving Darius), and at Aristagoras's instigation Miletus has now openly rebelled from the Persians. We here join in progress a long section about Aristagoras's attempt to win over as allies first Sparta, and then Athens. The map of Asia that Aristagoras brings with him is an extraordinary detail: the first Greek to draw a world map was said to have been Anaximander, only a couple of generations earlier. Cleomenes was but one of two Spartan kings; his co-ruler, Demaratus, is saved for later in the tale (we will see him first at 7.3).

As the Spartans tell the story, it was in the reign of Cleomenes that 5.49
Aristagoras, tyrant of Miletus, came to Sparta, and he came to speak with Cleomenes himself, bringing with him a bronze tablet engraved with a map of the whole world, containing the whole of the sea and all the rivers too. When he was admitted to the king's presence, Aristagoras had this to say: "Cleomenes, don't be surprised that I come here with such urgency. The situation stands so: the sons of Ionians are slaves, not free men, a painful, disgraceful state of affairs not only for us but for all of Greece, and especially for you, who are Greece's champions. So now, by the gods of Greece, save the Ionians, your kinsmen, from slavery. Success can easily be yours. The Persians are no great warriors, whereas in affairs of war you have reached the highest pinnacle of excellence. They fight with bows and short spears, wearing pants and stiff peaked hats as they march to battle[1]—you can see how easy it will be to defeat them. Moreover, those who live on that continent have riches beyond all others, beginning with gold, but including silver and bronze and embroidered clothing and oxen and slaves—everything your heart could desire! Look here"—pointing to the map on the engraved tablet that he had brought—"how the peoples are situated, how next to the Ionians are the Lydians, who inhabit a land fertile and with more silver than any other. And look here," he said, "next to the Lydians to the east are the Phrygians, of all the peoples I know those with the most flocks and the greatest harvests. Next to the Phrygians are the Cappadocians, Syrians as we call them; and bordering those are the Cilicians, whose land extends to this sea here, do you see, the one around Cyprus—and they pay an annual tribute to the King of five hundred talents. Next to the Cilicians are these people, the Armenians, rich in flocks, and next to them the Matieni, who dwell in the land you see here. Cissia borders that territory, and there, next to this river, the Choaspes, is Susa, where the Great King passes his days, and where lie treasuries full of money. Capture that city and you need not fear to challenge Zeus for riches![2] Why must you fight over land that is neither great nor prosperous, and small in size, moreover against fighters who can match you for valor, Messenians and

1 Greeks thought pants exotic and rather ridiculous; note how Aristagoras neglects to mention the formidable Persian cavalry.
2 As Simon Hornblower puts it, the comparison to Zeus "would make a Greek reader or listener gasp" (see his commentary to book 5, ad loc.).

Arcadians and Argives, men who have neither gold nor silver, the sorts of things that men lust for enough to fight and die? Why choose that, when it is easily possible for you to rule over all of Asia?" So spoke Aristagoras, and Cleomenes answered, "Milesian stranger, I will take until the day after tomorrow and then give my reply."

5.50 That's as far as they got that day. But when the day appointed for the decision arrived and they met as arranged, Cleomenes asked Aristagoras how many days' journey it was from the Ionian seacoast to the king's palace. So far, Aristagoras in his cleverness had done well in duping the king, but here he stumbled. To get the Spartans to invade Asia as he wished, he needed to avoid the truth; but he told how it was, saying, "It takes three months." With that, Cleomenes cut off the rest of what Aristagoras was starting to say about the road to Susa, and said, "Milesian stranger, get yourself out of Sparta by sundown. You want to take the Lacedaemonians on a three-month journey into the heart of Asia, do you? No amount of eloquence could persuade them to a plan like that!"

5.51 That said, Cleomenes went home; but Aristagoras lay hold of a suppliant's bough[3] and went to the house of Cleomenes. Going inside he asked Cleomenes to honor his supplication and hear him out, and to send away the daughter, who was standing by Cleomenes' side. (Her name was Gorgo, a girl eight or nine years old and his only child.) But Cleomenes told him to say what he wanted and not mind the child. Aristagoras then began by promising him ten talents if he did as requested, and when Cleomenes shook his head, Aristagoras kept raising the price. He had gotten to the point of promising him fifty talents when the girl cried out, "Father, you must get yourself out of here or this stranger will make you a bad man!" Cleomenes was pleased with his daughter's advice, and went off to a different part of the house. Aristagoras had no further success in talking about the road up to Susa, and so he left Sparta altogether.

5.52 Now as for the road to Susa, here is what it is like. All along it are the king's way-stations and lovely inns with courtyards, and the whole road goes through country that is inhabited and safe. There are twenty way stations along the road as it stretches through Lydia and Phrygia, a distance of ninety-four and a half parasangs. On the far border of Phrygia is the river Halys; on its banks are gates that you have to pass through to cross the river, and there also stands a large guard-post. Crossing over to Cappadocia and traveling to the border with Cilicia, you find twenty-eight way stations along the way, a distance of one hundred and four parasangs. At the border, you go through two gateways, and pass by two guard-posts. After that, as you make your way through Cilicia, you pass three way stations, a distance of fifteen and a half parasangs. At the border of Cilicia and Armenia is a navigable river, called

3 An olive branch with wool was used as a traditional symbol of supplication.

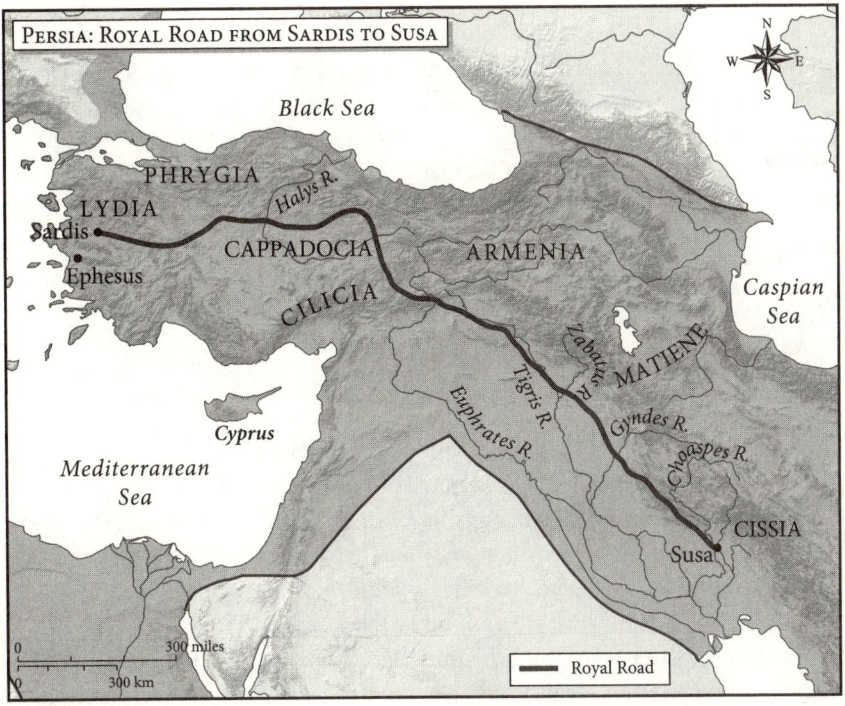

MAP 5.1

the Euphrates. And in Armenia are fifteen way stations or inns, a distance of fifty-six and a half parasangs; and along the way also a guard-post. Four rivers, all large enough to be navigable, flow through this land, all of which you have to cross: first, the Tigris, then a second and a third both called the Zabatus (these two are not the same river, nor do they come from the same source, one flowing from Armenia, the other from Matiene); and the fourth river is named the Gyndes, which is the one Cyrus once divided into three hundred and sixty channels. As you travel from Armenia to the land of the Matieni, you pass thirty-four way stations, a distance of one hundred thirty-seven parasangs. There are eleven way stations as you cross into the land of Cissia, forty-two and half parasangs, and there you come to the Choaspes, also a navigable river. On the banks of this river stands Susa.

The total number of way stations is, then, one hundred and eleven, and just so many are the places to rest as you make your way from Sardis to Susa. If my 5.53 measurements in parasangs are right, and if a parasang is thirty stades (which it certainly is), then the Royal Road stretches for thirteen thousand five hundred stades, or four hundred and fifty parasangs, between Sardis and the so-called Memnonian palace at Susa.[4] Assuming you travel one hundred and fifty stades a day, the calculation in days is exactly ninety.

4 About 1500 miles, 2400 km.

5.54 So, when the Milesian Aristagoras said to Cleomenes that the road inland to the king's palace took three months, he got it exactly right. But I will show how someone wanting to investigate further can make a more precise calculation—for we neglected to add in the distance from the coast at Ephesus up to Sardis. I can tell you that there are actually a total of fourteen thousand and forty stades if you measure from the coast up to Susa (for that is the city called the Memnonian), since the stades from Ephesus to Sardis number five hundred and forty. So, the length of the journey in fact is three days longer than the three months Aristagoras said. . . .

Athens and the Burning of Sardis

We rejoin the story as Aristagoras arrives in Athens. What must have seemed to the Athenians a relatively modest decision to send twenty ships to lend short-term aid to Miletus will become the main impetus for the Persian invasions of 490 and 480 BC. Note that the critical burning of city and temple are not part of the attackers' plan, but happenstance, which speaks resoundingly to the capriciousness of fate, as well as to human impotence in face of inevitable forces.

5.97 At the very time when the Athenians had fallen out with the Persians, Aristagoras, the Milesian—right after he had been driven away from Sparta by Cleomenes—came to Athens. Besides Sparta, Athens was, after all, far more powerful than any other Greek city. Aristagoras approached the assembly of citizens and told them—just as he had told the Spartans—all about the riches of Asia, and about the Persian habits of warfare, how they used neither shield nor spear, and so were easily defeated. To that he added the point that Miletus had originally been settled by Athenian colonists, and thus it was right that the Athenians, great in their power, come to their defense. So very in need was he that there was nothing he did not promise, and in the end he brought them over. Truly it seems that it is easier to fool a crowd than one man, seeing that Aristagoras was unable to deceive the Spartan king Cleomenes, but had success with thirty thousand Athenians. So, the Athenians were taken in, and voted to dispatch twenty ships to help the Ionians, appointing as their commander Melanthius, an entirely upstanding citizen. And these very ships were the beginning of troubles between Greeks and barbarians. . . .[5]

5.99 The twenty Athenian ships arrived in Ionia, bringing with them five triremes from the Eretrians—who were joining the fight not to please Athens, but to repay what they owed the Milesians. (Earlier Miletus had allied with Eretria to fight against Chalcis, a war in which Samos was the Chalcidians' ally.[6]) Once these ships were present, and the rest of the allies had arrived

5 This echoes a passage in the *Iliad* (5.62–64) that speaks of the troubles brought back to the Trojans by Paris's ships when he abducted Helen—likewise a relatively small action that led to a mighty conflict between Greece and Asia.

6 This is the Lelantine War, which is ancient history, at least 4 or 5 generations earlier and perhaps as long ago as 2 centuries. The relationship between Miletus and Eretria thus is old and revered in contrast to the ad hoc Athenian alliance.

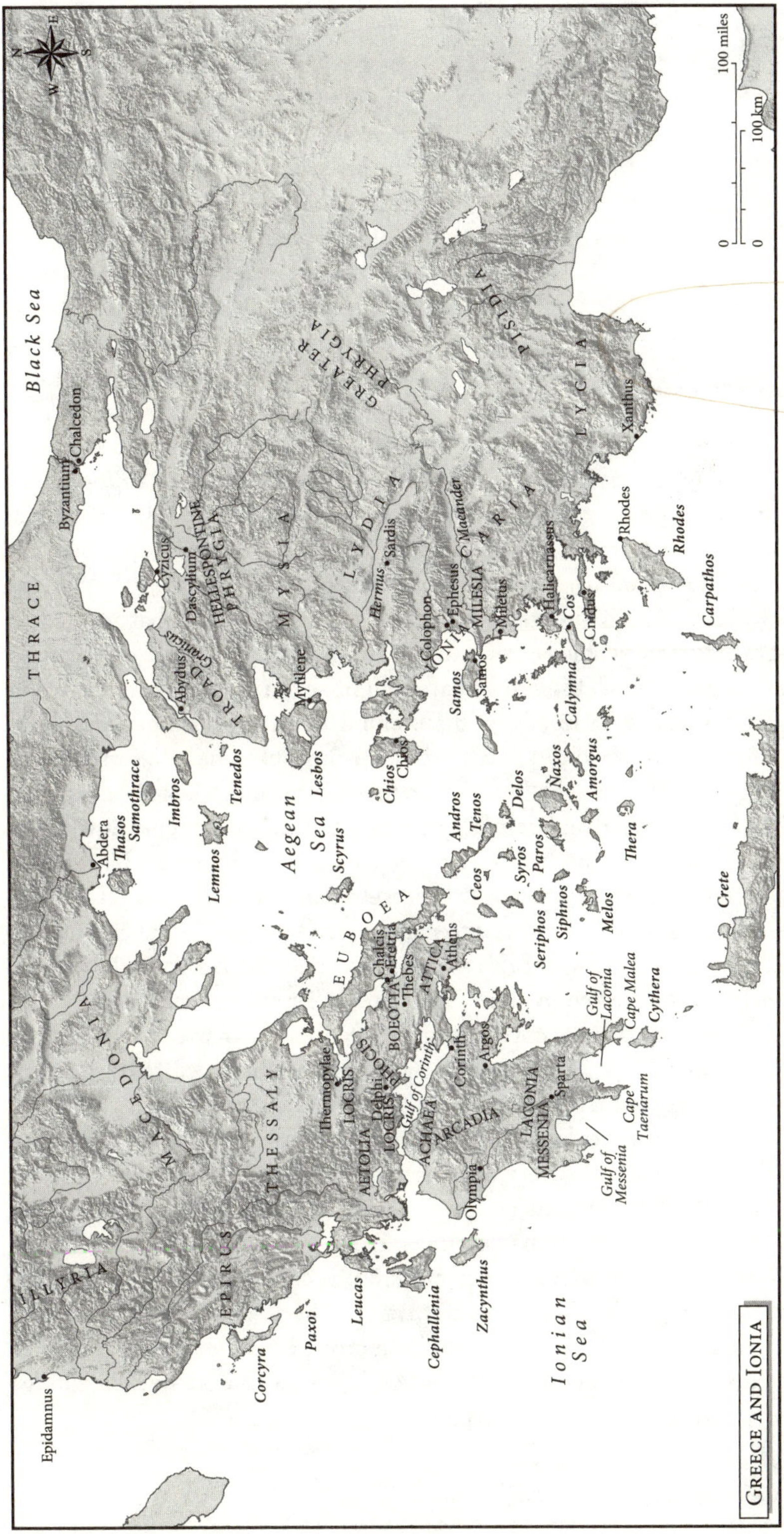

GREECE AND IONIA

MAP 5.2

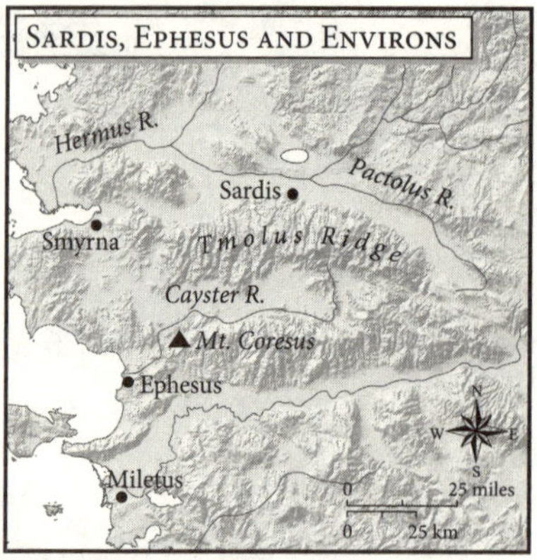

MAP 5.3

too, Aristagoras launched the attack on Sardis. He did not go himself, though—he stayed in Miletus. Instead, he appointed as commanders his brother Charopinus and another Milesian named Hermophantus.

5.100 Once the Ionian forces got to Ephesus, they left the transport ships behind near Mt. Coresus, still in Ephesian territory, and made their way upcountry with a large force, using Ephesians as their guides. They went along the banks of the river Cayster, climbed over the ridge of Tmolus, and thus arrived at Sardis—which they took unopposed, capturing everything, except the acropolis, which was defended by Artaphrenes himself[7] with a not inconsiderable body of men.

5.101 But as it turned out, they got no plunder at all, despite capturing the city, and here's why. In Sardis many homes are made of reeds, and those that are made of mud-brick have roofs made of reed-thatch. Some soldier set fire to one of these, and as soon as he did, the fire spread from house to house across the whole town. With the city ablaze, the Lydians and what Persians happened to be in town were beset by fire on all sides, and had no way out—the blaze extended all the way to the outer parts of the town. So they poured down into the open marketplace, next to the river Pactolus, a river that brings bits of gold down from Mt. Tmolus and flows through the marketplace down to the river Hermus, and from there to the sea. Packed in the marketplace alongside the Pactolus, the Lydians and Persians were forced to make a stand. But when the Ionians saw the enemy taking a stand and also a large force coming down from the acropolis to help, they retreated in alarm, back to Mt. Tmolus. From there, they re-
5.102 turned to their ships under cover of night. So Sardis was burned to the ground, and along with it the temple of the local goddess, Cybebe[8]—which the Persians would later claim as their excuse when they set fire to Greek temples in return.

All the Persians who dwell to this side of the river Halys, already notified of the disaster, now got together and came to help the Lydians. They arrived, however, to find the Ionians no longer there. So, they followed the Ionians' trail and caught up with them in Ephesus. There, the Ionians formed a line and joined battle, but were much overmastered: the Persians put many to the sword, including men of great repute, among whom was Eualcides, the general of the Eretrians, a man who had been crowned in the games and much lauded by the poet Simonides of Ceos. And those who were not slaughtered ran away and scattered, each to his own city.

7 Satrap of Sardis.

8 Often identified with Cybele, the famous mother goddess of the Lydians and Phrygians.

That then is how the battle went. After it the Athenians abandoned the Ionian cause altogether, refusing to help them further, despite the many entreaties sent them by Aristagoras. With the Athenians no longer their allies, the Ionians nonetheless—since there was no going back on what they had done to Darius—pressed on with their fight against the king. They sailed to the Hellespont, where they subjugated Byzantium and all the other cities there. Then, sailing out from the Hellespont along the coast of Caria, they added many an ally to the cause. After the burning of Sardis even Caunus, which before had not wanted to be part of the rebellion, joined up with them. . . . 5.103

When Darius heard the news that Sardis had been captured and burned by the Athenians and Ionians, and that the leader who had collected the troops and 5.105

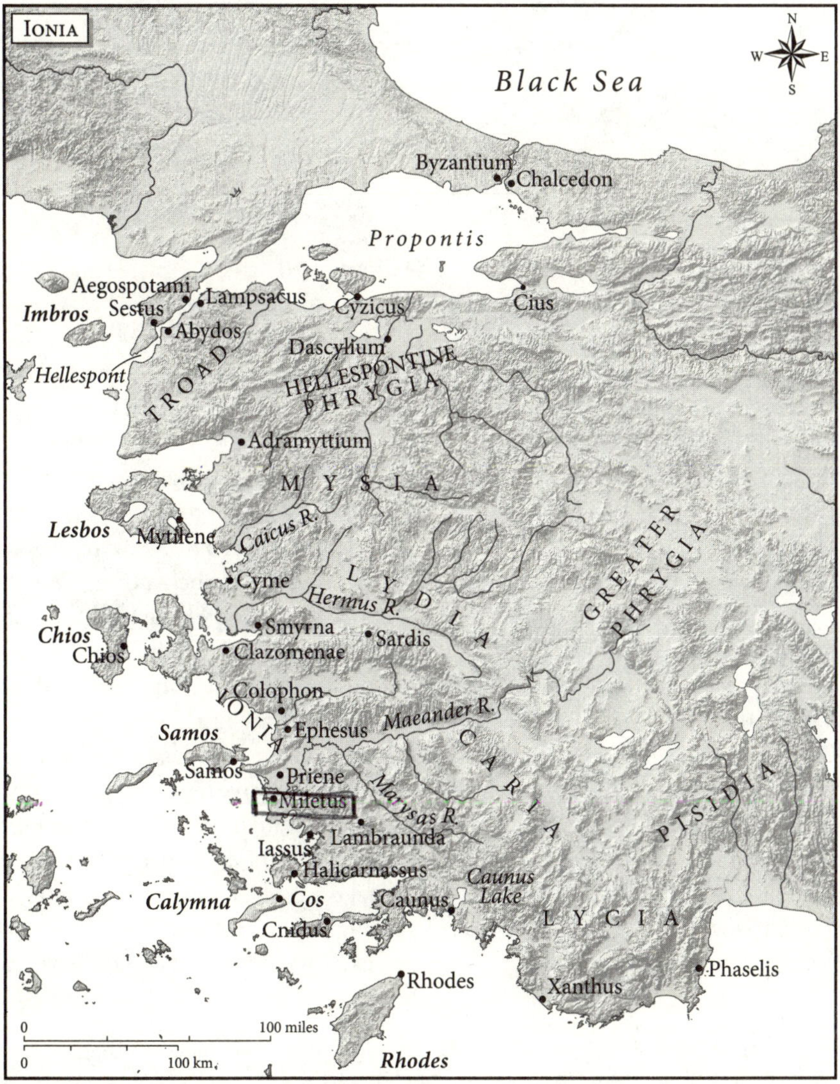

MAP 5.4

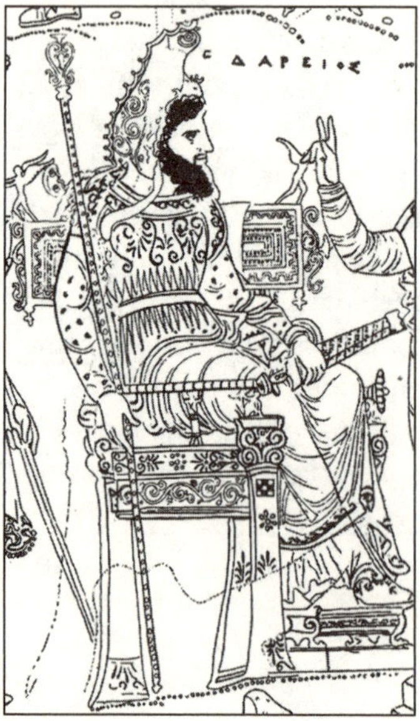

FIGURE 5.1 Darius

devised the scheme was the Milesian Aristagoras, it is said that he first brushed aside the Ionians, knowing full well that they would not go unpunished for their revolt; rather, he asked, "Who are these Athenians?" When he was told, he called for his bow. Taking it, he fit an arrow to the string and fired up into the sky, and as he shot the arrow aloft he said, "Zeus, grant me revenge upon the Athenians!" Then, he ordered one of his servants to come to him each time a meal was laid, and to say three times over, "Master, remember the Athenians!"

Histiaeus Hoodwinks Darius

Histiaeus, tyrant of Miletus, tricked the Scythians and now tricks Darius; this deception will not be his last.

5.106 Such was Darius's command. Next, he summoned to his presence Histiaeus, the Milesian tyrant who accompanied Darius to Susa long ago. "Histiaeus, I have learned that your deputy, the one you set up as tyrant at Miletus, has been engineering a revolt against me. He brought in men from mainland Greece and Ionians too—who will pay for it, you can be sure—and convinced them to follow him. And thus he has robbed me of Sardis. Now how does this fine situation look to you? How could he have done any of this without your involvement? Watch your step, or you'll find yourself to blame." To that Histiaeus said, "King, what a thing to say![9] That *I* plotted to bring harm to you in any way great or small? What do I lack that I should do such a thing? What am I in need of? Everything that is yours is also mine, and I have the honor of being your counselor in all deliberations. No, if my deputy is doing the sorts of things you report, know that he does this on his own. I for one find hard to believe this news that the Milesians and my deputy are in revolt against you. But, my king, if they *are* doing that, and what you have heard is true, clearly it was you who brought this to pass—by keeping me captive here, away from my home on the sea. Out from under my watchful eye, the Ionians, or so it seems, have done what their hearts have long desired. Now if I had been in Ionia, not a single city would have stirred a finger. So, let me travel to Ionia immediately! In that way, I can re-establish control, and hand over to you the deputy of Miletus who has devised this. Moreover, once I have finished all you have in

9 Greeks will have recognized this as a phrase echoing Homer, a favorite expression of Hera's when she is countering Zeus. Often it is said coquettishly, almost comically, and in the context of denying some sly trick Hera is trying to pull; that is probably the tone here.

mind, I swear to the gods—the gods sacred to the king!—that the tunic I wear down to Ionia will not come off my back until I also make Sardinia, that greatest of islands, your tributary."[10] So spoke Histiaeus, trying to trick the king— 5.107
and Darius was taken in. So, Darius sent off Histiaeus, telling him to come back to the court at Susa once he had done all he promised....

The Persians Move to Re-establish Control Even as the Revolt Spreads

We here revisit the strategic question of whether it is best to cross the river and fight with the river to your back or to have the enemy cross. Here, the answer is opposite from Cyrus's decision in the Massagetae campaign (1.206–208), but the result is equally disastrous for the side that makes the choice. The episode seems then to raise, again, a metaphysical question as to what sort of advantage we can expect from even the best human thinking and planning.

Meanwhile the Persian commander Daurises, who had married into the 5.116
house of Darius, and Hymaees and Otanes, two others who also had married daughters of Darius, were pursuing the Ionian force that had attacked Sardis. These they overwhelmed in battle and drove back to their ships.[11] From there, the three Persians divided up the Ionian cities and proceeded to sack them.

Daurises made for the cities about the Hellespont, and there captured 5.117
Dardanus and Abydos and Percote and Lampsacus and Paesus. He captured them one a day, but as he was marching from Paesus against Parium news came that the Carians, in solidarity with the Ionians, were also revolting. So, turning away from the Hellespont, he marched his army to Caria.

As it turned out, the Carians 5.118
learned of Daurises' march before he got there. So, they massed together at a place called the White Pillars, at the river Marsyas, which flows into the Maeander from Idrian territory. Many were the plans put forward to the men there assembled, but the best, or so it seems to me, was that of Pixodarus son of Mausolus, a man from Cindya who had married the daughter of the Cilician king Syennesis. His view was that they should cross the Maeander, and join battle with the river at their

MAP 5.5

10 Sardinia is the largest of Mediterranean islands (9300 sq. mi., 24,000 km^2), located in the Tyrrhenian Sea west of Italy; thus Histiaeus promises to bring under control not only all of the Greek islands off Ionia, but also this enormous island far to the west, an extravagant, again almost comical, claim.

11 We now return to the action described in 5.102.

backs—"In that way," he said, "the Carians will have nowhere to flee and will have to stand their ground. They thus will fight even more bravely than nature has made them." But his view did not prevail. Rather, it was decided that the Persians and not they should have the Maeander at their back; in that way, if the Persians were turned and defeated in the battle they would not return home, but fall to their death in the river.

5.119 Soon the Persians came and crossed the Maeander, and the Carians and Persians joined battle next to the river Marsyas. Hard did they fight, and long, but in the end the Carians were overwhelmed by superior numbers. In the battle, two thousand Persians fell, but ten thousand Carians. And after that, those who had fled the battlefield were trapped at Labraunda at the sanctuary of Zeus, God of the Army, a large and holy grove of plane trees. (The Carians are the only people I know of who sacrifice to Zeus, God of the Army.) So, trapped there, they tried to plan for their safety: was it better to surrender
5.120 to the Persians, or to leave Asia altogether? But even as they were trying to decide, the Milesians and other allies arrived. The Carians then put aside their planning, and got ready to enter the fight anew. The Persians attacked, the Carians and allies joined battle, and the defeat was far worse than before. And of all the many that fell, the Milesians lost by far the most. . . .

5.122 Now Hymaees, who was the second of the Persian commanders to pursue the attackers of Sardis, marched to the Propontis and took the city of Cius in Mysia. After that, he learned that Daurises had left the Hellespont and was marching on Caria. So, he left the Propontis and marched to the Hellespont. There, he took captive all the Aeolians who lived about Troy, as well as the Gergithes, who were the descendants of the Teucrian Trojans of old. But once he had taken these peoples captive Hymaees himself fell sick and died, there in the area about Troy.

5.123 After Hymaees died, Artaphrenes, the satrap of Sardis, and Otanes, the third of the Persian commanders, were assigned to attack Ionia and neighboring Aeolia. They then captured the Ionian city of Clazomenae and the Aeolian city Cyme.

5.124 It became plain then that Aristagoras, the tyrant of Miletus, was a man of little mettle. It was he who had roused Ionia and stirred up these great troubles, and yet as he saw the cities falling to the Persians he made plans for an escape—it seemed impossible to defeat King Darius, he thought. So, he summoned his fellow rebels and took counsel, telling them they needed to have some refuge in case they were forced out of Miletus. "Would it be better to go from here to Sardinia and set up a colony? Or to Thrace, to Myrcinus, that city of the Edoni that Histiaeus fortified, when he got it as a present from Darius?"
5.125 In answer, Hecataeus son of Hegesander, a thinker and writer, offered his opinion: "Neither of these is the right path to follow; instead, you should build a fortification on the island of Leros and, if you are forced out of Miletus, lie low there. From there, you can come and return to Miletus later on."

5.126 Such was Hecataeus's advice, but Aristagoras thought it best to go to Myrcinus. So, Aristagoras handed over Miletus to Pythagoras, a leading citizen, and he then took all who were willing and sailed to Thrace, where he occupied Myrcinus as planned. From there he launched an attack on a neighboring town and he and all his men were killed by the Thracians—precisely because he continued to lay siege to their city though the Thracians were perfectly willing to sign a treaty and leave.

Histiaeus Joins the Revolt

Histiaeus is, ironically, a tyrant who joins the fight for freedom from the Persians, but in this passage it becomes clear that in keeping with his tyrant's role he really is fighting for himself. As a tyrant, he naturally inhabits a world marked by duplicity, scheming, and brute force.

Such then was the end of Aristagoras, the man who had started the Ionian revolt. Meanwhile Histiaeus, the tyrant of Miletus, was released by Darius, and so appeared at Sardis. When he arrived from Susa, Artaphrenes, the satrap of Sardis, asked, "What do you think made the Ionians revolt?" Histiaeus said he didn't know, that the rebellion had taken him by surprise—pretending that he knew nothing of the circumstances. So, Artaphrenes, seeing that he was scheming and knowing full well the truth about the uprising, said, "This, Histiaeus, is the fact of the case: it was you who stitched the sandal, and Aristagoras who put it on." 6.1

That then is what Artaphrenes said about the uprising. Histiaeus was alarmed by how much Artaphrenes knew, and so he ran away at first cover of night, down to the coast. His promise to conquer Sardinia, that largest of islands, was but a trick; his real plan was to make himself the leader of the Ionians in their war against Darius. But when he crossed to the island of Chios, he was put into chains by the Chians, since they supposed that he, as Darius's agent, was involved in some plot. The Chians released him, however, as soon as they heard the whole story—that he was now at war with the king. 6.2

But then they asked Histiaeus what made him so eager to get Aristagoras to revolt and bring so many pains upon the Ionians. In reply, he did not give the real cause, but said that King Darius had made plans to resettle the Phoenicians in Ionia, and the Ionians in Phoenicia—this, then, was his reason for ordering the revolt. In fact, the king had no such plan; by saying this Histiaeus was trying to heighten their fears. 6.3

Next, Histiaeus, using Hermippus of Atarneus as his messenger, sent letters to certain of the Persians in Sardis (those he had spoken with earlier about the revolt). But Hermippus did not deliver the letters to the men appointed; instead, he took them and handed them over to the satrap, Artaphrenes. Artaphrenes thereby learned everything that was happening. He then told Hermippus to deliver the letters to the men he was carrying them to, but to deliver to him the Persians' replies. With the plot now exposed, Artaphrenes had a great many of the Persians executed. 6.4

6.5 Such, then, was the turmoil round and about Sardis. His hopes dashed, Histiaeus next asked the Chians to bring him to Miletus to be restored as tyrant. But the Milesians, glad to be rid of Aristagoras, were by no means ready to embrace another, now that they had had their taste of freedom. So Histiaeus tried to take Miletus by force, under cover of night—but the result was that he was wounded, in the thigh, by one of the Milesians. So, driven out of his own town, Histiaeus came back to Chios. From there, after failing to persuade the Chians to give him warships, he crossed over to Mytilene, where he did convince the men of Lesbos to provide them. Manning eight triremes, he and his men now sailed to Byzantium. There they stationed themselves, and

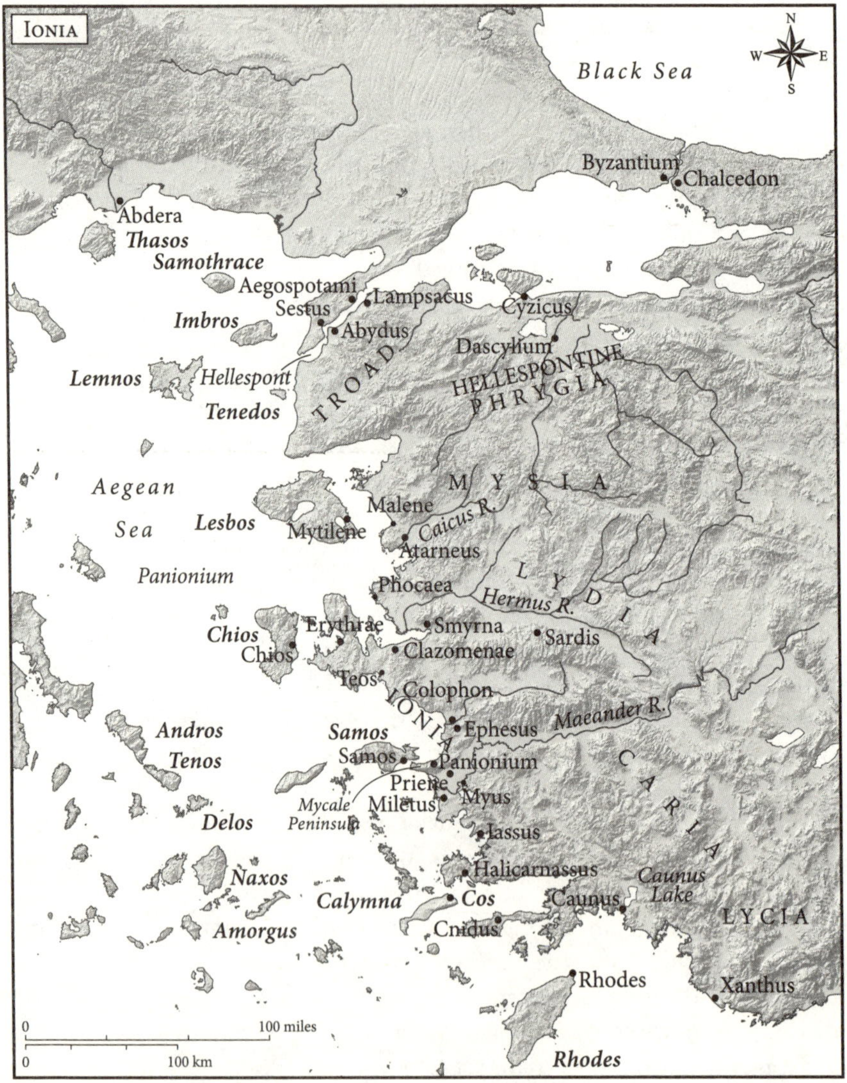

MAP 5.6

seized every ship that sailed down from the Black Sea—unless, that is, they declared themselves ready to accept Histiaeus as their commander.

Sea Battle at Lade and the Fall of Miletus

The sea battle here prefigures the battle of Salamis, which will be the decisive contest between Greeks and Persians in the great invasion to come. But at Salamis, almost all of the Ionian ships will be fighting on the Persian side, and it is in this scene that we start to understand how that situation came about. Throughout the revolt, we have seen the lack of any coordinated action or strategy on the part of the Ionians, but, ironically, as they here finally present a united front we are shown a near total absence of true commitment and strength of purpose. The scene involving Dionysius, in particular, repays scrutiny, as it functions as a sort of meditation on the hard work, discipline, and profound resolve necessary to achieve collective freedom in the face of tyranny, as well as the gulf between what freedom means for an individual and what it means for a people.

So much then about Histiaeus and the Mytileneans. Meanwhile, Miletus 6.6
was anticipating a large-scale attack by land and by sea. The Persian commanders, you see, had come together and combined forces into a single army, and were even now marching on Miletus, thinking the other cities less crucial. As for the navy, the Phoenicians were the most willing of the participants, but they were joined by sailors from Cyprus (recently conquered), Cilicia, and Egypt.[12]

Such then were the forces marshaled to attack Miletus and the rest of Ionia. 6.7
When the Ionians found out about it, they all sent delegates to gather at Panionium.[13] The delegates arrived and deliberated, and decided not to raise an army to oppose the Persians, but to let the Milesians use their walls to protect themselves by land; as for the fleet, however, they were to man every ship, omitting none, and gather as soon as they could at Lade, so as to protect the seaside of Miletus. (Lade is a small island situated near Miletus.)

So, the Ionians, and as many Aeolians as live on Lesbos, arrived with their 6.8
manned ships. Here's how they formed the battle line. The Milesians themselves held the east wing of the fleet, with eighty ships; next to them were the men of Priene, with twelve ships, and the men of Myus, with three ships; next to the Myesians were the men of Teos, with seventeen ships, and next to them the Chians, with a hundred. Next to these, the Erythraeans and Phocaeans were stationed, providing eight and three ships, respectively. Next to the Phocaeans were the Lesbians, with seventy ships, and at the end, holding the west wing, the Samians were stationed, with sixty ships. The total count of all the triremes was, then, three hundred and fifty-three.

These were the ships on the Ionian side; on the Persian side the ships num- 6.9
bered six hundred. But when the Persian ships arrived at Miletus (and the

12 These are the four great naval powers of the Persian empire, a formidable force.

13 The Panionium is a sacred sanctuary near Mycale where Ionian city-states would meet to consider collective action.

whole army with them), the Persian commanders learned the size of the Ionian fleet, and grew worried that they would not be able to defeat them at sea; and, without control of the sea, they could hardly capture Miletus—in which case the reprisal from Darius could be harsh. Such were their thoughts. So, they summoned the Ionian tyrants, the ones who, when Aristagoras deposed them, fled to the Medes—for these were with the army marching on Miletus. When they were all there, the Persian commanders spoke: "Men of Ionia, now is the time for you to make plain your good service to the king's household. We want each of you to try to split your countrymen from the rest of the Ionian alliance. Propose to them that, if they withdraw, they will suffer no harm from the rebellion, and neither their temples nor their houses will be burned, nor will they have any more constraint than they had before. But if they refuse, and go through with the battle, then tell them in no uncertain terms what will happen to them: when they are defeated, they will be enslaved; their boys we will castrate; their girls we will carry as captives to Bactra, at the far reaches of our empire; and we will distribute their land to some other people."

6.10 Thus spoke the Persians. So, that night each tyrant worked to get the message to his countrymen. The Ionians got these messages but stood firm, unwilling to yield to such treachery, even though each thought that they alone were getting this proposition from the Persians.

6.11 All this happened just after the Persians arrived at Miletus. But after that, the Ionians gathered at Lade held various councils, and at these, I suppose, many spoke, but most remarkable was what the Phocaean commander Dionysius had to say: "Men of Ionia, we have come to the tipping point, where we decide whether we are to be free men or slaves—and runaway slaves at that. Now if you are willing to accept hardship, in the short term you will have the pain of work, but you *will* be able to overcome the enemy and to be free. But if you are soft and irresolute, I have no hope for you—there is no way the king will not punish you for your rebellion. Come then, obey me, entrust yourselves to me. In return—as long as the gods treat us fairly—I expect that either the enemy will not fight, or if he does he will come off much the worse."

6.12 The Ionians listened and decided to entrust themselves to Dionysius. Every day, he led the ships into the battle line, so that he could have the oarsmen practice the "sailing through" maneuver, and the marines practice bearing their heavy armor; and for the rest of the day he had the ships sit at anchor in the hot sun. Thus did the Ionians get hardship all the day long. For seven days, they obeyed him and did what they were told. But on the eighth day the Ionians, not used to such discipline, and worn out by the hard work and constant sun, began to talk among themselves: "Which of the gods did we offend that we have to put up with *this*? Have we lost our minds? Surely we are crazy to have entrusted ourselves to this loudmouthed Phocaean charlatan—a man who comes here with only three ships! Since taking command, he has treated us so brutally that we'll never recover: many of us are already ill, and many more likely will be. It would be better to suffer anything other than what we suffer now—better to

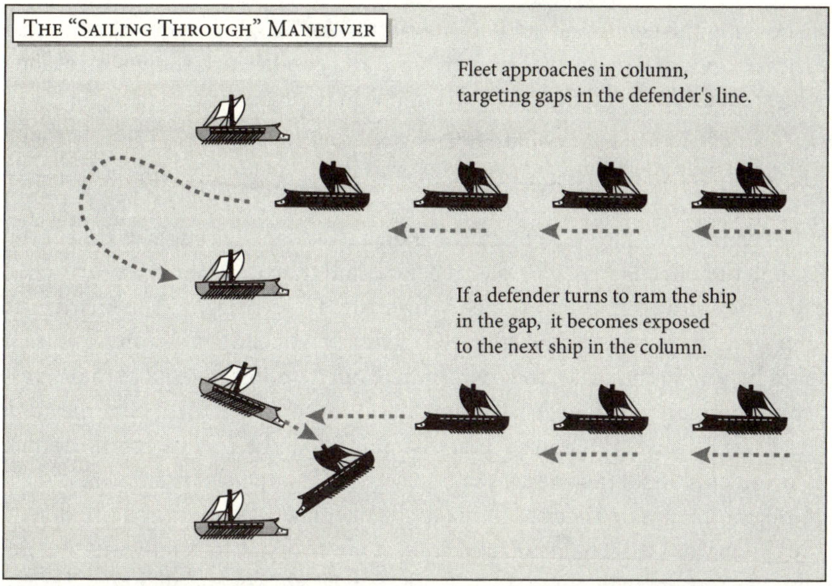

FIGURE 6.1 The "sailing through" maneuver (*diekplous*) consisted of breaking through the enemy line and then turning suddenly so as to ram the ship from behind

wait and see what some future slavery might bring than to put up with the slavery already upon us. Come, let's not listen to him any more." Such were the things they said, and from that day no one would obey Dionysius. Instead, they set up tents on the island, like an army camp, so that they could have shade, and were no longer willing to man the ships or to practice.

When the Samian commanders heard what the sailors were doing, they 6.13
decided to accept the proposal from Aeaces son of Syloson—the one that Aeaces had sent earlier at the Persians' bidding, suggesting that they abandon the Ionian alliance. Not only could they see that the Ionian cause was in considerable disarray, but they also thought it obvious that it was impossible to defeat the king: they understood full well that if Darius's present fleet was defeated, they would face another, fivefold the size. So, when they saw the Ionians unwilling to cooperate, they seized on this as their excuse, thinking it more expedient to act to protect their own temples and houses. (Aeaces, the one who sent the Samians the proposal, was the son of Syloson son of Aeaces, and he had been the tyrant of Samos before he, like all the other Ionian tyrants, was deposed by Aristagoras of Miletus.)

Now when the Phoenician ships began their attack, the Ionians put out to 6.14
sea with their ships in battle formation. They approached each other and joined battle, but from there I am not able to record accurately which of the Ionians were brave men in the fighting, and which cowards—for they all blame everyone else. It is said, though, that the Samians, just as they had agreed with Aeaces, raised their masts and sailed away from their station, back to Samos—all except eleven ships. The captains of these eleven stayed and fought,

disobeying the commanders. Because of this the people at Samos engraved a stele in honor of the captains, as men brave and good, listing their names along with their fathers'; and that stele still stands in the marketplace there.

But meanwhile the men of Lesbos saw the Samians, who were next to them, sailing away, and so they did the same. And then most of the Ionians followed this lead.

6.15 Of those who stayed to fight, the Chians had far the roughest time, even though their deeds were glorious to behold and they were not in any way cowards. They provided, as mentioned before, a hundred ships, and on board each ship were forty men, picked from the citizenry. When they saw most of their allies betraying the cause, they determined not to follow the lead of these cowards, but to sail out alone, with only a few allies, and fight. And fight they did, breaking through the enemy line and ramming their ships, until, despite taking a number of the enemy's ships, they had lost most of their own.

6.16 So, the Chians fled back to their own land with what ships they had left. And the Chian ships that could not follow, being too crippled, took refuge in Mycale, with the Persians in pursuit. There they beached the ships and abandoned them, and made their way overland by foot. But when in the course of their journey the Chians reached the territory of Ephesus, it was nighttime, and the women were celebrating the festival of the Thesmophoria.[14] The men of Ephesus, knowing nothing of what had happened to the Chians, saw this armed force crossing their borders and assumed that they were marauders coming after the women—and so they marched out in full force and killed the Chians.

6.17 Such then were the misfortunes that beset the Chians. The Phocaean commander Dionysius, meanwhile, once he understood that the Ionian cause was lost, captured three of the enemy warships and sailed, not to Phocaea (since he knew full well that it would be enslaved just like the rest of Ionia) but as directly as he could to Phoenicia. There he sunk several merchant ships and seized a lot of money, and then sailed to Sicily. He established himself as a pirate, working out of Sicily, but never robbing a Greek—only Carthaginians and Tyrrhenians.

6.18 Once the Persians had defeated the Ionians in the sea battle, they besieged Miletus by land and sea, digging under the walls and bringing to bear siege engines of every kind. And they captured it, citadel and all, in the sixth year from the rebellion started by Aristagoras.[15] They then enslaved the city, and with this the prophecy that had been given Miletus was fulfilled.

6.19 The Argives, you see, had asked the oracle at Delphi about the safety of their own city, to which a double oracle was given, the first having to do with the Argives, but with a second added for the Milesians. I'll report about the one having to do with the Argives when I get to that part of the story, but about the Milesians (who were not present) the prophecy went like this: *O Miletus, contriver of evils, a time will come / when you will provide a feast and*

14 A religious festival in honor of Demeter and her daughter Persephone.

15 494 BC.

shining gifts for the host / of long-haired men whose feet your women will bathe; / and others will tend to our temple in Didyma. And that was what now befell the Milesians: most of their men were killed by the Persians, men who wear their hair long; the women and children were made captives; and in the sanctuary at Didyma both temple and oracle were plundered and burned. . . .

After the sea battle for Miletus, the Phoenicians at the Persians' bidding restored Aeaces son of Syloson as tyrant of Samos, a man of much importance to them because of the great service he had rendered. And because in the battle their ships had deserted, the Samians alone among the rebellious states had neither their city nor their temples burned by Darius. Also, as soon as Miletus had fallen, the Persians occupied Caria, with some of the cities surrendering of their own accord, and others added by force. 6.25

The Fate of Histiaeus

That, then, is how all that came about. But meanwhile Histiaeus of Miletus, who had been settled in Byzantium seizing all the Ionian merchant ships sailing out from the Black Sea, got the news of what had happened at Miletus. So, he handed over what he was doing at the Hellespont to Bisaltes of Abydos, son of Apollophanes, and he himself took the Lesbians under his command and sailed to Chios.[16] When the Chian outpost at that part of Chios called the Hollows did not let him pass, he joined battle and killed a great many. And as for the rest of the Chian force—which had been much weakened in the sea battle—Histiaeus and his Lesbians overmastered them too, using the town of Polichne as his base. 6.26

The divine, it seems, is wont to give forewarning, when a great evil is to come about for a city or a people. And to be sure the Chians had had great forewarnings before all this. They sent to Delphi a chorus of a hundred youths, but only two of them came back home—the other ninety-eight were taken by the plague and died. Also at the same time in the city, a little before the sea battle, a roof collapsed upon children studying their letters, such that out of one hundred and twenty schoolchildren only one escaped. Such were the signs the god gave in advance. Thereafter, the calamity of the sea battle brought the city to its knees. And following that came Histiaeus with the men of Lesbos, who easily overpowered the beleaguered Chians. 6.27

Histiaeus next sailed against Thasos, in command of a great many Ionians and Aeolians. But while he was besieging Thasos a message came that the Phoenicians were sailing from Miletus to attack the rest of Ionia. When he heard this, Histiaeus left Thasos uncaptured, and hurried to Lesbos with his army. But the army was starving, so from Lesbos he crossed over to the mainland, to harvest the grain from Atarneus and the Mysian part of the Caïcus plain. But as it happened Harpagus, the Persian general, was there, with a 6.28

16 The unlucky Chians are the Greeks who originally took in Histiaeus when he fled the Persian court and joined the revolt.

large army. After they landed, Harpagus attacked them and took Histiaeus alive, destroying a great part of his army.

6.29 Now the way that Histiaeus was captured alive was this. The Greeks had battled the Persians at Malene, in the territory of Atarneus, for a long time, but then the cavalry, arriving late, swooped down and fell upon the Greeks. This action proved decisive: the Greeks turned and ran away. But Histiaeus didn't expect the king to kill him for his present transgression, and so showed a craven love of life. As he was running away, he was caught by a Persian, and even as the Persian was about to put him to the sword, he spoke out—using the Persian tongue—making it clear that it was he, Histiaeus, the Milesian.

6.30 If now he had been brought as a captive to the court of Darius, he would not have suffered any great harm, or so it seems to me, and Darius would have forgiven his crime. But as it was, precisely because of that—so that he could not escape and become an important man at the king's court again—Artaphrenes, the satrap of Sardis, and Harpagus, the one who had caught him, had him impaled as soon as he arrived at Sardis. His head they mummified, and this they sent to King Darius in Susa. When Darius heard what had happened, he greatly blamed those who had done this, because they did not bring him alive back to his sight. He ordered them to wash and adorn the head of Histiaeus, and to bury it with due care, as that of a man who had rendered much great service to Persia and its king.

The Final Subjugation of Ionia

6.31 That then was the end of Histiaeus. Now meanwhile the Persian fleet had stayed the winter in Miletus. Putting out to sea the following year[17] they easily captured the islands that lie near the mainland, Chios and Lesbos and Tenedos. And whenever they captured an island, the Persians would round up all the people. This is how they do that. Every man holds the hand of another in a line from the north coast down to the south, and then they walk across the entire island, flushing everybody out. Similarly, the Persians captured the Ionian cities on the mainland, but there they didn't round up all the people, it not being logistically possible.

6.32 Then the Persian commanders did not fail to make good what they had threatened the Ionians, back when the armies were encamped opposite one another. As the cities came under their control, they selected the most comely of the boys and castrated them, making them eunuchs instead of men. The most beautiful girls they sent as captives to the king. And once they had done that, they burned the cities to the ground along with the temples. And so for a third time the Ionians were enslaved: first by the Lydians, and then twice in succession[18] by the Persians. . . .

17 493 BC.

18 The first Persian subjugation of the Ionians was by Cyrus after he overthrew Croesus and took Sardis.

BOOK 6 (CONTINUED)

The First Invasion of Greece: Mardonius and Marathon

By 493 the Persians had dealt sufficiently with the Ionians, and Darius's attention returns to the need to punish Athens and Eretria on the mainland, in retaliation for their involvement in the burning of Sardis. As the paradigm of the Ionian Revolt has shown us, the question of unity is paramount in countering the Persians, both in terms of concerted action between city-states and in the dangers inherent to internal strife. The dangers of factionalism will be highlighted by the fatal result that the lack of internal unity brings to Eretria (6.100), and the same danger of disunity is latent in Athenian politics as well (6.109). What sets Athens apart is that it has now rid itself of tyrants and has established a flourishing democracy, hardly ideal (recall that they can easily be fooled: 5.97) but founded on the sound principle of equality among men. The Athenians therefore can stand and fight the Persians as equals. We sense that Greek freedom hinges on Athenian freedom, even as we are led to reflect further on what freedom entails. As for coordinated action, the ready agreement by Sparta (a traditional rival) to come to aid the Athenians is as encouraging as their delay in doing so is frustrating. The tension over whether the Greeks can retain a sense of national purpose will become a dominant theme in the books to follow.

Herodotus from this point now writes a different sort of history. The actions are well known—the Athenians trumpet their victory at Marathon as often as they can—and near contemporary, and he will have had access to many who lived through these events. (Herodotus was probably born in the decade following the battle.) The narrative becomes different too: more linear in its movement, less prone to digression (though there are some significant sections on earlier Athenian history that we skip over), more neutrally descriptive. Largely dropped from the text are those characteristic markers of uncertainty or active inquiry ("so they say," "my narrative forces me to inquire") that, earlier, drew constant attention to the problems of access to historical truth. The narrator, that is, starts now to resemble more the sort of third-person persona that Thucydides and future historians will adopt as the quietly authoritative voice of the *historian*.

The Invasion of Europe: Mardonius's Misadventure

Note that the first great loss suffered by the Persian fleet comes by a sort of divine intervention. The puzzle of why Mardonius dethrones the tyrants and establishes democracy in Ionia is perhaps best resolved so: democracy under continuing Persian domination leads to lack of strong leaders and true mob rule (as the Constitutional Debate tells us: 3.81–82); by contrast, democracy strengthens the Athenians, who are actually free and thus can foster leaders who are not tyrants.

6.43 The next spring,[1] King Darius dismissed the other generals and appointed Mardonius son of Gobryas, a young man recently married to his daughter Artozostra, to march down to the sea with a very large army and a large fleet as well. When Mardonius, at the head of this army, reached Cilicia, he got into one of the warships and traveled with the fleet, while other commanders marched the foot soldiers to the Hellespont. So, Mardonius sailed along the coast of Asia, and when he got to Ionia, he did something utterly astonishing—or so Greeks would think who do not accept that Otanes presented to the Seven his view that Persia ought to be a democracy:[2] Mardonius deposed the Ionian tyrants and made the cities democracies. After that, he hurried on his way to the Hellespont. And when a great number of ships, and a great many foot soldiers, were collected there, they used the ships to cross the Hellespont and marched into Europe, heading for Eretria and Athens.

6.44 Eretria and Athens were, at any rate, the excuse for the expedition. But really they had in mind to conquer as many Greek cities as they could. The fleet conquered Thasos without encountering resistance; and the army added the Macedonians to its bounty of slaves. (The peoples east of Macedonia were already their subjects.) From Thasos the fleet sailed along the southern coast of Europe as far as Acanthus, and setting forth from there, they tried to round the cape at Mt. Athos. But as they sailed round the cape a great, violent wind from the north fell upon them, more than the ships could manage, tossing them about and driving many a ship upon the mountain. Three hundred ships were lost, it is said, and over twenty thousand men. The sea round about Athos is infested with sharks, and so some were caught and eaten, while others were dashed against the rocks. Moreover, some did not know how to swim and died because of that; and yet others died from the cold.

6.45 While that was happening to the fleet, Mardonius and his army were encamped in Macedonia, where they were ambushed at night by the Brygi, Thracian men. The Brygi killed a great many of them, and wounded Mardonius himself. Even so the Brygi did not escape slavery at the hands of the Persians—Mardonius did not leave these lands before making them his subjects. Still, after conquering them, he led his forces back, in the face of the disaster visited upon the army by the Brygi, and the very great disaster inflicted on the fleet at Athos. And so the expedition, marred by these ugly setbacks, returned to Asia in disgrace. . . .

1 492 BC.

2 In the Constitutional Debate, at 3.80.

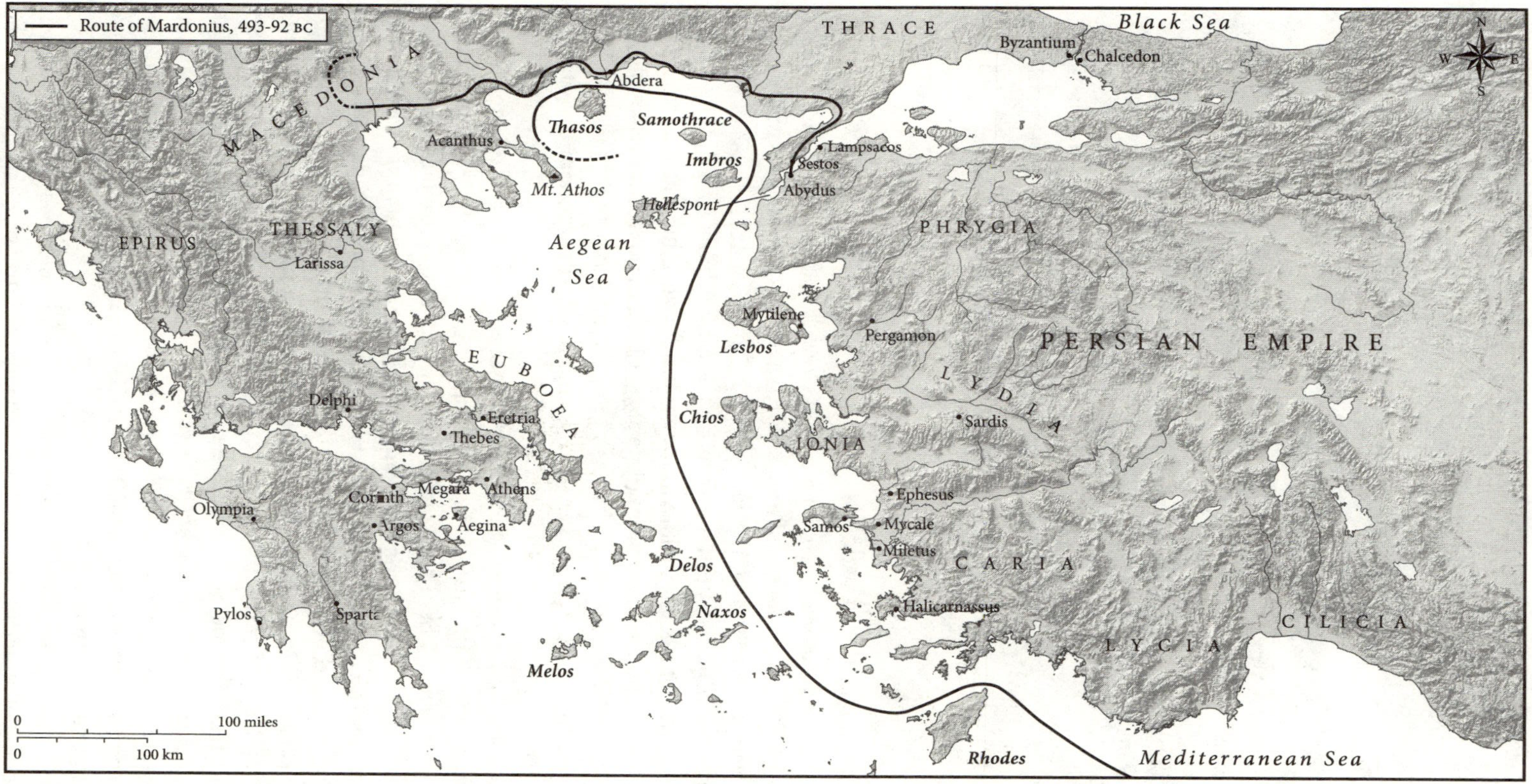
Route of Mardonius, 493-92 BC
N
E
S
W
THRACE
Black Sea
Byzantium
Chalcedon
MACEDONIA
Abdera
Thasos
Samothrace
Imbros
Acanthus
Mt. Athos
Hellespont
Lampsacos
Sestos
Abydus
THESSALY
EPIRUS
Larissa
Aegean
Sea
PHRYGIA
Mytilene
Lesbos
Pergamon
PERSIAN EMPIRE
EUBOEA
LYDIA
Delphi
Eretria
Thebes
Chios
Sardis
IONIA
Corinth
Megara
Athens
Olympia
Argos
Aegina
Ephesus
Samos
Mycale
Miletus
CARIA
Delos
Pylos
Sparta
Naxos
Halicarnassus
CILICIA
LYCIA
Melos
0
100 miles
0
100 km
Rhodes
Mediterranean Sea

MAP 6.1

FIGURE 6.2 Mt. Athos

Subjugation of the Cyclades

Delos, notionally at the center of the ring of Greek islands known as the Cyclades, was, with Delphi, the holiest of sites, said to be the place where Leto gave birth to the Olympians Apollo and Artemis.

6.94 Since Mardonius had done such a poor job with his expedition, Darius relieved him of his command, and appointed two other generals to attack Eretria and Athens: his nephew, Artaphrenes son of Artaphrenes, and Datis, who was a Mede. He sent off these two, giving them their orders, "Take Athens and Eretria captive, enslave the men, and bring them back for me to see."

6.95 So, the two appointed generals made their way from the king's court to the Aleian plain in Cilicia, each bringing with him a large and well-equipped army. There the soldiers encamped, and to each army came an entire fleet, as well as transport ships for the horses, which the year before Darius had bid his subjects get ready. The transport ships took on the horses, the soldiers went aboard the others, and with six hundred ships they set sail for Ionia. From there they did not, however, keep close to the mainland, sailing straight for the Hellespont and Thrace, but, once they set out from Samos, they made their way across the Icarian Sea through the Cyclades, mostly (or so it seems to me) out of fear of the cape at Mt. Athos—it was rounding that cape when, the year before, they had met with such a great disaster. And, beside that, Naxos forced their hand, since it had yet to be captured.

6.96 Once the Persians had crossed the Icarian Sea and reached Naxos (their plan being to attack Naxos first), the Naxians, mindful of what had happened

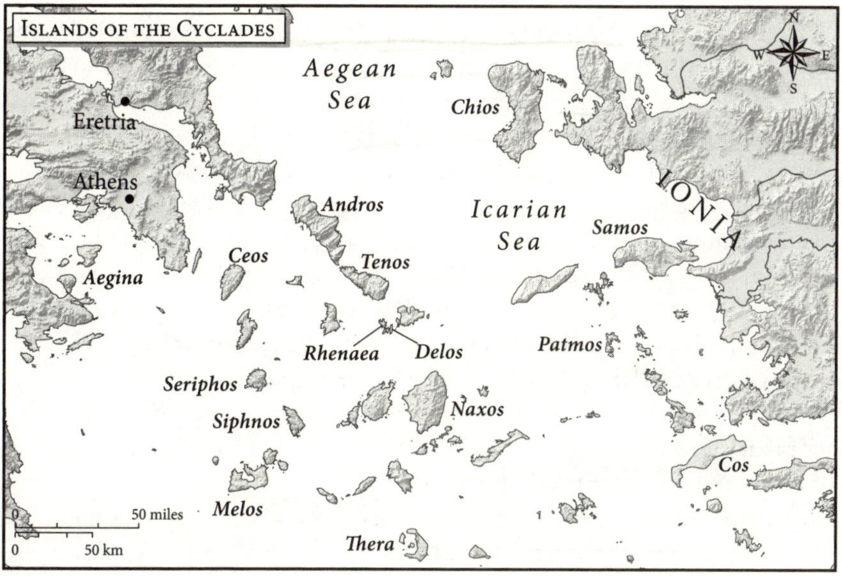

MAP 6.2

earlier,[3] fled to the mountains, not staying to fight; and so the Persians captured everyone they could find, and set fire to the temples and the city. With that done, they set sail for the other islands.

While the Persians were busy with Naxos, the Delians abandoned Delos 6.97
and fled to Tenos. As the Persian fleet was making its way, Datis, who was in the lead, forbid the ships from putting in at Delos; instead, he made them anchor across the way, at Rhenaea. And when he found out where the Delians were, he sent a messenger to tell them this: "Men of sacred ground, why do you flee? You judge me wrongly. What I myself think and what the king commands is this: in this land the two gods were born,[4] and so we will harm nothing, neither the land itself nor its inhabitants. So, now, go back to your homes and live on the island." Such was his message to the Delians, and afterward he heaped up and burned upon the altar three hundred talents of costly incense.

FIGURE 6.3 Delos

Once that was done, Datis 6.98
sailed with his army to attack Eretria first, bringing along with him Ionians and Aeolians. After

3 See 6.32 for the Persians' brutal treatment of the Ionian cities that had rebelled.

4 Apollo and Artemis.

he had sailed away, Delos was struck by an earthquake—and according to the Delians, this was something Delos, neither before nor after, at least up to my time, had ever experienced. The god sent this portent, I suppose, to make manifest the ills that were about to fall upon mankind. Indeed, in the time of Darius son of Hystaspes and Xerxes son of Darius and Artaxerxes son of Xerxes—three successive generations—more evils befell Greece than in the twenty generations that came before, some at the hands of the Persians, and others at the hands of the leading Greek states as they warred for dominion.[5] Thus it was no great wonder that an earthquake shook Delos, something it had not previously experienced. Besides, there was an oracle in which it was written, *I will make Delos quake, Delos which has never quaked before*. . . .

6.99 Sailing from Delos, the Persians put in at the islands, where they conscripted soldiers and took the islanders' children as hostages. Once the circuit of the islands was complete, they put in also at Carystus, a Euboean city, where the citizens would not give hostages and said they could not join the fight against their neighbors—by which they meant Eretria and Athens. There the Persians laid siege and razed the land until the Carystians were persuaded to their point of view.

Subjugation of Eretria

The quick siege of Eretria could be a tale of the formidable might of the Persians, but becomes instead a tale of betrayal. Either way, the swift conclusion to this part of the campaign bodes ill for Athens.

6.100 Now when the Eretrians learned that a Persian force was sailing against them, they asked the Athenians for help. And the Athenians did not refuse the alliance: they sent in support four thousand citizens who had been given the land of the wealthy Chalcidians.[6] But even though they had sent to Athens, the Eretrians had no sound strategy, for they were of two minds. Part of the citizenry planned to abandon the city for the highlands of Euboea; while others, looking out for themselves and expecting a reward from the Persians, were plotting betrayal. But one man, Aeschines son of Nothon, the finest of the Eretrians, when he found out about these plans, went to the Athenians as soon as they arrived and told them how things stood. He concluded: "Go back to your own land; otherwise, you die." And the Athenians followed Aeschines' advice.

6.101 So, the Athenians crossed over to Oropus and saved themselves. Meanwhile the Persians landed their ships at Tamynae and Choereae and Aegilia, all in Eretrian territory; and, having secured these places, they immediately got the

5 Probably a reference to the early years of the Peloponnesian War between Athens and Sparta (431–404 BC) though the so-called "First Peloponnesian War" (460–445 BC) may also be in view. Darius reigned 522–486, Xerxes 486–465, and Artaxerxes 465–424.

6 In an earlier action (in 506 BC), Athens after defeating Chalcis seized the land of its wealthiest citizens and distributed it to these 4,000 citizens. Since Chalcis is adjacent to Eretria, this is a logical deployment.

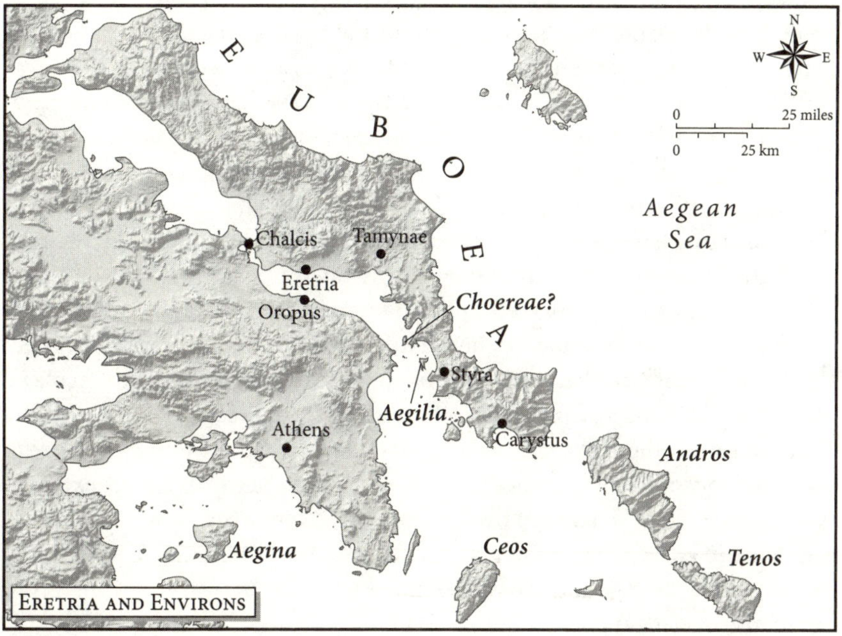

MAP 6.3

horses off the ships and prepared to engage the enemy. But the Eretrians had no desire to come out and fight—"if only the walls can protect us!" was their only concern, now that the plan to leave the city had been abandoned. Many on both sides fell over the next six days as the Persians attacked the walls in force; and on the seventh day, Euphorbus son of Alcimachus and Philagrus son of Cyneas, both citizens of good repute, betrayed the city to the Persians. When the Persians entered the city they looted the temples and set them ablaze, in reprisal for the burning of the temples in Sardis, and they enslaved the men, as Darius had commanded. Having overpowered Eretria, the 6.102
Persians rested for a few days; then they sailed to the land of Attica, supposing that, with much already accomplished, they would do to the Athenians what they had just done to the Eretrians.

The Battle of Marathon

This classic David and Goliath story is framed as one of Athenian resolve, which interestingly, however, hangs on the slender thread of one man's vote and another man's ability to persuade. The fragility of the Athenians' critical decision to stand and fight for freedom is thereby highlighted.

ATHENS ASKS SPARTA FOR HELP

Marathon was the most suitable part of Attica for cavalry maneuvers and also closest to Eretria, so it was to that spot that Hippias the son of Peisistratus

6.103 guided the Persians. When the Athenians got news of the landing, they too marched out to Marathon. Ten generals led them, and the tenth of these was
6.105 Miltiades. . . . But before they left the city, the generals had sent a messenger to Sparta, named Philippides, an Athenian man, specially trained as a long-distance runner. This was the man whom once the god Pan fell upon near Mt. Parthenium above Tegea (as Philippides himself claimed and reported to the Athenians). The god, he said, shouted out " Philippides!" and bid him proclaim these words to the Athenians: "Why do you pay me no heed? I look upon you kindly, and I have often helped you in the past, and will help you in the future." The Athenians believed him and so, once prosperity returned, they set up an altar to Pan next to the Acropolis, and, because of this message, they honor Pan every year with sacrifices and a torch race.

6.106 It was this Philippides, the one who said that Pan had appeared to him, who now was sent off by the Athenian generals, reaching Sparta the next day.[7] Arriving there, he declared to the magistrates: "Men of Sparta, the Athenians ask that you come to their aid and not allow the oldest of Greek cities to fall into slavery at the hands of the barbarians. As it is, Eretria is now captured and her men enslaved, and Greece is weakened by the loss of a noble town." Such were his words, as he had been commanded. The Spartans were happy to lend aid to the Athenians, but (they explained) it was impossible for them to do so immediately, since they were unwilling to relax their custom—it was the ninth of the month, and custom forbade them march to war until the fifteenth, when the cycle of the moon was complete.[8]

HIPPIAS HAS A DREAM VISION

Hippias was a son of Peisistratus, the tyrant of Athens we met in book 1, and was himself tyrant from 527 until the Athenians expelled him in 510. He assists the Persian forces in hopes of being reinstated.

6.107 So, the Spartans awaited the full moon. As for the Persians, they were being guided to Marathon by Hippias the son of Peisistratus. In the passing of the night, Hippias saw a vision in his sleep: he dreamed that he lay in bed with his own mother. By his analysis, the dream meant that he was to descend on Athens and win back the rule, and thus grow to an old age in the bosom of his motherland—that was his interpretation. The next day, acting as guide and leader for the Persian force, he first landed the prisoners from Eretria on the Styrean island called Aegilia, and then he brought the ships to Marathon, where he had them anchor. He then had the troops go ashore and get into battle formation. But as he was working on this, an unusually violent sneezing

7 That is, he ran there, able to do so by virtue of his special training, a distance of 150 miles. Later writers had this same Philippides (under the variant name Phidippides) run from Marathon to the city of Athens after the battle, to announce to the citizens their victory—whereupon, they say, he died from exhaustion. It is that tale that led to our name for the long-distance race, Marathon to Athens being a distance conventionally measured at 26.2 miles.

8 The battle happened to fall during the festival of the Carneia, during which Spartans and other Dorian Greeks held back from warfare; the festival lasted from the seventh of the month through to the full moon.

and coughing came upon him, and, as an older man, several of his teeth were loose—and a particularly strong cough made one fall out. It fell in the sand, and he took great pains to find it; but the tooth was nowhere to be seen. Groaning, he then said to those around him, "This land is not ours, and we will not be able to bring it under our sway: whatever share I had in it now rests with the tooth, which lies in its motherland." It was by this means, then, that 6.108
Hippias thought the dream vision fulfilled.

THE PLATAEANS ARRIVE TO HELP

Meanwhile, the Athenian troops had mustered at the area sacred to Heracles when the Plataeans joined them in full force. The Plataeans, you see, had put themselves under the protection of Athens, and the Athenians had already done much work on their behalf. This is the story of how they became allies. The Plataeans were being threatened by the men of Thebes. They first asked Cleomenes son of Anaxandrides and his Lacedaemonians[9] to protect them. These, however, dismissed the request, saying this: "We live far away, and such an alliance would bring cold comfort to you. You could be enslaved many times over before any of us so much as heard of it. We advise you therefore to ask the Athenians for protection, who are your neighbors, and no cowards if you need help." Such was the Lacedaemonian advice—but not out of good will; rather, they wanted the Athenians to bear the burden of fighting the

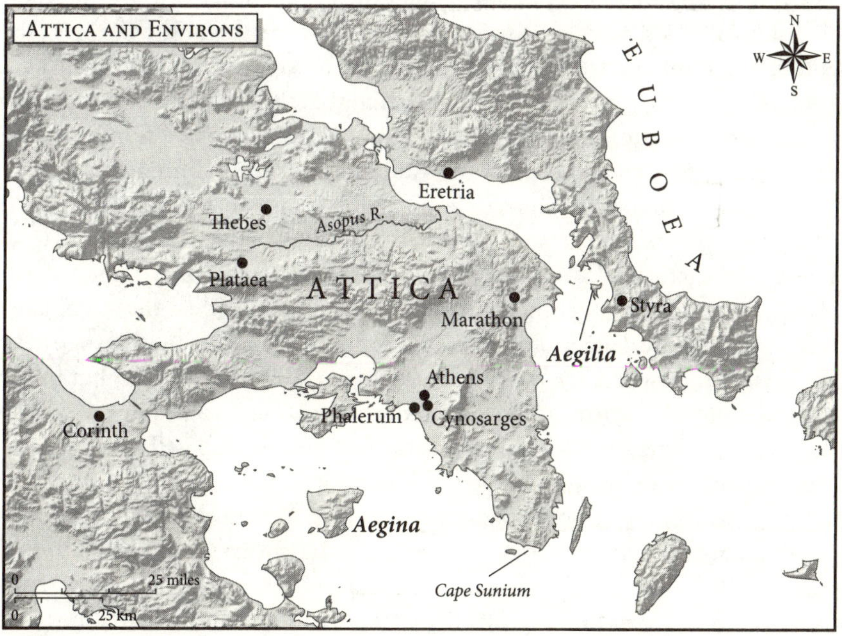

MAP 6.4

9 Lacedaemonian is an alternate name for a Spartan.

Boeotians. The Plataeans thought this a good plan. So, just as the Athenians were making sacrifice to the twelve Olympian gods in the city center, the Plataeans sat themselves as suppliants at the altar, and asked the Athenians for protection. When the Thebans heard this, they marched at once on Plataea—and the Athenians came to their aid. But even as they were about to join battle, the Corinthians (who chanced to be there) intervened. They negotiated a truce and with trust from both sides they set a boundary line between the two, but on the proviso that any Boeotians who so chose not be forced into the Theban-led coalition. The Corinthians, having so resolved the matter, left for home. The Athenians were on their way home too when the Thebans and Boeotians ambushed them—but in the battle the Athenians got much the better of it. The Athenians then crossed the border that the Corinthians had set for Plataea, and declared the river Asopus the boundary between Theban territory and the land of Plataea and Hysiae. That, then, is the story of how the Plataeans came to be allies with the Athenians. And so it was that they now came to Marathon to help.

MILTIADES URGES THE ATHENIANS TO STAY AND FIGHT

Note that the choice Miltiades presents for Athens is not merely between slavery and freedom, but between slavery and weakness, on the one hand, and freedom and power, on the other.

6.109 Now the Athenian generals were of two minds: some were against joining battle, thinking they were too few to fight the Persian force, while others, including Miltiades, were all for it. So, opinion was split, and the cowardly option was gaining the upper hand. There was, however, an eleventh who had a vote, the one chosen by lot as the polemarch (back then the polemarch had a vote along with the generals), and at this time Callimachus, a man of the Aphidnae deme, held the post. To Callimachus, then, Miltiades turned, saying this: "All now rests on you, Callimachus—it is yours to decide whether Athens will be enslaved, or whether it will be free, allowing us thereby to leave a memory that will last as long as mankind survives, such as not even Harmodius and Aristogeiton left.[10] Now is the moment when the Athenians face their greatest danger of all time: if they are laid low by the Persians, we know what they will suffer when they are handed over to Hippias; but if the city itself prevails, it can become supreme among the Greek states. How all this can be, and how yours has become the deciding voice, I will now explain. We ten generals are equally divided in our opinion: half are urging battle, and half are against it. If we do not fight now, I foresee the rise of factionalism, terrible infighting that will so shake Athenian courage that we will yield to the Persians. But if we fight—before the rot of discord sets in—and the gods treat us fairly, we can beat them in this battle. All now depends on you, it rests in

10 The tyrant slayers whose act conventionally marked the moment when the Athenians were delivered from one-man rule and became "free."

your hands. If you follow my advice, the fatherland will be free and the city the first among the Greeks. But if you go with those advising against the fight, you will get exactly the opposite."

With these words Miltiades won over Callimachus; and, with the 6.110
polemarch's vote in support, the resolution to join the fight prevailed. Thereafter, the generals who had supported the decision handed over to Miltiades their days of command (otherwise, the command would rotate daily). Miltiades accepted this, but still waited until his own day of command to launch the attack.

FIGURE 6.4 Hoplites running into battle. The shield-to-shield formation known as the *phalanx* was adopted by Greek armies in the 8th or 7th century BC and proved decisive at Marathon against the Persians, whose own shorter weapons and lighter armor proved no match for the long swords and spears of the tightly coordinated and heavily armed Greeks. In this magnificent depiction, we see the devastating charge that a phalanx formation could manage when it got within the enemy's arrow range. Black-figure Attic vase from the 6th century BC

THE BATTLE IS JOINED

6.111 When Miltiades' day came, the Athenians formed their battle line: the polemarch, Callimachus, led the right wing (as was customary then), and the Athenian tribes were arranged in the stipulated order one right after the other; and at the end the Plataeans were arrayed, holding the left wing—and ever since the time of this battle, whenever the Athenians celebrate with sacrifices the great quadrennial festivals, the Athenian herald lifts a prayer, that all things good come to the Athenians and Plataeans alike. So, at that time, in Marathon, the Athenians drew up their battle line, and it worked out like this: their army was ranged in a line equal in length to that of the Persians, and though their middle was thin in the ranks (here then was the weakest part of the line), each of the wings was in full force.

6.112 So, the battle lines were formed, and the sacrificial omens proved favorable. The Athenians, as soon as the commanders let them go, hurled themselves at a dead run against the barbarians, even though the distance between the armies was no less than eight stades.[11] The Persians saw them coming at a run, and prepared to meet the attack, but thought the Athenians crazy, even suicidal, being few and yet attacking at a dead run, without any horse or archers to support them. That at any rate was what the barbarians thought. But the Athenians, once they all managed to close with the barbarians, fought remarkably. To my knowledge, they were the first of the Greeks to use the dead run as a war tactic, and they too were the first to meet the Persians undaunted by their strange look and odd clothing—before that, even hearing

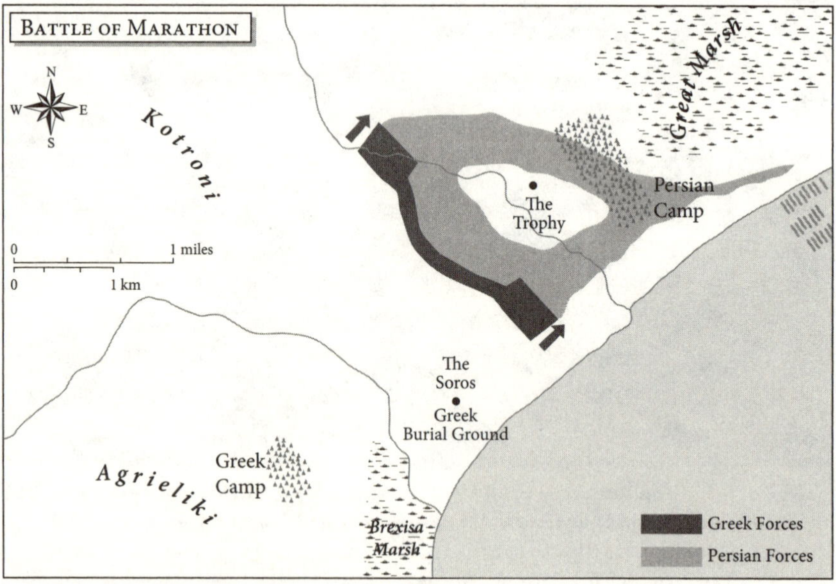

FIGURE 6.5 Battle of Marathon

11 Almost a mile (1½ km), a long way given the weight of the armor.

the name of the Persians brought fear to the Greeks.

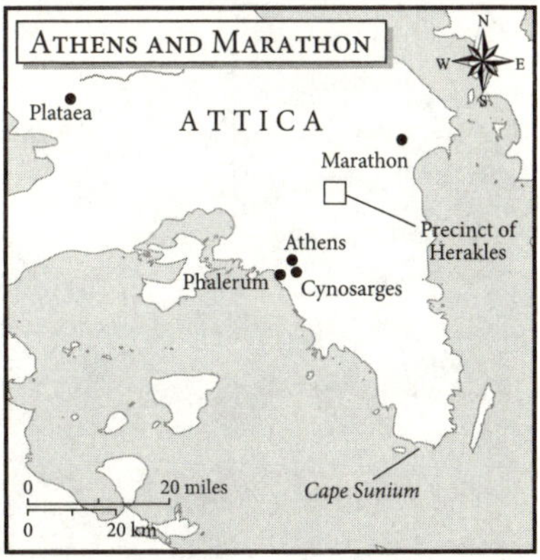

MAP 6.5

6.113 Long did the fighting go on at Marathon. The middle of the line was taken by the barbarians, where the Persians themselves fought alongside the Sacae, and when they broke through they chased after the Greeks, heading inland. At the wings, however, the Athenians and Plataeans prevailed, and when the barbarians turned and fled they let them go. Bringing together their two wings, the Greeks then turned to fight the part of the Persian force that had broken through the middle line; and the Athenians proved victorious. The Greeks chased after the Persians, cutting them down as they fled, and when they got to the sea they called for torches and started grabbing the ships.

6.114 It was in this action that the polemarch died, fighting bravely; as well as one of the generals, Stesilaus son of Thrasylaus. Cynegirus son of Euphorion[12] also fell, just as he was laying hold of a ship's figurehead, his hand cut off by an ax. And many other well-known Athenians also lost their lives.

6.115 In this fashion the Athenians took control of seven enemy ships. The rest, however, backed water and put out to sea, whereupon they picked up the Eretrian prisoners from Aegilia, and made sail round Cape Sunium, hoping to reach Athens before the Athenians got back. Rumor has it that the scheming of the Alcmaeonid clan was to blame for this strategy: it is said that they had arranged to signal the Persians once the ships were underway, by flashing with a shield.

So, the Persians rounded Cape Sunium, while the Athenians as quickly as their feet could carry them came back to the city to help—and they did get there before the barbarians arrived, relocating their camp from the precinct of Heracles at Marathon to that at Cynosarges. The Persians anchored their ships at Phalerum (this being the Athenian harbor at the time), and after riding at anchor for a while they sailed away, back to Asia.

6.117 At the battle of Marathon, six thousand four hundred died on the Persian side, and on the Athenian side one hundred ninety-two: such was the total count on both sides. A great wonder happened there, as it is reported: the Athenian Epizelus son of Cuphagoras was fighting bravely in the battle when he lost sight in both eyes, though his body was neither struck nor pierced; and for the rest of his life he was blind. I have heard that Epizelus tells this tale about his injury: a man appeared opposite him, huge and armed, whose beard covered his entire shield. The phantom passed him by, but killed the man next to him. This then is Epizelus's story, just as I heard it.

12 Brother of the famous tragedian Aeschylus.

DATIS RETURNS TO SUSA

FIGURE 6.6 Shadoof

6.118 So, Datis and his army were making their way to Asia, and when they stopped at the island of Myconos, Datis saw a vision in his sleep. What it was, no one says, but as soon as day broke, he had his men search the ships. There they found, in one of the Phoenician ships, a golden statue of Apollo. He asked which temple it had been taken from, and as soon as he found out he sailed to Delos in his own vessel. (The Delians had by that time returned to the island.) He set up the statue in the temple there and bid the Delians take the statue to Delium, a town belonging to Thebes, situated on the sea opposite Chalcis. So bidding, Datis then sailed away. But in fact the Delians did not bring back the statue; rather, the Thebans themselves returned it to Delium, twenty years later, at the behest of an oracle.

6.119 Now once Datis and Artaphrenes reached Asia with their ships, they marched the Eretrian prisoners of war inland to Susa. Before the Eretrians were taken captive, King Darius was terribly angry with them: it was the Eretrians, after all, who, earlier, had done the first wrong. But now, when he saw them led in, entirely at his mercy, he did them no further harm; instead, he settled them on some of his own land, at a place called Ardericca in Cissia, about two hundred and ten stades from Susa. That place was also about forty stades[13] from a kind of well that gives forth three substances: asphalt, salt, and a kind of oil. And here's how they get these from the well. A shadoof or sweep is used, but one with a bag from half a goatskin instead of a bucket. With the shadoof they scoop material from the well and then pour the contents into a tank; from this it flows into another in such a way that the constituents separate off into three different channels. The asphalt and the salt immediately turn hard. The oil, which the Persians call *rhadinace*, remains liquid. Such is the area where King Darius settled the Eretrians, and to my day they still lived there and have kept their old way of speaking. So much then for what happened to the Eretrians.

13 About 5 miles, 8 km.

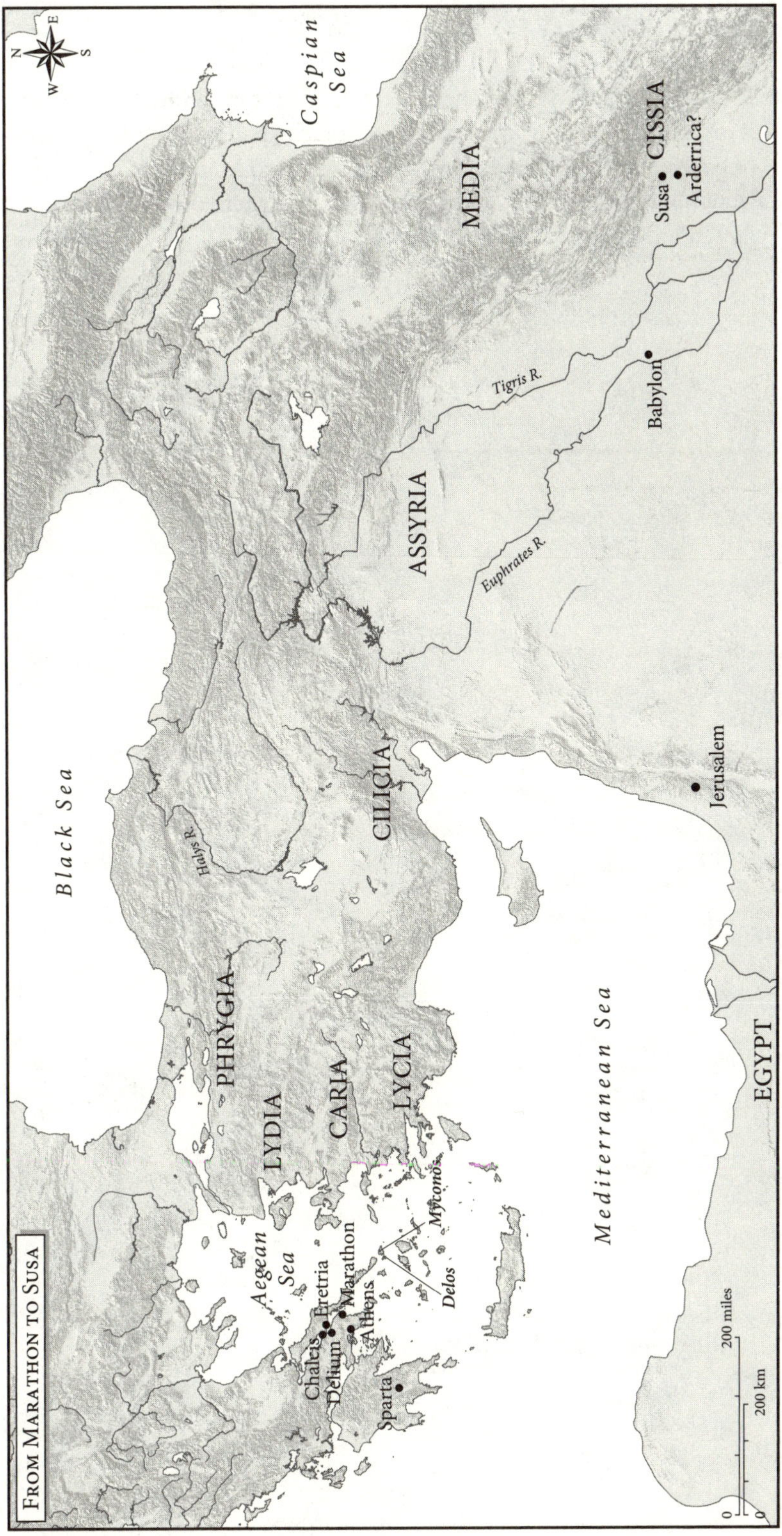
From Marathon to Susa
N
E
S
W
Caspian Sea
Black Sea
MEDIA
CISSIA
Susa
Arderrica?
Tigris R.
Babylon
ASSYRIA
Euphrates R.
Halys R.
CILICIA
Jerusalem
PHRYGIA
LYDIA
CARIA
LYCIA
Mediterranean Sea
EGYPT
Aegean Sea
Mykonos
Delos
Eretria
Marathon
Chalcis
Delium
Athens
Sparta
0
200 miles
0
200 km

MAP 6.6

THE SPARTANS ARRIVE

6.120 The Spartans did come to Athens, two thousand of them, once the moon was full; and so eager were they to get there in time, that they marched from Sparta to Attica in three days. They arrived too late for the battle, but wanted nonetheless to gaze upon the Persians. So, they marched to Marathon, and looked at the Persian dead. They then gave praise to the Athenians and their good work; whereupon they returned home.

BOOK 7
Xerxes Invades Greece

The invasion of Greece is the culmination of a host of earlier prefigurations, and thus revisits a long list of well-known themes and motifs. We are now trained to recognize many of these as anticipatory of disaster, such as the crossing of a water boundary, an insult to a god, the expression of greatness and display of excess, and so forth. It is perhaps worth remarking that just as Croesus was the fifth ruler from Gyges, so Xerxes is the fifth ruler from Croesus ("the man I myself know to have first initiated unjust deeds against the Greeks"—1.5). The three books describing the war with Greece and Xerxes's "fall" (books 7–9) have very much the sense of an ending, even as we also recognize the continuation of the various cycles (of reprisal, of rise and fall) that define the human condition.

Xerxes as King of Persia will embody the classic tragic dilemma: tradition and custom requires him, as the Great King, to display and exemplify greatness; but that very greatness inescapably marks him for reversal. As is typical, even this core theme is overdetermined: we now understand both that the cycle of human affairs is such that what was great in time becomes small, just as what is small can become great (a lesson we learned way back at chapter 1.5); and we also know that to think too much of oneself is to suffer *hubris*, and that the divine reaction to *hubris* is retribution (Artabanus will speak eloquently to this at 7.10(5) below, but we were first introduced to this dynamic in the story of Croesus in book 1).

We know almost nothing of the Persian invasion from eastern sources, so Herodotus's account is both the earliest and defining account of the war. Interestingly, Herodotus chooses to frame much of the narrative through Xerxes's conversations with a trio of wise advisor figures: first his uncle Artabanus (countered by Mardonius), then the dethroned and exiled Spartan king Demaratus, and finally (in the battles that follow) his ally, the ruler of Halicarnassus, Artemisia. These conversations, as the events themselves, also continually invite the reader to recall earlier expressions of the themes raised, and the contexts and outcomes of similar historical events. The whole becomes thereby a richly woven set of intimations on how human history seems to work, much more therefore than the story of one war.

Darius Decides upon a Full-Scale Invasion

It is precisely the fact that Darius decides to invade in angry retribution that allows Xerxes, when he becomes king, to reevaluate the wisdom of this action. In these stories we come to see the forces beyond Xerxes's control, human and divine, that are needed to convince—compel—him to act.

7.1 When the news of the battle at Marathon reached King Darius son of Hystaspes, he flew into a great rage—he was already provoked enough by the Athenian attack on Sardis!—and he became all the more determined to march on Greece. At once he sent messengers to all the cities, telling them each to muster an army and asking them to provide much more than before by way of warships and horses and grain and transports. At the proclamation, a whirl of activity gripped all Asia for three years,[1] as the cities chose and trained and equipped the best of their youth for the attack on Greece. But in the fourth year the Egyptians revolted—Cambyses, as you know, had made them Persian subjects. At that, the king was all the more convinced that he needed to be on the march—and against both.

A QUARREL OVER DARIUS'S SUCCESSION

7.2 But while Darius was making ready to attack Egypt and Athens, a great quarrel arose between his sons over who was to rule after him—since Persian law required that he appoint a successor before going out on campaign. Now before he was made king, Darius had had three sons from his first wife, the daughter of Gobryas,[2] and after he ascended the throne he had also had four others, from Atossa daughter of Cyrus. The eldest of the earlier children was Artabazanes, of the later children Xerxes, and it was these two, being sons of different mothers, who were involved in the dispute. For his part, Artabazanes argued that he was the oldest of all the children, and that the custom of all men was for the rule to pass to the eldest; but Xerxes argued that he was the son of Atossa daughter of Cyrus, and that it was Cyrus who had made the Persians free.[3]

7.3 So far Darius had not indicated his view of the matter, and it was at this very time that Demaratus son of Ariston happened to arrive in Susa, a man who had been removed from his kingship in Sparta and who had therefore exiled himself. When this man found out about the dispute between the two sons, the story goes that he went to Xerxes and advised him how to improve his side of the argument: "Say in addition that you were the first born to Darius after he was king and held sway over the Persians, but that Artabazanes was born to Darius when he was but a private citizen; it is therefore neither reasonable

1 489–487 BC.

2 Gobryas was one of the Seven (3.70).

3 Cyrus made them no longer subject to the Medes, thus making the Persian king a possibility in the first place. Xerxes is arguing that as the son of Cyrus's daughter he is the proper inheritor of the dynasty Cyrus founded, a dynasty that Darius married into and to which Artabazanes does not belong.

nor just that anyone but you get the rule. Moreover," Demaratus offered, "in Sparta there is the custom that, if there are sons born before the father assumes the kingship, but once appointed king he has another son, the kingship passes to the son born later." Xerxes tried Demaratus's suggestion, and Darius, seeing that what he said was just, appointed Xerxes his successor. Personally, though, I believe that Xerxes would have become king even without this suggestion—Atossa, after all, was the one with all the power.

At any rate, with Xerxes now appointed his successor, Darius turned his 7.4
attention back to the campaign. In the following year, however, even as he was making his final preparations, Darius died, having held the rule for thirty-six years.[4] It thus proved impossible for Darius to take revenge on either the rebellious Egyptians or the Athenians.

XERXES BECOMES THE PERSIAN KING

With Darius dead, the kingship passed to his son Xerxes. At first Xerxes had 7.5
no great enthusiasm for the attack on Greece, though he did continue to work on the expedition against Egypt. But ever alongside Xerxes was Mardonius son of Gobryas, Xerxes' first cousin (being the son of Darius's sister) and of all Persians the one with the greatest influence. Mardonius was always saying things like, "Master, it is not right that the Athenians, who have worked so many ills on the Persians, go unpunished. Finish the business you have in hand now; but when you have brought those insolent Egyptians to heel, then march on Athens. In that way, you will have fame for bravery and nobility, and none in the future will dare to march against your land." Such was his case for revenge, but Mardonius also added this to his argument: "Europe is an exceedingly beautiful place, with all kinds of orchards, and outstandingly fertile land, the sort of place that, among mortals, only the Great King deserves to have as his own."

So spoke Mardonius, with words driven by his love of adventure—and by 7.6
the fact that he wanted himself appointed as satrap of Greece. And in time he won out, convincing Xerxes that this was the thing to do. Several allies were enlisted to help bring Xerxes around. There were messengers who came from the Aleuadae, the kings of Thessaly, passionately offering support for his march on Greece. There were the descendants of Peisistratus, the Peisistratids, who traveled up to Susa, and said many of the same things as the Aleuadae, but added yet more inducements. And this is how. When the Peisistratids traveled to Susa, they brought with them Onomacritus, an Athenian who collected oracles—especially the oracles of Musaeus. Now by this time they and Onomacritus had set aside their mutual antagonisms. Earlier, you see, Hipparchus son of Peisistratus, though before a close friend, had exiled him from Athens. That was because Lasus of Hermione had caught him inserting a

[4] 522–486 BC.

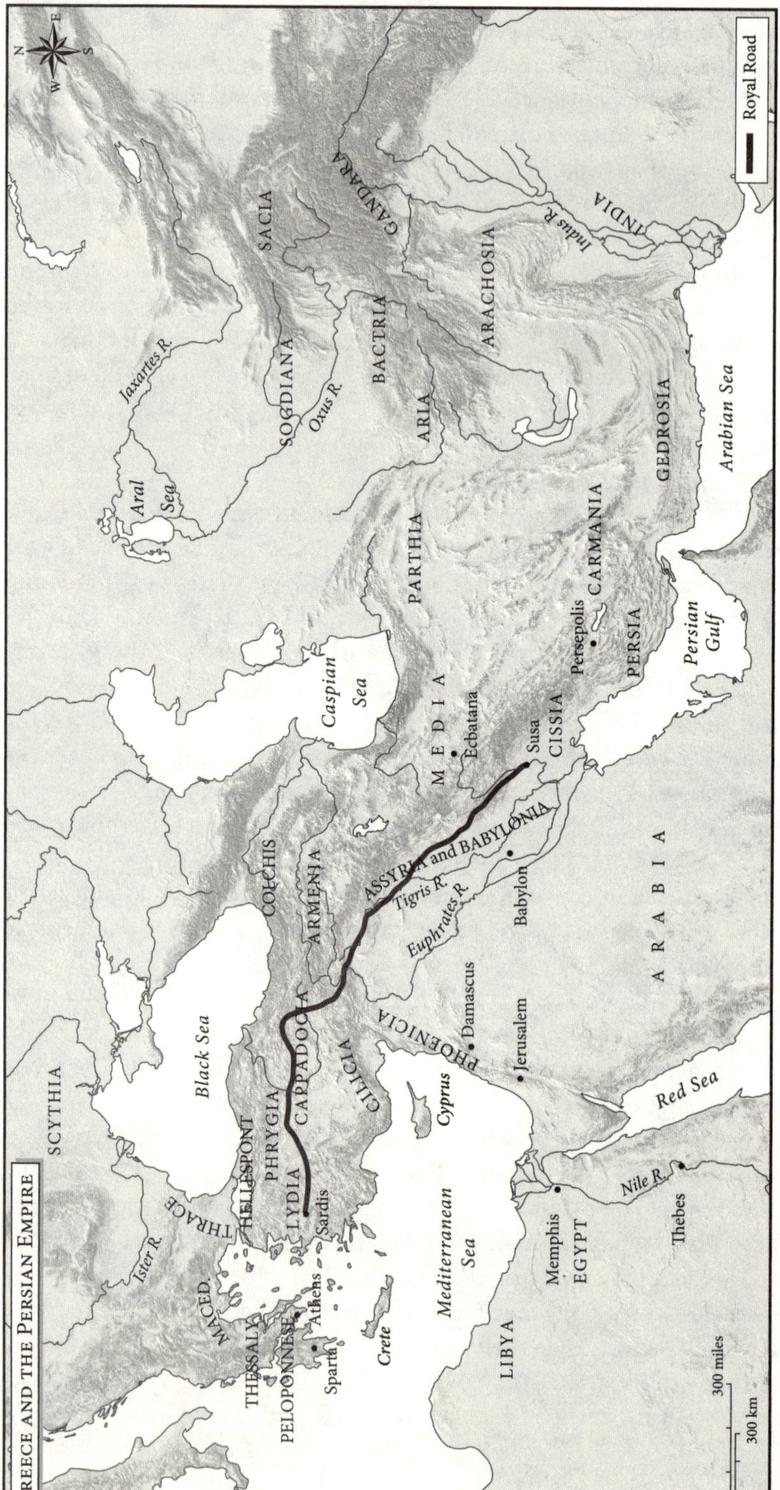
GREECE AND THE PERSIAN EMPIRE
N
E
S
W
Royal Road
SCYTHIA
THRACE
Ister R.
MACED.
THESSALY
PELOPONNESE
Athens
Sparta
Crete
HELLESPONT
LYDIA
Sardis
PHRYGIA
CAPPADOCIA
CILICIA
Black Sea
COLCHIS
ARMENIA
Cyprus
Mediterranean
Sea
PHOENICIA
Damascus
Jerusalem
LIBYA
Memphis
EGYPT
Nile R.
Thebes
Red Sea
ARABIA
Euphrates R.
Tigris R.
ASSYRIA and BABYLONIA
Babylon
MEDIA
Ecbatana
Susa
CISSIA
Caspian
Sea
Persepolis
PERSIA
Persian
Gulf
PARTHIA
CARMANIA
GEDROSIA
Arabian Sea
Aral
Sea
Jaxartes R.
SOGDIANA
Oxus R.
ARIA
BACTRIA
ARACHOSIA
SACIA
GANDARA
Indus R.
INDIA
0
300 miles
0
300 km

MAP 7.1

prophecy into Musaeus's oracle book (to the effect that the islands lying off Lemnos would disappear into the sea). At any rate, they now traveled together to Susa, and when they were in the king's presence the Peisistratids would speak of him in reverent terms. Onomacritus, in turn, would go through several prophecies, omitting, however, any that spoke of Persian calamity. So, taking only the omens of good fortune, he told how it was fated that a Persian man would bridge the Hellespont, and described the march on Greece. The oracles of this man, together with the advocacy of the Peisistratids and Aleuadae, helped to bring Xerxes along.

Xerxes was now convinced to march on Greece. So, in the year following 7.7
the death of Darius, he first set out with his army to crush the revolt in Egypt.[5] That he did, putting the whole of Egypt under far more strict control than in Darius's time, and handed the command to his brother Achaemenes, Darius's son. (Achaemenes, while still satrap of Egypt, was later murdered by a Libyan, Inarus son of Psammetichus.)

Council of the Persians

The council is both like and unlike a Greek assembly, with speakers presenting contrasting arguments in the Greek style, but with the constraint of the fear of speaking freely in front of the king. Xerxes's words that "some god guides" the Persians toward constant imperialist expansion are as ominous as they are fatalistic and will be picked up by the dream vision that follows.

After the subjugation of Egypt, just as he was about to take in hand the 7.8
expedition against Athens, Xerxes convened an extraordinary council of the leading Persians, both to learn their thoughts and to let them all know what he had in mind. Once they were gathered, Xerxes spoke as follows.
"Men of Persia, I have no intention of putting to you some new way of doing 7.8(1)
things; rather, I will follow the ways of my forefathers. Never yet have we rested on our laurels, or so the elders tell me, not since we first took control from the Medes, when Cyrus deposed Astyages. Some god guides us in this way, and by following him we work many things to our betterment. The peoples that Cyrus and Cambyses and my father Darius conquered and added to our empire, one need hardly mention to you, who know it full well. But I, ever since I took up the throne, have had in mind not to fall short of what others in this office have accomplished, nor to add any less to the Persian dominions. So, I now have found a plan that not only brings us glory and adds more land to our territories—land as large and fertile as our own land, or even more so!—but also allows us to exact vengeance and retribution. That, then, is the reason I have gathered you here: so that I can tell you what I am planning to do.

[5] 485 BC.

7.8(2) I am going to bridge the Hellespont and march an army through Europe to attack Greece. My purpose is to make the Athenians pay for what they did to the Persians and to my father. You all saw that my father was directing his army against these men. But he died and was unable to take vengeance himself. Therefore I, for his sake, and on behalf of all the Persians, will not rest until I capture Athens and burn it to the ground. The Athenians were the ones who started it, by wronging my father. First, with Aristagoras—our slave!—as their general, they came to Sardis and burned the sacred groves and temples. As for what they did next, when Datis and Artaphrenes landed in their territory with our army, that you all know, I should think.

7.8(3) These then are my reasons for the invasion, but also, as I think it through, there is a wealth of good to be found in this plan. If we subdue the Athenians, and also their neighbors who live in the land of Pelops the Phrygian,[6] we will make the Persian territories coextensive with the heavens: the sun will look down to find us without neighbors, since I, once I work my way through Europe, will have made all lands part of our own.[7] I have found out, you see, that with those I have just mentioned out of the way, there is not a single other city or people left who will be able to stand against us in battle. Thus, be they guilty or innocent, all will put on the yoke of slavery and become our subjects.

7.8(4) All of you then will please me by doing this: as soon as I send word that it is time, present yourself, ready and willing. And whoever comes with the army most finely equipped I will present with the most costly gifts our land can offer. All this then is what needs doing and how to do it. But so that I do not seem to be making plans all on my own, I put the matter now before you, asking that whoever so wishes make his mind known." With that he stopped.

7.9 Next Mardonius spoke: "Master, not only are you the most noble of all Persians ever born, but of all Persians yet to be. Every word you have spoken is excellent and gets to the very truth of the matter: that you will not allow those vile Ionians who live in Europe[8] to make fools of us. It would indeed be a dreadful business, if we hold subject the Sacians and Indians and Ethiopians and Assyrians and many other great peoples, none of whom did us the least injustice—having conquered them only because we wanted to extend our empire—and yet will not take vengeance on the Greeks, who first and of their own accord did us harm.

7.9(1) And what is there to dread after all? What great massing of a host? What power and resources? We know how they fight, we know how weak is their power. We have conquered and hold subject their descendants and kin, those colonists that they call Ionians and Aeolians and Dorians, who live here in

6 In other words, the Peloponnesians (named for Pelops), with the Spartans especially in mind.

7 Xerxes imagines the heavens as a bowl over the flat disk of the earth. Thus the Great King would rule over the whole earth just as Zeus rules over the heavens.

8 By European Ionians, he means the mainland Greeks. Note the Persian point of view. (From a Greek viewpoint, Ionians are Asian Greeks, and mainland Greeks are simply Greeks.)

Asia, our territory. And I myself have made trial of them, when your father ordered me to march against these men; and though I marched as far as Macedonia, within striking distance of Athens itself, not a one came out to face me in battle.

Yet wars the Greeks do wage, and, as I now understand, in an idiotic fashion, with willful incompetence. Once they declare war on each other, they find a fine, level open space, and there they meet and fight. The result is that the ones who win go back with grave losses; and as for the ones who lose, I cannot begin to describe—they are simply annihilated. But they ought to resolve their differences through heralds and messengers or by anything other than fighting—they speak the same language, after all! And if they really must fight each other, they ought to find a place where each side can best defend itself, and contend there. Such are the useless ways of the Greeks, and thus it was that when I marched deep into Macedonia, they never so much as thought about fighting me. 7.9(2)

Who then is going to oppose you, King, when you march in at the head of a mighty fleet and a host drawn from all of Asia? My guess is that the Greeks will not muster the courage. But even if I am wrong, and they, roused by their folly, come to meet us in battle, they will learn that we are the greatest warriors on earth. So, let the venture begin. Nothing happens on its own: it is only by venturing that anything is gained." 7.9(3)

With that Mardonius stopped, having smoothed the way for Xerxes' view to prevail. The rest of the Persians kept quiet, not daring to voice an opinion contrary to Xerxes' proposal. But then Artabanus, Xerxes' uncle (and relying on that fact), rose to speak. 7.10

"King, without hearing both the argument for and the argument against, it is impossible to decide and choose the better; rather, one must take whichever argument has been articulated. Hearing both arguments, however, does make it possible to judge—just as we cannot know how impure gold is in isolation, but by rubbing two pieces against a touchstone we can judge which is better. 7.10(1)

I advised your father, too, my brother Darius, not to march on Scythia, on grounds that they were men without any cities in their territory. But he did not listen to me, expecting to conquer that nomadic people, and by the time he came back from that expedition he had lost many good men. Now you, King, intend to march against men far better than the Scythians, men said to have exceptional valor both on land and on sea. And so, it is right that I explain this very question: what there is to dread from them.

You say that once you bridge the Hellespont you will march an army through Europe to attack Greece. But let's think this through. Suppose you are defeated, whether on land or on sea, or on both. These men are said to be brave fighters, after all, and we can measure this by the fact that the Athenians all by themselves destroyed the army, great as it was, that Datis and Artaphrenes brought to the land of Attica. But no—let's suppose not that they prevail on both land and sea, but only that they attack with their ships and win a single 7.10(2) naval battle. In that case they will sail to the Hellespont and destroy your bridge. This then is one thing for the king to dread.

7.10(3) I come to this conclusion through no special cleverness of my own, but by the example of something that very nearly happened to us. Your father once bridged the Bosporus at Thrace, and making a bridge over the river Ister he crossed over to attack the Scythians. But the Scythians then did everything they could to get the Ionians (who were on guard duty at the Ister bridge) to destroy the passage over the river, and thus trap the Persians. And if Histiaeus the Milesian had followed the advice of the other Ionian leaders instead of acting in opposition, the Persians would have been finished. Even just to hear the story is a thing to dread: that the survival of the Persian empire and its king depended on one man.

7.10(4) So: do not willingly take such a risk when there is no need, and listen to me. Dissolve this assembly. Some other time, whenever it seems best, and once you have thought deeply about this on your own, announce what course seems best to you. I find that the greatest profit lies in good planning: even if things turn out for the worse, at least the plans were good, and it is only chance that makes it go wrong; but if the planning is bad, even if chance favors you, the result is no more than luck, since the planning was still badly done.

7.10(5) You see that among living creatures it is the great ones that the god strikes down, and whose grandeur is not allowed to shine. The lowly creatures irritate him not. You see how the greatest houses and tallest trees are the ones he hits with his lightning. To curb the overweening is the god's way. In just such a way is a mighty host destroyed by a small one: the god, begrudging their might, hurls panic upon them, or the thunderbolt itself, and they are ignobly cut down. The god suffers none other to think himself great.

7.10(6) Hurrying this matter will breed missteps, and from that great losses will come. Holding back is the right thing to do, even if it doesn't seem so at the moment. One can find what is the best course only with passage of time.

7.10(7) Such is my advice to you, my King. But as for you, Mardonius son of Gobryas, stop your foolish words about how the Greeks are contemptible—it's not worth hearing. You stir the king himself to war by slandering the Greeks, with, it seems to me, utter recklessness. Let this stop. Slander is, after all, another thing to dread, and very much so, since there are two people doing wrong, and one being wronged. The slanderer does wrong by denouncing someone not there to defend himself, and his audience does wrong by being convinced before knowing the facts. And then there is the one wronged, even though he is not there to hear it: for he has been denounced by one, and thought a bad man by another.

7.10(8) But if it is truly necessary to march against these men, come, let the king stay in the Persian lands, and, with the two of us staking our children's lives on the outcome, you make the campaign yourself. Choose what men you will and take an army as big as you like. And if the king's affairs turn out in the way you suggest, let my children be cut down, and me along with them. But if things go as I predict, let your children be the ones to suffer, and you with them—if you get back home, that is. But if you are unwilling to risk your children, and you lead another expedition to Greece anyway, I tell you that those left behind will hear this of Mardonius: that he worked a great disaster for the Persians, and that his body lies torn by dogs and birds,[9] somewhere in the land of the Athenians or in that of the Spartans, or perhaps even earlier on the way there, having come to know what sort of men you now advise the king to make war upon." So spoke Artabanus. 7.11

And Xerxes flew into a rage, saying: "Artabanus, you are the brother of my father—that's all that will protect you from a punishment in keeping with these foolhardy words. But this dishonor I *will* set on you—you spiritless coward!—you will not join me in my expedition against Greece, but will stay here, with the women. And even without you I will bring to pass everything I said. May I not be the offspring of Darius son of Hystaspes son of Arsames son of Ariaramnes son of Teïspes son of Cyrus son of Cambyses son of Teïspes son of Achaemenes, if I do not take vengeance on the Athenians, knowing full well that if we keep the peace, they will not. No, they will attack our land, if one can judge by what they started, when they marched on Asia and burned Sardis. There is no way either side can back down now: in the struggle before us we will either act or be acted upon—either all our empire will be subject to the Greeks, or theirs subject to the Persians. Our mutual hatred admits no middle ground. We were the victims earlier, and it is but honorable that we now take our revenge. In that way I can also learn about the 'dread' that I will feel, when I have marched on these men, and have conquered them. These, after all, are the men whom even the Phrygian Pelops—a slave of my forefathers!—subjugated so thoroughly that to this day people and country are called by the name of their conqueror."

Xerxes and the Dream

Artabanus gets it right—he learns from the history of Cyrus's attack on the Massagetae and Darius's on the Scythians—but it matters not: some divine guide will force Xerxes to act against the wise advisor, and against his own best interests. Cultured Greeks will have recognized here an allusion to the opening of the second book of the Iliad, *in which Zeus sends a dream to Agamemnon, who stands over him to announce, falsely, that Zeus will now let the Greeks take Troy. Agamemnon obeys and musters his troops, but to disastrous consequence—in accordance with the will of Zeus. The allusion reminds us once again that the full sweep of motivations for the invasion includes the long chain of reprisals that, after some snatchings of women, becomes earnest with the Greek invasion of Asia in the time of the Trojan War.*

9 This is an allusion to the beginning of the *Iliad* (1.4–5), which invokes exactly this horrifying image of a body abandoned on the battlefield and mutilated by scavengers. The tone is mockingly heroic.

7.12 With that the argument ended. Afterward, though, Xerxes calmed down and Artabanus's advice began to trouble him. Thinking about it that night, he found that the attack on Greece was not at all what he should be doing. With that decision in mind he fell asleep and in the night he saw a dream vision. The Persians say that it went like this. Xerxes dreamed that a man, tall and handsome, stood over him, saying, "Are you changing your mind, O Persian king, no longer planning to invade Greece, even though you already told the Persians to muster an army? You do not do well in this change of heart, nor will he who stands beside you forgive you for doing this. No, go back to the path that you planned to take when still it was day."

divine intervention

7.13 So spoke the man, and, as it seemed to Xerxes, he then flew away. With the daylight, Xerxes thought no more of the dream. He called the Persians together, the very ones he had assembled before, and said this: "Men of Persia, pardon me if I change my plans. But my sense of judgment is not yet mature, and those who urge me on this course give me no rest. When I heard Artabanus's advice, my youthful temper boiled over, and I lost control, hurling unseemly abuse at an elder. Now, though, I give way and will take his advice. I have changed my mind. There will be no invasion of Greece, and you can stay at peace."

7.14 On hearing that, the Persians rejoiced, got on their knees, and bowed. But when nightfall came, the same dream again stood over Xerxes as he was sleeping and said, "Child of Darius, do you show yourself among the Persians, speaking against the invasion and taking no account of my words, as though I were a nobody and you never heard them? Now hear this, and make sure you understand. Unless you march at once, this will be the result: just as you and your people became great and mighty in a short time, so with all speed will you be laid low again."

7.15 Xerxes, thoroughly terrified by the dream, raced out of bed and sent a messenger to summon Artabanus. When he arrived, Xerxes said: "Artabanus, for a short time I was out of my senses and spoke some foolish words to you about your counsel; but not long afterward, I changed my mind, and decided that I had to do exactly as you suggested. I, however, cannot do this, even though that is what I want. You see, since I changed my mind, a dream keeps haunting me in my sleep, forbidding me to act as you advise. And just now too it has made a threat and then gone away. Now I figure that if a god is the one sending this, and it is very much his desire that I march on Greece, then this same vision will come to you, and command you as it did me—as long as you put on all my kingly garb, then sit on my throne, and afterward go to sleep in my bed."

7.16 So spoke Xerxes. Now Artabanus would not do the first bidding—it was not right, he said, for him to sit on the kingly throne[10]—but Xerxes continued to press and in the end he did as he was told. And this then is what Artabanus

10 By Persian law it was a capital offense for someone other than the king to sit on the throne.

said: "In my view, it is all the same, whether a person has good sense or is will- 7.16(1)
ing to listen to those who give good advice; and you do well in both respects. But you were surrounded by bad men who led you astray, much as the sea, by nature man's greatest benefactor, cannot keep true to itself when beset by strong breezes. As for me, the strong words you uttered did not cause me nearly so much grief as the fact that there were two proposals before the Persians, one expanding our excess and arrogance, the other putting that to rest and arguing that it was a bad thing to train our spirit always to want more than what we have—and that of these proposals you chose the one fraught with danger for both Persians and yourself.

So now, when you have changed your mind for the better, you say that by 7.16(2)
the guiding hand of some god a dream comes to haunt you, just as you were abandoning the attack on Greece, and that this dream vision forbids that you give up the expedition. But this is hardly something from a god, my child. As I am much your elder, let me teach you about the things that drift into the minds of men as they sleep. What we see in our dreams is very much wont to match what we are thinking about in daylight hours. And in the past days our hands have been full of the business of this military campaign.

But if this explanation of mine is not the 7.16(3)
right one, and the dream is in some part divine, you have already voiced the heart of the matter, that we let the dream appear and give its bidding to me just as it did to you. Yet the prospects are no better if I wear your clothes any more than if I wear my own, nor if I rest in your bed rather than in mine—if the dream is really inclined to appear. Surely this thing that appeared to you in your sleep, whatever it is, is not so silly that it will look at me and think, just because I have your clothes on, that I am you! What we need to find out is whether it will pay me no attention and not deign to make an appearance, and, regardless of whether I am in my clothes or yours, refuse to come. If, on the other hand, it does come to me after coming to you, I too will agree that it is sent by some god. But, come now, if you think it best, and I cannot convince you that it is unnecessary for me to sleep in your bed, then let me do as you say and may the dream appear to me in this way. Until it comes, though, I will keep to my present opinion."

FIGURE 7.1 Xerxes's kingly garb

7.17 So spoke Artabanus, and he did as he was told, expecting to prove Xerxes
mistaken. So, putting on Xerxes' kingly garb and sitting on the royal throne, he
next lay in his bed—and to him came the same dream vision that had visited
Xerxes. Standing over him, the vision said, "Are you then the one who convinced Xerxes not to march against Greece, thinking to work in his interest?
You will not go unpunished, not in future nor right now, for trying to avert what
needs must be. As for Xerxes himself, I have already made known what he must
7.18 suffer if he does not obey." And even as he made these threats, the man in the
dream took up hot irons and turned to burn out Artabanus's eyes. Bellowing,
Artabanus leaped up from the bed and, seating himself next to Xerxes, described in detail the vision he had seen in his sleep. Then he said, "King, I recognize, as much as a mortal may, how often the greater is toppled by the lesser;
and I did not want you to succumb entirely to the impetuousness of youth,
since I know well how bad it is ever to want more. I remember Cyrus's attack on
the Massagetae, how that turned out; I remember too Cambyses' disastrous
attack on the Ethiopians, and I marched with Darius against the Scythians. In
full knowledge of all this, I took the view that if you remained at peace all men
would count you blessed. But now some divine impulse intervenes, and a god-
driven disaster, so it seems, comes down upon the Greeks. Thus even I have had
a change of heart and mind: tell the Persians what the god has made manifest,
bid them carry out the preparations you ordered earlier, and, even with the god
on your side, make sure that nothing is lacking in your planning."

Such were his words, and so, goaded on by the dream, at daybreak Xerxes told the Persians the whole story; and Artabanus, the man who before was the only one arguing against the expedition, now made himself conspicuous in his support for it.

7.19 With Xerxes now eager for war, a third vision appeared in his sleep. The Magi, when he told them, interpreted it as meaning that it pertained to the whole earth, and that all men would become his slaves. And this was the vision: Xerxes dreamed that he wore a crown of olive, and that from the crown branches grew and stretched over the whole earth; later in the dream, the crown on his head disappeared. Such anyway was the Magi's interpretation.

So now all the Persian nobles rushed from the council, each back to his own country, where each applied himself to carry out the king's orders, keen to get the gifts that Xerxes had promised earlier. Thus did Xerxes go about mustering his army, scouring every land on the continent in gathering his forces.

Xerxes Prepares to Invade

At the front of this section, the theme of reprisals returns again: Darius's invasion of Europe, the Scythian invasion of Asia, the Greek invasion of Asia at Troy, and, now, the Persian invasion of Greece. The use of the superlative ("greatest") bodes ominously, to a Greek. Note that the narrative once again returns to highlight Sardis, with its now deep associations.

TABLE 7.1: TIMELINE OF PREPARATIONS FOR THE PERSIAN INVASION

490 BC autumn	Marathon
489–487	Darius prepares for a full-scale invasion of Greece (3 years)
487	Revolt of Egypt
486	Death of Darius
485	Xerxes reconquers Egypt
484–480	Xerxes prepares for invasion of Greece (4 full years)
480 spring	Xerxes invades

For a full four years after the conquest of Egypt did Xerxes muster his army 7.20
and get together all that was needed, and as the fifth year came on he began his march, leading a great host. Of all the military expeditions that I myself know of, this was far the greatest: Darius's attack on Scythia seems nothing in comparison, nor the Scythian force, when they, in pursuit of the Cimmerians, invaded Media and lived there, having conquered almost all of upper Asia (this, you recall, is the reason Darius later tried to take vengeance on them); nor, at least according to the stories that are told, was the expedition of the sons of Atreus against Troy anything to compare, nor the expedition of the Mysians and Teucrians that happened before the Trojan War—when they crossed over the Bosporus into Europe and conquered all of Thrace, marching down to the Ionian Sea and then as far south as the river Peneus.

All of these together, even if we added others, were not comparable to this 7.21
one expedition. What people indeed did Xerxes *not* lead from Asia to attack Greece? What body of water was not drunk dry by this army, save only the great rivers? Some provided ships, others foot soldiers; some were asked to bring cavalry, others horse transports as well as men to fight; some were to bring long ships for the pontoon bridges, and others grain and the merchantmen to carry it.

And for roughly the three years before, Xerxes had also made advance 7.22
preparations near Athos, all because the Persians had met with disaster when they first rounded the cape at Mt. Athos.[11] First he had his ships anchor at Elaeus at Thracian Chersonese. Using that as a base, all the various peoples in the army worked—under the lash—to dig a canal, each working in turn; and the people who lived near Mt. Athos dug too. Bubares son of Megabazus and Artachaees son of Artaeus, both Persians, were the overseers of these works. This Athos is a large, impressive mountain that stretches down to the sea, and whose slopes are inhabited. At the place where the mountain ends on the mainland side, there is a sort of peninsula and a narrow isthmus of only twelve stades.[12] This part is level with only small hills, running between the sea by Acanthus and that opposite Torone. On that isthmus lies the Greek town Sane, and there were other towns that lay seaward of Sane yet inland of Athos—which the Persians now set out to make island towns and no longer

11 In Mardonius's failed invasion before Marathon, in 490 BC (6.45).

12 About 1.5 miles, 2.4 km.

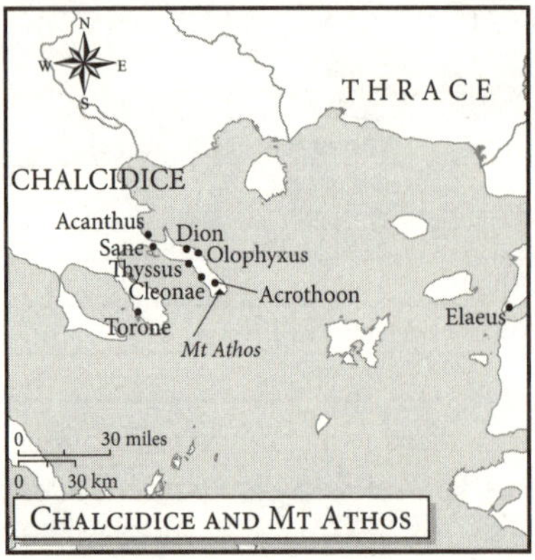

MAP 7.2

part of the mainland. The names of these towns were Dion, Olophyxus, Acrothoon, Thyssus, and Cleonae.
7.23 Such were the towns of those who dwelt on Athos.

The Persians assigned different parts of the canal to different peoples, and this is how they went about the digging. They dug a channel in a straight line right alongside the town of Sane. When the channel grew deep, they positioned men at the bottom to dig, and alongside were men who passed the dirt as it was excavated up to others who were standing on a step; these took it in turn and handed it to yet others, until they reached those standing at the top. The ones at the top then hauled it away and dumped it. Now to all but the Phoenicians, the sheer wall of the canal would cave in and so made for double the work—since they made the opening in the canal the same width from top to bottom, this was bound to happen. But the Phoenicians, always clever when it came to such works, showed here remarkable ingenuity. When they were assigned their section of the canal, they dug the upper opening twice the width necessary for the finished canal, and as they proceeded they made it ever narrower: thus by the time they got to the bottom, the width of their section matched that of the others. There was also a meadow in the vicinity, where they set up a market and a canteen, stocked with plentiful flour brought from all over Asia.

7.24 I have thought this over, and here is what I have concluded: it was out of self-pride that Xerxes ordered the digging of this channel, driven by the desire to demonstrate his power and to leave a memorial for all time. It was possible to drag the ships over this isthmus—hardly any bother at all—but instead he ordered a channel dug from sea to sea, wide enough for two warships to row along side by side.[13]

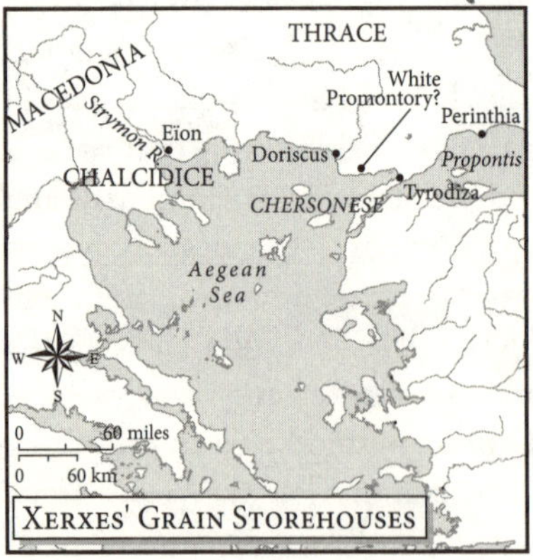

MAP 7.3

To the same group that dug the channel, Xerxes also assigned the job
7.25 of bridging the river Strymon, and

13 The digging of this canal has been doubted, but joint British–Greek excavations in 1991–2001 have definitively established its historicity.

once that was done, he had the Phoenicians and Egyptians get ready papyrus and flax to make ropes for the bridge over the Hellespont. Xerxes also had grain brought and stored for the army, wanting neither men nor oxen to go hungry as they marched to Greece; he searched everywhere for the best places to store the grain, and had transports and cargo ships bring it from all over Asia to storehouses scattered along the route. Most of it he had brought to a place called the White Promontory, in Thrace; but stores were also brought to Tyrodiza in Perinthia, Doriscus, Eïon on the river Strymon, and to Macedonia.

And even as these were busy with their appointed work, all the foot soldiers 7.26
had gathered and now began their march with Xerxes to Sardis, starting off from Critalla in Cappadocia—that's where, they say, the whole army, from all over Asia, gathered as they were about to set off with Xerxes. As to which of the satraps gathered the army of best equipage and got the prize offered by the king, I cannot say—for starters I do not even know whether the matter was ever decided. In any case, the soldiers crossed the river Halys and made their way to Phrygia. Traveling from there they came to Celaenae, where the springs of the river Maeander spill forth, as well as that of another river no smaller, whose name is the Catarrectes; and that river rises from a spring at the city center of Celaenae, whereupon it flows down to the Maeander. In that town also is hung the skin of the satyr Marsyas, who—according to the Phrygian tale—was skinned by Apollo, and it was he, Apollo, who hung it up there.[14]

It was in this very town that the Lydian Pythius son of Atys[15] waited, and 7.27
when they arrived he held a lavish feast for the king's entire army and for Xerxes himself, and also of his own accord offered to provide money to support the war. At the offer, Xerxes asked the Persians present who this Pythius was and how much money he had that he could propose such a thing. And they said, "King, this is the man who gave your father Darius the plane tree and grape vine made from gold, and even now he remains the richest man of any we know, after you."

The last of these words amazed Xerxes—the next richest man in the 7.28
world!—so he next asked Pythius directly how much money he had. And Pythius said, "King, I will not hide this from you, or pretend not to know the extent of my wealth. I know it full well and I will tell you precisely how much. As soon as I heard that you were on your way down to the Aegean coast, I had it counted, since I wanted to give money in support of the war. And here's what I found: I have two thousand talents of silver, and four million Daric staters of gold, except that I am seven thousand short. And all this will I give you—as for me, I have enough livelihood from my slaves and farmlands."

So spoke Pythius, and Xerxes was pleased at the words. "Lydian friend," he 7.29
said, "since I left the Persian land, I have so far met with no man who wanted

14 In Greek myth, Marsyas discovers the *aulos* (a reed pipe, usually played as a pair: see Figure 4.2) and challenges the god Apollo to a music contest. When he is defeated, Apollo flays him alive, in punishment for the *hubris* of daring to try to compete with an Olympian.

15 Atys is probably the unfortunate son of Croesus we met at 1.34, thus Pythius the grandson of Croesus, whose vast wealth he had inherited.

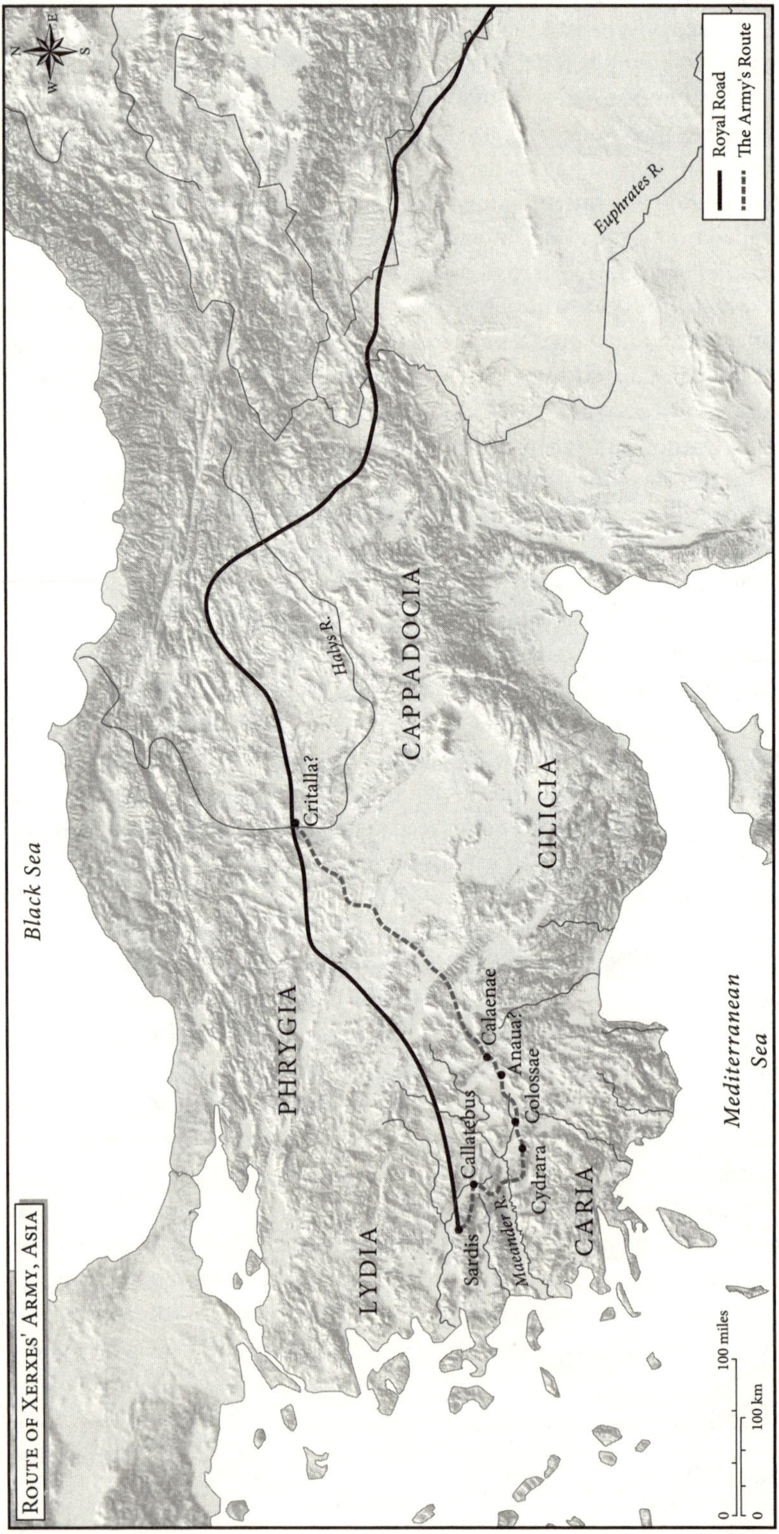
Route of Xerxes' Army, Asia
Black Sea
Royal Road
The Army's Route
Euphrates R.
Halys R.
CAPPADOCIA
CILICIA
PHRYGIA
LYDIA
CARIA
Critalla?
Calaenae
Anaua?
Colossae
Callatebus
Cydrara
Sardis
Maeander R.
Mediterranean Sea
0
100 miles
0
100 km
N
E
S
W

MAP 7.4

to lay a feast for my army, nor has anyone stood in my presence wanting to offer money to support the war, except for you. You, on the other hand, have feasted us grandly and you also make a grand offer of support. So, in return, I grant you this gift: I hereby make you my guest-friend, and I will top off your four million staters, giving you the seven thousand from my own stores, so that your four million will no longer be short, but evened off to a round number. Keep then what you have, and keep in mind ever to be such as you are today: if you do so, neither now nor in time will you have cause for regret."

So saying, Xerxes gave orders to make his words true. He then marched 7.30
ever farther along the road, passing by the Phrygian town called Anaua and the lake and salt flats there. Next he came to the great city of Phrygia, Colossae. There the river Lycus disappears into a hole in the earth, reappearing about five stades away, whereupon it too flows into the Maeander. From Colossae, the army made its way to the dividing line between Phrygia and Lydia, coming to the town of Cydrara; there a pillar set up by Croesus still stands, with an inscription announcing the border.

Once the army crossed into Lydia from Phrygia, the road split, with the left 7.31
fork running to Caria and the right to Sardis. Taking the right fork, they crossed the Maeander (there was no avoiding it) and went by the town of Callatebus, where the artisans make a sort of sweet from tamarisk and wheat. Along the way, Xerxes came upon a plane tree, of such exceptional beauty that he decorated it with golden ornaments and assigned it a caretaker for all time. After arranging that, he went on his way and the next day he reached the Lydian capital.

Once at Sardis, Xerxes first sent heralds to demand earth and water from the 7.32
Greeks, and to give them advance notice to make ready meals for the king. To all of the Greek lands he sent this message, excepting only Athens and Sparta. Now the reason he made his demand for earth and water a second time was that he fully believed that the Greeks who had refused earlier were now frightened enough to give in. So, wanting to find out if this was so, he sent out the heralds.

Bridging the Hellespont

The king's attempt to assert control over the Hellespont signals a man who does not understand his mortal limitations, a theme also suggested by the enormity of the forces Xerxes has assembled.

Xerxes next made preparations for the march to Abydos. It was during this 7.33
time that his men were building the bridge over the Hellespont to connect Asia and Europe. In the area of Hellespontine Chersonese, between Sestos and Madytus, lies a broad headland that stretches down into the sea opposite Abydos. And that very headland was the spot where, not long afterward,[16] the Athenians under the command of Xanthippus son of Ariphron seized

16 In 478 BC, at the tail end of the war. The story will be told at the very end of the work, 9.120.

FIGURE 7.2 The Hellespont

Artaÿctes, the Persian governor of Sestos, and nailed him alive onto a board, crucifying him, because he was in the habit of bringing women to the temple of Protesilaus at Elaeus and doing ungodly things with them there.

7.34 This in any case was the headland where they now made two bridges, starting on the Abydos side, one built by the Phoenicians using ropes of flax, the other by the Egyptians using ropes of papyrus, and stretching over a span of seven stades from Abydos to the coast opposite. But when the strait was bridged, a mighty storm arose, breaking everything into pieces and utterly destroying all the work.

7.35 When Xerxes heard what had happened he flew into a rage, and ordered his men to lay three hundred lashes upon the Hellespont with a whip, and to lower into the sea a pair of shackles—and I once heard a story that he also sent men with hot irons to brand the Hellespont. As they were laying on the lashes, the men were instructed to speak these outlandish and blasphemous words: "O bitter water, your master sets you this punishment, since you did him wrong when he did none to you. King Xerxes will cross you,[17] whether you wish it or not, and it is but just that no man tenders you sacrifice, with your muddy, briny waters." Xerxes then ordered those who had punished the sea also to seize the men who had supervised the building of the bridges and to cut off their heads.

Other engineers are brought in to rebuild and the 2 pontoon bridges are described in detail.

Xerxes Marches into Europe

7.53 Xerxes now summoned the leading Persians and, when they were assembled, he spoke as follows. "Men of Persia, I summoned you to demand this, that you be men noble and brave, and that you not disgrace the Persians of the past, who worked deeds great and glorious; nay, let us, each and all, be eager to join the fight. The noble cause that spurs us on is shared by all alike. I command you to fight with every ounce of your being, and it is with good reason: the men we fight, I am told, are brave, but if we overmaster them, there is not another army in the world that can stand against us. So, let us pray to the gods appointed, and then—cross into Europe!"

17 In the Greek this is a double entendre: the word means "cross over" but also "transgress."

FIGURE 7.3 Xerxes's bridge. Temporary bridges using pontoons or ships as floating mechanisms were commonly deployed in military campaigns throughout the ancient Mediterranean. The size of Xerxes's bridges is, however, extraordinary. Modern analyses conclude that the bridges must have been at least half again the length reported by Herodotus (6 stades = 3/4 mile, 1.2 km). The required materials—twin anchor weights and cables for each of the 674 ships; thick cables to attach to land; wide, heavy planks and earth for the road—would have been enormous, and the technological hurdles, given the strength of current and depth of the strait (300 ft., 90 m), considerable

For all that day they then made ready for the crossing; and on the next, 7.54
while waiting to see the sun rise, they burned incense upon the bridges, of all kinds, and strewed myrtle branches to cover the way. And when the sun lifted over the horizon, Xerxes made a libation from a golden cup, pouring the wine into the sea; and he prayed to the sun god, "Grant me, god, that no accident of fortune stop me in my subjugation of Europe before I reach its farthest borders." With that prayer, he threw the cup into the Hellespont, and along with it a golden bowl and a sword, of the Persian type known as the *acinaces*. Now as to whether Xerxes threw these into the sea as a dedication to the sun, or instead was giving an offering to the Hellespont, regretting the whipping he ordered—I find that hard to judge with any confidence.

Once Xerxes was done with the offerings, the Persians began the crossing, 7.55
with all the infantry and horse passing over the bridge closest to the Black Sea, and the supply train and servants passing over the bridge on the Aegean side. Leading the way first were the Ten Thousand, all with wreaths on their heads,

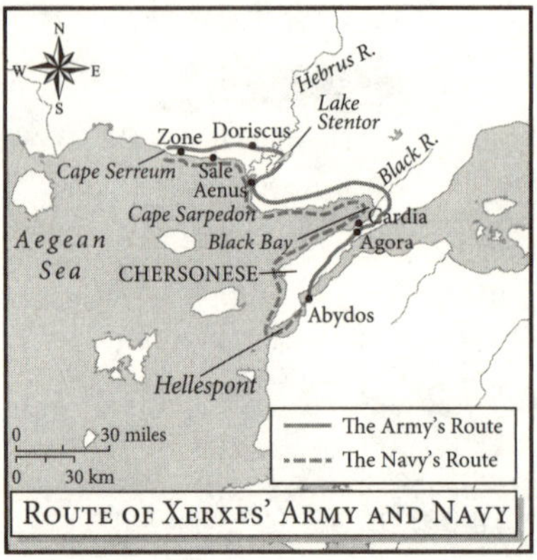

ROUTE OF XERXES' ARMY AND NAVY

MAP 7.5

and after them a mixed host of peoples from many lands. All that day they crossed, and on the next day first came the cavalry and the men who march holding their spears down to the ground; and these too wore garlands. Following them came the sacred horses and chariot, and, behind them, Xerxes himself with his bodyguards and thousand horse; and thereafter the rest of the army. The fleet meanwhile pushed off and sailed to the coast opposite. I also once heard a different story, that the king crossed over last of all.

7.56 When Xerxes had made the passage into Europe, he watched as the main army now crossed, urged on by whips. For seven nights and seven days, without pause, the army streamed across the bridge. A tale is told that when Xerxes had finished the crossing a Hellespontine man said, "Zeus, why do you come in the guise of a Persian man and use the name Xerxes instead of your own, and why bring the whole world with you? If you wish to upturn Greece, surely you can do so without them."

7.57 When all were across, as they started on their journey a great portent appeared, and this Xerxes ignored, even though it was easy to interpret. This was the portent: a horse gave birth to a hare. And the obvious interpretation was thus, that Xerxes, proud and vainglorious, would march off with his army to attack Greece, but that he would return to this same spot running for his life. And there was another portent that happened at Sardis: there, a mule gave birth to a foal with twin sets of genitalia, male above and female below.[18] But Xerxes paid no attention to either portent, and journeyed on his way, taking the infantry with him.

7.58 The fleet, once outside the Hellespont, sailed close to the land, and thereby moved in a direction opposite to the infantry. They sailed due west, until they got to Cape Sarpedon, and there, following their standing orders, they anchored. Meanwhile, the army made its way by land due east toward the rising sun, through Chersonese, keeping the tomb of Athamas's daughter Helle to their right, and the city of Cardia to their left, and marching right through the middle of the town called Agora. From there, they rounded the Black Bay and came to the Black River (which shares the name of the bay); but the river did not hold out—the army drank it dry. So, they crossed the river, and now turned to march westward, skirting the Aeolian town of Aenus and Lake Stentor. Finally, they arrived at Doriscus.

18 Mules are sterile and cannot bear foals, so the portent is doubly strange. The mule is the Persian dynastic founder, Cyrus, as we recall from book 1 (1.55, 91), and so this seems to suggest that Xerxes (and his enterprise) combines male and female attributes, of strength but also weakness. In the fight to come at Salamis, watch for the comment that his men fight as women and his women as men (8.88).

Xerxes Counts and Reviews the Host

Scholars agree that the numbers given here are wildly exaggerated.

Doriscus is a large coastal plain in Thrace, through which flows the great river Hebrus. There a walled fortress had been constructed by the Persians, which goes by the name Doriscus, where a Persian watch had been posted by Darius from the time when he invaded Scythia. Xerxes then had the thought that the plain there would be perfect for marshaling and counting his army, so he did as follows. He had the ship captains bring all the ships there, to the beach near Doriscus, where is situated Zone and the Samothracian town of Sale; at the end of the beach is the impressive headland known as Cape Serreum. This area of old had belonged to the Cicones.[19] Landing the ships there, they dragged them up on the beach, to dry and refit the timbers. Meanwhile, in Doriscus Xerxes made a count of his army. 7.59

Now what the count was for each nation in the host, I am not able to say with accuracy—no one reports this. But as for the total count of the land army, that appears to be one million seven hundred thousand. And this is the way the count was made. They assembled in one spot ten thousand soldiers. Then, pushing them together in as tight a formation as they could they drew a circle around the outside. They then let the soldiers go, and built a low fence along the circle they had drawn, up to the height of a man's waist. When the fence was finished, they led the rest into the enclosure, ten thousand at a time, until they had counted them all. 7.60

And once the count was made, they marshaled the troops, arranged by nations.

Following are 39 chapters enumerating the army and fleet, nation by nation. Greek readers will have recognized this as a reflection of Iliad, *book 2, which is a full catalogue of the Greek and Trojan forces that met at Troy.*

When Xerxes had finished counting and marshaling the troops, he conceived the desire to drive through on his chariot and review the host. So, after the troops were all marshaled, nation by nation, he mounted his war chariot and drove through the army. For each people he came to he asked, "What is your nation?" and his scribes wrote down the name, continuing until he had gone from one end to the other of both horse and infantry. When that was done, and the ships dragged down and launched, Xerxes got down from his war chariot and seated himself on a Sidonian ship, under a golden awning, sailing along the prows of the ships. For each ship he asked the same question as he had posed the infantry, and had the name recorded. The ship captains had put out from shore about four hundred feet, and there rode at anchor, in line, with each prow turned to land, and the marines on board all in armor as if for war. So, Xerxes made his review, sailing between ships and shore. 7.100

19 Odysseus and his men go ashore in the land of the Cicones in book 9 of the *Odyssey*.

Xerxes and Demaratus

What follows is a fundamental discussion on the nature of "freedom" in a polity, which makes clear how a monarchy like Sparta and a democracy like Athens, despite differences, remain on one side of a great divide, with the despotic rule in Persia on the other. We met the banished Spartan king Demaratus at chapter 7.3, and his very state of exile demonstrates that even when king he had to answer to the Law, as a higher master. He now replaces Artabanus as the wise advisor figure.

7.101 When Xerxes had sailed past them all, he disembarked, and then sent for Demaratus son of Ariston, who had come with his army as they marched on Greece. When he was summoned, Xerxes asked him this: "Demaratus, it would give me pleasure to ask you a question. You are a Greek, and as I know from talking with you and other Greeks, you come from a city by no means the least or weakest of Greek polities. So, now, tell me this: will the Greeks stay and try to resist? To my way of thinking, even if you put all the Greeks together, and with them everyone living to their west, they still are no match for my onslaught—at least so long as they are not united. Nevertheless, I want to hear what you have to say about them." To his question, Demaratus replied, "King, should I tell you the truth, or should I say what will please you?" Xerxes bid him speak the truth, promising that he would be no less favored than before.

7.102 Hearing the king's reply, Demaratus said, "King, you bid that I speak the truth, the whole truth, shunning anything that will later be proved a lie. This then is what I have to say. Poverty has ever been the natural state of Greece, and Greece's excellence and nobility is something earned, molded from wisdom and strict adherence to the law. It is by virtue of this earned excellence that Greece has driven off both Poverty and Despotism. I honor all Greeks who inhabit the Doric lands, but I am now going to speak not about all, but only about the Lacedaemonians: I say, first, that they will never accept terms that bring slavery to Greece; and, second, that they will stand and fight you even if every other Greek goes to your side. And as for numbers, it is pointless to inquire how many they are that they can do this. Even if they march with a thousand men, they will fight you; and they will fight with fewer, and they will fight with more."

7.103 Hearing this, Xerxes laughed out loud. "Demaratus," he said, "what a thing to say—that a thousand men will fight a host as vast as this! Come, tell me. You say that you once were the king of these men. Are you willing then—right now—to fight ten of my men? But, no, if your Spartan state is as you describe, you as king should by right of law take a double share,[20] and fight twice as many. So, if each Spartan is a match for ten of my soldiers, then I'd want you to be a match for twenty—only then could your claim be proven. But if the Spartans who think so much of themselves are like in size and build to the Greeks that visit my court, or to you for that matter, then you should watch that your bluster does not get you into trouble. Look at the matter reasonably. How

20 Spartan kings famously got a double share in many contexts: two votes in the assembly, twice the servings at public feasts, and so forth. Herodotus had described this in an earlier passage dealing with Demaratus, in book 5, that we did not read.

could one thousand or ten thousand or fifty thousand men withstand such a host, especially since they are all free, on equal footing, ruled by no one man? Why, if there were five thousand Greeks, we would outnumber them by more than a thousand to one! Now if they were subject to one ruler, like we are, fear of their master might get them to fight beyond themselves, and a smaller force could be pressed by the whip to go up against a larger. But as it is, with these men free to do as they like, neither of these things can happen. My own view, then, is that even if they were equal in number, the Greeks would find it hard to fight with the Persians alone. Indeed, we are the only ones who have the talent you mention, but it is rare, by no means common. For we do have men among my spearmen who would gladly fight three Greeks single-handed. But clearly you don't know a thing about this, or you wouldn't be speaking such nonsense."

why Xerxes thinks Persia will win

To that Demaratus replied, "King, from the start I knew that in speaking the truth I would say things not to your liking. But, since you forced me to speak nothing but the truth, I told you how it is with the Spartans. And yet you yourself know well that I have no love lost for these men, who stripped me of my office and patrimony and have made me an exile, a man without a city to call his own; and it was your father who welcomed me and gave me lodgings and livelihood. A man of sense does not reject good will when it is offered, but requites it with loyalty and affection. As for myself, I do not promise that I am capable of fighting ten men, or even two, and I would not willingly fight with one. But if I had to, or some contest drove me to it, I would best like to fight one of those who claims to be a match for three Greeks. As for the Spartans: when we fight one on one, we are as good as anyone, certainly no worse; but when we fight as a group, we are the best warriors on earth. To be free, you see, is not to be free in every respect. The Law[21] is their master, and they fear the Law far more than your subjects fear you. They do whatever it commands, and the Law always commands the same thing: that soldiers not run away from the fighting, regardless of the odds, but remain in their ranks and fight and win, or fight and die. So, if I seem to you to speak nonsense, I am willing to keep silence in the future; but at present you forced me to speak. Nonetheless, may everything turn out as you desire, King."

Nomos is King

7.104

Such was Demaratus's reply, and Xerxes laughed, bearing him no ill, but sending him away in all kindness. After the conversation, Xerxes appointed Mascames son of Megadostes satrap of Doriscus, relieving the governor appointed by Darius, and then marched his army through Thrace to make his attack on Greece....

7.105

21 The Greek word here, *nomos*, means written law, but also the custom of the land, those traditions that inform the social structure. In traditional societies like Sparta, the two can be interchangeable in many contexts.

Artemisium and Thermopylae

We now come to the first significant battle action of the war, first involving the fleet (Artemisium) and then the army (Thermopylae). Herodotus lived through these events, if only as a small boy and across the sea, and the sources are now entirely contemporary, though as prone as any account to embroidering or propaganda. Persian sources are entirely silent. The narrative moves forward in a way that feels comfortable to us as "history," in chronological fashion with alternation of focus and perspective from Greek to Persian and back.

FIGURE 7.4 Leonidas, King of Sparta

Council at the Isthmus

The Greeks have just chosen to withdraw from Thessaly, where 10,000 had started to make a stand, but retreated at the advice of the Macedonian king. They now gather at the Isthmus of Corinth to plan their next steps.

At the Isthmus,[22] the Greeks met to decide where best to make a stand. The 7.175
prevailing opinion was to defend the approach into Greece at Thermopylae: the pass there was narrower than the one they had thought to defend in Thessaly, and closer to their homes as well; and as for the path around the mountain, by which the Greeks were to be trapped and defeated, that they knew nothing about until they got to Thermopylae and the Trachinians told them. So, they decided they would keep the Persians from entering Greece by securing the pass at Thermopylae; and also that the fleet would sail to Artemisium, in the territory of Histiaea. In that way, being nearby, the army and fleet could keep in touch with each other.

The overall topography is like this. First, Artemisium. From the waters off 7.176
Thrace the open sea contracts to a narrow strait lying between the island of Sciathus and the coast of Magnesia on the mainland; farther along this strait is a strip of the coast of Euboea known as Artemisium, where also stands a temple to Artemis. As for Thermopylae, the approach through Trachis into Greece is but fifty feet wide there, and yet the part in front and behind Thermopylae itself is even more narrow: behind, near Alpeni, the road is wide enough only for a single cart, and in front, along the river Phoenix and near the town Anthela, is another section only one cart wide. To the west of Thermopylae lies an impassable mountain, tall and sheer, that runs over to Mt. Oeta; while to the east of the road lies the sea and some marshes. There are hot springs at the pass, which the locals call *Chytri*, the Cauldrons, where also stands an altar to Heracles. Across this part of the pass a wall had been built, and in ancient times a gateway stood there as well. The wall was built by the Phocians, in fear of the Thessalians, when they came from Thesprotia to settle in the Aeolian territory they still occupy. This, then, was the Phocian line of defense in face of the Thessalian incursion, and they also diverted water from the hot springs, to make the pass full of streams and gullies. The old wall was built long ago and much of it had fallen to ruins over time; and so they now rebuilt it, thinking that they could use it to keep the Persians out of Greece. The closest village to the road is called Alpeni, and from there, the Greeks reckoned, they could get provisions.

As the Greeks looked at the situation and thought it over, these two places 7.177
seemed well suited for their purposes—in both, the Persians would be able to use neither their strength of numbers, nor their cavalry. Here then they resolved to make a stand against the invaders. And when they found out that the Persian king was already in Pieria, they broke up the gathering at the Isthmus and went on their way, those on foot to Thermopylae and those on ships to Artemisium.

22 The Isthmus of Corinth is the small strip of land that joins the Peloponnese to the rest of Greece.

MAP 7.6

7.178 So, the Greeks rushed to the two posts appointed as quickly as they could. Meanwhile, the Delphians, alarmed for themselves and for all of Greece, consulted the oracle; and the god prophesied, "Pray to the winds: they it will be who fight alongside Greece." With that, first the Delphians announced to the Greeks, all those still fighting for their freedom, what had been prophesied—and by this announcement won their eternal gratitude, terrified as they were of the Persians. Next, the Delphians dedicated an altar to the winds, at Thyia, where lies the sacred precinct of Thyia daughter of Cephisus (wherefrom it gets it name), and made sacrifices to win them over. And even now the Delphians continue to propitiate the winds in memory of this prophecy.

Artemisium

After a tremendous setup—almost seven full books!—the Greeks and Persians are finally about to engage in full force. But the first action reads more like a battle between men and divine forces than between Greeks and Persians.

THE ADVANCE GUARD

Xerxes' fleet now set out from the town of Therma, and the ten fastest of their 7.179
ships laid their course straight for Sciathus, where three Greek ships formed an
advance guard, one each from Troezen, Aegina, and Attica. And as soon as the
Greeks sighted the Persian ships they turned about to flee. The ship from Troezen, 7.180
captained by Prexinus, was immediately chased down and captured by the
Persians, and the Persians then seized the finest of the marines on board, led him
to the prow, and put him to the sword—sacrificing the first and finest of their
captives as the first fruits of victory. The man's name was Leon, and it may be
perhaps that his name was in part responsible for their choice of victim.[23] The 7.181
ship from Aegina, captained by Asonides, gave them some trouble, however,
since that day the marine Pytheas son of Ischenous proved an exceptionally brave
man. When the ship was taken, he resisted so valiantly that in the end he was
fairly well cut to pieces; and even when he fell he did not die but kept breathing.
The Persian fighters, struck by his bravery, then very much wanted to keep him
alive; and so they smeared his wounds
with medicaments and wrapped them
in linen bandages. And when they got
back to their own camp, they showed
him off admiringly throughout the
camp and treated him well. The rest of
those captured from this ship, however,
were treated as slaves.

So, two of the Greek ships were 7.182
captured. But the Athenian captain
Phormus sailed the third to the mouth
of the river Peneus, and ran the ship
aground. The Persians thus captured
the vessel, but not the men—for the
Athenians leapt off the ship as soon as it
was aground, and then made their way
through Thessaly back down to Athens.

Fire beacons were now flashed 7.183
from Sciathus to let the Greeks at Artemisium know what had happened.
In considerable panic, they changed
their anchorage from Artemisium to
Chalcis, where they set a guard over
the Euripus, and also stationed lookouts about the high points on Euboea.

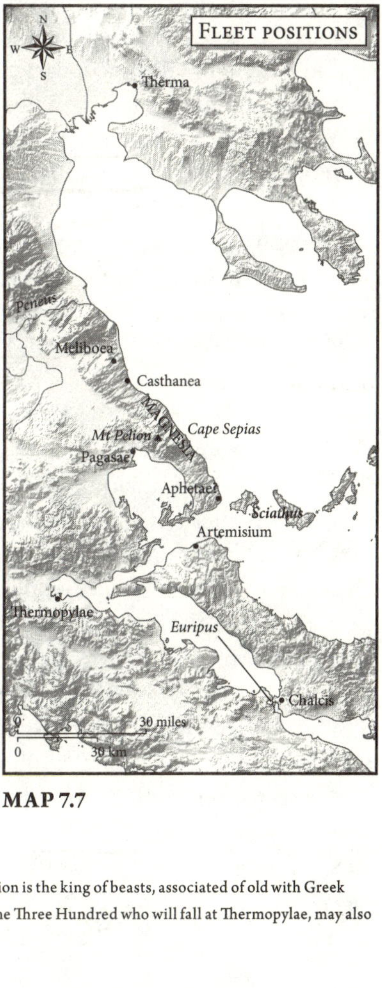

MAP 7.7

23 *Leon* means lion. What is meant here is not entirely clear, but the lion is the king of beasts, associated of old with Greek royalty as well. The echo with *Leon*idas, the Spartan commander of the Three Hundred who will fall at Thermopylae, may also help motivate this remark.

Of the ten Persian ships, three ran aground on a reef that runs between Sciathus and Magnesia, that they call *Myrmex*, the Ant. The Persians hauled a stone pillar there and set it up to mark the reef. The whole fleet then sailed from Therma, with the way now clear, leaving eleven days after Xerxes had marched on with the land army. Pammon, a Scyrian man, guided them through the reef, which runs right into the channel. Sailing all day long the Persians reached Sepias, in the territory of Magnesia, anchoring at the beach between the city of Casthanea and the Cape of Sepias.

THE ENORMITY OF THE PERSIAN FORCES

7.184 Up to this point, with the navy now at Sepias and the army at Thermopylae, the Persian forces had suffered no losses. As for the total size of all the Persian host, I estimate as follows, using a combination of evidence and inference. The ships supplied from Asia numbered 1207, and thus, to start with, had 241,400 of their own people on board, if you reckon about 200 men per ship. But, in addition to their own people, there were also thirty marines on each ship, Persians or Medes or Sacae, and this group adds up to another 36,210. I need also to add, in addition to these two counts, the men from the transports, putting them at about 80 men, on average, for each ship. There were 3000 of these transport vessels, as I mentioned earlier, so these ships carried 240,000 men. So much then for the fleet supplied from Asia, being all told 517,610. As for the infantry, there were 1,700,000 foot soldiers and 80,000 horse. To that we need to add the Arabian camel drivers and the Libyan charioteers, who add up to another 20,000. The total count of naval and land forces is then 2,317,610. Such then are the forces that are said to have come from Asia, without counting the servants who came along or those who sailed in the grain transports.

7.185 But we still need to add to this total the forces that came from Europe, and there some guesswork will be necessary. For ships, the Greeks from Thrace and the islands lying off the Thracian coast provided 120, and so 24,000 men sailed with them. For the infantry, I'd guess there were about 300,000 from the various peoples, including Thracians, Paeonians, Eordi, Bottiaei, Chalcidians, Brygi, Pierians, Macedonians, Perrhaebi, Enienes, Dolopes, Magnesians, Achaeans, and the tribes who live along the Thracian coast. Adding these to the total from Asia, the grand total for all the armed forces is 2,641,610.

7.186 Such then is the count for the armed forces. As for the servants who came along and those on the small grain transports and all the other supply ships that sailed with the army, my guess is that the total is not less, but more, than that for the armed men. But I will put them at the same size, no more no less, and on that assumption, the grand total of men who followed Xerxes son of Darius to this point in his advance—the navy to Sepias and the army to Thermopylae—was 5,283,220.

7.187 Such then is the count for the total force under Xerxes' command. But as for the women who cooked for them, and the concubines, and the eunuchs—no one can give a total with any accuracy. Nor is it possible to give a count for the oxen and other beasts of burden, or for the Indic dogs that followed along. It is, then, hardly a surprise that the water in the rivers along the way ran out, but rather the surprise lies in that the food never ran out for so great a multitude. If you assume that each man took one choenix of grain every day, no more, then I calculate that they used 110,340 medimni each and every day[24]—and I'm not even counting the women or eunuchs or oxen or dogs. These then are the numbers for the men in Xerxes' army, and out of them all, there was no man in nobility or stature more worthy than the Great King himself to hold the command.

THE STORM

So, the fleet had now sailed forth and come to land at the territory of Magnesia 7.188
on the coast between the city of Casthanea and Cape Sepias. The first line of ships moored to the land, but the rest had to anchor next to them—the beach was not broad enough, and thus they anchored with prows turned seaward, in lines, eight deep. In that way they spent the night, but with the dawn there arose from a clear and breezeless sky a mighty storm, that fell upon them with the sea boiling and great winds blowing out of the east, a kind of gale that the locals around there call a *Hellespontian*. When they heard the wind rising, those whose moorings allowed it, or who took action in time, got their ships up on the beach and survived, both men and ships; but those taken to the high seas were shipwrecked, some driven on the reefs at Ipni under Mt. Pelion, or on the coast thereabouts, others on Cape Sepias itself; and yet others washed ashore near the town of Meliboea or Casthanea: the might of the storm was simply more than the ships could stand.

A story is told that the Athenians had summoned Boreas[25] against the Per- 7.189
sian fleet, roused by an oracle that bid them ask their son-in-law for help. According to Greek legend, Boreas took as wife an Attic woman, Oreithyia daughter of Erechtheus.[26] Because of this legend, then, the Athenians thought Boreas their in-law, or that's what they say at least, and so, at their station at Chalcis, when they heard the storm coming, or even before that, they made sacrifices and called on Boreas and Oreithyia to come to their aid and wreck the Persian fleet—just as he had done earlier, off Mt. Athos.[27] Now whether for this reason Boreas came down on the Persians as they lay at anchor, I cannot say. But this in any case is what the Athenians say—that the North Wind came to their aid and worked destruction both earlier, at Athos, and at this time; and when they got home, they set up a shrine to Boreas, next to the river Ilissus.

24 A medimnus had 48 choenices, thus Herodotus makes a rare if also minor mistake in his calculation (110,067 is the correct quotient). A choenix is a dry measure roughly equal to 2 pints; a medimnus equals about 1.5 bushels. This is a lot of wheat: in weight, about 5000 tons a day!

25 The North Wind.

26 Legendary founder and first king of Athens.

27 See 6.44.

7.190 In this disaster, those who give the most conservative counts say that no fewer than four hundred ships were lost, as well as countless men and an enormous amount of money. For Ameinocles son of Cretines, a Magnesian man with property near Cape Sepias, the wrecked ships proved a great bounty, since he picked up many drinking cups of gold and silver that washed up there later, along with Persian treasure chests and other riches beyond reckoning. But though these lucky finds made him a wealthy man, he was not altogether fortunate—an unhappy mishap came to bring him pain, the unintended murder of his own child.

7.191 So much for the wrecked warships; of the wrecked grain transports and other such vessels, no count was possible. The fleet commanders now grew anxious that the Thessalians might attack them in their beleaguered state, and they therefore moved the wrecked ships to form a protective barricade around themselves. For three days the storm raged; the Magi made offerings to the wind, plied magical charms, and sacrificed to Thetis and the Nereids, and finally, on the fourth day, got it to stop—or maybe Boreas let up on his own. They sacrificed to Thetis because of a story they heard from the Ionians, that she had been taken from this very spot by Peleus, and that the whole of Cape Sepias was under her sway, along with the rest of the Nereids.

7.192 So, on the fourth day the wind stopped. The Greek lookouts meanwhile, who had been posted on the highlands of Euboea, had come down from the hills at a run on the day after the storm started, to tell all about the wrecking of the Persian ships. And when the Greeks heard this, they prayed to Poseidon as their Savior, and poured libations. And they hastened back to Artemisium, expecting to find few ships there to oppose them.

And so the Greeks came a second time to station their ships at Artemisium; and from that point still to this day they have called Poseidon "Our Savior."

FURTHER PERSIAN LOSSES

Again, it is chance rather than a battle that brings woe to the Persian fleet.

7.193 The Persians, once the wind had died down and the waves grew calm, launched their ships and sailed down along the coast; rounding the Magnesian cape, they sailed straight into the bay leading to Pagasae. On this bay there is a spot where, legend has it, Heracles while off getting water was left behind by Jason and his fellow Argonauts, when they were sailing to Aea in Colchis in quest of the golden fleece. This was the spot, then, where they watered the ship before launching out onto the high seas; and from that the place is named the Launching Spot, *Aphetae*. Here it was that Xerxes' men made their anchorage.

7.194 It happened that the last fifteen of the Persian ships, coming along far behind the others, somehow looked south to the Greek ships at Artemisium and thought these were their own; so, making sail for Artemisium, the Persians fell into enemy hands. These were under the command of Sandoces son of Thamasius, satrap of Cyme and that part of Aeolia. Years before

Sandoces had been one of the royal judges, but King Darius had had him seized and nailed alive to a cross when he was caught rendering an unjust verdict for a bribe. Yet even as Sandoces was hanging on the cross, Darius mulled things over and concluded that on balance he had done more good than bad to the king's interests. So, realizing that he had acted with more haste than wisdom, Darius had Sandoces released. Once then, Sandoces had escaped death, at the hands of King Darius, but now, sailing down to the Greek ships, he was not going to escape a second time: as soon as the Greeks saw the Persians approaching, they grasped what had happened, and so put out to sea and easily took them captive.

On board one of the Persian ships, they caught Aridolis, tyrant of the city 7.195
of Alabanda in Caria, and on another Penthylus son of Demonous, the Paphian commander. Penthylus had brought twelve ships from Paphos, but lost eleven of them in the storm off Cape Sepias; it was the one surviving ship that he now sailed down to the Greeks to be captured. The Greeks interrogated the prisoners, to find out all they could about Xerxes' army, and then sent them in shackles to the Isthmus at Corinth.

Meanwhile the Persian fleet, except for the fifteen ships under Sandoces' 7.196
command, arrived at Aphetae. Three days earlier, the infantry had marched through Thessaly and Achaea, and invaded the territory of the Malians. . . .

Thermopylae

Thermopylae and the 300 under Leonidas is a story best left to tell itself.

And it was in Malian Trachis that King Xerxes set up his camp, even as the 7.201
Greeks were setting up theirs in the pass called by the natives and locals the Gates, *Pylae*, but by most Greeks the Hot Gates, *Thermopylae*. So, each army set up its camp, the king controlling the area to the north all the way down to Trachis, and the Greeks holding the area from there to the south, on this, the Greek side of the mainland.

THE GREEK FORCES

The Greeks that awaited the Persian king there were as follows. There were 7.202
three hundred Spartan hoplites and a thousand from Tegea and Mantinea (each providing half that number), and from Orchomenus in Arcadia one hundred twenty, with a thousand from the rest of Arcadia. From Corinth there were four hundred, from Phlius two hundred, and eighty from Mycenae. That was the total from the Peloponnese, and from Boeotia came seven hundred from Thespiae and four hundred from Thebes.

In addition, the Locrians of Opus were asked to provide as many hoplites 7.203
as they could, and a thousand were requested from Phocis. The Greeks had put out a summons to these two allies, saying by messenger: "We ourselves have come in advance of the others, with the rest of the alliance expected any day; the Athenians and Aeginetans and the rest of the assembled fleet are

MAP 7.8

providing you protection by sea. There is nothing for you to fear. It is, after all, not a god who invades Greece but a man; and there is not and never will be a mortal who does not have from the moment of birth bad mixed in with the good—and for the greatest men the worst is mixed in with the best. We should expect that this invader, too, since he is mortal, must surely fail in such great expectations." On hearing this, the Locrians and Phocians sent men to help the Greeks at Trachis.

7.204 Each of the cities had its own general, but the most admired, and the supreme commander of the whole contingent, was the Lacedaemonian general Leonidas, son of Anaxandrides son of Leon son of Eurycratides son of Anaxander son of Eurycrates son of Polydorus son of Alcamenes son of Teleclus son of Archelaus son of Hegesilaus son of Doryssus son of Leobotas son of Echestratus son of Agis son of Eurysthenes son of Aristodemus son of Aristomachus son of Cleodaeus son of Hyllus son of Heracles. Leonidas had
7.205 come to hold the kingship at Sparta unexpectedly, having had not the slightest thought of becoming king, since he had two older brothers, Cleomenes and Dorieus. But Cleomenes died, without male issue, and at that point Dorieus was already gone, having ended his life in Sicily. So, the kingship devolved on Leonidas, both because he was born before Cleombrotus, the youngest of Anaxandrides' sons, and because he had taken to wife Cleomenes' daughter.[28]

Leonidas brought with him to Thermopylae the three hundred men dictated by Spartan law,[29] all of whom were men with sons to succeed them. He also brought with him the Thebans whose count I mentioned earlier, under the command of Leontiades son of Eurymachus. The reason why Leonidas made an arrangement to take along the Thebans, alone of all the Greeks, was that they were under grave suspicion of going over to the Persian side. So, wanting to know whether they would send troops or openly betray the Greek alliance, he summoned them to accompany him to the war. The Thebans did send troops, but their sympathies were elsewhere.

The Spartans sent Leonidas and his men first, so that the allies, on seeing them, would join the fight and not go over to the Persians (which they might if they found the Spartans hesitating). At present the celebration of the Carneia[30]

28 Cleomenes's daughter was named Gorgo; see 5.51, 7.239. Though of the same father, Cleomenes and Leonidas had different mothers.

29 The Spartan king traveled with a bodyguard of 300 Spartiates (i.e., full Spartan citizens).

30 This 9-day festival in honor of Apollo was also the reason for the Spartans delaying and thus missing the battle of Marathon: see 6.106. If true that Spartans were forbidden to wage war during this sacred festival, the dispatching of the Three Hundred is a remarkable exception.

was in the way, so their plan was to come later, once the festival was over, in full force and all speed, leaving but a garrison at Sparta. The rest of the allies, however, had pretty much the same thing in mind—since the festival at Olympia coincided with the invasion as well. So, not at all expecting the battle at Thermopylae to be decided so quickly, they dispatched only this advance guard.

Such in any case had been the Peloponnesian plans. But the Greeks at 7.207
Thermopylae, thinking the Persian attack imminent, grew alarmed and started to plan a retreat. To all the Peloponnesians except the Spartans, it seemed best to return to the Peloponnese and set up defenses at the Isthmus. But Leonidas, seeing the Phocian and Locrian outrage at the proposal, voted to stay there, and he sent messengers to the cities bidding them bring help at once—they were too few to stop the army of the Medes.[31]

Even as they debated, Xerxes decided to send a man on horseback to scout 7.208
out the size of the Greek force, and to see what they were up to. Back in Thessaly on his way here, Xerxes had already heard that a small force had gathered, and that it was under the command of the Spartans and Leonidas, a descendant of Heracles. When the horseman approached the camp, he looked but could not see the whole of it—some of the Greeks were stationed behind the wall, which they had now restored, and he could not see over it. But he did learn about those who were posted in front of the wall, with their weapons stacked on the ground. At that moment, these were the Spartans. The scout watched as some stripped for exercise, and others combed out their long hair. Amazed at what he saw, he made an exact count of their number and then rode away. And he rode away in peace—no one gave chase or paid him any attention. When he got back, he told Xerxes all that he had seen.

XERXES AND DEMARATUS

Xerxes listened but could not take in the plain truth—that the Spartans were 7.209
getting ready to fight to the best of their ability, to kill or be killed. In his view what they were doing seemed ridiculous. So, Xerxes sent for Demaratus son of Ariston, who was with him in the camp, and questioned him closely, wanting to uncover what the Lacedaemonians were up to. Demaratus replied, "You heard me talk about these men before, when we were setting out to invade Greece, and you thought my words risible, even though I foresaw how things were going to turn out. My entire goal, King, is to tell you nothing but the truth. Hear me again now: these men have come to fight us for possession of this pass, and they are ready to do so. It has always been their custom to carefully dress their hair when they are about to risk their lives. But know this: if you defeat these men and those left in Sparta as well, no other nation will lift their hands to resist you, King. You now are meeting up with the best of warriors, from the most noble kingdom and city in Greece." But to Xerxes what he said seemed beyond belief,

31 Herodotus sometimes, as here, uses "Medes" to refer to the whole of the Persian force.

and so for a second time he asked how so few men would fight his army. To that Demaratus replied, "King, treat me as a liar, if things do not turn out as I say."

THE PERSIANS ATTACK

7.210 Yet Xerxes remained unconvinced. He now let four days pass, expecting each day that the Greeks would take flight. But on the fifth day, since they showed no signs of leaving and seemed determined to stay—those impudent fools!—he angrily sent the Medes and Cissians to attack. "Capture them alive and bring them here to my sight!" But when they rushed upon the Greeks, many Medes fell, even as others came up to take their place; and though they did not retreat, the assault proved a great disaster. They made it clear to everyone, and not least to the king himself, that although he had many people in his army, he had few men. And so throughout the day the fighting continued.

7.211 The Medes, badly beaten, at length withdrew. Taking their place was a picked body of Persians, the ones the king calls his Immortals,[32] under the command of Hydarnes, and they attacked, thinking that they would make short work of the Greeks. But when they joined battle with the Greeks, they fared no better than the Medes—it worked out just the same, since they were fighting in a very narrow space and had spears shorter than the Greeks, unable therefore to use their force of numbers. For their part, the Lacedaemonians fought remarkably, skilled fighters against unskilled, showing among their many tricks this one: they would turn their backs and run in a group, pretending to flee; the Persians would see this and race after them with shouts and

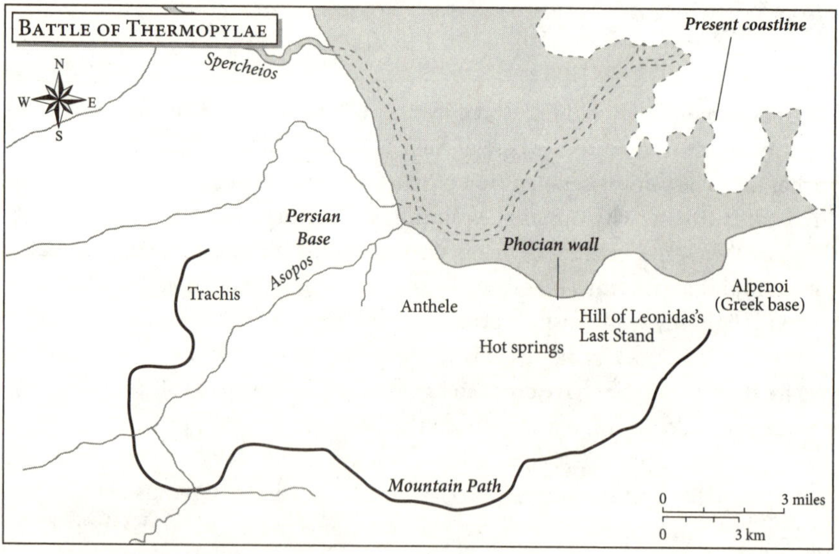

FIGURE 7.5 Battle of Thermopylae

32 The elite fighting force among the Persians, called the Immortals because as soon as a man fell, a substitute was added, thus keeping the group's strength at exactly 10,000.

commotion; but just as the enemy started to overtake them, they would whirl around and cut down Persians beyond count. The Spartans for their part had but few losses. The Persians, thus, were unable to take the pass, try though they might, attacking in waves and every other way—and so they retreated.

During the Persian assault, the king, they say, while watching thrice leaped up from his throne, frightened for his army. 7.212

That then was the fighting that day, and on the next the Persian army had no better success. Since there were not many Greeks, they attacked in the hope that enough had been wounded to make further resistance impossible. The Greeks, however, were deployed by divisions and nations, and each fought in turn—except the Phocians, who were stationed as guards at the path over the mountain. So, the Persians found nothing different from what they had seen the day before, and at the end of the day they drew back.

EPHIALTES AND THE PATH OVER THE MOUNTAIN

Xerxes was now at a loss as to what to do under the circumstances, and at that moment a man from Malis, Ephialtes son of Eurydemus, approached him. Thinking to get a big reward from the king, he told him about the path that goes over the mountain to Thermopylae—and thereby caused the deaths of all the Greeks who would stay to fight. Afterward, this Ephialtes, fearing the Lacedaemonians, fled to Thessaly; and while he was in exile representatives of the Amphictyonic council, meeting at Thermopylae, set a price on his head. Later, he returned to Anticyra and was killed by a Trachinian man, Athenades. Actually Athenades killed him for a different reason (which I'll explain later),[33] but he was honored by the Spartans anyway. 7.213

That in any case is how Ephialtes died, later on. There is a different tale told, though, that it was a Carystian man, Onetes son of Phanagoras, and an Anticyrean named Corydallus, who told the king and led the Persians over the mountain. But I don't believe it. One must weigh the fact that the Amphictyonic council set a price not on Onetes' head nor on Corydallus, but on Ephialtes the Trachinian, presumably after making exacting inquiries. And we know that Ephialtes was the one trying to escape punishment. True, Onetes, even though not from Malis, *could* know about this path, if he had strong ties to the area. But, no, Ephialtes was the one who led the Persians along that path, and I record him as the man responsible. 7.214

Now Xerxes was exceedingly pleased by what Ephialtes proposed, and he at once dispatched Hydarnes and the Immortals; so, just as the time came to light the torches, they set out from the camp. The path had originally been discovered by local Malians, and it was by this path that they led the Thessalians to attack the Phocians, at a time when the Phocians had barricaded 7.215

33 Herodotus never gets to this, one of a very few such unfulfilled promises in the work, sometimes taken as a sign that the work was not quite completed by the time of his death.

Thermopylae with a wall and thought themselves safe from invasion. From so early on, then, had the deadliness of the path been known to the Malians.

7.216 The path runs like this: it begins at the river Asopus at the point where it flows through a gorge, and the name of the mountain there is the same as that of the path, Anopaea. The path then runs along the ridge of the mountain, and ends near Alpenus (the Locrian town nearest to Malis), where stands the rock formation named after Melampygus and the Cercopes. There it is at its most narrow.

7.217 This then was the path the Persians took, crossing the Asopus, and marching all night, with the mountains of Oeta on the right and those of Trachis on the left. Daybreak found them at the summit of the ridge. And it was along this very mountainside, as I mentioned earlier, that one thousand Phocian troops stood guard, protecting their own territory and also keeping watch over the path. The road below was defended as I've described; but here, at the path through the mountains, the Phocians stood on duty, just as they had promised Leonidas.

7.218 Here's how the Phocians found out that the Persians had climbed up to the ridge. At first, the marching army went unnoticed, since the whole mountainside was obscured by oak trees. But there was no wind, and so gradually a great deal of noise arose, as you might guess, with so many leaves under foot. The Phocians sprang up and began putting on their armor—and just then the Persians appeared. And when the Persians saw men in the midst of arming themselves, they were astonished: they had expected not a soul there to oppose them, but here was an army! Hydarnes, fearing that the Phocians might be Spartans, asked Ephialtes whose army this was; and when he found out, he ordered the Persians to attack. Thick and fast, arrows hailed down upon the Phocians, and so they turned and ran for the crown of the hill, thinking that the attack was meant for them all along; and they prepared to die. Such was their thinking. But the Persians with Ephialtes and Hydarnes ignored them, and trekked off down the mountain as quickly as they could.

SOME GREEKS DECIDE TO DEPART

7.219 As for the Greeks at Thermopylae, first the seer Megistias, on examining the sacrificial entrails, declared that this dawn would bring them death. Next were the deserters, who came with news of the Persian march around the mountain. All that happened while it was still nighttime. But third came the lookouts, who raced down from the peaks as daylight came on. The Greeks then tried to formulate a plan of action, and opinions were divided. Some said they should not leave their post, others arguing the opposite. In the end they went their separate ways, some leaving and scattering, each to his own city, but others readying themselves to stay there with Leonidas and fight.

7.220 The tale is also told that it was Leonidas himself who sent them away, out of concern that they not die there, even if for himself and the Spartans it was unthinkable to abandon the post that they had come to defend. But here I am much more inclined to think that Leonidas ordered them to leave when he saw the lack of heart in the other soldiers and their unwillingness to risk battle.

For him to leave, he thought, was unsupportable; and indeed, he gained great glory by staying, and the future prosperity of Sparta as well.[34] You see, the Spartans had consulted Delphi about the war, right at the beginning when it first broke out, and the Pythian priestess had issued a prophecy: either Lacedaemon would be conquered by the Persians, or the Spartan king would die. The hexametric verses of the oracle went like this:

O ye residents of bounteous-landed Sparta, hear what is fated:
either your much-famed citadel will be sacked by the sons
of Perseus, or, if that not be, then the land of Lacedaemon
will mourn the perishing of a king from Heracles' line.
No might of bull or lion can stop the invader, strength against strength,
for he has the might of Zeus. No one, I say, will stop him
before he has had his fill of one or the other, Sparta or its king.[35]

Leonidas, I think, thought about these very verses, and so sent away the other soldiers, wanting to keep the glory for the Spartans alone—and also thinking it better to send them away in orderly fashion than to have them leave quarrelling and in confusion. A proof of this, and a strong one, is that Leonidas is 7.221
known to have sent away the seer who came with the army, so that he would not die alongside them—Megistias, an Acarnanian, reputedly a descendant of Melampus,[36] and the one who told them from the entrails what was to happen. Though bidden to go, Megistias refused; instead he sent his son, the only one he had, who was one of the soldiers on the campaign.

The rest of the Greek soldiers then went on their way as Leonidas had or- 7.222
dered, with only the Thespians and Thebans staying alongside the Lacedaemonians. The Thebans stayed quite against their wishes: Leonidas held them as though they were hostages. The Thespians, however, very much of their own accord refused to leave and thus abandon Leonidas and his men. So, they stayed and died. And their commander was Demophilus son of Diadromes.

LEONIDAS AND HIS 300 MAKE A STAND

At sunrise Xerxes poured libations, but then held back the attack until mid- 7.223
morning—such was the timing Ephialtes had advised, knowing that the path down the mountain is far shorter and quicker than the way up and around. And when the barbarian forces under Xerxes began their advance, the Greeks under Leonidas, coming out to face certain death, formed their line at a broader spot in the pass. Earlier they had used the wall to retreat to, and so in previous days had

34 In the *Iliad*, too, Achilles faces the choice of dying young and winning great fame (*kleos*), or going home without great battle deeds or fame. Cultured Greeks will have seen the epic resonance in Leonidas's decision and in the hand-to-hand combats to come.

35 The Persian foe is likened to a ravening monster feasting on the Greeks. As before (7.180) the "lion" is a play on the *Leon* part of Leonidas's name.

36 A legendary seer.

come out only to the narrow part just in front. But now, with the battle joined along a wide front, a great many of Xerxes' men died, everyone pressed on from behind, forced ever onward by the whips and canes of their commanders. Many fell into the sea too and perished there, and still more were trampled under foot by one another, with no thought given to who was being killed. On their side, the Greeks knew well that death was to be theirs, at the hands of those who were coming around the mountain, and so they put on display all the strength they could muster—wild, reckless, crazy in their fight with the Persians.

7.224 Many of the Spartans by this point had shattered their spears, but they fought on, using their swords to cut down the Persians. And now Leonidas fell in combat, the best and finest of warriors, and other Spartans of note, men so worthy that I have learned all their names—indeed, I know the names of all the Three Hundred. The Persians also lost many a distinguished man, among them two sons of Darius, Habrocomes and Hyperanthes, both born of Phratagune, daughter of Artanes. (This Artanes was the brother of King Darius, and son of Hystaspes son of Arsames; when he gave his daughter to wed Darius, he
7.225 gave his every possession as dowry, she being his only child.) These two, then—brothers of Xerxes—were among those who fell in combat.

7.225 Now around the corpse of Leonidas a great pushing and pulling arose, until the Greeks bravely dragged off the body and four times turned back the enemy.[37] And so it went, up to the time that Ephialtes and the Immortals appeared. Once the Greeks found out that they had arrived, the fighting shifted: they retreated to the narrow part of the pass, and then positioned themselves up on a small hill past the wall, all bunched together (except the Thebans). The hill is right there in the pass, where now the stone lion stands memorializing Leonidas. Here they tried to defend themselves with short swords if they still had them, or with bare hands and teeth if they did not, even as the Persians buried them with arrows and spears, some coming up in front of them, knocking down the wall, others stationed all around, shooting at them from every side.

7.226 Such then was the brave fighting of the Lacedaemonians and Thespians. For all that, one man, a Spartan named Dieneces, is said to have been the bravest of all. Of him they tell this tale: that before the fighting began, he heard from one of the Trachinians that when the Persians fire their bows, there are so many arrows that they block out the sun; untroubled, Dieneces made light of the numbers of the Medes, saying, "You, my friend, come with good news, if truly the Medes will cover up the sun and our battle can be fought in the shade."

7.227 They say that the Lacedaemonian Dieneces left this and other such sayings as his memorial. After him two Spartan brothers are singled out for bravery, Alpheus and Maron, the sons of Orsiphantus. As for the Thespians, the best report is given of a man named Dithyrambus son of Harmatides.

37 This fighting over the fallen corpse is a familiar scene from the *Iliad*, where it plays out many times, but in its most prolonged scene over the body of Achilles's comrade Patroclus. Whatever the historicity of this part of the struggle, the tone here is decidedly heroic.

The Greeks were buried right there where they fell in battle, as well as those 7.228
who died earlier, before anyone left at Leonidas's bidding. Over them stands an inscription that reads:

Here against three hundred ten thousands[38] *did*
four thousand men from the Peloponnese make a stand.

That inscription was for all who defended the pass, but there is another for the Spartans alone.

O stranger passing by, tell the men of Sparta
that, having obeyed their commands, we here lie.[39]] law, nomos

There is also a third inscription, for the seer.

Here stands the memorial of famed Megistias, a man killed
by the Medes after they crossed the river Spercheius, a seer,
who though he saw clearly that Death was on its way,
could not abandon his Spartan commander.

The pillars with these inscriptions, except for the one about the seer, were set up by the Amphictyonic council; the one about the seer was composed and set up by Simonides son of Leoprepes, in honor of their friendship.

THOSE WHO SURVIVED

A story is told of two of the Three Hundred, Eurytus and Aristodemus, who 7.229
had been removed from camp by Leonidas and were laid up at Alpeni with a bad eye ailment. Now if they had agreed on their course of action these two could have reached Sparta safely together, or, if they didn't want to go home, could have died with the others. But as it was, they could not agree. So, when they heard that the Persians had gotten around the mountain, Eurytus called for his armor, put it on, and ordered a helot to guide him to the battle; once they got there, his guide ran away, but he joined the melee and was killed. Aristodemus meanwhile, faint of heart, was left behind. Now if Aristodemus had been the only one sick and had gone back to Sparta, or if the two had both made the journey together, I think the Spartans would not have been so indignant. But as it was, with one dying, and the other escaping death—while having only the same excuse his comrade might have offered—they were unavoidably incensed at Aristodemus's conduct.

38 In other words, 3,000,000.

39 The word here for "commands" (*rhêtra*) in Spartan society implies obedience to their laws and customs. Recall that Spartan law dictates that the Spartans must stand and fight, even if it means certain death (7.104).

7.230 That Aristodemus returned safely to Sparta and used his eye ailment as an excuse is not, however, the only report. Others say that he had been dispatched as a messenger, and though it was possible to get back when the battle started, he deliberately lingered on the road and so survived; and that Eurytus was with him, also as a messenger, but returned in time for the battle and died.

7.231 In any case, when Aristodemus got back to Lacedaemon he met with disdain and public humiliation: no one would give him a light to kindle his fire nor would they talk to him; and they gave him the nickname "Aristodemus the Faint-Hearted." But in the battle of Plataea he put right all the ignominy that had attached to him.

7.232 Another such tale is told, of one of the Three Hundred who was dispatched to Thessaly as a messenger and thus survived. His name was Pantites, and when he returned to Sparta, he too met with public humiliation; and so he hanged himself.

7.233 As for the Thebans under Leontiades, they fought against the Persians under compulsion as long as the Greeks were alongside. But when they saw the Persians gaining the upper hand, and the Greeks under Leonidas being pushed up the hill, they broke away and went up to the Persians with outstretched arms, telling them what was very much the truth, that they were on the king's side—they had been among the first to offer him earth and water!—that they had been forced to come to Thermopylae, and that they were blameless for the harm done to the king. And so saying, they survived; they had the Thessalians to back up the story, after all. Yet it was not entirely a happy ending. The Persians seized them as they approached, and some they killed on the spot, while most of the others Xerxes had branded as slaves, beginning with the commander, Leontiades, putting on them his royal mark. And later,[40] Leontiades' son Eurymachus would take the city of Plataea with four hundred Thebans under his command, but then be killed by the Plataeans.

Xerxes and Demaratus

Once again, Xerxes has the opportunity to avoid imminent disaster by following wise advice.

7.234 That then is how the Greeks fought at Thermopylae. Xerxes now summoned Demaratus to ask him a question, but prefaced it with this: "Demaratus, you are a good and trustworthy man. The facts prove it: all that you predicted has come to pass. But now tell me this: how many Lacedaemonians are there, and how many fight like this—or is it all of them?" Demaratus replied, "King, great are the numbers and many are the cities in all Lacedaemon. But here is what you want to know. In Lacedaemon there is a city, Sparta, with about eight thousand men, and these are all very like the ones who fought here. The rest of the Lacedaemonians

40 Much later: 431 BC at the outbreak of the Peloponnesian War. The story is told in Thucydides 2.2–5.

are not like this, though brave." To that Xerxes said, "Demaratus, how can we overmaster these Spartans with the least trouble? Come, tell me: as their former king you know the ins and outs of their strategy."

He replied, "King, if you are seeking my advice in all seriousness, it is but 7.235
right that I tell you the plan that is best. I would that you send three hundred ships from the fleet to the land of Laconia.[41] An island lies just off there called Cythera, and one of the wisest among us, a man named Chilon, once said of it that for the Spartans the greatest boon would be if it sank beneath the ocean; he always expected, you see, that something would come from it such as I am suggesting, not foreseeing your invasion in particular, but fearing in general such an attack. It is from this island that you should launch a campaign of terror against the Lacedaemonians. With a war of their own so close at hand they are not to be feared—even if your army captures the rest of Greece, they will not come to help. And, when the rest of Greece is under your sway, an already weakened Laconia is all that is left. But if you do not follow my advice, expect this to happen. The Peloponnese has a narrow isthmus. There, with all of the Peloponnesians joining forces to resist you, expect other battles like the one here, or even worse. But if you do as I say, the isthmus and the cities will surrender without a fight."

Now Achaemenes, commander of the fleet and Xerxes' brother, happened 7.236
to be at that conversation. Worried that Xerxes might be persuaded to follow this advice, he spoke next. "King, I see you listening to a man jealous of your successes, or even ready to betray you. That, you know, is exactly how Greeks love to be, ever envying good fortune and hating their betters. Now in the present circumstances, with four hundred ships wrecked, if you send three hundred to sail around the Peloponnese, our adversary becomes our equal. If, however, the fleet stays together, it will present them with insurmountable difficulties: they will not be able to challenge us in combat, and the fleet and army can buttress and assist each other, the two working in tandem. Split them up, though, and you will be of no use to them nor they to you. My counsel is to keep track of your own concerns, and not to think too much about the enemy, where they will make a stand, what they will do, or how many they are. Let them sort that out for themselves, and let us

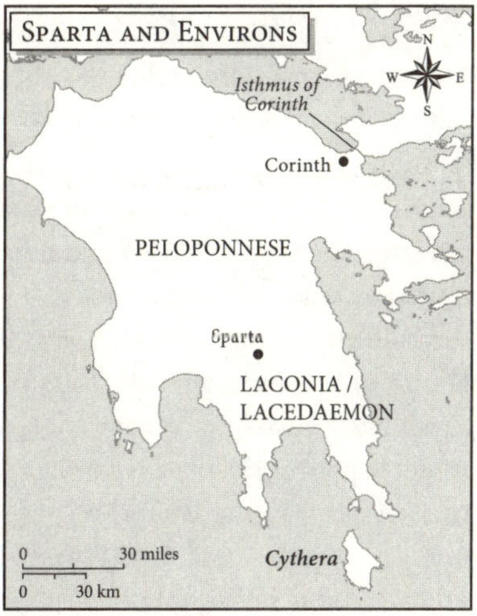

MAP 7.9

41 Laconia is another name for Lacedaemon, the region around Sparta.

focus on our own affairs. And if the Lacedaemonians do come to face the Persians in battle, they will surely not heal the hurt they suffered here."

7.237 Xerxes replied, "Achaemenes, what you say makes sense and I will do as you suggest. But Demaratus is saying what he thinks will turn out best for me, even if your advice is better. I reject the notion that he has in mind anything but my best interests, judging both by what he has advised in the past and by this fact: a fellow countryman may indeed envy the successes of another, and when advice is needed, he may angrily keep quiet, refusing to give the best course of action—unless he is remarkably noble, but such people are rare. A man from a different country, however, is unmatched as a supporter when things go well for his foreign friend, and when advice is needed he gives the best he can. So, I command you in the future to keep to yourself such slander against Demaratus, a foreigner whom I have taken in as my friend."

7.238 With that, Xerxes proceeded to walk through the battlefield and inspect the corpses. And when he came to Leonidas, hearing that this was the king and commander of the Lacedaemonians, he ordered his men to cut off his head and fix it to a pole. Many other pieces of evidence, but particularly this deed, convince me that Leonidas enraged King Xerxes more than any other man, at least while he was alive. Otherwise, he would not have done something so outrageous to the corpse, since Persians, more than any other people I know, honor men who fight bravely. But those to whom it was appointed did as Xerxes had ordered.

7.239 I now need to return to an earlier part of my narrative. The Lacedaemonians were the first to find out that the Great King was invading Greece, and thus they were the ones who sent to the oracle at Delphi and got the prophecy I mentioned a bit earlier; but how they found out about the invasion is an amazing tale. When Demaratus son of Ariston fled in exile to the Medes, he was not, in my view and with probability as my ally, well disposed toward the Spartans—and one can therefore reasonably guess whether what he did was in friendship or by way of gloating. Now at the time when Xerxes decided to march on Greece, Demaratus was in Susa, and when he found out about the invasion, he wanted to be the one to tell the Lacedaemonians. But he didn't have any way to communicate—it was dangerous if he was exposed. So, he devised this scheme. He took a diptych tablet and scraped off the wax. On the wood underneath he wrote out what the king had in mind, and when he was done he melted wax back on top of what he had written. In that way, the tablet, apparently blank, could be carried without danger of trouble from the border guards. But when the tablet reached Lacedaemon, the Spartans couldn't figure it out, until (as I have learned) Gorgo, Cleomenes' daughter and Leonidas's wife, guessed the truth and made a suggestion: "Scrape off the wax," she bid them, "and you will find something written on the wood." Doing as they were told, they found the message and read it; and then wrote to tell the rest of the Greeks. Such is the story of how that came about.

BOOK 8
Salamis

The Persian occupation and destruction of Athens, and especially the burning of the Acropolis, including Athena's temple (the "Old Temple"), was a defining event in the life of the city. After the war, the Athenians left the Acropolis in its ravaged state for years, as a constant reminder of this ultimate violation, and when they did finally rebuild the walls and buildings on the Acropolis, they incorporated into the north wall remnants of the Old Temple, including visually striking rows of 29 enormous column drums that anyone in the central meeting area of the city would look up and notice (and very much visible today). The abandonment of Athens was a difficult but necessary military decision. The buildup of the Athenian fleet to a formidable force of 200 ships was a policy pushed by Themistocles, an influential politician who would become fleet commander in the years running up to the Persian invasion. It was this that made the evacuation of the city possible to countenance. With the city destroyed, however, it became desperately critical to Athenian survival that they defeat the Persians by sea, and this is an important part of the dynamic that plays out, by which the Athenian leader Themistocles insists on fighting it out here, at the island of Salamis, opposite the Athenian port, and in full view of Athens' Acropolis.

As so often, there is an interesting correlation between the Greek military strategy and the Delphic oracle. The oracle (as Herodotus described in a section we did not read, 7.141) predicts the fall of the city and advises the Athenians to withdraw, but in reply to Athenian supplication, adds that Athena has approached Zeus on their behalf and that *far-seeing Zeus grants to Athena that the wooden wall alone will remain intact, and give help to you and your children*. Themistocles and his supporters seized on this as meaning that the Athenians should retreat to the wooden ships, and rely on naval power. We cannot know, of course, but many scholars suppose that there was some explicit coordination between the Delphic priestess and the scheming Themistocles.

After Thermopylae and preliminary to Salamis, the Persians and Greeks fight an indecisive series of sea battles at Artemisium, in which, however, the Greeks show their superior command of naval tactics, and the Persians lose yet another 200 ships to the caprice of a god-sent storm. When the defeat of Leonidas is announced to the Greeks, the fleet decides to retreat from Artemisium.

The Greeks Evacuate Athens

8.40 At the request of Athens the Greek fleet sailing from Artemisium now put in at Salamis. The Athenians asked that the fleet make its anchorage at Salamis for two reasons: so that the ships could ferry the women and children from Attica, and because they wanted to discuss what needed to be done—given the current circumstances they intended to hold a council. The Athenians, you see, had a mistaken impression: having assumed that they would now find the Peloponnesians in full force in Boeotia, waiting to make a stand against

MAP 8.1

the Persians, they found nothing of the sort; rather, they learned that the Peloponnesians were busy building a wall across the Isthmus, clearly privileging the survival and defense of the Peloponnese, and giving up on the rest of Greece. For these reasons, then, had the Athenians made their request to station the fleet at Salamis.

So, the fleet anchored at Salamis, all but the Athenians, who anchored 8.41
across the strait in their own harbor. And after the fleet's arrival, they issued a proclamation, telling the Athenian citizens to get their children and households to safety by whatever means possible. Most were sent off to Troezen, but some to Aegina, and yet others to Salamis. They hurried to evacuate them in deference to the oracle to be sure, but also because of a remarkable thing that had happened. A large snake lives in the temple of Athena, standing guard over the Acropolis, or that at any rate is what the Athenians say; and since they think the guardian snake exists they have a monthly ritual in which they set out an offering to it, a cake made of honey. Now at this time the honey cake—which before had always been eaten—was left untouched. So, when the priestess revealed this, the Athenians vacated their city with yet more urgency, thinking that even Athena had abandoned the Acropolis. And when they had gotten everyone out, they sailed over to the main encampment.

When the ships from Artemisium had taken up station at Salamis, the rest 8.42
of the Greek fleet, as soon as they heard, joined them, streaming over from Pogon, the harbor at Troezen which had been their appointed gathering spot. Far more ships were now assembled than had fought at Artemisium, and from more towns as well. The fleet commander remained as at Artemisium, the Spartan Eurybiades son of Eurycleides, even though he was not of the royal line. It was Athens, however, that provided far the greatest number of ships, as well as the best trained crews.

The Greek Fleet

The catalogue of Greeks here effectively defines the "true" Greece under attack by the Persians, and largely matches the peoples inscribed on the so-called Serpent Column set up as a memorial to the defenders of Greece after the Persian War. The Greeks have great plurality in their fragile unity, with marked differences in region and ethnicity (as the remarks here on Dorian versus Ionian Greeks, etc., make clear). What unites them is, then, not simply language and customs, but also a commitment to national freedom in the face of tyranny.

The ships that comprised the fleet are as follows. First from the Pelopon- 8.43
nese: sixteen ships came from Sparta, forty from Corinth, the same count as at Artemisium, fifteen from Sicyon, ten from Epidaurus, five from Troezen, three from Hermione. All but Hermione are Dorian and Macedonian Greeks, the last to migrate from Erineus and Pindus and Dryopis. The people of Hermione are Dryopian Greeks, who were driven by Heracles and the Melians from the land now known as Doris.

8.44 Such then was the Peloponnesian contingent. From the Greek mainland, the Athenians sent one hundred and eighty, half of the whole fleet. They worked the ships by themselves: the Plataeans did not fight with the Athenians at Salamis (as they had at Artemisium) because, when they were leaving Artemisium and were near Chalcis, the Plataeans had disembarked at the shore opposite, in Boeotia, to try to evacuate their families; these, busy with the rescue effort, had been left behind. The Athenians are Pelasgians:[1] in the time when the Pelasgians held what is now Greece they were called Cranaï, then when Cecrops became king the Cecropidae, and only when Erechtheus assumed the throne did they change their name to Athenians; and when Ion son of Xuthus became their general, they took from him the name Ionians.

8.45 From Megara came twenty ships, the same number as at Artemisium; and seven from Ambracia joined the alliance, as well as three from Leucas. The Ambraciots and Leucadians are Dorian Greeks originally from Corinth.

8.46 From the islands, Aegina sent thirty ships. They had other ships in their command, but these they needed to guard their island, so they sent the thirty ships with the best crews to fight at Salamis. The Aeginetans are Dorian Greeks originally from Epidaurus, and earlier the name of their island was Oenone. Next came twenty ships from Chalcis, the same number as at Artemisium, and seven from Eretria; these people are both Ionian Greeks. From Ceos came seven; and these too are Ionians, originally from Athens. Four came from Naxos: these had been sent by their citizens to join the Medes, just as the rest of the islanders had done, but—at the instigation of Democritus, an outstanding citizen and at that time the naval commander—the Naxians ignored their orders and came to join the Greeks. The Naxians are Ionians, originally from Athens. Styra sent the same number of ships that they had at Artemisium, and Cythnus one trireme and one penteconter; both of these are Dryopian Greeks. Seriphus, Siphnus, and Melos also joined the fleet: these alone among the islanders had refused to subject themselves to the Persian king by sending earth and water.

8.47 Of those who dwell to this side of the river Acheron and the land of the Thesproti these then are all the ones who joined the fleet. The Thesproti are neighbors of the Ambraciots and Leucadians, the most distant lands to join the alliance. Beyond that boundary, the men of Croton[2] were the only ones to join the Greek cause, sending a single ship; and their captain was Phaÿllus, a man who had thrice won at the Pythian games. The Crotoniats are Achaean Greeks.

8.48 In every case triremes were the ships sent to join the fleet, except the Melians, Siphnians, and Seriphians, who sent penteconters: the Melians (of Lacedaemonian stock) sent two, the Siphnians and Seriphians (Ionians of Athenian lineage) sent one each. The total count of all the ships, penteconters

1 By Greek tradition, the original inhabitants of Greece.

2 Croton is at the southern tip of Italy, a Greek colony to the far west.

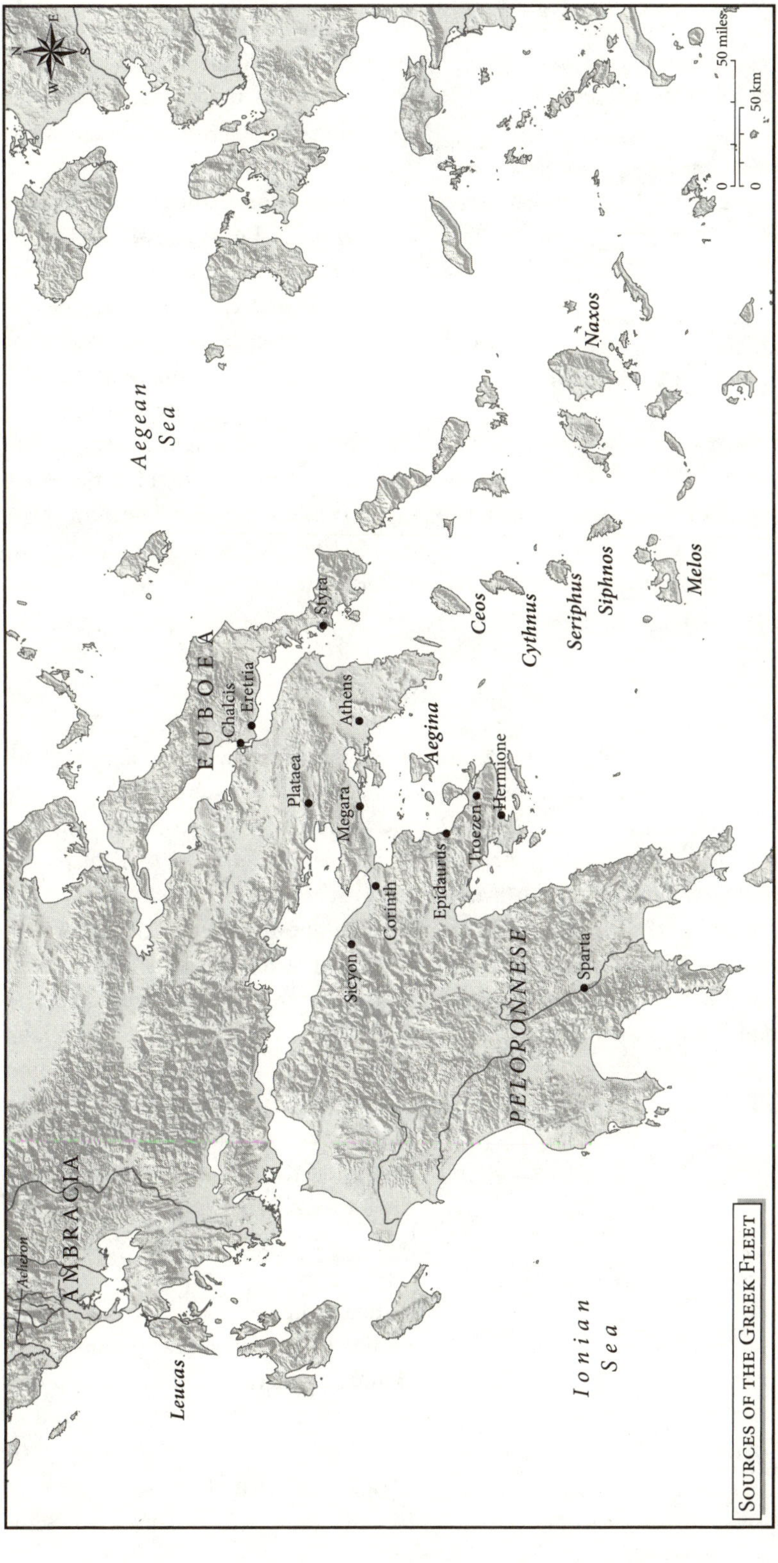

SOURCES OF THE GREEK FLEET

MAP 8.2

aside, was three hundred and seventy-eight.

FIGURE 8.1 The Olympias, a full-scale reconstruction of a trireme. Note the three banks of oars and the metal ram at the bow. A penteconter was an older ship: similar, but with only two banks of oars

8.49 When the captains from all these towns were gathered at Salamis, they held a council. The fleet commander Eurybiades spoke. "Let whoever so wishes offer an opinion on this question: where, of the areas we control, does it seem most expedient for the fleet to make its stand?" Attica was already lost, so it was about the rest that he was inquiring. Most of those who spoke were of one mind, that they should sail to the Isthmus and battle for control of the Peloponnese. A central consideration was this: should the fleet be defeated, at Salamis they would be trapped on the island and there would be no help in view; but at the Isthmus those shipwrecked would be cast ashore on their own territory.

The Persians Occupy Attica and Burn Athens

The way that the Acropolis is taken should remind the reader of Sardis; not, however, the burning by the Athenians, but its initial capture, by Cyrus. This is but one example of the way Herodotus draws together historical events remote in time and place, so as to suggest larger patterns. Here, the correlation serves to highlight the pivotal position of Sardis and Athens in his overall account.

8.50 But even as the commanders from the Peloponnese were debating this question, an Athenian man came to tell them that the Persians had reached Attica and were putting the whole countryside to the torch. Xerxes' army, he said, had made its way through Boeotia, burning the city of the Thespians (who had abandoned it and come to the Peloponnese) and likewise Plataea, since the Thebans had told them that these towns refused to join the Persian cause. Now the Persians had come to Athens and were laying waste to everything there.

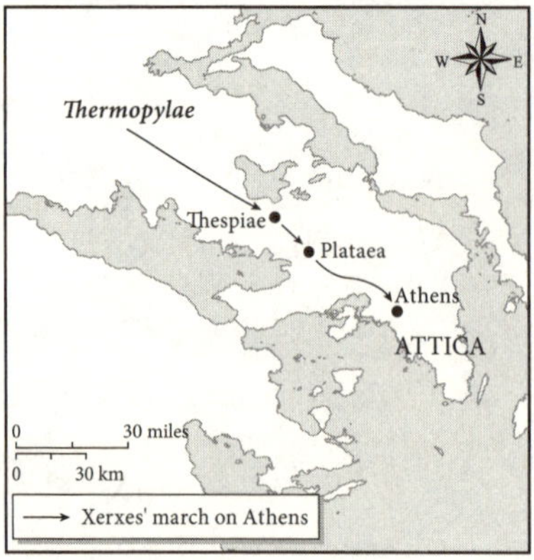

MAP 8.3

8.51 From the crossing over the Hellespont where they launched the invasion, the Persians had taken one month to march across Europe, and three more to make their way to Attica. We can fix the date as the year that Calliades was the archon in

Athens.[3] They captured a deserted city, finding only a few Athenians still in the temple, the keepers of the temple and some penniless people. These had barricaded the Acropolis entrance with planks and doors to keep out the attackers, not evacuating to Salamis both because of their lack of means and believing to have discovered what the oracle meant to say—the wooden wall that would be impregnable. The barricaded Acropolis, they thought, was the refuge the oracle intended, and not the wooden ships.

The Persians took up position on the hill opposite the entrance to the 8.52
Acropolis, which Athenians call the Areopagus. Here's how they went about the siege. They tied flax to their arrows to make a sort of wick, set them on fire, and then shot them at the barricade. The Athenians under attack nonetheless held their position, even though the barricade had failed them and they were now in desperate straits. They refused the offers for a treaty brought to them by the kinsmen of Peisistratus, and held on, using every scheme they could think of, including rolling down great boulders when the Persians tried to approach the gates. Xerxes was unable to defeat them, and thus for a long time was at a loss as to what to do.

But in time a way out of this impasse presented itself to the Persians—for, 8.53
to fulfill the prophecy, it was necessary that *all* of mainland Attica be under Persian control. At the front side of the Acropolis, behind the gates and the entrance, there was a spot left unguarded since no one expected any ever to climb up there. But some of the Persians did manage that climb, even though the way was precipitous, reaching the top near the temple of Aglaurus daughter of Cecrops. When the Athenians saw that the Persians had scaled the sheer cliff up to the Acropolis, some threw themselves down from the walls to their deaths, while others raced back to Athena's temple to take position as suppliants. The first Persians to scale the cliff turned to the gates, opened them, and then put the suppliants to the sword. And when all the Athenians had been killed, they looted the temples on the Acropolis and set everything ablaze.

With Athens entirely under his control, Xerxes sent to Susa a horseman to 8.54
announce to Artabanus his success. The next day, however, he summoned the Athenian exiles traveling with the army and bid them to mount the Acropolis and perform the customary sacrifices. It is not clear whether he ordered this because of a vision he saw in his sleep, or whether he was having regrets about burning down Athena's temple. In any case, the exiles did as commanded.

Let me explain why I mention this detail. On the Acropolis lies a temple of 8.55
Erechtheus the Earthborn (as he is called), and in its precinct there is an olive tree, and a well that gives forth saltwater. The Athenians say that these are relics that memorialize the contest between Poseidon and Athena over their land.[4] Now the olive tree and temple had been totally destroyed when the

3 480 BC. The archon was the chief magistrate of the city.

4 Legend has it that Poseidon and Athena competed to be patrons of the city, Poseidon bringing a salt spring and a horse, Athena the olive tree. Athena, of course, won.

Persians set the Acropolis on fire. But by the very next day, the Athenian exiles ordered by the king to make their sacrifices climbed up to this temple—and there saw a sprout shooting up from the stump, about a foot and a half long. The exiles then reported what they had seen.

8.56 Back at Salamis a great uproar arose when the Greeks heard about the burning of the Acropolis, and some of the captains did not so much as stay to vote on the resolution before them—they scrambled onto their ships and raced away under full sail. The captains who were left then resolved to fight at the Isthmus in its defense. Night fell, the assembly was dissolved, and the captains went back to their ships.

The Greeks Deliberate. Themistocles Tries to Persuade Eurybiades

Themistocles was a hugely controversial figure, a populist and as we see here more than a bit of a bully. As mentioned, he was the architect of the Athenian strategy of relying on their fleet, which he enacted over the objections of Aristeides, whom Themistocles and supporters had had ostracized and exiled. After the Persian War, Themistocles will be ostracized himself and then denounced as a traitor, fleeing eventually to Persia, where he would live out his life as a governor in service to Xerxes's successor Artaxerxes. Herodotus's readers will have known all about the scandals and controversy attached to this remarkable Athenian leader. The fragility of the Greek alliance is here on full display, and the deliberations show the unruly side of "freedom," warts and all, including cajoling, officiousness, threats, subterfuge.

8.57 An Athenian named Mnesiphilus then spoke with Themistocles when he came on board, asking what had been decided by the captains. When he heard that they had resolved to take the ships to the Isthmus and fight for the Peloponnese, he said, "If they set sail and leave Salamis, you will no longer be fighting for a common fatherland. Instead, each will turn to protect his own city, and neither Eurybiades nor any one else can keep them from scattering, thus breaking up the fleet. Greece will be lost through such utter folly! If there is anything you can think of, come, try to get this decision rescinded—see if you can convince Eurybiades to change his mind and stay here."

8.58 Now Themistocles was exceedingly pleased by Mnesiphilus's suggestion, so without saying a word he went straight to Eurybiades' ship. When he got there, he said he wanted to confer on a point of mutual interest; so, Eurybiades told him to come aboard if he liked. Taking a seat, Themistocles went through all the points Mnesiphilus had raised, though talking like they were his own, and adding many more. Finally, his very urgency convinced Eurybiades to step down from the ship and reconvene an assembly of the ship captains.

8.59 When all were present, before Eurybiades could say a thing about why he had summoned the captains, Themistocles poured out a torrent of words, urgent in his plea. But as he was talking a Corinthian captain, Adeimantus son of Ocytus, spoke up, saying: "In foot races, Themistocles, those who jump the starting line are punished with a cane." Defending himself, Themistocles replied, "Yes, and those left behind at the starting line do not get the victor's crown."

So far, then, he made the Corinthian but a mild retort. Turning now to 8.60
Eurybiades, he included nothing of what was said earlier—with the allies there, it would be impolitic to say that if the fleet sailed from Salamis the allies would run away. Instead, Themistocles pursued a different argument, which
went like this: "Saving Greece is in your power, if only you can be persuaded 8.60(1)
not to move the ships to the Isthmus, but to stay here to fight. Listen, and judge between the two plans. Fighting at the Isthmus you will fight in the open sea, which is least to our advantage, with our less maneuverable boats and lesser numbers. Moreover, you will lose Salamis and Megara and Aegina, even if we are successful in the fight. And their fleet travels in tandem with the land army and thus you yourself will draw them down to the Peloponnese,
and thereby endanger every part of Greece. But if you do as I suggest, you will 8.60(2)
find much to like. First, fighting here, in a narrow strait with our few against their many, we will be able to beat them, or that at least is what reason dictates. Fighting the sea battle in a narrow strait is to our benefit; fighting in the open sea is to theirs. Moreover, Salamis will continue to be ours, and that's where our women and children are. And there is also this point, which you should especially attend: if we stay here and fight, we will be defending the Peloponnese just as much as if we move to the Isthmus—but, by being smart about
this, you will not be drawing them down to the Peloponnese. Indeed if, as I 8.60(3)
expect, we win the sea battle, neither will you see the Persians at the Isthmus, nor will they march farther than Attica, but they will retreat in disorder; and we will have gained the rescue of Megara and Aegina—and Salamis, where the oracle told us we would get the upper hand over our enemy. For men who plan sensibly, everything they want can come to pass. But the god does not gladly come to the aid of men who do not."

After Themistocles' speech once again the Corinthian Adeimantus ob- 8.61
jected, telling him to keep quiet since he was now a man without a country and telling Eurybiades that it was impermissible to take a vote on a motion made by a cityless man; Themistocles, he said, must first find himself a city before participating in such a council; and he pointed out that Athens had been captured and occupied. At that, Themistocles said many a strong word about Adeimantus and the Corinthians, making it clear that Athens and Attica remained far greater than the land of Corinth, as long as they had a full complement of two hundred ships. Not a single one of the Greeks, he said, could stop them if they chose to attack.

After making that clear, he turned to Eurybiades, and spoke with yet more 8.62
passion: "If you stay here, you will show by staying that you are a fine and noble man. If not, you will bring about the downfall of Greece. The whole war depends entirely on our ships. So, heed what I say. And if you do not, we will

take our families and sail at once to Siris, in Italy, which has belonged to us of old, and where the oracles say we need to make a colony. And you, once stripped of allies like us, will remember my words."

8.63 At these words, Eurybiades decided to change his mind. I think the main reason for his change of heart was his fear that the Athenians would abandon them if he moved the ships to the Isthmus. Without the Athenians, the remaining fleet was no match for the Persians. In any case, Eurybiades chose this plan, to stay and fight at Salamis.

Signs from the Gods

The Greeks believed that after death great warriors—heroes—retained special powers. These were, however, local: you had to be at the tomb, or have the cult figures with you, for the hero to be able to exercise power on your behalf.

8.64 So it was that the Greeks hurled words back and forth at Salamis. But with Eurybiades' decision, they now got themselves ready to fight right where they were. The day came on and—just as the sun rose over the horizon—an earthquake shook land and sea. They then thought it best to pray to the gods and to enlist the sons of Aeacus as their allies. And they did just as they had resolved: praying to all the gods, they called on Ajax and Telamon from Salamis,[5] and then sent a ship to Aegina to fetch the cult images of Aeacus and his sons.

8.65 There is a story told by Dicaeus son of Theocydes, an Athenian in exile who was well respected among the Medes at this time. He says that when the Attic lands were being ravaged by Xerxes' army and all the Athenians had left, he chanced to be with Demaratus the Lacedaemonian on the plain of Thria, and there saw a cloud of dust moving from Eleusis as though an army of thirty thousand was marching, and that they were astonished, not understanding what men could be producing such a cloud. Just then, he said, they heard a voice, and the voice seemed to him the mystic cry of the Eleusinian cult. But Demaratus was unfamiliar with the rites of Eleusis, and so he asked Dicaeus what this cry was. "Demaratus," he said, "without any doubt some great harm is in store for the king's forces. Clearly some divinity has spoken—Attica is deserted, after all—and comes from Eleusis to avenge the Athenians and their allies. If the cloud descends upon the Peloponnese the king and the land army will be in danger, but if it turns toward the ships at Salamis, the king may well lose his fleet. Every year Athenians celebrate a festival for Demeter and her daughter Persephone, and any Greek who so wishes can become an initiate into the cult. The voice that you hear is the mystic cry raised in that festival." To that Demaratus said, "Keep quiet and tell no one else about this. If this story is reported to the king, you will lose your head, and neither I nor anyone else will be able to save you. So keep your peace, and as for the fate of the

5 Well-known heroes from Salamis. Ajax is a central character in the *Iliad*; Telamon, his father, was one of the Argonauts, and son of King Aeacus of Aegina.

armed forces here, that will be the gods' concern." Such was his advice, and from the dust cloud and voice arose a cloud high above, that was borne to Salamis, to the Greek camp there. By this the two came to know that Xerxes' fleet was to be destroyed. Such is the story Dicaeus son of Theocydes told, with Demaratus and others as his witness.

The Persians Deliberate. Artemisia Tries to Persuade Xerxes

The Persian council could not contrast more with the free-for-all we witnessed among the Greek leaders. Here, Xerxes does not even speak directly with his commanders, who sit at a distance in strict order of rank. The ruler of Halicarnassus, Artemisia—yet another of the remarkable women leaders in the Histories—rotates in as the final wise advisor to Xerxes on his Greek campaign. In an ironic twist, after Eurybiades autocratically makes the decision for the wrangling Greeks, Xerxes makes his decision in keeping with the majority view (and against his advisor).

When the captains of Xerxes' fleet finished their inspection of the Laconian 8.66
losses at Thermopylae they crossed over to Histiaea, and after pausing for three days they sailed through the strait at Euripus; and in another three days they made it to Phalerum, the port of Athens. As it seems to me, the Persians attacked Athens by land and by sea with no fewer soldiers than when they first reached Sepias and Thermopylae. For every man lost in the storm or killed at Thermopylae or in the sea battle at Artemisium, you can add men who more recently joined the king, the men from Malis and Doris and Locris and all the Boeotians, in full force excepting the Thespians and Plataeans, and to that you can also add the men of Carystus and Andros and Tenos and all the rest of the islanders—excepting only the five whose names I mentioned earlier.[6] In fact, the deeper the king proceeded into Greece, the more nations were added to his army.

When all his forces had reached 8.67
Athens and anchored at Phalerum (except the Parians—they had remained behind at Cythnus and were waiting to see how the war turned out), Xerxes went in person to the ships, wanting to talk with the men and learn their views. When he got there, he sat before them on a throne, and the tyrants of the various nations and captains of the ships came at his summons and sat in the order the king allotted, first the Sidonian king, next the king of Tyre, and so on for the rest.

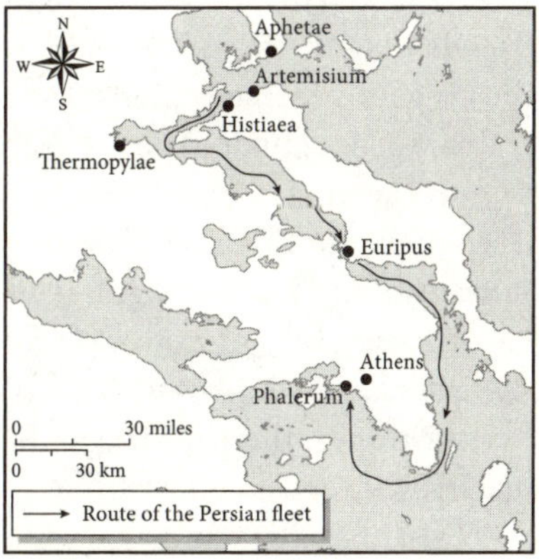

MAP 8.4

6 At 8.46 (where, confusingly, six are mentioned).

When they were seated, in order of rank one after the other, Xerxes sent Mardonius to test them, asking each whether or not he should order the fleet to attack.

8.68 So, Mardonius went around with his questioning, beginning with the Sidonian king, and everyone conveyed the same opinion, bidding the king to make the attack—everyone, that is, except for Artemisia, who said this.
8.68(1) "Mardonius, tell the king for me that I have this to say, as one whose courage and service in the sea battle off Euboea were second to none. Master, it is but right for me to make my view known to you, whatever I in fact think best for your affairs. And this is what I say to you: spare the ships and do not attack. In matters of the sea these men are stronger than yours as much as men are stronger than women. What pressing need is there for you to risk a sea battle? Do you not hold Athens, the very reason for which you launched your invasion? Do you not hold the rest of Greece? No one now stands in your way, and those
8.68(2) who did stand against you have reaped the reward they deserve. I will now tell you how I think matters will turn out for our enemy. If you do not press a sea battle, but keep the ships here close to land or even move them down to the Peloponnese, then, Master, you will easily get what you have in mind. The Greeks will not be able to hold out for long; no, they will scatter, each running back to his own town. They have no stores of grain on the island, I hear, nor is it likely that the Peloponnesians will stay here if you march your army to attack the Peloponnese—no, they will not care to fight in their ships to defend
8.68(3) Athens. But if you do immediately press on with a battle, I fear that if your fleet is badly beaten you will lose your army too. And lay this in your heart, my King: slaves are wont to be useless for good men, and useful for bad. Since you are the best of all men, your slaves are particularly useless—and I mean the so-called allies, the Egyptians and Cyprians and Cilicians and Pamphylians. These are of no help to your cause."

8.69 When Artemisia finished talking with Mardonius, those who were her friends were dismayed at her words, certain that she would be punished by the king for speaking against the attack; and those filled with envy and hate because of her honored position among the allies were delighted at her objection to the attack, equally certain that she would die. But when the views were conveyed to Xerxes, he was exceedingly pleased at what Artemisia had said: thinking her excellent even before, he now praised her to the skies. Nonetheless, his orders were to follow the majority opinion, thinking that at Euboea they had proven themselves cowards because he was not there to oversee things; this time he would arrange it so that he could watch the battle in person.

8.70 When the command was given, the Persians brought their ships up to Salamis and calmly positioned them in order of battle. But by then there was not enough of the day left to begin the battle, and night fell. So, they continued to get ready, but for the next day. Meanwhile dread and fear gripped the Greeks, and particularly those from the Peloponnese—panicky because they

were going to sit there at Salamis and fight a battle over the land of Athens, and if they were defeated they would be trapped and besieged on an island, leaving their own land without protection. And on this very night the Persian army 8.71
was marching down to attack the Peloponnese.

And yet everything possible had been devised to keep the Persians from invading by land. As soon as the Peloponnesians heard of the fate of those with Leonidas at Thermopylae, they raced from their cities to take up a post at the Isthmus, under the command of Leonidas's brother, Cleombrotus son of Anaxandrides. Once established there they destroyed the Scironian road,[7] and next, as resolved in council, they built a wall across the Isthmus. There were many, many thousands of them, every man working hard, and so they managed to complete the task, bringing in stones and bricks and logs and buckets full of sand. And those helping with the construction of the wall worked night and day, never stopping. . . .

The Greek Resolve Wavers. Themistocles' Message to Xerxes

Themistocles's ruse here was, as one can imagine, hotly debated among the Greeks: was it a brilliant and necessary maneuver or arrogantly treasonous?

Such was the great effort made by those at the Isthmus, determined to fight 8.74
to the very end, and not expecting the ships to win the day. Hearing of these great efforts made the men at Salamis all the more uneasy, however, fearing now not so much for themselves, but for the Peloponnese. For a time men would step aside and speak quietly with one another, marveling at the folly of Eurybiades. But in the end the quarrel broke out into the open. A council was called, where they rehearsed many of the same arguments as before, some saying that they needed to make sail for the Isthmus and defend the Peloponnese, and not stay to fight for a land already under occupation; while the men from Athens and Aegina and Megara argued to stay and fight at Salamis.

When Themistocles saw that the Peloponnesians were not to be convinced, 8.75
he quietly slipped out of the meeting and sent a man called Sicinnus by boat to the Persian camp; Sicinnus was his servant, the tutor of his children, and he had given him instructions as to what he needed to say. Much later than these events, when the Thespians were taking on new citizens, Themistocles would make Sicinnus a Thespian, and a wealthy man to boot. But now he sent him off in a boat, and when he landed, Sicinnus said to the Persian commanders, "One of the Athenian commanders has decided to side with the king, and wishes your affairs rather than the Greeks' to succeed; and so, without the other Greeks knowing, he has sent me to tell you that the Greeks have panicked and are planning to run, and that now is your chance for a most glorious victory, as long as you do not let them get away. They are no longer of one mind, and they

7 A narrow road from Eleusis and Megara that becomes a ledge along the cliffs that run down to the Isthmus; it was thus easy to make impassable. In this period this was apparently the only road large enough for wagons.

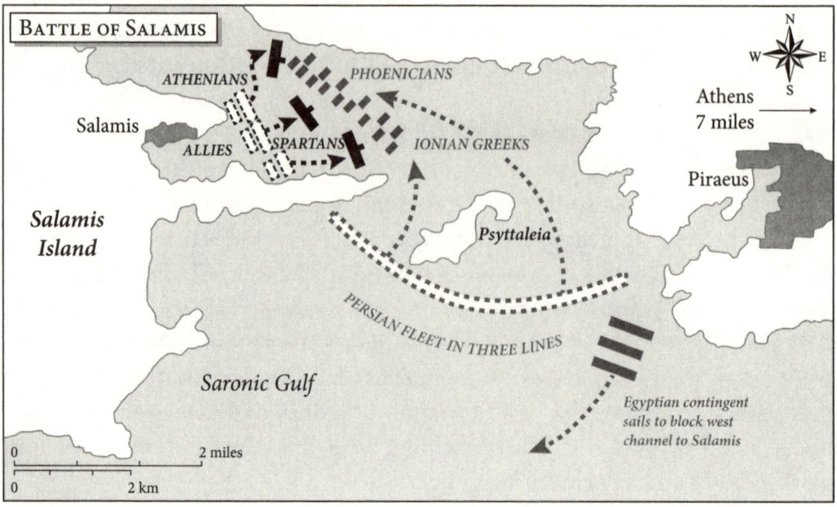

FIGURE 8.2

will not be able to resist you: in the battle you will see that they will fight against each other, those who have joined your side against those who have not."

8.76 Having delivered his message, Sicinnus departed. The intelligence seemed credible to the Persians, so they landed a large number of troops on a small island, Psyttaleia, that lies between Salamis and the mainland, and, while it was still the middle of the night, had the west wing move up toward Salamis, to encircle the Greeks; and they also had the ships stationed off Ceos and Cynosura sail over, to occupy the whole eastern side of the strait, as far as Munychia. They commanded these ship movements to make it impossible for the Greeks to escape: trapped in the strait at Salamis, the Greeks would pay the price for their success at Artemisium. The troops were landed on the little island called Psyttaleia with this in mind: during the battle, as the current brought down men and wrecked ships (the island lying as it does in the very channel where the battle was to be fought) they could rescue their own and kill the others. All was done in silence, so that the enemy would not find out. So, throughout the night, without taking any rest, the Persians made ready for the battle.

8.77 Now as for oracles, I cannot argue against their truth, nor wish to try to discredit them, when I look at examples like this, where the meaning is clear:

After the slaughter of shining Athens, wild with hope
will lines of ships stretch like a bridge from the sacred headland
of golden-sworded Artemis to the beach of Cynosura.
Then will divine Justice crush Glut, offspring of Excess,
strong, terrible, lustful, thinking to swallow up all;
bronze will clash with bronze, and Ares will purple
the sea with blood. That is the time when far-seeing Zeus
and mistress Victory bring to Greece its day of freedom.

The meaning of Bacis's prophecy thus is clear, and with such examples in mind, I dare not speak against oracles, nor give credit to those who do.

8.78 Meanwhile, a huge dispute arose among the captains at Salamis. So far they did not yet know that the Persians had surrounded them during the night—no, they thought the Persian ships were in the same arrangement as when they had last seen them in the daylight. But in the midst of this dispute, 8.79 an Athenian, Aristeides son of Lysimachus, sailed over from Aegina. This Aristeides had been ostracized and exiled by the people of Athens, but I have studied his character and, by my way of thinking, he was the best and most just man that Athens had. In any case, Aristeides was standing at the entrance to the meeting of the captains, and called over Themistocles. They were by no means friends—rather, the worst of enemies—but because of the magnitude of the present peril, he quietly called him over to confer. He had heard that the Peloponnesians were hurrying to make sail for the Isthmus. So, when Themistocles came over, Aristeides said, "Our rivalry, now more than ever, must focus on this: which of us can do the most good for our country. It matters not whether they argue a little or a lot about sailing back to the Peloponnese, let me tell you. I speak now as an eyewitness: neither the Corinthians nor Eurybiades himself will be able to sail away, regardless of what they want—for the enemy has surrounded us. Now go in and tell them."

result

8.80 Themistocles said, "Your advice is excellent, and you bring good news too: indeed, you come as the eyewitness to exactly what I wanted. The Medes' actions here, you see, are my doing. There was no choice: since the Greeks would not join the battle willingly, they will now stand by us whether they want it or not. And, since you have come with this excellent news, you yourself tell the captains. If I tell it, they will think that I am making it up, and I won't convince them—they will think the Persians are not doing this at all. So, you go in and tell them how things stand. And when you've given your news, if they are convinced, that's all to the good, but if they don't find it credible, it won't matter: they can no longer run after all, if we are in fact surrounded on all sides as you say."

all Greeks have to fight

8.81 So, Aristeides went in and spoke, telling them that he had come over from Aegina and had only barely escaped detection as he sailed through the Persian blockade. "Our position," he said, "is now surrounded by Xerxes' fleet. I advise you to get ready to defend yourselves." Aristeides then left the meeting, and at once a fresh dispute arose, with most of the captains finding the news hard to believe.

8.82 But even as the captains were refusing to believe Aristeides' report, a trireme came over, deserting from the Persians, of men from Tenos under the command of a certain Panaetius son of Sosimenes, and they gave a detailed account of how things truly were. And it is for this deed that Tenos is inscribed on the tripod at Delphi among those who defeated the Persian king.[8] With this

8 Herodotus here refers to the so-called Serpent Column, which once supported a golden tripod. The column still exists, and on it (not the tripod) we find a list of the defenders of Greece, and that list does in fact include Tenos.

ship deserting to join the Greeks at Salamis, and with a ship from Lemnos earlier deserting at Artemisium, the final tally of Greek ships was fully three hundred and eighty—before that, the count had been short by two.

The Battle of Salamis

In a sea battle, triremes did not use sails except in flight. Tactics involved maneuvering into position so as to suddenly push forward with the oars, thus ramming an enemy's ship in the side and sinking it. If the ships got tangled up, then the hoplites on board (the marines) would try to board the enemy ship and fight. "Backing water" means to use the oars to move backward, which was part of the sparring as the ships tried to get into position. The beaks at the prow were made of heavy planks of wood covered in metal, so there was no profit in head-to-head ramming.

8.83 What the Tenians reported was convincing to the Greeks, and so they prepared to fight. As the light of dawn appeared in the sky, they called together the fighting men, and among the speakers, Themistocles told them of the success he foresaw. His whole speech had to do with the contrast between better and worse, in men as individuals and in the human condition at large; and he urged them to choose the better. Having wound up this speech, he ordered them to board ship. The marines were going aboard, when the warship from Aegina—the one that was bringing back the sons of Aeacus—returned to join the fleet.[9]

8.84 Then the Greeks launched all their ships, and as they rowed out the Persians immediately fell upon them. All the rest of the Greeks backed water, running the ships back ashore, but Ameinias, an Athenian from Pallene, moved forward and rammed a ship. And when the two ships were tangled up and not able to get away from each other, others came to help Ameinias—and thus the battle was joined. That in any case is how the Athenians say the battle got underway; the Aeginetans say that the ship coming back from Aegina was the one that began the battle. And yet another story is told of the start of the battle: that a vision of a woman appeared to them, calling out in a voice that the whole Greek force could hear with this reproach: "Men, what madness is this? How much longer will you be moving backward?"

THE BATTLE FROM THE PERSIAN PERSPECTIVE

8.85 The Phoenicians were lined up opposite the Athenians, on the wing next to Eleusis, to the west, and the Ionians opposite the Lacedaemonians held the wing to the east, next to Piraeus. A few Ionians heeded Themistocles' request and shied away from the fight, but most did not.[10] I can list the name of many

9 That is, the cult images of Ajax and Telamon (see 8.64, above); a good omen, since they now have the spirits of the heroes to fight alongside them.

10 After Artemisium, Themistocles had had his men leave inscriptions at the places where ships stop to load water with a message asking the Ionians to defect, or at least to fight without heart. (See 8.22, not part of our selections.)

a captain who captured a Greek ship, but I will mention only Theomestor son
of Androdamas and Phylacus son of Histiaeus, both Samian men. For his feat
in the battle, Theomestor was set up by the Persians as the tyrant of Samos;
and Phylacus was recorded as a royal benefactor (*orosanga* to use its Persian
name) and given a great deal of land. These two then did well, but the great 8.86
multitude of Persian ships were wrecked at Salamis, many destroyed by the
Athenians, many by the Aeginetans. And it was inevitable that it turn out that
way, since the Greeks continuously fought with disciplined movements and in
battle formation, while the Persians soon were fighting in no line at all nor
with any sense of strategy. And yet on that day the Persians proved better men
than they had at Euboea, and surpassed themselves, every man eager to please
Xerxes and scared to displease, each man thinking that the king had his eyes
on him.

I cannot say in precise detail how each of the Greeks and Persians fought, 8.87
but I can say what Artemisia did, and how by so doing she enhanced her
repute with the king still further. At a moment when the king's forces were in
utter chaos, Artemisia's ship was being chased by an Attic vessel. She was
unable to get away, since hers was the ship closest to the enemy line and the
Persian ships, her allies, were in her way. So, she formulated a plan of action,
an action that would turn out to her profit. As she was being chased by the
Attic ship, she rammed full tilt—but into one of her allies, a Calyndian ship
with their king Damasithymus on board. Now whether she harbored him ill
will because of some quarrel that arose while they were still at the Hellespont,
I cannot say, nor whether she had targeted him in advance or the Calyndian
ship happened to be the one that came along. But at any rate she rammed and
sunk the ship, and in so doing—and by good luck!—brought a double benefit
to herself. First, when the captain of the Attic ship saw her ramming an enemy
vessel, he thought that either her ship was Greek or she had defected and was
fighting on the Greek side; so, he wheeled his ship about and turned to fighting others.

That then was the first benefit, to escape and not be killed, but it happened 8.88
also that by working this evil deed Artemisia's reputation with Xerxes, already
good, was made even better. It is said that the king, as he was watching the
battle, observed the ship that had just done the ramming; and that one of
those there said, "Master, do you see how well Artemisia fights, how she has
now sunk an enemy ship?" Xerxes then asked whether this was truly Artemisia's doing, and those present said that, yes, they knew her ship's figurehead
very well; and naturally they believed the wrecked ship to be the enemy. So,
Artemisia enjoyed good luck in many respects, and not least in this, that not a
single man from the Calyndian ship survived to be her accuser. Xerxes, the
story goes, then said, "My men have become women, and my women men."
Such were Xerxes' words.

In the battle, Xerxes' brother and a son of Darius, the fleet commander 8.89
Ariabignes, died, along with many other distinguished Persians and Medes

FIGURE 8.3 Xerxes. Servants here hold a parasol to keep the Great King comfortable in the strong Mediterranean sun. The king has a cylindrical crown made of metal (probably silver or gold) upon his oiled locks and wears the long court robe traditional to the Persian monarch. (Curiously, the Persian king wears this robe even when depicted in battle, a sign of his difference and authority.) This stone relief resides in the Hall of the Hundred Columns, at the king's palace in Persepolis

and their allies; and some few Greeks as well. The Greeks knew how to swim, so they could swim over to Salamis if their ships got wrecked—so long as they were not killed in the hand-to-hand combat. But most of the Persians did not know how to swim, and so perished in the sea. The greatest number died when their battle line first was turned and they were trying to flee: the ships that were drawn up behind, in their eagerness to join the ships in front and show the king their mettle, entangled their allies as they were trying to get away; and so, many died.

In the chaos of battle, some of the Phoenicians who had lost their ships 8.90
came to the king to accuse the Ionians: "Our ships were lost because they betrayed us!" But the upshot was that the Ionian commanders were not put to death, and that those of the Phoenicians doing the slandering got the reward I will now describe. Even as they were talking, a ship from Samothrace (that is, an Ionian ship) rammed an Attic vessel. The Attic ship began to sink—but then a ship from Aegina came on at full tilt and sank the ship from Samothrace. The Samothracians, however, had spearmen, who from the deck of their sinking ship attacked the Aeginetan marines, knocked them off, and then climbed up and took control of the vessel. This event saved the Ionians: for when Xerxes saw the great feat wrought by the Samothracians, he turned to the Phoenicians, ready to blame them all in his frustration and rage, and ordered his guards to cut off their heads—saying that he would not have men who are cowards slandering their betters. Xerxes noticed the Samothracians since, throughout the battle, he was sitting on the mountain opposite Salamis, called Aegaleos, and whenever he saw one of his ships displaying a feat of courage in the battle, he found out who the captain was, and had his scribes record name, father's name, and city. And yet another contributing factor to the Phoenicians' wretched fate was that Ariaramnes, a Persian but also a
friend of the Ionians, was alongside. In any case, the guards now turned to 8.91
take care of the Phoenicians.

THE BATTLE FROM THE GREEK PERSPECTIVE

As Herodotus turns to look at the battle from the Greek point of view, an ironic contrast develops between Xerxes's careful observation and recording of the Persian actions and the conflicting accounts of the Greeks. Even in the context of their greatest sea victory of all time, the Greek unity of purpose remains fragile; and for the historian the truthful account hard to find.

The Persians, then, had turned to flee and were trying to sail off to safe harbor at Phalerum, when the Aeginetans, who were lying in ambush in the narrows, displayed remarkable feats of courage. In the chaos of battle, the Athenians were wreaking havoc among the enemy staying to fight as well as those who were trying to flee, but it was the Aeginetans who worked ruination on those trying to get out of the strait—for any ship that got away from the Athenians sailed at full speed into the Aeginetan line.

8.92 And it was then that the ship of Themistocles, in hot pursuit of a ship, came alongside that of Polycritus son of Crius, an Aeginetan man, as it was ramming a Sidonian vessel. Earlier,[11] the Sidonian ship had captured a ship from Aegina, posted as an advance guard at Sciathus, and had on board one of their marines, Pytheas son of Ischenous, that badly wounded man whom the Persians were keeping alive in tribute to his courage. The Sidonian ship was conveying this man along with the Persians when it was rammed and taken, and thus it was that Pytheas was rescued for Aegina. Now as Polycritus was attacking the Sidonian vessel, he recognized the insignia of the Athenian flagship as it passed, and so he called out to Themistocles and scornfully said, "This then is the way that Aegina joins cause with the Persians!"[12] Such was the taunt Polycritus hurled at Themistocles even as he was ramming the Sidonian ship.

As for the Persian ships that got away, they now fled to make safe harbor at Phalerum, where the land army offered protection.

8.93 In the sea battle off Salamis, the Aeginetans were by all reports best among the Greeks, with the Athenians coming next; and best among the men were Polycritus of Aegina and the Athenians Eumenes of Anagyrus and Ameinias of Pallene—the one who had chased down Artemisia. Now if Ameinias had known that Artemisia was on board, he would not have left off his pursuit, but would have taken her, or been taken himself. Special orders to that effect had been given to the Athenian captains, and there was even a price on her head—ten thousand drachmas for the man who took her alive.[13] So terrible, in Athenian eyes, was it that a woman was making war on Athens! But she escaped, as was mentioned before, and now she, along with the rest of the surviving Persian ships, was safe at Phalerum.

8.94 A story the Athenians tell is that the Corinthian commander Adeimantus, right at the start of the battle, when the battle was first joined, panicked, hoisted sail, and ran away; and the rest of the Corinthian captains ran too, when they saw their flagship in flight. But in the midst of their escape, as they neared the temple of Athena Sciras on Salamis, they came upon a small boat. It seemed heaven sent: no one is known to have dispatched it and at that point the Corinthians knew nothing of what was happening with the fleet. This in any case is why they thought some deity was involved. When the ships drew near, those on the small craft called out, saying, "Adeimantus, you turned and set your ships to flight, forsaking the Greeks, but these are even now winning a victory, beating the enemy decisively just as they prayed they would." That's what they called out, but Adeimantus did not believe it, and so they spoke again, inviting him to take them as hostages and kill them if the Greeks were not victorious for all to see. So, he turned his ship around, and the others with

11 At Artemisium; the story of Pytheas was told at 7.181.

12 Ten years before Athens had accused Aegina of siding with the Persians, with Polycritus's father Crius blamed in particular.

13 Soldiers made about 1 drachma a day, so this represents almost a lifetime of wages for the marines on board.

him, and arrived at the Greek position just as the action had ended. That's the story the Athenians tell. The Corinthians, however, dispute this, and consider themselves among the first to join the battle—and the other Greeks all confirm what the Corinthians say.

Aristeides son of Lysimachus, you recall, was the one I just now singled out as the most outstanding man in Athens, and here is what he accomplished. As the battle raged about Salamis he took many of the hoplites stationed on the beach there, Athenians, and landed them on the island of Psyttaleia. The hoplites then slaughtered the Persians on that isle, every one of them.[14] 8.95

When the sea battle was finally over, the Greeks on Salamis—sure that the king would call on the ships he had left—got ready for another attack, pulling ashore as many of the wrecked ships as were still afloat. But many of the shipwrecks had been carried by the wind, a breeze from the west, to the Attic coast at a place called Colias. And thereby the prophecies were entirely fulfilled, including those about the sea battle spoken by Bacis and Musaeus, but also one spoken many years earlier about the shipwrecks cast ashore here, by an Athenian seer named Lysistratus, a prophecy that had been forgotten by all the Greeks. It ran, *Oars will the women of Colias use when they roast their barley.* And that is what was to come to pass when the king marched away. 8.96

Xerxes Decides to Return to Susa

When Xerxes grasped the enormity of the disaster, he grew anxious that one of the Ionians would suggest to the Greeks—or have the thought themselves—to sail to the Hellespont and tear down the bridges. And, if he were trapped in Europe, he might lose his life; so he planned an escape. Wanting it not to be obvious—to the Greeks, but also to his own men—he tried to fashion a causeway over to Salamis, by tying together Phoenician transport ships as a sort of pontoon bridge and wall, and in general arranged things as though he was going to fight another battle at sea. And when they saw what he was doing, everyone believed Xerxes' full resolve to stay and carry on the war—everyone but Mardonius, that is: nothing escaped him, since he knew Xerxes' ways of thought so well. 8.97

And as Xerxes was doing all this, he also sent along news of the present setback to the Persians. Now there is nothing faster than the message system invented by the Persians, at least nothing that is mortal. They say that there are exactly as many horses and riders stationed along the Royal Road as the days it takes to travel it, one horse and one rider for each day's stretch of road. Neither snow nor rain nor heat nor gloom of night stops them from the swift completion of their appointed segment.[15] The first rider hands over the 8.98

14 Hoplites are soldiers in full armor, trained to deploy in phalanx formation. The more mobile but lightly armed Persians faced an insurmountable challenge with so little space to maneuver.

15 The U.S. Postal Service motto, inscribed on New York's James A. Farley Post Office Building, is taken from this passage in Herodotus. The Royal Road from Sardis to Susa was over 1500 miles long; see 5.52–53.

message to the second, and the second to the third, and from there it goes along the whole way, passing from one to the next, much as the relay race with torches that the Greeks hold in honor of Hephaestus. The Persians call this posting system the *angareion*.

8.99 When the first message arrived at Susa, announcing that Xerxes had captured Athens, the Persians left behind in the capital rejoiced, covering all the roadways with myrtle branches, burning incense, and busying themselves with sacrificial feasts and celebrations. But the arrival of the second message upended all that: everyone tore their clothes asunder, wailed and moaned unceasingly, singling out Mardonius for blame. And they did all this not so much
8.100 in grief for the lost ships as fearing for the life of Xerxes. The lamentation continued among the Persians for this entire stretch of time, until Xerxes himself brought it to an end by his arrival at Susa.

Now Mardonius could see that Xerxes considered the sea battle a great catastrophe, and he suspected that he was planning an escape from Athens; and he also privately thought that he, Mardonius, would certainly be punished for convincing the king to march on Greece. So, he thought, better to take a gamble: either to conquer Greece or at least to play for high stakes and die gloriously—though his expectations inclined toward the former. Reflecting on this, he brought a proposal to Xerxes: "Master, do not grieve so, and do not think that there is any great misfortune in what has happened here. Things made of wood[16] are not the important test of strength for us, but horses and men. There is not a one of our enemy here—who now suppose to have total victory!—who will get off their ships and fight man to man, nor anyone from this continent. No, those who have dared to stand and fight have reaped their reward. Let us attack the Peloponnese at once, if that's what you think best; or, if it seems better to wait, that too is fine. But do not lose heart: the Greeks cannot possibly escape paying for the things they have done now and in the past, and becoming your slaves. Such, then, is your best course of action. But if, as the case may be, your intent is to march the army back, I can offer a different plan. Do not let the Greeks take the Persians for fools, my King. The *Persians* have not done the least harm to your affairs, nor can you say that we are cowardly in some way. If the Phoenicians and Egyptians and Cyprians and Cilicians[17] proved themselves cowards, that misfortune has nothing to do with the Persians. So then, seeing that the Persians are not to blame, listen to me: if you have in fact decided not to stay in Greece, march back home taking the bulk of the army, but let me, with three hundred thousand picked men, stay and enslave Greece on your behalf."

8.101 At these words, Xerxes was happy and pleased—at least so far as the circumstances allowed—and he told Mardonius that after consultation with others he would let him know which plan of action he preferred. As he was

16 That is, the ships.

17 The four naval powers that formed the core of the Persian fleet; see 6.6.

consulting with his councilors, he decided to send for Artemisia and consult with her too, since in the last council she was the only one who in fact understood the best course of action. When Artemisia got there, Xerxes dismissed his other councilors, and his bodyguards as well, and spoke as follows: "Mardonius suggests that I stay here and attack the Peloponnese, saying that the Persians and the land army share no responsibility for this defeat, and would like to have the opportunity to prove themselves. That's one course of action he urges. But there is another option: he himself is willing, if he can take three hundred thousand select troops from the army, to enslave Greece on my behalf; and urges me to march with the rest of the army back home. You advised me well about the recent sea battle, telling me not to fight. So now too consider this and tell me which plan I would most wisely follow."

To his request, she said, "King, it is hard to say what is the best, and yet in 8.102
the present circumstances I think you ought to march back to Susa, and for Mardonius, if that's what he wants and he is willing to make the attempt, to stay here with the troops he requests. If he defeats those he says he will, and succeeds as he thinks and says, the achievement will be yours, Master—for the ones who will have done this are your slaves, after all. If, on the other hand, things go wrong, and all turns out opposite to what Mardonius expects, it will be no great misfortune, as long as you are alive and your household and kingdom survive. So long as you and your dynasty lasts the Greeks will many times have to race for their lives. If Mardonius dies, no one will care much; and not even if the Greeks win will they have the victory, for they will have only killed one of your slaves. But you will march away having burned Athens to the ground, the very reason you made this expedition."

The advice pleased Xerxes—she gave voice to exactly what he himself was 8.103
thinking. Now in my view, Xerxes would not have stayed even if every man and woman advised it—he was that scared. In any case, he heaped praise on Artemisia, and sent her off by ship to Ephesus, and on board were his own children, some bastard sons who had come with him on the expedition.

The war will continue under Mardonius's leadership, and in the summer of 479 BC the Persians will lose decisively at Plataea, where Mardonius is killed, and at Mycale (opposite Samos in Ionia), where the entire Persian naval force is also lost. The Persian forces will break up and retreat in disarray, and the Greek victory will, by Herodotus's account, be complete. It is interesting to reflect, however, how all this would be seen from a Persian standpoint. Greece was, after all, far at the edge of what was a vast empire stretching from the Caspian Sea to the Persian Gulf and from India to Egypt. Artemisia's advice suggests a suitable official line that could even claim Persian victory: Eretria ravaged and Athens burned in reprisal for the burning of Sardis, the king alive and well with his army, and the defeat of Mardonius of no real consequence. Indeed, she might have added the Persian victory over the Spartans and the killing of their king.

BOOK 9
Coda

Below are the final chapters of Herodotus's *Histories*. Not so long ago, Greek literature was understood poorly enough that some thought the (to us) odd ending to Herodotus's work to be a sign of incompletion. Scholars now understand it very differently. The quiet close is consistent with the way that Herodotus has ended the sections of his work all along. More tellingly, the reprise of Troy through the figure of Protesilaus—the first Greek to put his foot on Asian soil in the attack on Troy, and the first Greek to die—reminds us of the focus on the Trojan War at the very beginning (1.4), as well as the many allusions and reminders along the way. This evocation of the work's beginning is now recognized as a characteristic feature of early Greek literature in general, and the *Iliad* in particular (scholars call this *ring composition*). The open-ended way the work ends is also characteristic of such writing: the ring is closed, but of course reprisals and conflict will continue.

Very striking among what follows is the crucifixion toward the very end, a brutal punishment that seems more in keeping with the Persians, or at least Thracians, than the Athenians who order it. By the time Herodotus was composing his work, Athens was still a democracy, but had established a sometimes ruthless empire, and many readers see the crucifixion scene as implicit criticism of the Athenian imperialist behaviors in evidence by that time. The curious final paragraph may also have in view the newfound opulence of the Acropolis, with its Parthenon and other splendors—all paid for by tribute money collected from Greek states now effectively subject to the Athenians (on tribute and slavery, see 1.27). In this vein, it is worth remarking that the end of the *Histories* returns quietly but emphatically to the rich reflections throughout the work on the theme of tyranny and freedom. The final word in the Greek is *douleuein*, "to be enslaved."

last word
opposite of happy, prosperous
shows who is most prosp (solon), those not enslaved

Setting out from Mycale to sail to the Hellespont, the Greeks first dropped anchor near Lectum, driven off course by the winds. Sailing from there they reached Abydos, where, however, they found that the bridges—which they had thought to find intact and which were the main reason they had come to the Hellespont—had already broken apart.[1] The Peloponnesians under Leotychides thought it best to sail back to Greece, but the Athenians under the command of Xanthippus[2] preferred to remain and attack Chersonese. So, some of the Greeks sailed away, but the Athenians crossed over to Chersonese and began to lay siege to Sestos. 9.114

When they heard that the Greeks were there, men from towns round about gathered at Sestos (which had the strongest defensive wall of the towns there) and among them a Persian from Cardia, Oeobazus, who had brought there the cables from the bridges. Sestos was held then by the native Aeolians, but Persians and a great crowd of other allies also came to help. 9.115

Over this territory Xerxes' satrap, the Persian Artaÿctes, ruled like a tyrant, a cunning man prone to reckless deeds. Back during Xerxes' march on Athens, he had even played a trick on the king, and thereby gained control over the money in Elaeus that belonged to the hero, Protesilaus son of Iphiclus.[3] In the Chersonese at Elaeus is Protesilaus's burial mound, and around the mound a sacred precinct, and there lies a great deal of money as well as gold and silver bowls, bronze, robes, and other offerings. These Artaÿctes stole, with the king's consent. But the consent was gained by deceit, for he told the king this: "Master, nearby lies the estate of a Greek, who attacked your territory, and for that he paid the price of death. Give me his estate, so that people will learn not to attack your lands." With these words he was bound to easily convince Xerxes to hand over the estate, since Xerxes had no clue what Artaÿctes had in mind. And what Artaÿctes was thinking when he said that Protesilaus "attacked the king's territory" was this: that Persians consider all Asia to belong to them and to whoever the ruling king might be. When the king gave his consent, Artaÿctes had the money taken from Elaeus to Sestos, and the holy precinct put into cash crops from which he took the profits; and he would go down to Elaeus and copulate with women in the most sacred inner part of the hero's shrine. But now the Athenians had him under siege and since he had not prepared for a siege nor expected the Greeks, he was powerless as they pursued their attack. 9.116

But when the siege continued into autumn, the Athenians grew impatient, being away from home for so long and yet unable to take the fortified town; and so they asked the generals repeatedly to take them back, but the generals refused—not, they said, before we capture the town or the Athenian citizenry recalls us. So, the soldiers acquiesced. 9.117

1 The bridges had been broken up by storms.

2 Xanthippus was the father of Pericles, the great Athenian leader who consolidated the Athenian Empire, built the Parthenon, and guided Athens through the beginnings of the Peloponnesian War.

3 Protesilaus was the first Greek to die at Troy, thus the first casualty in Greece's first attack on Asia. Note that Herodotus assumes everyone knows who he is, such is the fame of Homer and Troy among the Greeks.

9.118 But those inside the walls had come to extreme deprivation, such that they were boiling the leather straps from their beds to eat as food. When they no longer had even that, the Persians, including Artaÿctes and Oeobazus, left under cover of night, climbing down at the back side of the wall where there were the fewest enemy troops. And when it was day, the men of Chersonese mounted the towers, signaled to the Athenians what had happened, and opened the city gates. The greater part of the Athenians went in pursuit of the Persians, leaving the remainder to secure the town.

9.119 Oeobazus got as far as Thrace, where a Thracian people, the Apsinthi, captured him and sacrificed him to their local god, Pleistorus, in their customary fashion; the men traveling with him, they slaughtered in some different way.

Artaÿctes and his men had taken flight later and were captured just a little beyond Aegospotami, where they fought back for a long time—but in the end all were taken, some dying and others captured alive. The captives were shackled and hauled back to Sestos, among them Artaÿctes, also in chains, along with his son.

A story is told by the men of Chersonese that one of Artaÿctes' guards was 9.120
frying dried fish when a great marvel occurred: the dried fish as they were lying over the fire started to flap about and wriggle, like fish freshly caught. Men crowded around in wonder, but Artaÿctes on seeing it called over the man doing the frying and said, "Athenian stranger, fear not this portent: it is revealed not for you, but for me—it means to signify that Protesilaus at Elaeus, though dead and a dried-out corpse, holds the power from the gods to punish those who do wrong. So, I now want to offer recompense: in return for the money I stole from the shrine a hundred talents for the god; and I will give the Athenians two hundred talents in return for my life and the life of my son."[4] But with these promises he failed to move the Athenian commander Xanthippus. The men of Elaeus demanded that he be killed in vengeance for Protesilaus, and Xanthippus was likewise inclined. So, they led him to where Xerxes had bridged the Hellespont—or, as some say, to the hill above the town of Madytus—and hung him nailed to a board, crucifying him; and his son they stoned to death before the father's eyes.

With that done, they sailed back to Greece, carrying all their plunder and 9.121
money, including the cables from the bridge, intending to hang these up in a temple. And in that year nothing further happened.

Artembares was an ancestor of this Artaÿctes, the one who was crucified, 9.122
and he once sketched out a proposal for the Persians that they liked and thus brought to Cyrus.[5] It ran like this: "Zeus gives sovereignty to the Persians, and, now that you have deposed Astyages, he gives sovereignty to you above all, Cyrus—and yet we inhabit a small territory and even this is rugged. Let us move elsewhere, and take possession of a better land. Many are the lands nearby, and many far away, whose possession would make us more admired among men. It is but reasonable that the powerful do this: and when will be a better time than now, when we rule many peoples and all of Asia?" Cyrus listened, but found little to admire in these words. He told them to go ahead and do it, but advised them in that case to get ready to be not the rulers, but the ones ruled. "It is the way of things," he said "that soft men come from soft lands; it is not the way of nature for the same land to yield wondrous crops and men good at fighting." So, defeated by Cyrus's argument, the Persians yielded and withdrew, choosing to live on poor land and be the rulers, rather than to sow crops in fertile fields and be slaves to others.

4 An enormous sum, almost half what the Parthenon cost to build. By "god" he means the hero Protesilaus.

5 The narrative now returns to the early years of the reign of Cyrus, at a time before he had begun his conquests.

Bibliography

HERODOTUS IN GREEK

For those with even a bit of Greek, it is not hard to develop fluency in reading this very enjoyable author.

Selections from Herodotus, Amy L. Barbour (Oklahoma, 1977). Reprinted many times, this contains a selection of well-known passages in Herodotus, along with notes intended for the intermediate Greek reader. This remains the best text for starting to read Herodotus in the original.

Herodoti Historiae, ed. Charles Hude (Oxford Classical Texts, 1927). Still the standard Greek text for the entirety of Herodotus.

A Lexicon to Herodotus, J. Enoch Powell (2nd ed., Hildesheim, 1977). An extraordinary piece of work, and very helpful. Available without cost at the website of the *Thesaurus Linguae Graecae.*

HERODOTUS IN TRANSLATION

There are several competent contemporary translations to the whole of Herodotus. My two favorites are a bit older. De Selincourt is eminently readable and often a genius in bringing out clearly the meaning of a passage; Grene is more prettified in his language, but serves well to convey the dignity and charm (and sometimes also the quirkiness) of the original.

Herodotus: The Histories, trans. by Aubrey De Selincourt (Penguin Classics, 1954), rev. with introduction by John Marincola, 2003.

Herodotus: The Histories, trans. by David Grene (Chicago, 1988).

INTRODUCTIONS TO HERODOTUS

Much of the foundational contemporary scholarly work on Herodotus was done in the 1980s, and the best general introductions are from that era. Immerwahr's landmark study remains useful for its clearheaded exposition of the structure of the *Histories.*

J. A. S. Evans, *Herodotus* (Boston, 1982).

John Gould, *Herodotus* (New York, 1989).

H. R. Immerwahr, *Form and Thought in Herodotus* (Cleveland, 1966).

Donald Lateiner, *The Historical Method of Herodotus* (Toronto, 1989).

READINGS IN HERODOTUS

The scholarly bibliography on Herodotus is as massive and wide-ranging as the monumental history itself. Below are but a few starting points for further investigation.

Egbert J. Bakker, Irene J. F. de John, Hans van Wees, edd., *Brill's Companion to Herodotus* (Brill, 2002). An enormous collection, with several important articles, and a vast bibliography.

Emily Baragwanath and Mathieu de Bakker, edd., *Myth, Truth, and Narrative in Herodotus* (Oxford, 2012).

Deborah Boedeker, "Herodotus's Genre(s)," in M. Depew and Dirk Obbink, *Matrices of Genre, Authors, Canons and Society* (Cambridge MA, 2000) 97–114. A fundamental discussion of the problem of genre.

Peter Derow and Robert Parker, edd., *Herodotus and His World* (Oxford, 2003).

Carolyn Dewald, "Narrative Surface and Authorial Voice in Herodotus' Histories," *Arethusa* 20 (1987) 147–170. A landmark study of authorial persona in Herodotus's history.

Carolyn Dewald and John Marincola, edd., *The Cambridge Companion to Herodotus* (Cambridge, 2006).

Nino Luraghi, ed., *The Historian's Craft in the Age of Herodotus* (Oxford, 2007).

Rosaria Vignolo Munson, *Telling Wonders: Ethnographic and Political Discourse in the Work of Herodotus* (Ann Arbor, 2001).

Rosaria Vignolo Munson, ed., *Oxford Readings in Classical Studies*, vols. 1 and 2 (Oxford, 2013). An excellent collection of widely diverse scholarly readings of Herodotus.

Rosalind Thomas, *Herodotus in Context: Ethnography, Science and the Art of Persuasion* (Cambridge, 2000). Studies the intellectual context to Herodotus's world.

FURTHER READING

Oxford Bibliographies Online offers an excellent and extensive topical guide to the bibliography for Herodotus, compiled by Emily Baragwanath and Mathieu de Bakker. Here will also be found references to various learned commentaries, including those edited by Ashieri, Lloyd, How and Wells, Hornblower, and others.

NOTE ON THE SELECTIONS

In this relatively slim volume are assembled selections that aim to give the reader a representative sampling of Herodotus's monumental original, along with enough magisterial guidance to make these materials accessible for those approaching Herodotus for the first time. The practical goal was to limit the compilation to about one-third of the original; and to pick passages that contained essential features of the whole, not merely an illustrative diversity of subject matter. Thus, for example, I have carefully selected passages that have rich associations—parallels and contrasts and recurrent themes—with other passages, so that the reader can witness the ways by which our historian constructs deep resonance and meaning from the historical materials he has gathered. This can take place at a high level of detail: the passages culled from the Egyptian ethnography, for example, will be seen to have substantial crosstalk with the ethnographical materials in the Scythian narrative. I have also preferred long runs of text wherever feasible, so that the reader can get a sense of the charming flow characteristic of Herodotean narrative.

One additional practical note: those using this book in the classroom will want to know that the sections are by design roughly equivalent in length, so as to facilitate assignments. The materials for books 2, 3, 4, 5–6, 7, and 8–9 are all similar in length, as are the tales of Cyrus from book 1; the tales of Croesus at the front of book 1 are about twice that length.

Several good translations to the whole of Herodotus are in print. The full text of Herodotus runs about 600 pages, and with notes and introduction these translations tend to run over 700, even 800 or 900 pages. This book will have succeeded best if it persuades the reader to want to read carefully through the whole, and if, after the guidance here presented, that reader finds him- or herself able to navigate the text with confidence and to see with clarity its richness and brilliance. As a teacher of ancient Greek, I will also point out that Herodotus is relatively easy Greek to read, and that for those up to the challenge of learning an ancient language, reading him in the original is pure joy.

For convenience, I list on the page following chapter numbers for what is included in the selection and, in brackets, what has been omitted.

Book 1

Prologue: 1.1–1.5

Croesus and Tales of Lydia: 1.1–56.1 [1.56.2–58] 1.59–94

Tales of Cyrus and the Rise of the Persians: 1.95–103 [1.104–106] 1.107–130 [1.131–200]

Cyrus's Last Campaign: 1.201–216

Book 2

Cambyses and Tales of Egypt: 2.1–9 [2.10–18] 2.19–27.1 [2.27.2–34] 2.35–36 [2.37–64] 2.65–79 [2.80–81] 2.82–88 [2.89–111] 2.112–128 [2.129–182]

Book 3

Cambyses Invades Egypt: 3.1–7 [3.8] 3.9–15.2 [3.15.3–26] 3.27–38 [3.39–60]

Crisis and Constitutional Debate: 3.61–88 [3.89–160]

Book 4

Darius Invades Scythia: 4.1–5 [4.6–7] 4.8–11 [4.12–59] 4.60–65.1 [4.65.2–67] 4.68–80 [4.81–82] 4.83–90.1 [4.90.2] 4.91–92 [4.93–96] 4.97–102 [4.103–109] 4.110–142 [4.143–205]

Books 5 and 6

The Ionian Revolt: [5.1–96] 5.97 [5.98] 5.99–103 [5.104] 5.105–106 [5.107–115] 5.116–120 [5.121] 5.122–126, 6.1–19 [6.20–24] 6.25–32 [6.33–42]

The First Invasion of Greece: Mardonius and Marathon: 6.43–45 [6.46–93] 6.94–98.2 [6.98.3] 6.99–102 [6.103–104] 6.105–120 [6.121–140]

Book 7

Xerxes Invades Greece: 7.1–35 [7.36–52] 7.53–60 [7.61–99] 7.100–105 [7.106–174]

Artemisium and Thermopylae: 7.175–196 [7.196–200] 7.201–239

Book 8

Salamis: [8.1–39] 8.40–8.71 [8.72–73] 8.74–102 [8.103–144]

Book 9

Coda: [9.1–113] 9.114–122

NOTE ON THE TEXT

The Greek text used for the translation is the *Oxford Classical Text* by C. Hude (1908). Listed below are the few places where I felt the need to diverge from the Oxford text (small disagreements that do not materially affect the translation are not noted).

1.12.2 Deleting as a gloss τοῦ καὶ Ἀρχίλοχος . . . ἐπεμνήσθη with Wesseling (see Ashieri's commentary, ad loc.).

1.38.2 Retaining τὴν ἀκοὴν with the MSS.

1.84.3 Retaining τὸ χωρίον with the MSS.

2.26.1 Reading ἑαυτῷ with Lloyd.

2.36.3 Retaining καὶ τὴν κόπρον ἀναιρέονται with most MSS. (Legrand supposes a lacuna prior to these words.)

2.68.3 Retaining κατὰ λόγον τοῦ σώματος with all MSS.

2.78.1 Deleting πάντῃ with Stein.

2.79.1 Reading ἔνεστι with most MSS, reading ἐπεζωσμέναι with some MSS, here and at 2.85.2.

2.116 Reading κατά (= καθ' ἅ) περ ἐποίησε with Reiz.

2.121δ.2 Deleting τῶν ὄνων as a gloss.

2.127.2 Deleting as a gloss δι' οἰκοδομημένου . . . Χέοπα.

3.68.3 Reading Φαιδύμη, not Φαιδυμίη (see argument in Rosén's app. crit. ad loc.).

4.11.2 Reading δέον μένοντας for δεόμενον with Valckenaer.

4.64.3 Reading δέρμα δὲ ἀνθρώπου καὶ παχὺ καὶ λαμπρὸν· ἦν ἄρα σχεδὸν δερμάτων πάντων κτλ., a punctuation suggested by M and followed in the Aldine edition.

4.125.6 Expunging ἀπείπαντας with Corcella (see his commentary ad loc.)

4.127.3 Omitting περὶ τῶν τάφων as a gloss.

6.102.1 Reading κατεργάζοντες with some MSS.

6.119.3 After ἔλαιον, supplement for the lacuna is *exempli gratia*.

7.191.2 Reading γόησι with the MSS instead of Madvig's βοῇσι.

7.236.2 Reading <ἐκ> τῶν with Baehr.

8.76.1 Retaining Ψυττάλειαν with the MSS.

8.77.1 Reading πίεσθαι for πιθέσθαι with Duentzer.

8.82.1 The addition of <Τήνιος> by Krueger, accepted by Hude, is unnecessary. (See Bowie's commentary ad loc.)

Acknowledgments

I would like to thank those who reviewed the initial proposal for this book: Richard Fernando Buxton, Charles Lipson, Adam Kemezis, Sheila Murnaghan, Jonathan Perry, Martha C. Taylor, Gregory Viggiano, and Robert Zaretsky.

I am deeply thankful for those who agreed to read the manuscript in draft: James Andrews, Emily Baragwanath, Christopher Baron, David Branscome, Charles Chiasson, Joseph Roisman, and Mack Zalin. Their interventions saved me from errors great and small, though of course errors remain, and these are now fully my fault.

I also wish to thank Charles Cavaliere, Sara Birmingham, and Marianne Paul at OUP, for unflagging help, encouragement, and patience.

Photo Credits

1.1 Vix Crater, bronze, c. 500 BC. Musée du Pays Châtillonnais. Credit: akg-images / CDA / Guillot.

1.2 Detail from red-figure Attic amphora, c. 490 BC. Attributed to the Berlin Painter. Metropolitan Museum of Art. Credit: Image copyright © The Metropolitan Museum of Art. Image source: Art Resource, NY (56.171.38).

1.3 Athenian Treasury, Delphi. Inset: reconstruction of the Siphnian treasury.

Credit: PHOTO BY Christian Delbert/Alamy Stock Photo.

1.4 Lustral basin (*perirrhanterion*) from the archaic Temple of Poseidon at Corinth. Marble, 7th century BC. Corinth Museum.

Credit: Courtesy of The University of Chicago / Excavations at Isthmia.

1.5 Detail from red-figure Attic amphora, c. 525 BC. Antikesammlung Berlin.

Credit: bpk, Berlin / Antikensammlung/Photo: Ingrid Geske-Heiden/ Art Resource, NY.

1.6 Detail from red-figure Attic amphora, c. 480 BC. Attributed to Myron. Musée du Louvre Paris.

Credit: Gianni Dagli Orti / The Art Archive at Art Resource, NY.

1.7 Bas-relief of Cyrus II, from the palace of Cyrus at Pasargadae.

Credit: North Wind Picture Archives / Alamy Stock Photo.

2.2 Bronze figure of the cat-goddess Bastet. Egyptian, c. 6th–4th century BC.

Credit: Werner Forman. Heritage Image Partnership Ltd / Alamy Stock Photo.

2.3 Crocodile mummies. Egyptian, c. 6th–4th century BC. Musée du Louvre, Paris.

Credit: © RMN-Grand Palais / Art Resource, NY.

2.4 The god Thoth, painted limestone, from the Tomb of Prince Khaemwaset II, son of Ramesses III. Egyptian, 12th century BC. Valley of the Queens, Thebes, Egypt.

Credit: Valley of the Queens, Thebes, Egypt / Bridgeman Images.

2.5 Detail from red-figure kylix from Tanagra. c. 520–510 BC. Attributed to the Skythes Painter. Musée du Louvre, Paris. Photo: Erich Lessing.

Credit: Photo Credit: Erich Lessing / Art Resource, NY.

2.6 Gold mask of Tutankhamun. Egypt, 18th dynasty. Egyptian Museum, Cairo.

Credit: Scala / Art Resource, NY.

2.7 Pyramid of Menkewre (left), pyramid of Chephren (center), pyramid of Cheops (right). Giza, Egypt.

Credit: Walter Rawlings/Robert Harding.

3.1 Detail of the Behistun Relief, depicting Darius I before the defeated Magi, c. 520 BC. Kermanshah Province, Iran. Photo: Zev Radovan.

Credit: Photo © Zev Radovan / Bridgeman Images.

3.2 The deceased worshipping a standing sacred Apis bull, private painted limestone stele from the Serapeum at Memphis, 21st Dynasty, 1075–945 BC. Musée du Louvre Paris.

Credit: Gianni Dagli Orti / The Art Archive at Art Resource, NY.

3.3 Behistun Relief, depicting Darius I, c. 520 BC. Kermanshah Province, Iran.

Credit: akg-images / ullstein bild / ullstein—Archiv Gerstenberg.

3.4 Relief from the north facade of the Apadana Stairway, Persepolis, depicting Darius I, c. 470 BC. National Museum of Iran, Tehran.

Credit: National Museum of Iran, Tehran, Iran / Bridgeman Images.

4.1 Scythian vase from Kul'-Oba Kurgan, Crimea. Gold or electrum, 4th century BC.

Credit left: Archives Charmet / Bridgeman Image.

Credit center: Photo © Boltin Picture Library / Bridgeman Images.

Credit right: © Boltin Picture Library / Bridgeman Images.

4.2 Tondo of red-figure kylix. Attributed to the Euaion Painter, c. 460–440 BC. Musée du Louvre, Paris.

Credit: Erich Lessing / Art Resource, NY.

4.3 Scythian cup. Gold, 7th century BC. Hermitage, St. Petersburg.

Credit: De Agostini Picture Library / A. Dagli Orti / Bridgeman Images.

4.4 Detail from Scythian horse diadem. Gold, amber, and glass, 5th century BC. Natural Science Academy, Kiev.

Credit: Alfredo Dagli Orti / The Art Archive at Art Resource, NY.

4.5 King's stele with inscription and relief depicting King Sennacherib praying in front of the divine symbols, 705–681 BC. From Nineveh. Archaeological Museum, Istanbul.

Credit: © Tarker / Bridgeman Images.

4.6 Statue of wounded Amazon. Roman marble sculpture, 1st century AD copy from a Greek original by Pheidias. From the sanctuary of Artemis in Ephesus. Musei Capitolini, Rome.

Credit: Ghigo G. Roli / Art Resource, NY.

4.7 Scythian plaque depicting a mounted Scyth armed with a spear. Gold, 4th century BC. From Kul-Oba, Russia. Hermitage, St. Petersburg.

Credit: Werner Forman / Art Resource, NY.

4.8 Bridge using ships as pontoons.

Credit: North Wind Picture Archives.

5.1 Darius I, drawing from a Greek painting, 4th century BC.

Credit: From August Baumeister, Denkmäler des klassischen Altertums zur Erläuterung des Lebens der Griechen und Römer in Religion, Kunst und Sitte, vol. 1 (1885) Tafel VI.

6.2 Aerial view Agion Oros, Mount Athos, Chalkidiki, Greece.

Credit: © Airphoto | Dreamstime.com.

6.3 House of Cleopatra and Dioscourides in Delos, Greece.

Credit: Photo by Bernard Gagnon. Licensed under the Creative Commons Attribution-Share Alike 3.0 Unported license. Found at https://commons.wikimedia.org/wiki/File%3AHouse_of_Cleopatra%2C_Delos.jpg.

6.4 Detail from black-figure Attic vase, 6th century BC. Naples, Museo Archeologico Nazionale.

Credit: The Art Archive / Alamy Stock Photo.

6.6 Print reproduced from Amelia B. Edwards, *A Thousand Miles up the Nile* (Routledge: London, 1890), p. 73.

7.1 Drawing of the Persian royal dress. Antique hand-colored print.

Credit: Copyright © North Wind Picture Archives—All rights reserved.

7.2 Satellite image of the Hellespont.

Credit: NASA.

7.3 Illustrated by Victor and Maria Lazzaro.

7.4 Leonidas Monument, Thermopylae. This monument celebrating the heroism of Leonidas and the Spartans was commissioned in 1955 by Paul, King of Greece. Thermopylae, Greece.

Credit: © Vanni Archive/ Art Resource, NY.

8.1 The Olympias, a modern reconstruction of a trireme.

Credit: ©AAAC / TopFoto / The Image Works.

8.3 Relief on a doorway of the hall of the Hundred Columns, Persepolis.

Credit: Werner Forman Archive / Bridgeman Images.

Maps

Index to Place Names

Below is a list of places located on the maps, keyed to the map number.